06/12/9

Terri W. Lee

Best wishes

always

ON WINGS AND PRAYERS:

Living With Diabetes

One Sugar at a Time

a novel by

TERRI WOOD JERKINS

LANGMARC PUBLISHING · AUSTIN, TEXAS

ON WINGS AND PRAYERS:
Living With Diabetes One Sugar at a Time
BY TERRI WOOD JERKINS

Cover Artist: Aundrea Hernandez

Copyright©2001 Terri Wood Jerkins
Permission is granted by MiniMed Inc.
to use the MiniMed® name • www.minimed.com
Permission is granted by Eli Lilly and Company to use
names of Humalog™ insulin and Humalog mix 75/25™
First Printing 2001
Printed in The United States of America

Published by
LANGMARC PUBLISHING
P.O. Box 90488
Austin, Texas 78709-0488
1-800-864-1648 • www.langmarc.com

Library in Congress Cataloging-in-Publication Data

Jerkins, Terri Wood.
    On wings and prayers : living with diabetes one sugar at a time : a novel
/ by Terri Wood Jerkins.
        p. cm.
    ISBN 1-880292-64-5 (alk. paper)
    1. Diabetes--Patients--Fiction. 2. Indians of North America--Fiction. 3.
Space Shuttle Program (U.S.)--Fiction. 4. Astronauts--Fiction. I. Title.

PS3560.E67 O5 2001
813'.54--dc21

                                                                2001029326

DEDICATION

TO HERBERT SLOAN

AND ALL THE PEOPLE WHO HAVE DIABETES
AND STILL HAVE THE COURAGE
TO LOOK FOR A
LIFETIME OF SOMETHING WONDERFUL.

Chapter 1

The morning Laurel Wolfe met Jackson Driver, she never dreamed she was meeting her destiny. She was simply hoping to improve her grade in her college photography course. She had always believed God moved in mysterious ways, but little did she realize when she met Mr. Driver, she was beginning one of life's mysteries that wouldn't be solved for quite some time.

Laurel's job as a hostess at an upscale restaurant in Gatlinburg helped her pay her bills, but she had dreams of a better, more fulfilling future. She had come to Gatlinburg at age nineteen with neither money nor contacts. She had rented a room from a widow who took her under her wing until Laurel had found a job. After saving her money for a year, Laurel enrolled in day classes at the local community college and moved to her own apartment. She had started with basic freshman courses, but the arts attracted her attention.

Her new dream was to become a professional photographer. Her course instructor in advanced photographic techniques had given his students an assignment to create the most unusual photograph and setting they could find. Laurel immediately had thought of the helicopters that flew over the Smoky Mountains.

Early on a Saturday morning in July of 1999, Laurel drove past the crowded vendors in Pigeon Forge to Sevierville. She stopped at Driver's Flight Service because she was fascinated with the bright red helicopter.

Her compact car and a pickup truck were the only vehicles in the parking lot. Apparently the pilot didn't expect early morning trade because he was busy servicing the helicopter. He crawled from underneath it when he saw Laurel approaching. He was tall and lanky with wavy black hair that hung almost to his shoulders. He had a striking face with high flat cheekbones and arched black eyebrows over grayish eyes. He was wearing a well-worn blue jumpsuit that looked like it had been part of a uniform.

"So do you want a ride?" he asked.

"I'm a photographer," Laurel said. "Well, actually I'm working towards a photography profession, and I need to get some unusual pictures for a class I'm taking. Most of my final grade is riding on this project. I'm hoping to get some shots while the mist is still hanging over the mountaintops."

"It's fifty bucks, cash up front," the pilot said flatly. "I'm not cheap, but I'll make it worth your while."

Laurel dug into her jean pocket and pulled out sufficient funds. "When do we leave?"

"I don't like to waste time either," the pilot said as he took the money. "Give me about five minutes. There's coffee in the office if you want a cup."

"Thanks. I believe I will. It's kind of early for me. I work late on the weekends." Leaving him to complete his maintenance tasks, Laurel walked past him to the small block building at the hill's crest.

The office was a surprise. She paused at the door to look around. The decor spoke to her roots. Woven southwestern rugs in a pattern she knew was Pueblo were hanging on the walls. A tape of the wind over-dubbed with flute music was playing. Laurel listened intently as she poured a cup of coffee and stirred in artificial sweetener and powdered creamer. The pilot appeared as she added cold water to the cup to make the temperature tolerable.

"It does get hot," he commented as he bent over a logbook. "What's your name? I need it for my records."

"Laurel Wolfe. Do I get to know who you are?"

"Jackson Driver at your service." His flippant attitude was incredibly abrasive, and Laurel focused on her surroundings to avoid a reflex response. She examined a piece of pottery on the rough wooden shelving.

"Are you a Native American?"

"Not to the degree that would invite me to live on the reservation," he said cryptically. "Are you?"

"Yes," she said, feeling insulted by his glib come-back. It seemed to be the remark of a man who didn't appreciate his heritage. Laurel had been raised to treasure her family's heritage. "I'm darn proud of it."

"If you are so proud, then why aren't you on the reservation?" Driver asked.

"If you aren't proud, then why did you choose this decor?" Laurel retorted.

"Touché. Let me run to the john, and I'll be ready to go," Driver said.

Laurel contemplated leaving with or without her money. While the infuriating pilot was otherwise occupied, she convinced herself to make him earn her fifty dollars. She steeled herself to be as abrupt and forceful as he was. She walked around the office, scanning the other contents dispassionately. The photo on his desk caught her eye. It was a picture of Jackson Driver in a military uniform with his arm around a tall, blond girl. He looked happy, and it occurred to Laurel that the pilot didn't seem particularly happy at present, at least on the surface.

Jackson emerged from the bathroom and gestured toward the door. "Let's go. The mist is burning off while we hang around here." He didn't wait for a response. He flipped off the tape player and strutted to the helicopter as if he were certain she would follow. His attitude irritated Laurel anew. Without a word, she climbed into the helicopter and glared at him as he slammed the door.

"So how does a jerk like you keep customers?" she asked as he climbed into the pilot's seat.

He laughed as he started the engine. "They come for the view and not for the company, babe. You might want to look for that great photo opportunity and ignore the scenic beauty in here."

"Just let me out," Laurel said. "I'd rather fail the class."

"Chill out," he said as they took off. "And fasten your seat belt. It's only an hour. You can stand anything for an hour, can't you?"

"Some things are pretty unbearable," she said as she removed her camera from its case. She kept calm by focusing on the blue outline of the mountains. They were home to her in a way that people who had not lived in the mountains could never understand. The noise of the helicopter blades prevented conversation even if Laurel had wanted to make small talk. She was content with the incredible view. She had never flown before that day.

They passed over Pigeon Forge and could see the distant outline of Gatlinburg off to the right. Driver handed her some headphones with a microphone. She donned them, expecting to hear some sort of radio noise. Instead she heard his voice.

"You have to use these or scream," he said. "Usually

I just cruise over the mountaintops, but I had the feeling you were looking for something specific."

"The new rock slide near Klingman's Dome," she said. "There's a tree clinging to the mountainside. It's almost horizontal."

"I hadn't noticed, but we'll make a low pass over it. There isn't much wind to get in the way. Anything else?"

"A sky shot of a waterfall might be nice."

"We'd have to go south for that. From the air you can see the big one on the South Carolina border. Let's do the rock slide first and see how much time we have left."

He was a very adept pilot, and he was obviously willing to help Laurel obtain the best possible angle for her photographs. She knew the terrain like the back of her hand and focused her camera several times before they were close enough to the rock slide for her to snap her pictures. The tree was still there, tenaciously clinging to the mountainside for whatever time remained. Driver turned the helicopter and held his position until Laurel had taken several shots. When she lowered her camera, he turned south and flew the forty miles to the tallest waterfall in North Carolina. Laurel snapped several more shots before consulting her watch. They had been in flight for over forty minutes.

"I guess we're going overtime," she said.

"Them's the breaks." Driver shrugged. "Tell you what. Give me a copy of your pictures when you get them developed, and we'll call it even." He smiled at her surprise. "I can be a gentleman when I'm in the mood." He pointed down as they crossed Nantahala Lake and allowed her to take several shots of a vintage train crossing the old bridge. He continued to point out sites as they made their way back to Sevierville. Laurel forgot to feel resentment during the last half hour of flight time.

Once on the ground, Driver jumped out and hurried into the office, leaving Laurel to extricate herself. By the time she had reached her car, he emerged from the office and handed her a business card.

"Give me a call when you have the pictures developed. Otherwise I'll have to send you a bill." The words were intended as a subtle invitation, but Laurel was still on the defensive and took his remarks as another goad.

"I'll have them done this afternoon," she said brusquely. "I'll bring yours back so I won't have to worry about being billed."

The expression on Driver's face revealed that she had made the wrong assumption. For a brief moment, he looked as if she had slapped him. Then he retracted the card and walked away without a word.

Guilt washed over Laurel, and she called out. "Hey, Driver. What about the pictures?"

"Forget it," he snapped. "Don't put yourself out." The slam of the office door punctuated his sentence.

As she drove away, she lectured herself on the perils of codependency. Then she reassured herself she didn't owe the cocky arrogant pilot anything. As she passed the church, its steeple reminded her of her faith.

She stopped at a local cave and participated in a tour just so she could finish the roll of film. By noon she was at a one-hour photography shop having the roll of film processed. She lectured herself again in the drive-through line of a hamburger joint, but she knew what she would have to do. As soon as she finished her burger, she picked up the developed photographs and drove to Jackson Driver's office.

As she pulled into a parking place, a customer drove out of the parking lot. Driver was nowhere in sight. Laurel entered his office without knocking, and he hurriedly concealed several items on his desk before speaking to her.

"Do you know how to knock?" he said sharply.

"Do you hate everybody or is it just me?" she asked. She fumbled while opening the envelope and managed to drop all forty-eight pictures on the floor. As she began picking them up, he bent down to help her.

"Sorry," he said as he gathered the pictures near him. "We've kind of been in each other's faces since we met."

Another sharp reply crossed Laurel's mind, but as she looked into his eyes, she suppressed it. His eyes weren't just gray. They had patches of brown scattered around each iris. She had never seen such an unusual color. As she stared into his eyes, she felt oddly attracted to him despite their abrasive beginning. She had no idea that Driver was feeling the same attraction.

He stood abruptly and extended his hand to help her stand. When their hands met, the chemistry intensified. He was much taller than she was, yet she didn't feel intimidated as she looked up into his face. She felt powerless to release his hand or look away from his eyes.

"So, did they turn out as good as you thought they would?" He smiled at her blank expression, but the smile was not mocking. "The pictures," he prompted her.

"Yeah. They're not bad." She moved to the desk and divided them into two even piles. She put one pile back into the folder. Driver examined the second pile with an intense interest.

"They're better than not bad. You've got talent." Driver looked at her as if he were trying to read her thoughts. "I'd like to make up for being so abrupt this morning. I haven't had time to eat lunch. Would you like to go across the street with me? The cafe has decent food. We could leave the hostility here."

"I think shots were fired from both directions," Laurel admitted. "I already had lunch, but I could take another cup of coffee."

"Let me pull the distributor cap off my chopper, and I'll be right with you." He left her standing in his office beside the photo of him with the blond. When she picked up the picture, she saw a used syringe he had pushed behind it. Syringes meant only one thing to Laurel. While she waited for Jackson, she wondered how to tactfully walk away from someone who was obviously on drugs.

Jackson returned to the office and hurried to lock a mechanical part in his desk. "I used to leave the helicopter parked and not worry. That was before a drunken tourist hijacked it while I was eating supper. I was lucky to get it back in one piece. That was when I gave it the sixties paint job. It won't be easy to hide a bright red helicopter, and obviously it will be easier for the police to follow if it disappears again." He held the door for her and then locked it behind them. "Do you live in Sevierville?"

"Gatlinburg," she said. She was haunted by her memory of the syringe. "I wanted to get away from home but not too far away, if you know what I mean. I'm from Cherokee."

"I kind of figured that after what you said about being Native American. Your quantum of blood has to be enough to get you housing on the reservation."

"It would if I wanted it. I'm full blooded." Laurel hesitated to tell Driver anything more about herself yet she continued. "My mother died a few years ago, and my dad remarried. I'm not crazy about my stepmother. Anyway, I'm a big girl now. It was time for me to have my own place. The pay is better in Gatlinburg." She glanced at him as they started across the highway. "You aren't from around here, are you?"

"I'm from everywhere. My father is in the Air Force. His last post when I was living with him was in Charleston. I was smitten by this part of the country."

"You were in the Air Force, too?"

"Yeah. I guess you saw the picture. It was taken just before I got out. That's how I got so much flight experience. First I flew helicopters and small planes, and then I went to flight school and flew fighter jets. My time in the Air Force is a good memory. The blond is not a good memory, but I still like the picture. So tell me about yourself."

They entered the restaurant before she decided what to say. The hostess ushered them to a booth, allowing Laurel extra time to choose her words. She spoke when they were alone.

"I guess I'm a little nervous." She looked into his eyes again and said, "I saw a needle thing on your desk, and I was wondering if you do things you shouldn't. I'm really opposed to that kind of life-style."

He reached into his jacket pocket and pulled out a zippered case. After he opened it, he pushed it toward her. "I'm addicted to insulin. I can't come off it, and I've tried." His face was very tense in that moment, even though he was trying to make his confession into a joke. Laurel was too relieved to notice.

"Whew. I was thinking I had just gone flying with someone who was already flying. I wasn't sure I wanted to tell you about myself when I was thinking you were keeping company with sister morphine."

"Never got into that kind of thing. I guess I couldn't be a politician because I didn't light it or inhale it. I thought I was a pretty healthy guy until I developed diabetes. I don't drink or smoke, but I definitely take a drug." He put the case under the table and drew up a dose of insulin as the waitress came to take their order. Laurel never saw him take it, and he moved hurriedly past further discussion of his illness.

"So, are you in school full time?"

"I have to work to pay the tuition. I take classes at the community college in Gatlinburg. I'm a hostess at the Mountain Mist Restaurant from six until midnight. Hopefully I won't have to be there much longer. If my professor likes these shots, I just might end up with a good grade in the course. I am trying to earn a scholarship so I can work fewer hours and spend more time on my courses. This morning's project is kind of the final exam."

"You don't look old enough to be in college. How old are you? I don't want to get arrested if I ask you out."

"I'm twenty-two and completely legal. How old are you? I might be too mature for you," Laurel said.

"Thirty-three." He smiled. "I do this by day, and at night I study aerodynamics and astrophysics. Actually I just got my pilot's license back last year. That was when the powers that be decided a pilot could fly planes and take insulin. Prior to that, only drugs and alcohol were allowed in the cockpit." The comment was intended as a joke, but Laurel could feel his bitterness. Her intuition was good.

"I guess that's why you aren't in the Air Force now."

"Bingo! I'd have to say 1996 was a very bad year for me. Over a period of two months, I found out I had diabetes, lost my career, and was dumped by the blond." The words hung between them as the waitress placed their food and coffee on the table.

"So I guess it was good that you asked about the tools of my condition," he said when they were alone again. "If you have a problem with extra sweet guys like me, I'd rather know now than later."

"I don't see that as a big deal," she said as she studied his face. "I just wanted to know that your drug of choice was legal. Why did the blond see it as such a big deal?"

"I still don't know," he admitted. "I imagine she thought I'd be sick all our lives. Nobody believes you can have diabetes and a normal life. Everyone assumes you'll be blind and lose your kidneys if you take insulin. She said she was worried about it passing to our kids. It wasn't any more specific than that. I got a 'Dear Jackson' letter. I was stationed overseas when I became ill, and the first thing the Air Force did was ground me. I called her for emotional support, and I thought she sounded weird. Then she wrote me. I knew what the letter said before I read it."

"What did you do?" Laurel was appalled. "I guess it was better to find out she was a gold digger before rather than after the wedding, but that had to have been rough."

"Yeah. It isn't something I like to think about. We'd been together for three years. You think you know somebody after that long." He paused and then began eating his lunch. Laurel had the feeling he might have communicated more than he had planned.

"I've never been married either, but I've never really been that close. I lived at home until my father remarried. My brothers are a lot older than I am so for a long time after my mother died it was just my dad and me. When Mary made us a threesome, I thought I should give them some space. Since then I've just been trying to find myself. I guess that sounds childish."

"Everybody has to do self discovery sooner or later," Driver said. "I guess I'm telling you about Alyssa so you'll understand why I wasn't particularly endearing at first. I tend to stall when I'm attracted to someone now."

Laurel was flattered, and she smiled spontaneously. "I don't stall. I just get nervous and drop things—like pictures."

"I'm really glad you brought them back. I didn't think you would." He glanced at his watch. "I'll have to get back to work in about ten minutes." He took his business card from his pocket and placed it on the table beside her coffee cup. "I'd like to get to know you better. Why don't you think about it and, if you feel the same, let me know."

Laurel was startled by the unusual proposition. "I've never asked out a guy. I think that would be a little too weird. If you want to ask me out, I'll probably say yes. Just remember I work every night except Sunday nights."

"Or after midnight," he said. "Well, Laurel, I guess we're on the same wavelength. May I call you?"

Before leaving the diner, she wrote her phone number on half of a deposit slip. She was surprised at her feeling of regret as she left Jackson Driver. The customers waiting for him didn't give her the option of lingering because she had to be at work at 6 P.M. She was lost in thought as she drove to her apartment. She placed Jackson's business card on her dresser before dressing for work.

In a tourist town, summer Saturday nights were busy in the local restaurants. Laurel wasn't waiting tables, but she was on her feet for six hours. At midnight, she was too tired to do anything other than clock out. She was unlocking her car door when she heard a voice call out to her.

"Hey, Miss Wolfe. You said you might go out with me. How about now?"

Laurel would have been frightened if the parking lot hadn't been full of other restaurant employees. The security guards were also looking in her direction, so she turned to acknowledge Jackson's presence.

"Do you ever sleep, Mr. Driver?"

"Not when I can look at the stars," he said with a smile. "I have some friends with a very large telescope. Would you like to come with me? You can follow in your car. We're just going to the end of Blueberry Road."

She glanced at the starry sky and agreed to star gaze,

even though she was tired and her feet were aching. As she followed Jackson Driver up Blueberry Hill Road, she wondered if she had lost her mind.

Chapter 2

Laurel had not realized there was an observatory in Gatlinburg until she spotted it on the hilltop that evening. Jackson parked near the entrance and directed her to park beside him. He opened her car door for her and offered her his hand. His eyes had captivated her, and Jackson Driver's hand projected a feeling of magnetic connection she had never felt before. She walked close to him hoping he would put his arm around her. She was disappointed when he didn't.

"Hey, Jack," a man called out as they entered the dimly lit observatory. "Did you come to see Jovian moons?"

"Can you see them? I was worried about the cloud cover." It was obvious from their greeting that Jackson had visited there frequently. Jackson pulled Laurel forward. "This is Laurel Wolfe. Laurel, meet George Connor. He's studying for his Ph.D. in astronomy."

"Nice to meet you, Laurel. Go on back. Ken's viewing one of them on the scope right now, but with the clouds no one knows how long it will last."

Jackson led Laurel into a room lit only by starlight through the open dome. They spent the next two hours viewing objects Laurel had seen only in pictures. She forgot to feel tired. She kicked off her high-heeled shoes and made herself comfortable.

The three postgraduate students and Jackson had knowledge of the solar system that astounded Laurel. The first object she saw was Io, a volcano-covered moon orbiting Jupiter. She was able to see several Jovian moons and details of the giant planet. She viewed the rings around Saturn and the tiny pebble-like moons orbiting it. When the students were through studying the solar system, Jackson persuaded them to focus on galaxies and distant objects in the Milky Way.

Laurel was shocked when she realized it was 3 A.M. "I guess I need to head home. I attend church on Sunday mornings."

"Me, too," Jackson said. He held her elbow as she stepped into her shoes, and he wrapped his arm around her as they walked out of the observatory. A misty rain met them at the door. Laurel moved closer to the warmth of his body.

"I don't have an umbrella, Laurel. Do you want me to drive your car up to the door?"

"No. I won't shrink." She hesitated and then said, "Why don't you come over to my place for a little while? I'd like to repay you for this great adventure."

"Are you sure?" he asked uncertainly. "I mean, I'm not going to put any moves on you, but I don't want to ruin your reputation."

"No one will be awake in my complex at this time of night. I can brew some cappuccino."

"You're making me an offer I can't refuse. Give me one minute to check my sugar. I don't like to drive without testing first."

"You've got it. That will give me just enough time to change shoes." She hurried through the rain and unlocked her car. She waited one minute without looking in his direction and then started her car engine. When he did the same, she proceeded from the parking lot. She drove home slowly and tried to remember if she had left the three rooms in shape to entertain a guest. She had never invited a date into her apartment. When she turned on the light, she was relieved there was evidence of a recent dusting.

Jackson was quiet until she closed the door, and then he moved past her to the stereo. "If I keep the volume down, may we have some music?"

"Absolutely. I hope our tastes are compatible." As she headed for the kitchen, she glanced at her reflection in the living room's full-length mirror. The image told her that her black dress was wrinkled, and her long black hair was escaping the careful up-do she had created.

"I'll start the espresso and then change my clothes, if you don't mind. I look like I worked all night."

"Don't bother for my sake. You look really good. I was having a hard time staying on my side of the telescope." He pushed "play" on the stereo and the soft sounds of a Saint-Saens concerto filled the room.

"Do you like classical music?" Laurel asked.

"A lot. I play the piano. Since I never lived in one place for more than two years, I can truthfully say I've studied piano all over the world. Do you play?"

"The flute. No worldwide experience, but I was in the North Carolina All State Band when I was a senior. Several of us get together and do the chamber music thing once a month. We don't have a pianist. You can come if you want to."

"I'd like that." Jack sat at the kitchen bar and watched her make the coffee. "I was thinking you might like to go flying with me tomorrow. I have some real plane flying planned for tomorrow night."

"Night?" She stood at the opposite side of the counter, leaving the coffee brewing. "Is it a good idea to fly at night?"

"Hey, I've got hundreds of hours of night flying in a fighter plane. It's actually more fun at dusk when the weather is good. You don't have to worry about the other idiots who are up there not knowing what they're doing. You aren't scared of heights, are you?"

"Never," she replied indignantly. "I used to go rock climbing. You know, Native American people used to do all the high steel work on skyscrapers because heights don't bother us." She studied his face. "You never answered me about why your office is in the southwestern motif."

"I'm a quarter Navajo," he said. "I like the decor and the music. Other than that, I don't know much about that part of my heritage. My mother's father was one of the men who transmitted the Navajo language during World War II. That's what they used as a code because the Japanese couldn't translate it. The Navajo language isn't written. It's only spoken, and it's passed from father to son. My grandfather stayed in the service for ten years working with codes and code breaking after World War II. He and my grandmother retired to Window Rock, Arizona.

"We lived overseas much of the time when I was a kid, so I never had a chance to spend time with my grandparents. I really don't remember them. My mother died when I was seven. For a long time, it was my father, my brother, and me supported by various housekeepers. My dad remarried the year I started high school. My stepmother isn't interested in our ethnic background. I think she felt it wouldn't further her social position. I've never known more than I've just told you."

"You ought to find out. It's a part of who you are."

Her hand was close to his, and they moved at the same moment to touch each other. Their fingers entwined, and Jack pulled her toward him very slowly. Their first kiss took place with the counter between them, but Laurel couldn't feel anything but Jackson. The intensity of the attraction between them was overwhelming. He released her slowly like the ebbing of a tide, and she closed her hands over his shoulders. There was no need to speak as they looked into each other's eyes.

"I think the espresso is calling," he said reluctantly. When she didn't move, he walked around the counter and began steaming the milk. "Where do you go to church?"

Laurel glanced at the clock and giggled. "In about four hours I'll need to be there. Sometimes I go home to Cherokee, but lately I've been going to the Christian Church in Townsend. It's really nice. Of course, I might fall asleep tomorrow or rather today. Where do you go?"

"I don't have a home congregation yet, but I haven't missed a Sunday since I had to start my life over again. I'd like to go with you tomorrow. Then I won't have to worry about staying awake. You've been keeping my attention most of the day." He poured the espresso and topped each cup with milk. "Do you have artificial sweetener?"

She reached behind the coffeemaker and pulled out a box. The movement caused her arm to wrap around Jackson. She pulled him close until their mouths were touching. Laurel felt as if a fire were burning between them. She could feel his response was as strong as hers from the pressure of his hands on her back. Their bodies were pressed tightly together.

"I've never acted like this before," Laurel stammered.

"I think I probably should take my coffee and go," Jackson said. "For a minute I was thinking I didn't want to leave, but I gave you my word I wouldn't put any moves on you."

"I'm glad you're trustworthy." Laurel smiled and then closed both her hands around her cup. "I'm also really glad you came."

"I'll be back at 8:30 with your cup." He placed his arm around her shoulders and propelled her gently toward the door. It was difficult to say good night. Even four hours seemed like a long time. She watched out her window until his truck disappeared into the night. She crawled into bed and set the alarm for 7:30 A.M.

The telephone awakened Laurel. She muttered "Hello."

"Since I don't see a light in your window, I have the feeling you might still be asleep. You didn't forget our date, did you?"

"Oh, no," Laurel groaned. She glanced at the nightstand and noticed the alarm clock was missing. Further search revealed it was on the floor. "I think I may have murdered my alarm clock. What time is it?"

"Closing in on 8:30 A.M.," Jackson said. "I'll run by one of the fast food restaurants and pick up some break-fast for us while you shower. I can trust you to get out of bed when I hang up, can't I?"

"Yeah, you can trust me. I'm sorry. I'll be ready in fifteen minutes. Don't forget to come back."

"I'll see you in fifteen minutes, sleeping beauty."

Laurel hung up and ran to the shower. She stepped under the water before it warmed up. She was clean but cold when she emerged three minutes later and hur-riedly slipped into her underwear, slip, and hose. She was struggling to zip her skirt and tuck in her blouse when the doorbell rang.

"Coming," she shouted as she snatched her hair-brush and gave her hair a cursory brushing. She tried to compose herself, but when she opened the door she laughed. Jack stood there wearing an expression resem-bling a somewhat stern school teacher.

"Okay," she admitted. "Maybe I need more than fifteen minutes." Jackson laughed and leaned on the doorframe.

"I'll give you another five, and then we've got to hit

the road or miss church. I'll make some super quick espresso while you finish up." He followed her into the living room and closed the door.

Laurel hurried to her bedroom and brushed her hair until it lay in a shimmering mass. She thought her hair was her best feature, but she was modest in her assessment. She was a strikingly beautiful girl. It was a fact Jackson Driver appreciated.

"You look definitely worth waiting for." He poured two cups of coffee and pushed a breakfast sandwich in her direction. "We've got about ten minutes to spare. I was actually here a little early. It's an air force habit." He pulled off his sports coat and removed the small black kit from his pocket. "I need to check my blood sugar. May I borrow your bathroom?"

"You can check it right here if you want to," she said. "Blood doesn't freak me out, and I'd like to see how you do it."

Jackson sat down and took out a lancet device and a small rectangular electronic device. He inserted a strip into the device and it turned on. Then he used the lancet to draw blood from his fingertip. Laurel had never noticed how rough his fingertips were. They were covered with a myriad of stick marks. He deftly applied a drop of blood to the glucose strip and pressed his fingertip against a folded tissue in the kit. It was marked by at least ten other bloodstains. The machine counted down and gave the reading, 89mg percent. Jackson recorded the number in a logbook and took out two vials of insulin.

"How often do you have to test?" Laurel asked.

"Every time I eat, drive, or fly. Usually I test about six times a day. When I fly planes, I have to test every hour while I'm in the air. The strips are fifty cents to a dollar a piece, so it's a big financial deal." He drew insulin from each bottle and administered the injection through his shirt.

"Don't you have to use alcohol or something?"

"Not unless I'm feeling masochistic. Alcohol makes it burn. It's not like people don't get little wounds every day without getting infected." He tucked away the bottles, syringe, and glucose meter. His eyes revealed the concern he was trying to hide when he asked, "Did it bother you to watch?"

"No. Did it bother you to show me?"

"Actually it did," he admitted. "It was a vulnerable moment. I'm not good with vulnerable moments." He finished his sandwich and watched as she finished hers.

"What's your blood sugar supposed to read?" Laurel asked with interest.

"It's supposed to be 80 to 120, just like yours. I try to keep it there. If I do, having diabetes won't change anything else about my life. Other than the first couple of months when I had my denial reaction, I've kept it under control. I have a blood test every three months to look at the average and, according to my doctor, I'm practically perfect. Of course, he knows me only from a blood sugar standpoint."

Laurel laughed as she carried the dishes to the sink. "Let's go."

"Bring some out-of-church clothes, and we'll change before we go flying."

She threw her clothing into a bag along with her camera and two rolls of film. She also packed her flute without really knowing why. They left Gatlinburg at 8:50 and reached the church in Townsend as the services began.

Laurel's belief in God was very important to her. In many ways, she had left her family on a wing and a prayer. She was the youngest of three children and the only daughter. Her father had been her best friend after her mother's death from leukemia. When Lawrence Wolfe had started dating Mary Kinnard, a widow from their church, Laurel had felt abandoned. Out of jealousy she had allowed her relationship with her high school sweetheart to progress to a marriage proposal. Her father had approved of Jimmy Wilson and had encouraged her to commit to him. She had not been ready to make that commitment. Instead Laurel left her home and family. On the rebound, Jimmy soon married a local girl.

For a year Laurel had expected her father to beg her to return home. During that year of isolation and resentment, her landlady had helped her understand her father's motives. Lawrence had married Mary eight months after Laurel's departure. With prayer, Laurel was finally able to accept that his remarriage was best for her father and was also none of her business.

Laurel had dated several men in Gatlinburg including several students at the community college, but nobody had moved her until Saturday, July 14. In church, she tried to surreptitiously study Jackson from the standpoint of his faith. Faith was a deciding factor for her in every relationship. At the end of Sunday school she had to believe Jackson was as committed to Christianity as she was. His involvement in the Bible study showed he had spent time studying on his own. His well-worn Bible confirmed that impression.

They made small talk as they drove to Jack's home in Sevierville. She expected an apartment and was very surprised to approach a house with a generous yard.

"Your rent must be awesome," she commented as she climbed out of the truck.

"Not really. I own it. Come on and I'll show you around." He led her to the front door and whistled as he unlocked the door. A large black and tan German shepherd appeared at the door and examined Laurel's knees with his cold wet nose.

"Laurel, this is Kennedy." Jack turned on the lights and led her to his guest room. "Get changed while I pack some lunch. We'll go do the afternoon tourist trade and leave at six for the airport."

Laurel changed into jeans and a Cherokee tee shirt. She lingered in the room, then in the hallway and his study to examine the photographs. She was sure Jackson came from a wealthy family even before she saw his diploma from the Air Force Academy and his picture with an older man who was obviously his father. Jackson's father was wearing a general's uniform. Beside that picture was a photograph of Jack in a flight suit with a helmet tucked under his arm and his hand resting on a jet. The jet's fuselage read "Major Jack Driver, Wildfire." There was a picture of Jackson in uniform with his arm around another man in uniform. Their resemblance prompted Laurel to think they were related, probably brothers. She returned to the living room and sat down at the baby grand piano. She was perched at the piano when Jackson returned from the kitchen.

"I think I'm sort of intimidated," she said. "You're rich."

He sat down beside her and ran his fingers over the keys agilely. "My father's wealthy. My mother's parents were well to do. They had a huge ranch in Arizona. I get by on my share of my mother's inheritance."

"Do you have other family?" she asked.

"My brother, Lucien, is a captain in the Air Force. He's stationed at Cocoa Beach. My dad and stepmother live in D.C., and I have a couple of stepsisters who aren't worth mentioning. They buy into the concept of position. Charlotte and Caroline. Their names even sound like American princesses, don't they?" He stood. "We ought to go. I'll show you more tonight." He was inside the truck when he realized her discomfort for the first time.

"You know what I have doesn't change who I am, Laurel. I'm not into money and power. I have dreams, just like you do. I was thinking you could be in them, but maybe you don't want to be. I hope you'll be totally honest and tell me."

She moved close beside him as if touch were the easiest way to communicate. When she kissed him, the embrace increased in intensity until she could feel him breathing.

"I've never really let myself get involved with a man before now, so this is all new," she said. "I guess I thought the racial line was the only one I would be crossing."

"The way I see it, we have more in common than we have differences between us." He kissed her again and then jammed the key into the ignition. He pulled out his glucose kit almost as an afterthought. "Okay, I've got to put my brain in gear first."

They both laughed while he ran the test and recorded the results. It bothered Laurel only because she wished it weren't necessary for Jackson to do something so unpleasant so often. The ride to his office passed quickly while they talked about Jackson's father.

"He's been in the Air Force for forty years now. He's been at the Pentagon for the last five years. He moves in all the right political circles for Charlene and her two princesses. Actually, that's how I met the blond. I should've known she was bad news because the princesses revel in her companionship even now.

"My dad's full name is Jack Roman Driver. He didn't like the idea of the junior thing so I'm Jackson. You know, Jack's son. Apparently my mother contributed the Daniel middle name. That was her father's name. He was the Navajo. My brother is Lucien Roman Driver."

"I guess you're the older son."

"Yeah. I was going to do all these things to make the old man proud. Diabetes was not in the plan. I did the denial. He did the rage. At first, I honestly think he blamed me for getting it."

"How did you find out you had it?"

"I went into a coma while I was in Saudi Arabia. I'd been there twice before, but the heat seemed to get to me much worse the last time. I was always thirsty. I think I was drinking a gallon of water a day and living in the bathroom. I lost about eighteen pounds in six weeks. That's how it starts.

"I have the kind of diabetes children usually get. You can get it at any age. It comes from your body making antibodies against the cells that make insulin. They think you get exposed to something like an infection and when your body fights the infection, it gets confused and makes antibodies against the insulin-producing cells. Your blood sugar starts to rise, and your body tries to dump the extra sugar in your urine. It acts like a water pill and makes you go to the bathroom constantly. Since a lot of your calories are coming out in your urine, you lose weight even if you eat more. Finally, you can't make enough insulin to let any sugar into your cells. You start to starve to death and burn your fat to have fuel to keep you alive. Fat burning builds up ketones in your blood, and they make you nauseated.

"When I got to that phase, I thought I had the stomach flu. I didn't know anything about diabetes then. By the third day of not being able to drink, I was so weak that I couldn't walk to the infirmary. The base was on alert status, but we weren't flying. I'm really lucky I didn't die. By the time someone reported me to sick call, my blood sugar was over thirteen hundred. I was in a coma so I don't remember being treated there or flown to Germany on a medic flight.

"I woke up in the base hospital in Germany three days later. Dad had flown to Germany the day after they flew me in. I remember he was yelling at everyone. He kept saying the doctors were supposed to fix the blood sugar. 'It can't be fixed, General,' the doctor told him.

'Your son has insulin dependent diabetes. He'll either take insulin for the rest of his life or die.'

"It was the only time in my life that my father really let me down. I needed him to tell me I was still a man and still his son, but he couldn't do it. He couldn't talk to me at all, and he left for D.C. as soon as they were sure I was going to live. He said he had to get to a meeting.

"I called Alyssa because I was lost. I didn't know where to go and what to do. I needed somebody to keep me focused. When Alyssa sent her lovely 'Dear Jackson' letter, nothing mattered anymore. I went through a phase when I hoped I would die. I was raised to go to church, but I wasn't really a Christian then. Now I'm ashamed of feeling that way, but I like to think I'm stronger because of it. I stopped taking insulin and ended up in the hospital a day later. I tried it twice more before the doctors realized it was deliberate. The chaplain spent a whole night praying with me after the third go-around. I hadn't been able to talk to anyone except doctors until then.

"My brother couldn't get leave to come to visit me, and you know about my father and Alyssa. I raged and cried and finally I prayed. The next morning I started taking it one step at a time until I knew God was carrying me. It was hard, and some of it doesn't ever get easy. It's not the first shot that gets to you. It's knowing there won't ever be a last shot." He exhaled slowly. "You know the old saying that God never gives you more than you can handle. Sometimes I think He gives me more credit than I deserve, but here I am three years later still slightly too sweet but dealing with it."

"It looks like you're doing a good job," Laurel said.

"With the diabetes, but probably not everything else. I haven't been out with anybody in a long time, Laurel." He pulled into the parking lot. "Don't underestimate how I'm feeling. When you get a major rejection from someone you love, it's hard to take the risk again."

"I couldn't do that to you," she said sincerely. "I felt rejected once, and I couldn't do that to another person."

Laurel wanted him to keep talking. She felt hungry for his words, but there was a customer waiting for him. She sat in the office and manned the coffeepot and telephone for a good part of the afternoon. She didn't feel abandoned and didn't mind waiting for Jackson. Surrounded by his belongings, she felt as if she were a part of his life. She was hungry, but she knew they would eat lunch when Jackson took a break. A break never materialized, and briefly Laurel wondered if Jackson would be all right if he skipped a meal. She looked at him from a distance every time she heard the helicopter land, and he seemed all right. Later she learned his appearance could be very deceiving.

Business was brisk until 4 P.M. when the last customer left. Laurel looked out the window and saw Jack servicing the helicopter. He had hung up the CLOSED sign. After thirty minutes, he entered the office. He held a familiar part from the helicopter, but with very unsteady hands he dropped it on the desk. He sat down on the floor before Laurel could ask what was wrong. He began eating a roll of pink tablets. He looked dazed, and Laurel thought he was going to pass out. She moved to his side and kept her hand on his shoulder because she didn't know what else to do. After ten minutes, he was covered in sweat. The sweating scared her even more, and she thought of all the television shows she had seen where people had gone into diabetic comas. She reached for the phone.

"Don't," he pleaded. "It's going away." With difficulty he pulled out the glucose meter and took a reading. "It was 34mg percent."

"Is that too low?" Laurel asked.

"A whole lot too low." He wiped his face, leaving a trail of grease on his forehead. Laurel went into the bathroom and returned with a damp paper towel. She cleaned his face with her unsteady hands while praying she was doing the right thing. It took thirty minutes before his eyes cleared and he stopped sweating.

"I'm sorry," he said. "I want to control the blood sugar, but sometimes it still controls me. This was my fault. I should have stopped to eat. I knew better, but I was trying to pretend to be a normal human being. I'm not, and I'm not going to be until they find a cure."

"No one is perfect, Jackson," Laurel said slowly. "At least this is easy to fix. I was just scared because I didn't know what to do. Can you give me something to read?" She flushed and looked at her hands. "I mean, if we're going to see each other, I'd like to know how to take care of you—if you need me."

He had a strange look on his face. It was a look she would not really understand until much later. He took both of her hands and held them.

"I want to keep seeing you. I hope you still want to keep seeing me."

She embraced him with all of her emotions transmitted to him through her touch. She could feel he didn't want her to let go.

Chapter 3

Laurel thought Jackson would cancel their flight, but he had her drive them to the small private airport on the outskirts of Sevierville. They sat in the truck and ate. By the time they reached the twin engine plane, his blood sugar reading was 149mg percent.

"Is that too high?" she asked as he took a shot.

"It's not too bad now, but it's going to go a whole lot higher. When it crashes, I make a lot of adrenaline and other hormones to bail me out. It's called rebounding. I'll be lucky if I can keep it under three hundred." He sighed. "Live and learn. High is better than low when we're flying." He helped her into the plane and then walked slowly around the plane and checked every visible part. He climbed in and showed her a clipboard.

"This is the checklist. A pilot has to check all these things before taking off."

"Don't you have to talk to somebody before you leave?" she asked.

"We're not really going anywhere definite, so we don't have to file a flight plan, and this airport doesn't have a tower."

"So how do you know when it's clear to take off?" She tried to conceal her anxiety and knew she had failed even before he smiled.

"You follow the time-honored rules and look both ways." He handed her a set of headphones. "You need to help me make sure there isn't anything on the runway. Then you can either talk to me or sing 'Off we go into the wild blue yonder.'"

"I may have to rethink not being afraid of heights, Jackson." She pulled on the headphones and watched as he carefully examined the checklist. Ten minutes later they were airborne.

Laurel had never flown before her helicopter ride. This flight in Jack's plane was truly exhilarating as they climbed toward the stars. Although they were circling only a small area, she could imagine flying to exotic places she had never seen. Jackson taught her how to hold the plane's wheel and how to pull back to make it climb. He helped her negotiate two rather wobbly turns and showed her how to slow the airspeed to let their altitude fall. When they had been flying almost an hour, he let her hold the controls alone while he checked his blood sugar.

"What was it?" she asked with genuine concern.

"Climbing like the plane," he said. "I guess we'd better land. I've got to take more insulin." He negotiated a slow turn and lined up with the runway. "I'm working on getting an insulin pump. If I ever get it, we won't have to worry about filling syringes. I'll be wearing the insulin all the time." He glanced at her and saw she was staring at the full moon. He was relieved to see no reaction to his words. "What are you thinking?"

"I used to dream about being an astronaut," she said. "I read everything I could find about the National Aeronautics and Space Administration and every book in the library about space. I wondered what it would feel like to fly even higher. How high did you fly?"

"The highest was about sixty thousand feet. You can't really go much higher than that because the air is too thin to support fuel combustion. If you push the edge of that envelope too far, you'll flame out both of your engines, which is a spine-tingling experience. Even knowing that, I never felt like I could get high enough." He shrugged. "I did get to go real fast. I flew a prototype plane that could go to Mach II. That's way over a thousand miles an hour."

He set the plane down gently and taxied back to the hangar. They both removed their headphones at the same time. As Laurel handed her headphones to Jackson, she noticed a very strange expression on his face.

"What are you thinking, Jackson?"

"Fate, coincidence, or God moving in mysterious ways," he said. "Let's go to my place for a couple of hours, and then I'll take you home."

"Stop for food," she ordered. "I'm buying this time."

"No way," he replied. "You're driving and I'm buying." When they were in the hangar, he purchased a diet coke for each of them; he drank his before they left the airport. They stopped at a fast-food restaurant and picked up grilled chicken sandwiches and salads.

Laurel kept talking during the drive. She hadn't noticed Jackson was asleep until they pulled into his driveway. She was embarrassed to think he had been so bored by her one-sided conversation. He jerked awake as the truck engine stopped. He swore under his breath.

"I'm sorry. Let's go in, Laurel, and I'll explain my drowsy state to you when I sober up." His blood sugar was 489mg percent when he checked it again, and he took insulin without eating for the two hours that followed. As it finally began dropping, he felt self conscious.

"When your blood sugar goes high, it makes your blood thick. It's like the difference between lemonade and syrup. When your blood gets thick, you get blurred vision and an insatiable thirst. Then you get sleepy." He shook his head. "In church this morning, I was praying to know if you'd be okay with my little problem. Now you've seen both sides of it in about six hours. I guess I'll have my answer one way or another."

"I'm still here, Jackson," Laurel said. "There comes a point when I might get insulted if you think I'm like the blond. I really like you, so I guess I'll learn how to manage everything else. Why don't we quit talking about it, and then you can tell me what you were going to tell me when we were in your plane."

"Okay," he conceded. He left the room and returned with a file folder. He handed her the top paper and said, "Read it."

She was only halfway down the page when she realized it was a letter of acceptance into the space program.

"You were an astronaut?" she asked.

"I would have been. I was doing my last thirty days in the regular Air Force, and then I was to report to Houston for training. I'd wanted to do that all my life, and I almost made it. If I hadn't believed in 'All things working together for the good of them that love God' like it says in Romans 8:28, I don't think I could have handled the disappointment. I guess someday God will show me why."

"Maybe it was so we could meet," she whispered. "My mom used to say people have soul mates. Have you ever heard of that?"

"I've heard it, and I've always believed it. I just wasn't sure it could happen for me—until I met you." He pulled her into his arms and kissed her with his hands in her hair and then on her face. It seemed very natural to move closer together until their bodies made them think of getting too close. Stopping was not easy and, for a long time, they continued kissing and holding each other. When temptation was growing too great,

Jackson pulled away and said, "I need to take you home, Laurel. We're going too fast for our own good."

She wanted to protest, but she knew he was right. She gathered her belongings. Jack tested his blood sugar again and, with palpable reluctance, he drove her back to Gatlinburg. At her apartment, she kissed him gently and moved across the seat before the feeling could claim her again.

"Don't forget to call me," she said.

"I won't. What days do you go to class?"

"Tuesdays and Thursdays," she said. "But I still work every night except Sunday."

"That hasn't stopped me yet." He grinned. "Remember, this is the nineties. You can call me, too."

"Don't think you had to ask," she said softly. "I had a great time, Jackson." She walked away wanting to tell him she was in love even though the idea seemed crazy. Inside her apartment, she didn't care if she was crazy. She couldn't sleep until she focused on the memory of his face and of how he had made her feel.

All day Monday Laurel expected a call from Jackson. She made only one phone call all day. That call was to the Knoxville chapter of the American Diabetes Association. She asked for information on insulin dependent diabetes.

By some twist of fate, the daytime movie on cable was *Top Gun*. She felt as though she were watching Jackson Driver, and she wondered if he had been like the Tom Cruise character. His comment about pushing the edge of the envelope made her think he had been. Thanks to the movie, she now understood the phrase, "pushing the edge of the envelope." It was about taking risks. She missed Jack even more after the movie ended.

When Laurel drove to work, she consoled herself by thinking Jackson would come to the restaurant. Two of the waitresses she counted as friends had seen him in the parking lot, and they pumped her for information.

She was willing to rave about him. Then midnight came and there were no calls and no Jackson. On the way home Laurel felt like Cinderella after the ball. She walked slowly from the parking lot to her apartment. An envelope was taped to her door. The note was from Jackson. For a brief moment she wondered if she were going to be a recipient of a "Dear Laurel" letter.

Laurel,
My office phone is out of order. They're supposed to have it fixed by tomorrow, but we're not talking about infinitely reliable people. I have to go to Knoxville tonight. I didn't know until I got home or I would have told you yesterday. I'll be at the Parkerson Inn. The phone number is 423-296-4500. Call me when you get in if you get the chance. Okay. Make the chance. I really need to talk to you.
                              Jackson

It was almost 1 A.M. when Laurel let herself into her apartment and hurried to the phone. She dialed three times before she managed to get the number right. An answer was a long time coming.

"Parkerson's," a clerk said.

"I need to speak with Jackson Driver. He's expecting my call."

"I'll ring you through to his room."

The phone in Jackson's room rang only once before it was answered.

"Hi," Laurel said. She was suddenly at a loss for words. Jackson wasn't.

"Laurel, I'm really glad you called. I didn't want you to think I was giving you the brush off or anything like that, but I didn't know I would have to come here until after you left for work."

"Did something bad happen, Jackson? You left so suddenly."

"It was sudden, but it was good news. I've finished all the course work for my doctorate in aerospace engineering. They've had my dissertation for the last couple of months, and they asked me to come to defend it. It's like taking an oral examination. I was scheduled for next week, but the guy who was supposed to defend his dissertation this week got sick. I'll probably be here for the next three days. Say a big prayer for me. I'm really nervous."

"I will," Laurel said. "I guess it sounds stupid, but I miss you."

"No, it doesn't sound stupid. I've been feeling the same way. If I hadn't been on a tight schedule with flights, I would have closed my shop and come to see you. I have a friend who will be working the chopper until I get back, so maybe I'll just come over to your place if I get through early enough on Thursday. Do you think you could take off Friday night?"

"I'll ask in the morning. I never miss work so maybe the manager will have mercy on me." She held the phone tightly. "Call me tomorrow night if you're not too tired."

"I will. Wish me luck." He paused. "I don't want to hang up, but I've got to get some sleep or I'll be more of an idiot than usual. I'll talk to you tomorrow night."

"Good luck." She kept clutching the phone when the line went dead. Then she sat on the bed and tried to remember every detail of Jackson's face. She prayed for him before going to sleep.

Laurel's three-hour photography class at the community college began at 1 P.M. She had made enlargements of her two best shots and presented them for inspection along with the photos taken by the other twenty students.

"Very nice work, Miss Wolfe," Dr. Cotham said. "You really should sign up for the advanced course this fall. See me after class and we'll discuss it."

After class he informed her that he had submitted her name for a scholarship. "I'm certain you'll get it," he said. "You're a minority, and you've made straight A's in all your course work. You need to think of enrolling as a full-time student in the fall. You have enough hours to be nearing your junior year." He smiled at her expression. "Miss Wolfe, I have never known you to be this quiet."

"I'm just surprised," she admitted. "I didn't think I was good enough." She thought of Jackson and how it might be embarrassing to him to have an uneducated girlfriend. She made her decision. "I want to do it. What should I do next?"

Dr. Cotham gave her an envelope. "This is the application. Fill it out tonight and turn it in on Thursday at the latest. I'm going to enter your photograph in the school's competition." He smiled his dismissal, and Laurel floated to her car. The day just got better when she arrived at the restaurant. A dozen roses were waiting for her at the front desk. The card read, "So far so good. I'm missing you a lot. Don't forget to ask about Friday night."

Jane, one of Laurel's waitress friends, brushed past her humming "I Could Have Danced All Night."

"So, I guess he's making up for last night," Jane said.

"He definitely made up for last night." Laurel laughed. "I just wish he were here tonight."

The evening dragged, but she knew Jackson would call her when she got home. She asked for Friday night off, and her wish was granted. When she arrived home, Jackson didn't call. After spending two tortured hours wondering about their relationship, she fell asleep clutching the telephone. The telephone awakened her at 6 A.M. It was her stepmother, Mary.

"You need to come to Cherokee this morning, Laurie," Mary said. She sounded frantic. "Your daddy had a heart attack last night. He's in intensive care." The words brought an end to her illusion of joy like a hammer shattering a perfect piece of porcelain.

"I'm on my way," Laurel promised. She hurried to the shower and didn't hear the telephone ring for a second time. She didn't have an answering machine.

Jackson sighed as he hung up the telephone in his hotel room. He didn't have time to keep trying the call. As he gathered his briefcase and laptop, he wished he could gather his thoughts as easily. On the way to his meeting, his mind wandered. His years as a fighter pilot and endless prayers allowed him to refocus himself as the second day of inquisition began.

He hadn't been sure of his progress after the first day. He had been so mentally exhausted that he had fallen asleep before the appointed time to call Laurel. He knew he had been successful at the end of the second day because all the professors seemed to be running out of questions. Finally, they stood to congratulate him.

"I don't believe we'll need to continue this defense," Dr. Campbell said with a mentor's pride. "It's very obvious that you know your subject. If you'll see the department secretary, she'll give you instructions about graduation. I presume you'll want at least some of your recommendations mailed to NASA. I sent them a copy of your dissertation, and Colonel Asher seemed very impressed."

"I would appreciate any help you can give me," Jackson acknowledged. "I've just got to see what they'll say. If it doesn't work out, I've got a couple of other really nice offers. I'm not in a hurry to decide."

"If you're still here this evening, Libby and I would like for you to join us for supper," Dr. Campbell said.

"I wish I could, but I really need to get back. Since I didn't know I was going to be here this week, I had to quickly change arrangements. After graduation I'd like to take you and your wife to dinner."

"We'll plan on that, Jack. Good luck to you and let me know if you hear from NASA."

Decorum required that Jack speak to each participating professor before he departed. What he really wanted to do was shout "Thank God! I made it" and call all the important people in his life. Military training helped him keep his celebration to himself. It couldn't stop him from thinking about Laurel. Knowing her for just a few days, he didn't want a future without her.

When all the proper farewells had been said, Jack hurried to his truck and drove to the hotel. He took enough time to test his sugar and eat a snack. Then he was on the highway headed for Gatlinburg.

Laurel arrived at the hospital in time to hear the tail end of the first family conference with the doctor.

"Mr. Wolfe was having a massive heart attack. Fortunately the clot-breaking medicine we gave him allowed us to stop the heart attack before any permanent damage occurred. He's going to need to be transferred to a larger hospital so we can do an arteriogram and find out where his blockage is. I expect he will need at least balloon surgery and possibly bypass surgery. I've already spoken to a cardiologist in Knoxville, and I think that might be our best selection."

Laurel's brothers, Joseph and Peter, were obviously in charge. They made the decision without even consulting Mary. Joseph spoke for both of them. "Knoxville will be an easier drive for us. We'll be ready to go when you're ready to take him."

"We'll plan to transport him in the morning then. You can take turns visiting him, but no more than two at a time should visit. Please don't upset him."

Mary and her daughter, Suzanne, followed the doctor to intensive care, leaving Laurel with her brothers. Neither brother seemed particularly pleased to see her.

"Dad will be glad to see you," Peter said grimly. "He

was asking if any of us had heard from you on Sunday. How have you been, Laurie?"

"I've been fine. I talk to dad at least once a month. He didn't say anything about being ill." Laurel felt guilty, and it came through in her words.

"If he lives, I'm sure he'll tell you all about it," Joseph said sharply. "If you want to be a part of this family, Laurel, you need to be with the family. I think you need to grow up while dad's alive to see it. We all know the stress you put him under probably caused this."

They left Laurel alone as they went to see their father. Mary spoke to her politely, but no one sat with her. Visiting hours ended before she had an opportunity to visit her father. She started to walk to intensive care only to have Joseph block her path.

"I don't think you should go, Laurel. I was watching the monitor when I told him I had heard from you. His heart rate got faster and skipped beats. I don't think you need to add to his stress. If you want to help him, sit here and pray."

She was devastated by his words. She and her brothers had always been close, but now it was obvious they were very angry with her. She didn't know how to change that. Faced with four hours of isolation, she used the pay phone to call the Parkerson Inn in Knoxville and prayed Jackson wanted to talk to her. Learning that Jackson had checked out of the hotel was almost too much for her. She did, however, have the presence of mind to leave a message on his answering machines at home and at his office. Then she walked to the chapel and sat down. She felt less alone there.

Chapter 4

Jackson headed home in hopes of spending the afternoon with Laurel. His only stop was at the kennel to pick up Kennedy, who was happy to see his master. The dog followed Jackson through the house while he changed clothes. He was about to leave when he noticed the flashing light on his answering machine. He decided to listen to the messages before his departure in case Laurel had tried to call him. Her message was the last of five, and immediately her voice made him uneasy.

"Jackson, it's Laurel. I'm in Cherokee. My dad had a heart attack this morning. He's in intensive care. I called your hotel, and they said you had checked out. I didn't want you to worry when you couldn't reach me. I hope everything went well. I've been praying for you. I guess I'd better go. Pray for my dad."

He flipped off the machine. He felt sorry for Laurel. He was also disappointed because he had wanted to celebrate his graduation with her. He prayed for her father and then called his father and brother. He had to be content with leaving messages on their machines. Needing company, he headed for his office. While driving toward it, he decided to take the winding highway leading to Cherokee, North Carolina.

It was dusk when he drove through town, and he had to ask directions to the hospital. As he pulled into the parking lot, he realized he had missed lunch. He stopped to purchase a soft drink before looking for the intensive care waiting room. He was fairly sure his blood sugar was low, but he knew the sugar in the soda would buy him enough time to eat supper. A volunteer at the waiting room desk showed him to the chapel where he found Laurel sitting alone in the front pew. She didn't move until he sat down beside her. Her eyes registered surprised recognition just before she flung herself into his arms and started crying.

"I'm so glad you came," she sobbed. "My brothers are blaming me for this. I haven't gotten to see my dad at all. I don't even think he knows I'm here." She held onto him while he stroked her hair. It felt like coming home for Laurel when he held her close. Jackson had no desire to release her. He had never felt needed by another person. When Laurel could control her tears, she looked up into his eyes. "Why did you come?"

"I thought you might need a friend." He wiped her tears with his fingers and offered her a drink of his soda. "Let's go get something to eat before I fall out. Then we'll find some paper so you can write your dad a note. I'll bet one of the nurses will make sure he gets it."

She agreed, and he let her drive his truck while he checked his blood sugar. He finished the soda after entering the number in his logbook.

"Are you really low?" Laurel felt anxious.

"Not too bad. It's under seventy, but I've already had enough sugar to bail out." He watched her face in the shadowy light. "I passed, Laurel. I'll get to graduate next month."

"You're so awesome," she said. "I've never even been friends with a Ph.D. before. I got to thinking maybe you'd be embarrassed to have a girlfriend with nothing but a high school diploma."

"That's not true." He took her hand and held it firmly. "I'm eleven years older than you are, and I'm just coming to a place where I know what I want to do with the rest of my life. I might enjoy seeing how it happens for you. Did your professor like your pictures?"

"He really did. He has submitted my name for a scholarship for the fall. I was feeling good about everything and then my stepmother called." Laurel pulled into a restaurant parking lot and turned off the ignition. "I received the roses you sent. No one has ever sent me flowers before. You're the first for a lot of things in my life."

He pulled her close and kissed her without holding back any of his emotions. She could feel his desire as clearly as she could feel her own. He kissed her until she was hot and cold and trembling. She clung to him, not wanting to let go.

"I want to be first, Laurel," he whispered against her ear. "I want to be first in your life always." Their eyes were holding them together even more tightly than their hands.

"I want you to be first, Jackson," she said. Her eyes made him feel loved, and he acted on that feeling. He kissed her again, forgetting about food or any need other than holding her in his arms. When the car windows were fogging over, Laurel sat back reluctantly.

"This is a really small town. If we stay here like this, my reputation will be shot." She smiled. "I've never made windows fog up before."

"Like I said, I want to have all the firsts." Jack laughed as he took her hand. "Let's eat and go leave your father a note." He led her into the little diner to a corner booth and ordered for both of them. Neither of them saw her brothers until they came to the table.

"I guess we know why you've stayed away," Peter said with bitterness in his voice. "You knew dad wouldn't approve of where and how you're living."

Laurel flushed and started to protest. Jackson stood and faced her brothers. "I don't see how hurting Laurel will help anybody," Jackson said calmly. "You're mistaken about us. We're good friends and that's it. As far as I know, she lives alone in Gatlinburg. Even if you disagree with where she lives, she's still your sister."

"Why do you have any right to be here?" Peter said. "This is none of your business."

"I'm her friend. She needs one right now. Actually she needs her family, but that obviously isn't an option. You made it my business when you made your accusation." Jackson's voice was flat and in no way challenging, but Peter was distraught and not listening. He grabbed Jackson's shoulder. Laurel came to her feet and froze as Jackson easily spun her brother and pinned his arm between his shoulders.

"Don't go there, Mr. Wolfe," Jackson said tersely. "You're way out of your league. If you can't talk to your sister like a Christian man, just leave us alone." He released Peter and sat down as the waitress pushed past Laurel's brothers to bring their drinks.

"Go somewhere and cool off," she said to the brothers. "If you don't leave these people alone, the manager is going to call the police. It's your choice."

"Stay away from our father, Laurel," Joseph said sharply. "You walked out of his life and our lives. It was your choice. Stand by it."

Laurel's face was gray despite her dark complexion. Jackson drew up his insulin without looking at her while she made an effort to pull herself together.

"I don't think I can eat," she said.

"Then eat for me because I've got to eat." Jackson picked up his fork and looked at her. "I gather you left home against your dad's wishes."

"I felt lost when my mother died," Laurel admitted. "I needed her, and sometimes I feel like I still do. My dad was my best friend then. Peter is ten years older than me, and he got married when I was twelve. Joseph is seven years older, and he was in vocational school when I started high school. It was just my daddy and me. I cooked for him and kept house for him. I didn't think he needed anyone else.

"When he started dating Mary, I thought he was rejecting me. At first I tried to do more for him so he wouldn't need her, but it seemed like he spent even more time with her. Then I became really serious with my high school boyfriend mainly to make my dad jealous, but I think he knew what I was doing. Instead of talking to me about why, he told me I should marry Jimmy if we loved each other. He said he had asked Mary to be his wife. We're both stubborn like that.

"I knew I wasn't in love with Jimmy, and I believed my dad loved Mary more than he loved me so I left home. I moved to Gatlinburg and found a job. I stayed in the spare room of this older lady's house for the first six months. She was a widow, and her daughter had died. She was like my mother for a long time. She even had the same name as my mother—Miriam. She talked me into going back to school, so now I have enough credits to be a sophomore. I just didn't know what my major would be until recently.

"Miriam broke her hip about eight months ago and had to move into a retirement complex. Her son moved her to Nashville to be closer to him. She made me understand how my dad felt. Dad knew I would have to grow up, and he couldn't stand losing me. So he drove me away, and I let him. He loves Mary, and she's a good person. I just wish I could have my daddy back."

"If you apologized to your stepmother, you probably could," Jackson said quietly. "I know it isn't easy because I had to do it myself. At least your stepmother is human. Mine is like the stereotypic WASP in a bad sixties movie. She pretends that my dad has always been married to her, and I think she likes to forget he has

two sons who are darker complexioned than her comfort level. Actually she's the modern day equivalent of
Cinderella's stepmother, and she has the daughters to
prove it. Lucien and I stopped trying to see our father
after we left home. I had a few memorable confrontations with my stepmother.

"After I left the service and got dumped by the
blond, I really needed to feel less alone so I apologized
to Charlene. I got my father back. It was worth eating
crow, Laurel. Just swallow hard and pretend it's medicine. Someday you won't remember how it tasted." He
smiled wryly. "You know your apology will be easier
than mine. I'm pretty sure the quarter Navajo really
bothers Charlene and her friends. I've had people guess
I was part Navajo since I was a kid, but no one ever
made me feel ashamed of being part Native American
until I met Charlene and her contingent. Lucien looks
even more Navajo than I do. How do you spell bigot?"

"Oh, I can spell it," Laurel said. "I think that's why
most Native Americans live on reservations. I've had
the deed done to me more than once since I left home.
Now I analyze it. You have the arrogant bigot who
stoops to discuss your gene pool while carefully keeping his feet away from the slime. Then there's the stupid
bigot who knows you aren't white and has to guess
what you are. Finally you get the occasional Aryan
racist who calls anybody darker than he is a 'nigger.'"
Her dark eyes communicated her anxiety. "Your stepmother might disown you for hanging around with a
non white girl."

"Do you think I care?" Jackson said. Her eyes mesmerized him. They were very dark brown and rimmed
with long black lashes. "Remember my mother was half
Navajo so my dad should understand where I'm coming from. I actually think he knows how Charlene feels
because he tries to spend time just with me and Lucien
when we're home. I've wondered how he's stayed mar

ried to her, but he believes in keeping vows." He exhaled slowly, suddenly losing his own appetite and wishing he could recall the insulin he had given. "I've got to eat this or have fun like we had on Sunday."

"I'm sorry I made you upset," Laurel said. "I guess we've both had a trail of tears." She dug into her food with determination. "Your name will drive my father crazy. You know Andrew Jackson was the one who sent the Cherokee on the Trail of Tears. My father is like the chairman of the impeach Andrew Jackson posthumously committee."

"That's easy to fix," Jackson said. "I hate my name. I'd much rather be called Jack. Why don't we drop the son permanently? I was just plain old Jack Driver in the Air Force. My dad goes by J.R."

"I like your name," she said. "But I can't see it ever being plain old Jack. There must have been a title when you were in the Air Force. What was it?"

"Major," he said. "Major Jack Driver otherwise known as Wildfire. Pilots have a call name." He finished his food as he thought of the other things he needed to tell her. He decided they had both had enough gut wrenching for one night. The waitress refilled their coffee cups and loaned them a clean pad of paper and a pen. With Jack's help, Laurel drafted two letters. One was to her stepmother, and one was to her father. Long before the sun rose over Cherokee, they took both letters to the intensive care waiting room and left them for the volunteer to give to Mary Wolfe.

Laurel seemed lost. Jack put his arm around her. "Why don't you follow me back to my place? You can get some sleep there. After they leave, we'll call and find out which hospital they'll be taking him to. I can always fly you to Knoxville and avoid the traffic."

She agreed because she was exhausted. It was a battle to stay awake and follow Jack's dark blue truck across the mountains. When they reached his house, she stumbled getting out of her car and fell on the gravel driveway. Jack picked her up and carried her over the threshold of his house. Laurel closed her eyes and tried to pretend she was his bride. He laid her on his bed and sat beside her for a long tempting moment. When he started to get up, she held onto his arms.

"Don't leave," she begged. "I'm in love with you, Jack. Please don't leave me. Just hold me."

He caressed her hair from her forehead gently. "I'm in love with you, too, Laurel. Feeling that way makes me want to make love with you. If I try to sleep next to you, I don't think I'll be able to do the right thing. It's 2 A.M. Get some sleep and we'll talk some more when we're rested." He extricated himself from her grasp and covered her with a woven blanket. She could smell Jack's scent on the pillows and the blanket, and it was comforting. When she closed her eyes, she could pretend she was sleeping with her head on his chest. She was asleep before he left the room to seek sleep on the couch in the den.

The phone rang at noon and awakened Jack. He answered it groggily and then sat up as he recognized the voice.

"What do you want, Alyssa?"

"Just to talk, Jack. I've missed you. I've written to you more than once."

"Don't expect an answer, Alyssa. I've got better things to do than relive my mistakes. Call somebody who still cares." He was poised to hang up when he caught the beginning of her next sentence.

"Your dad said you got your doctorate. He's planning on flying down in the morning to surprise you. I think he's told everybody in D.C."

She had always known how to manipulate him, and Alyssa managed to land one tentacle with her words. Jack sat back still holding the phone reluctantly. "When is he leaving?"

"Charlene says he'll get into Knoxville at noon tomorrow. I just thought you would want to know. Take care of yourself, Jack. You know where to find me." She kept control of the conversation until the moment she hung up the telephone.

He could feel he was getting low. He went to the kitchen to eat and test before going to awaken Laurel. She looked like a sleeping angel. He stood at the door and watched her sleep. He wanted to lay down beside her. Because he cared about her, he suppressed those feelings and sat down on the opposite side of the bed before he touched her.

"You might want to wake up now," he said. "Morning has passed us by."

She smiled at him and said, "Good morning or afternoon."

"Afternoon is closer. It's almost 1 P.M. Do you have to work tonight? Can I talk you into staying here with me?"

"I really should go to work. I just want to know if my dad is all right. Let me call the hospital and find out where they took him."

Jack handed her the telephone and gave her privacy to make her call. He returned with a cup of coffee for each of them just as she hung up the phone.

"He's in Mercy Hospital in Knoxville. They said Mary left a note for me, but now I can't get it."

"Call them back and ask them to fax it to my office," Jack suggested. "We'll pick it up on the way to your apartment." He scribbled the fax number on a notepad by the bed and gave it to her.

"I'll be afraid to read the note."

"I'll read it for you if you want me to." He paused. "What did the restaurant manager say?"

"He wants me to work if I can. I'm still off tomorrow night, but I guess that doesn't matter now."

"Yes, it does," he said. "My dad is flying into Knox-

ville tomorrow. I want the three of us to have supper."
He hesitated, knowing the conversation with his father
might reveal things Laurel didn't know. "Make your
call to the hospital, and then let's talk. We've got a while
before we'll have to leave."

He finished his cup of coffee and poured another
while trying to think of how much to divulge to her and
how to say what he wanted to say. His reluctance came
from fear of being pushed away and fear of committing
himself, even when every fiber in his being told him he
should. She touched his shoulder as he stared out the
window at the summer day. He was searching for an-
swers that could only come from his heart.

"What are you thinking about, Jack?"

"I was thinking about how fast everything is happening between us," he said without looking at her. "I
know I'm getting serious much faster than I thought I
would or could. I guess before we go any farther, we
need to know how far we're willing to go. I've applied to
the space program again. I'm applying as a civilian
mission specialist because I wouldn't have any chance
as a pilot on insulin. If I'm accepted, it would mean
moving to Houston for as long as I was with NASA."

"That's great, Jack," she exclaimed. "Do you think
you'll get it?"

"I don't know. I have friends who think I will because I had already been accepted once. I have an
interview in a couple of weeks. I think they were waiting to see if I would pass my dissertation defense. If they
accept me, I'd have to move there by the end of the year
to start training." He turned to scan her face. "I guess I
need to know if you could live in Houston if the opportunity came to live there. I wouldn't ask now, but I don't
want either of us to get hurt by a major compatibility
issue. The training is very time consuming at first, and it
wouldn't be possible for me to come back here to see
you very often."

Laurel's eyes widened. His question seemed to be asking for a commitment to live together.

"I could live anywhere my husband needed to live," she said slowly. "I couldn't live with someone I wasn't married to. I couldn't even if I loved him."

"If he loved you, he wouldn't ask you to do that," Jack said. "I'm sorry. I guess that wasn't the best way to ask what you thought."

"I love you, Jack," she said. Her face had the quiet conviction of a young woman in love for the first time. "I wasn't sure of how I felt until you came to Cherokee. When you walked into the chapel, I knew you were the only person I wanted to see. I've never felt that way about anybody else. If I knew you loved me, I'd follow you anywhere you wanted to go in this world or out of this world."

Jack smiled and reached for her hand.

"I feel the same way, Laurel. I know some of it is chemistry, but that's not the biggest part of it. You make me feel like—like we're mirror images of each other. I've never felt that way before." He exhaled slowly. "Give me a minute." He went to the refrigerator and poured a half glass of orange juice, which he drained as if it were medicine. "I didn't eat enough, and I'm feeling a little stressed. Do you want something to eat?"

"Why don't I make something while you take a shower?" she suggested.

"Okay. When I get through, I'll lay everything out for you. Do you have a change of clothes?"

"I have a suitcase in my car. The keys are in my purse." Jack walked to her car and retrieved her suitcase. He set it right outside the bathroom door and then stepped into the shower hoping it would clear his head. He prayed about what to do and came out of the water feeling even more certain that he had met the woman he was supposed to marry. When he returned to the kitchen, she was setting soup and biscuits on the table.

"You're multitalented," he said. "I've never had anyone to cook for me other than the mess hall in the Air Force."

She stepped back to let him choose his seat. "Eat and I'll be right back."

"Wait," he said. "I was talking about how committed you could be, Laurel. I just wanted to know if you could live with the diabetes and all that it brings with it."

"If I couldn't, I wouldn't have said I love you," she said simply. "I'll be right back. Eat or you'll hurt the cook's feelings."

Eating had become a battle for Jack, but that meal wasn't. It felt like a gift of normalcy. When Laurel returned to the kitchen, she was dressed for work, but she sat beside him until they had both eaten. They cleaned up the kitchen together and then sat in his living room while he showed her pictures of when he had been in the Air Force. Several pages of the photograph album were empty, and they were pages Laurel knew had belonged to the blond. She was glad they were empty as she promised herself to get the blond's picture removed from Jack's desk.

"So do you ever think about your high school boyfriend?" Jack asked her.

"No. He was my friend. He had his feet firmly on the ground, and I had my head in the clouds. I love it in Cherokee, but I want to see other places. A lot of people like my dad never go anywhere except Qualla Boundary. He was in the service, but he came home without seeing anything else of the world. I guess I see myself living here someday, but not always."

"It's sort of the opposite of how I've lived," Jack told her. "I've lived in twenty different countries. I don't think of any place as home. I don't think my brother does either. After our mother died, there just wasn't any constancy. These mountains drew me the first time I saw them, but maybe that was your aura and I just didn't know it."

She moved closer to him and embraced him. "What's it like in Houston?"

"Flat, but it's close to the ocean. Have you seen the ocean?"

"In books and on television." Laurel smiled and looked into his eyes. "Maybe you're supposed to show me the world."

The words to commit himself rose inside Jack, and the clock on his desk struck five o'clock.

"We're out of time," Laurel moaned.

"I'll take you to work and go back to check the fax machine," he told her. "I'll pick you up at midnight. Then I'll have time to go see Buddy and find out what's been happening this week. I'll file a flight plan so we can fly to Knoxville in the morning."

"I'll have to get more clothes," she said. "This is a lot of trouble for you."

"No. I want to do it, and I would want you to come with me even if your father weren't in the hospital there." He led her out to the car. "If you go with me to live in Houston, I'll make sure you are enrolled in one of the colleges there. I wouldn't ask you to give up what you want for what I want."

She felt serene when he left her at the restaurant. It was hard to watch him drive away, but she felt like everything in her life was falling into place. Even though he hadn't really asked her to marry him, Laurel felt almost engaged. She couldn't keep from smiling every time anyone asked her about him, but most of the questions were about her father. Those were the questions that were hard to answer.

Chapter 5

Jack drove to his office and found a note from Buddy along with a bank deposit for half of the week's receipts. While pulling the fax messages out of his machine's memory, Jack called Buddy.

"Hi Buddy. How did it go?"

"Hey, Jack. I should be asking you that question. Did you do the deed?"

"Signed, sealed and to be delivered in two weeks. I really appreciate you minding the store for me. Did the chopper behave?"

"I think you need a new filter," Buddy said. "I'll pick one up on my way in tomorrow if that's okay. The engine's missing just a little more than it should."

"It probably does need a new filter," Jack said as he flipped through his maintenance log. "I changed it six weeks ago, but it's had a lot of miles since then. I've got to fly down and pick up my dad tomorrow morning. He's coming into Knoxville to help me celebrate. Can you finish out the week?"

"I was hoping you would ask me to," Buddy said. "I could use the money. School starts in a month, and I've got to earn another $800 to pay tuition."

"I'll probably be needing you a couple more times before you go back. Thanks, Buddy. I'll talk to you on Saturday night."

Jack walked over to the fax machine and pulled off the nine messages. The first few were reservations, and he recorded those on his calendar. One was a letter of congratulations from his brother.

July 19, 1999
Jack,

I was really excited to get your message. I knew you'd get it done. I've had the feeling that you were going to apply to NASA again. If my opinion counts, you should go for it. I have leave in three weeks, and I'll try to fly up to see you then. If you get a break, fly down here and spend some time on the beach. I have a bunch of good looking ladies panting to meet you. I also want you to meet my girlfriend, Julissa. I may need some backup with dad and Charlene. She's Hispanic, and I'm sure Charlene won't let dad approve of her. We're starting to talk about forever stuff. I hope you still believe in forever because we both know what happened with Alyssa wasn't your fault. I'm praying for you. Pray for me. You'll find this same message on your e-mail. I wanted to make sure you got to read it today.
Lucien

Jack folded the letter and stuffed it in his pocket, planning a lengthy response for his e-mail. The next fax was the message from Laurel's stepmother. He said a prayer before reading it.

Laurie,

I was really happy to get your letter. Your father was overjoyed to get his. I know he has been praying for the chance to make things right between the two of you.

Knowing you feel the same way made it easier for him to accept what's happening to him now. I'll take care of Peter and Joseph. They're men, and they don't understand how we feel. If you'll come to Mercy Hospital in Knoxville, I'll go with you to see your father. For myself, I've been praying we could someday be friends. I will be very glad to see you.

Mary

Jack was relieved at the response and sat down to reread the letter. Like Laurel, he felt as if everything were falling into place even before he read the last letter. It was from his contact at Houston.

July 19, 1999
Major Driver,
I received a letter and a phone call from Dr. Campbell this afternoon. He was effusive in his report of your dissertation defense and tells me your graduation is just a formality now. Of course, your situation with the agency has always been different from that of other applicants in that you were accepted into the program previously and voluntarily withdrew. For this reason, we have moved your interview ahead. We would like for you to come to Houston a week from Monday. You'll need to be here for approximately four days. Please be ready to have a physical examination and perform a fitness test under the supervision of our physicians. They will want an updated report from your endocrinologist and a recent glucometer record to document your compliance to treatment of your diabetes. I will need a confirmation of your intention to attend these meetings by Monday, 23 July. Good luck.
Sincerely,
Albert Asher
Colonel, United States Air Force

Jack sat with the letter in his hands and thought about how many years he had prayed for the chance to live his lifelong dream. He hadn't been praying to meet someone because he hadn't recovered from his divorce. He couldn't even think of how to speak to Laurel about his marital status. He had always believed divorce was wrong. He had married Alyssa with pomp and circumstance when he was twenty-six. He had known her for a year, and his father and stepmother had encouraged the marriage. Unfortunately, hindsight told him he hadn't really known the woman he had married. She was incredibly manipulative and smart enough to know how to work her audience.

Because of his role as a fighter pilot, they had endured long separations from the beginning of their marriage. Jack, however, did not believe that factor had played a role in Alyssa's actions, which had been completely unforeseen and unbelievably cruel. It was that sense of betrayal that made him fear commitment with anyone else. In fact, he had become a loner who had numerous acquaintances but kept his personal life strictly his own. He had confided in only two people—his brother and his former navigator, Rusty Carter. Rusty had been stationed in Southeast Asia so it was difficult to communicate.

Despite Jack's issues with trust, he knew he had been a breath away from asking Laurel to marry him after knowing her for only six days. He didn't see that desire as poor judgment. He saw their instant rapport as a sign she was different from any woman he had ever known. He had always believed in soul mates. He wondered if people so different in background could be meant to be together. After two hours of soul searching, he called the Knoxville airport and filed a flight plan for the following morning. His last call was to his father's home. He was so anxious about making the call that he checked his blood sugar while the phone was ringing.

Charlene answered, which provoked an adrenaline surge that belied the glucose of 104mg percent.

"Hello, Charlene. It's Jack. I wondered if dad's around."

"Of course, Jackson," she said in her syrupy voice. "And congratulations on your new achievement. Your father was absolutely delighted. Hold on for just a minute, and I'll see if I can find him for you."

"Thanks, Charlene. I really appreciate it." Jack said a prayer to suppress his response to his stepmother and focused on listening to the background noise. Unfortunately he was able to hear a muffled conversation taking place that obviously included more than Charlene telling her husband who was on the telephone.

"Jackson," his father said. "I was delighted to get your message. I can't tell you how happy you've made me."

"Thanks, Dad. I hated to just leave a message, but I couldn't wait to tell you. I heard you might be coming down tomorrow so I filed a flight plan for Knoxville. If you let me know if I'm right, I can meet your plane."

"I'll be there at 11 A.M.," his father said. "How did you guess?"

"Alyssa called me," Jack said grimly. "Hearing her voice put a damper on the news."

"Alyssa isn't the same person she was two years ago," the older Driver said. "I've spent some time with her, and she and the girls still spend a lot of time together. She really wants to see you again."

"Dad, I really couldn't ever see her again. I've prayed to forgive her, but that's the best I can do. She got the divorce, and she moved in with another man. That's called adultery. Let's not get into this now. Actually I'm seeing someone else, and I want to bring her with me so you can meet her."

"I'm not certain we'll have time for that, Jackson," his father said tersely. "I can only stay there until 7 P.M.

There's a summit in Zurich I have to attend on Monday. Why don't you meet me at the airport, and we'll take it from there."

Suddenly Jack regretted calling his father. J.R. had directed Jack's career from the time he had been accepted into the Air Force Academy. That had stopped when he had developed diabetes, but Jack hadn't forgotten his father's tactics. J.R. ignored or refused to discuss anything he didn't agree with. Jack knew Laurel had just been rejected sight unseen because she wasn't a part of the master plan. By remembering the fifth commandment, he managed to suppress the urge to tell his father off .

"I'll be waiting for you, Dad. Have a safe trip." When he hung up the phone, he knew he was probably going to be making a very unpleasant decision in the near future.

He drove to Gatlinburg and walked through the streets until he found a hair stylist to give him a haircut. Then he drove to the restaurant and waited in the parking lot. He was asleep when Laurel knocked on the window.

"I almost didn't recognize you, Jack," she said as he opened the door. "My manager said I could feed you if you showed up early. You didn't reenlist while you were gone, did you?"

"My dad is coming," he said as he stepped out of the truck and locked the door. "After forty years in the Air Force, collar length hair is long to him. He still has a crew cut. Growing mine long was a defiance thing. Dad wasn't amused when it was a couple inches longer than this last Christmas." He put his arm around her. "Actually I cut it now because of my interview. If I get the job at NASA, this would be about as long as it could get."

"You still look good." She wrapped her arms around his waist. "I missed you, Jack." She kissed him and then took his hands. "Let's get you some supper."

She led him into the dining room and introduced him to her manager and two of the waitresses. He almost forgot to give her the letter from her stepmother but pressed it into her hand before she returned to her station. After seating two parties, she read the letter and her smile was his reward.

Jack ordered his meal, tested his blood sugar, and then took insulin under the table. He watched Laurel and didn't think about having to eat. She was beautiful, and he knew it was a different kind of beauty than he had appreciated in the past. There was no pretense in Laurel, and there was no ego despite her appearance. When she smiled, she lit up the room. His watch told him it was eleven o'clock, but the time he sat at the booth seemed insignificant because he was watching her.

At midnight, she collected her purse and paycheck. Jack met her at the door. With his arm around her, they left the restaurant. When he slid into the truck beside her, she kissed him with her hands under his coat holding onto his body. Every time she touched him, he wanted her more.

"Don't change your mind about being with me," she whispered. "I want to be with you for the rest of my life, Jack. I've been thinking about it all night. I've been praying to find the right man, and I know you're the answer to my prayers."

"I've been thinking about it all night, too, and I don't think I could change my mind," he reassured her. "Let's go to your apartment and pick up some clothes. When we get to my house, we can talk more." He turned on the ignition only to have Laurel place his testing kit in his hand. For Jack, it was an intimate gesture because she had thought of it—and because he didn't feel disturbed about having her think of it. She recorded the reading while he was driving out of the parking lot.

They stopped in the apartment complex lobby and picked up her mail. A thick folder from the ADA was prominent among the letters. As she gathered her clothes and other belongings, Jack collected her flute case.

"So what did you get from the American Diabetes Association?" he asked casually.

"I requested information about insulin dependent diabetes. I thought it would be better if I knew more about it."

"I want you to know," he said. "I need to go by my endocrinologist's office, and I'll see what the educator has for you to read. Do you think you could give me a shot if you had to?"

"I don't know why not," she said as she emerged from the bedroom.

"There's an antidote to insulin. It's called glucagon. If I ever got really low, somebody else could give it to me. I don't keep it because I live alone, but I'd like to have it."

"I can do whatever you need me to do," she said in a determined voice. "What do you hate the most about it? I mean other than not being in the Air Force any more?"

"Not being able to go barefoot," he said. "I always liked going barefoot, and that's lesson one of foot care. Don't take the risk of going without shoes even in your own house. Always wear socks. Shake your shoes out before you put them on."

"Why do you have to do all that?" Laurel asked.

"You can lose some of the feeling in your feet even if your sugars are in fairly good control. If you lose any sensation, you could step on something and cut yourself or even get it stuck in your foot and not know it until you caused an infection. That's how diabetics lose their feet. It gets old remembering to always put on your shoes."

Laurel looked down at her own bare feet and realized she had never seen Jack go without shoes. She resolved to start wearing her shoes all the time to know how he felt. She slipped her feet into her clogs and picked up her suitcase. "I'm ready," she said.

Jack slid his arm around her again, and the embrace felt even more possessive as they walked to his truck. Laurel liked the way it felt, and she moved to the center seat to sit close to him during the ride to his house.

It never seemed awkward or wrong to be alone with him. Neither of them were tired so they sipped iced tea and sat on the sofa in comfortable silence.

"I never prayed to meet anyone else," Jack said quietly. "It meant a lot to me to know you'd been praying about it. I have to ask why you think I'm the answer to your prayer."

"Because we're so much alike," she said without hesitation. "I feel like I know what you'll say before you say it. It just feels right. It feels so wonderful being with you." She rested her head on his shoulder. "I'm still praying about it, Jack. God hasn't done anything to make me have second thoughts."

"It may not always be this easy," Jack said reluctantly. "I don't think it will be tomorrow." His hand tightened on her shoulder. "My dad has always tried to run my life. He quit when he thought my life was over, but I called him today. He's ready to start running me again. I think he's decided that I need to get back with Alyssa. He told her that he was coming down here, and she called me." He could feel Laurel trembling under his hands, and he pulled her into his lap.

"It's not like that, Laurel. I don't care what he wants. I want you. I just need you to know how he's going to act, and I need to tell you that Alyssa and I were married."

Laurel met his gaze without being able to conceal her feelings. Divorce was something her family had preached against from her earliest memory. She had the brief feeling that Jack's divorce might be a sign to pull back. When she saw the palpable expression on his face, she knew the divorce had not been of Jack's making.

"I was stationed all over the place after we got married. Technically I was at Langley Air Force Base, but I was overseas more than I was home. They do that when you're skilled in fighter jets. You get sent to all the hot spots.

"Alyssa stayed in D.C. with her family and friends. I thought she loved me—that is until I got sick. There were some things she did that got to me, but not to the point that I could see being abandoned.

"The base notified her when I was in intensive care. I think they weren't making any guarantees that I would live when I first got there. They offered to transport her to Germany, but she refused to go. By the time I returned to the States, she had filed for divorce and was living with another man. I've always believed divorce is wrong, but I didn't do anything wrong, Laurel. I never slept with anyone before I got married. I didn't cheat when I was married, and I haven't been with anyone since then. Alyssa has. She even brought one of them to divorce court with her.

"I'm sorry I didn't tell you sooner, but it's hard to talk about it when I know people should marry for life. I have the divorce papers if you want to see them. She didn't even try to lie about her reason: 'As Major Driver has become ill and is no longer able to perform his profession as a pilot, the plaintiff expects a significant change in her life-style, which is unacceptable to her.'" The words were incredibly cruel. Jack's face reflected how those words had hit him three years earlier and how they continued to hurt him undimmed by time.

"Don't," Laurel said. "Don't think about it, Jack. It doesn't matter to me. You didn't do anything wrong." She placed her hand on his face. "What about how your father feels?"

"I love you, Laurel. I can't understand how I could feel so much when we've only known each other a few days, but I know it's true. I want to marry you. I know what I want, but you should take all the time you need to decide if I am who you want. I'd prefer that you don't go with me tomorrow because I don't want you to be treated badly by my father. He doesn't hide how he feels. It won't be because he doesn't like you. He'll ignore you as if you aren't there because you are not a part of his plans, so therefore you don't matter."

"Tell me what you think I should do, and I'll do it," she said simply. "I already know how I feel about marrying you, Jack. I could get married tonight with no second thoughts, and I would be marrying you for the rest of our lives."

He held her tightly because he didn't trust himself to control his emotions. After a while, he knew she was asleep in his arms. He carried her to his room and laid her on the bed. Then he opened his computer and sent e-mail messages to his brother and to Colonel Asher in Houston.

Chapter 6

Laurel awakened in Jack's bed. She was alone. For a brief moment, she wished she would find Jack lying beside her even though she knew that would be morally wrong and devastating to their relationship. She found Jack dozing on the sofa. She lay down beside him with her head on his shoulder, and he moved to allow her more room. It felt good to him to hold her in the early morning light.

"What time do we have to leave?" she asked.

"By nine if you want me to drive you to the hospital. By ten if you take yourself. You need to either call your professor or send him an e-mail to explain why you missed class on Thursday. I don't want you getting kicked out of school for attendance issues."

Laurel looked at Jack's watch. "It's six o'clock. Why don't you take your shower, and I'll make us some breakfast. Then you can show me how to use your computer after I have my shower and change."

"I wish I could," he said, "but I need to go run first. The other letter I got yesterday was my invitation to Houston. I've got to be able to pass their idea of a health screen. If boot camp is any indication, I'm not ready."

"If you run, I run," she said adamantly. "I've got some shorts and a tee shirt. Check your sugar, and I'll be right back."

She changed and returned to find him eating glucose tablets.

"Are you too low, Jack?"

"Just perfect, but I'll be low by the time we finish running if I don't carbohydrate load. I've never gotten the amount right, and I have only one week to get it right."

"Why don't you spread them out more?" she asked. "I mean it seems like your body should release a little at a time."

He stopped and pocketed the tablets. "That makes sense." He whistled for Kennedy. "Let's go."

Sevierville lacked the mountains Laurel loved, but she was glad it was flat by the time they finished running. They jogged three miles in the early morning cool. When they returned to Jack's house, they were both drenched in sweat. Jack went to the bathroom and returned with a different glucose meter to test. The reading was 249mg percent.

"Not perfect yet," he said. "I did four tablets, but I'd done three when you made your suggestion. Tomorrow I'll try one every half hour."

"Why the different meter?" Laurel asked.

"They're going to download that one to have a record of how well controlled I've been. Last night I downloaded it and erased the memory. I need to be really good between now and when we go."

"We?"

"You and me, if you want to go. I hope you will."

"Then I'm going." She hesitated. "I have my photography final that week."

"I'll get you a copy of the letter from NASA. Maybe your professor will cut us some slack." He wiped her face with his towel and then kissed her. "Get a shower."

"You first. I'm the cook, remember."

They left at 8:30 and parked at the airport at 9 A.M. The walk around, checklist and last sugar check took ten minutes. They were airborne at 9:15 A.M.

"I'll miss the mountains," Laurel said quietly.

"We can fly back any weekend you want to. It only takes about four hours by jet. Even in this plane it wouldn't take more than ten hours with bad winds." He took her hand. "We're both jumping the gun a little. I've got to pass the interview and the physical. If we get accepted, the next few weeks are going to pass quickly." Her hand was cold and damp against his, and he glanced at her.

"I was just thinking about my dad," Laurel said.

"Stick with Mary and tell him how you feel. I bet you're going to have a better time than I'm going to have. Just don't get him irritated. As soon as he's feeling better, I've got to ask him for permission to marry you. I was thinking we could get married in Houston and head for Navajo country for our honeymoon."

"Or we could go somewhere tonight," she suggested. Jack had to force himself to look at the horizon and try to ignore her offer.

"Think about it, Laurel. I gave you a whole lot to think about last night."

"It didn't make any difference, Jack, and it won't." She studied his face as she tried to understand if he were still afraid she couldn't commit. Or was he having a problem taking the final step? In her heart, it seemed too right to have any doubts. "Do you believe me?"

"I do." He smiled. "The word choice wasn't by accident either. I'm just—I'm afraid of doing something wrong and making you change your mind. In some ways it doesn't seem fair to you. I want to believe this is God rewarding me for hanging in there." He glanced at her and saw she didn't understand.

"I used to think I had a perfect life. I was doing what

I wanted to do, and I was successful in my career. I made it to major before I was thirty, which doesn't happen very often. I was married, and Alyssa is attractive from a surface standpoint. I flew some really hairy combat missions in Desert Storm, but I always made it back. I felt invincible.

"Then this happened and, in just a few weeks, I lost everything I thought was important. That's what I meant when I told you I wasn't really a Christian then. I'd been going to church and praying all my life, but I hadn't been tested. When you don't have a reason to keep living except for your faith, you have to prove what you believe. I had to come to a point where I felt like this wasn't some kind of punishment. It just happened, and what happens after that depends on me and how hard I work and how hard I pray. I thought maybe I was supposed to go it alone, but now— I can't tell you how it feels to even have the chance to share my life with you."

He was telling her that he loved her in a way that touched her more than the words would have. Now Laurel wasn't afraid to face her father because she had Jack.

"Think about tonight," she said softly. "I'm ready to say forever, Jack. In my heart I already have."

The flight was short. They made their approach at 10 A.M. and followed two planes the tower called "heavies" onto the 9R runway. Jack explained that was air traffic controller slang for commercial airplanes. After they landed, Jack arranged for a tie-down at the hangar and called Laurel a cab.

"I'll come pick you up when my dad's ready to leave, but if it doesn't go well with your family just get a cab and come back here. I'll check here before I come downtown. You pray, and I'll pray." He kissed her as the cab pulled up to the hangar. She left for the hospital, and Jack began walking to the terminal.

Laurel prayed during the entire ride to Mercy Hospital. She continued praying as she approached the information desk. The attendant informed her that her father was in surgical intensive care on the fifth floor. On the elevator, Laurel took deep breaths and thought of Jack. His task was no easier than hers.

Laurel was calm when she reached the waiting room. She scanned the room until she saw her stepmother. Mary rose to meet Laurel before her brothers could. She put her arms around Laurel and held her until Peter and Joseph sat down again. Then she pulled Laurel aside.

"He's doing really well, Laurie. They did five bypasses yesterday afternoon, and he's already off the life-support equipment. We'll get to see him again at noon. I've been talking to Peter and Joseph since I got your letter. I think we should all go get some coffee and talk."

"I'll do whatever you think, Mary," Laurel said meekly. "I just want to make everything right again."

It had started as an act to get her father back, but Mary's arm around her shoulders communicated her stepmother's genuine care and concern for Laurel. Mary was able to command the respect and obedience of Laurel's brothers. They walked down to the coffee shop as if their problems had already been solved. The four of them settled at a table far from the other customers.

"I think you need to hold your tempers and let Laurel talk," Mary said. "Neither of you were living at home when your mother died, and neither of you were there when your father and I started seeing each other. You're in no place to judge her." She looked at Laurel. "Tell them what you told your father and me."

"I did everything wrong," Laurel said softly. "I took care of mom until she died. When she was dying, she made me promise to take care of daddy. I did it because I had promised mom and because I didn't have to dwell on thoughts about her being gone. I didn't do anything but take care of daddy. I went to school, and then I came home and did the washing and cooking and cleaning. I did it all for three years.

"Then I was a senior, and I think daddy knew it couldn't last forever. He knew it shouldn't last forever because I didn't have a life. He didn't have a life either.

"Daddy started dating Mary, and I felt as though he was rejecting me. I was desperate to keep doing my job since I'd promised mom I'd do it. So I tried to make him stop seeing Mary. When it didn't work, I ran away. I can't change what happened. All I can do is say I'm sorry. You both know I haven't had much of a life until now, so I think I've been punished as much as dad and Mary."

"More," said Mary. "You two men seem to forget Laurel was only seventeen when all this started. She was nineteen when she left home. Neither of you were perfect at that age. Don't delude yourselves because your father has told me all about those years. It's time to put the past in the past."

With a frown, Joseph looked at Laurel. "I had forgotten how hard you worked then. We should have been there to help you, Laurie, and I'm sorry we weren't. It was too much for somebody your age to take care of dad by yourself, and it was too much for you to take care of mom when she was dying. I just couldn't deal with all of it then, so I let you do it. I'm sorry for not being there then, and I'm sorry about the other night."

"I'm sorry too, Laurie," Peter said. "I was the oldest, and I should have been there. I just had so much on me then with being married and having a new baby. No excuse is good enough when I never gave you the chance for any excuse. You're a part of this family, and we didn't have the right to push you out. I'm glad you had the courage to push your way back in. Tell your friend I'm sorry about how I acted. I made a first-class jerk of myself. If he hadn't handled it well, we would have all ended up in jail."

They were still talking when the visiting hours were announced at noon. They went as a group to the intensive care unit. Laurel wasn't sure her father had seen her until he put out his hand. They both wept and let their tears wash away the stains of their mistakes.

Jack was at the gate when the flight from Washington, D.C. disembarked. His father was in first class and was quick to enter the terminal. He scanned the crowd around the gate and then raised his hand in greeting as he recognized his son.

"It's good to see you, Jackson. You look well."

"Thanks, Dad. I've been doing well. I know you don't have much time. I thought we could go somewhere for lunch."

"I want to go with you, Jackson, but I'm asking you to let my friend go with us. I want you to do this for me."

Jack cringed as he realized who would be the next person to exit the plane. He said a prayer as a tall, strikingly beautiful blond made her way through the crowd. He couldn't have forgotten her face because Alyssa had haunted him night and day until the morning he had met Laurel.

"Hello, Jackson," Alyssa said seductively. "It's really good to see you."

"Hello, Alyssa," Jack said tersely. "Let's get out of here. We can talk over lunch."

His father made certain Jack was sitting next to Alyssa during the cab ride. Jack was tempted to jump out of the moving car even before Alyssa started talking. Responses were unnecessary for his ex-wife. She was content with the sound of her own voice as she talked about all the people they had known as a couple. Jack kept his eyes on the highway during most of the ride. He glanced at his watch frequently because time had never seemed so interminable.

Jack had chosen the restaurant, expecting only his

father. They had to wait for a table that would accommodate three, and by then he knew his sugar was getting low.

Jack excused himself to go to the bathroom where he took his last two glucose tablets. When he could hold his finger steady enough to get a good test, the reading was 52mg percent. He drew up a dose of insulin with difficulty and put the syringe in his pocket. He knew he couldn't let them see him giving himself the shot. He took the dose of insulin without thinking his judgment was impaired by the low sugar reading.

"Get me through this," he prayed. He thought of Laurel and changed his prayer immediately. "Take care of Laurel. I can do this on my own."

He took two deep breaths as he walked back into the dining room. They had obviously ordered in his absence, and the order included a bottle of champagne. There was a filled glass at his place. Jack sat down as the waitress came to the table.

"I'll have a glass of unsweetened tea, please," he said.

"We thought champagne would be more appropriate," General Driver said. "This is a celebration after all."

"It was," Jack replied. "It isn't now because that's obviously not why you came. I don't drink, Dad. Insulin and alcohol don't mix very well. I still have diabetes in case both of you forgot. I don't even pray to be cured any more because there are too many people who've been waiting in line a lot longer than I have."

"We both came to celebrate your success, Jack," Alyssa said. She put her hand on his arm and caressed him. "I know you're angry with me, and you have every right to be angry. I made a terrible mistake when I let you get away. I treated you badly, Jack, but I was scared. Surely you can see I was terrified. I didn't know anything about diabetes then. Now I do. I know that you can take care of insulin dependent diabetes just like JFK took care of his Addison's disease. I was twenty-five when you got sick, Jack. How wise were you when you were twenty-five?" Jack jerked his arm away from her. "When I was twenty-five, Alyssa, I flew fighter planes, and I was ready to die for what I believed in," he said. "You didn't believe in me enough to stay with me when I needed you the most. Don't expect me to believe in you now." He glared at his father. The hypoglycemia allowed his emotions to be clearly visible.

"Dad, you need to realize I've had to survive on my own for the last three years. That included making all my own decisions. You chose to step out of my life when I was diagnosed with diabetes so don't expect to shove your way back in now. You obviously don't care about how I feel or what I want." Jack picked up the glass of champagne and raised it. "I think we should still celebrate. I'm getting married. Forgive me if I don't invite either of you." He drained the glass and stood as he looked at his father.

"Do you know what it feels like to drown, Dad? I've been there, and it was really hard getting back to the surface. Don't push me under again."

The general stood to protest, but he couldn't find the words quickly enough to stop Jack from leaving the restaurant. By luck or divine intervention, there was a cab in front of the restaurant. Jack climbed in and asked to be taken to Mercy Hospital. He gave the driver a twenty dollar bill and sat back feeling sick. With no food to protect him, the alcohol hit his bloodstream almost immediately and effectively blocked his body's ability to deal with the rapid fall in his blood sugar.

"Hypoglycemia unawareness can happen to anyone, Jack," his doctor had told him. "Eventually you'll have a low sugar, and you won't know it until it happens. People in tight blood sugar control are more at risk for those reactions because the body doesn't have as much time to react to the falling sugar when it considers a blood sugar of 80mg percent to be normal. You won't release adrenaline until you drop twenty points below your norm. At 40mg percent you're intoxicated. You'll know you're in trouble, but you won't remember what to do about it."

He had tested obsessively to keep the prediction from coming true, but in the cab it happened. By the time he made it into the hospital, he couldn't think of what to do or say. At the information desk, his hands and face felt numb.

"Page Laurel Wolfe," he slurred. "Please. Laurel Wolfe." The woman was looking at him strangely even as she called the operator.

"Are you all right, sir?" she asked. Her question was slow to penetrate his mind.

"No." He heard himself say the word just before the floor hit him. Then he couldn't feel anything. He heard a woman call his name and knew it was Laurel. It became hard to breathe.

His arm was burning all the way to his shoulder from the glucose solution they were giving him. He thought he could move it, but it was too heavy. His head had never hurt so much in his life, and when he could move, he threw up for what seemed like hours.

"Does he drink?" a male voice asked.

"No," Laurel said. "He never drinks alcohol."

"I'm having a hard time keeping his blood sugar up, ma'am. That doesn't happen unless the patient has another problem like Addison's disease or alcoholism."

"He doesn't drink," Laurel said fiercely. "We don't believe in it."

Her hands were on his face, and her voice was pleading. "Jack, please wake up. I'm really scared now."

It took all his will power to say her name, but he managed to voice the one word. "Laurel."

"Jack, are you all right?"

"I'm all right." He opened his eyes and tried to focus on her face. "I'm all right."

She held onto him then, and he could feel her hot tears on his chest. Gradually he could put his arms around her. "I'm sorry."

"Could you get the doctor?" he heard Laurel ask someone. "Tell him that Mr. Driver is awake now."

"Laurel." He felt as if her name were the only thing he could remember.

It was 7:30 P.M. when Jack was finally able to walk out of the hospital, and even then he was unsteady. "I can't fly," he said.

"It's okay," she told him. "We're going to a hotel for the night. We can go home tomorrow." She was holding his hand so tightly that it almost hurt him, but he was glad for any tangible sensation. "Just take us to the closest hotel," she told the driver.

Jack never remembered getting into the hotel or the bed. He felt Laurel stick his finger several times, but he was too tired to react to the sticks. After midnight, his sugar was 466mg percent, and Laurel shook him until he woke up.

"You need insulin, Jack. Your sugar is really high. It's over 400. Which kind should I give you? There's a cloudy one and a clear one."

"The clear one," he told her. "Eight units."

She was able to draw the insulin only because she had watched him do it so many times. She gave the shot through his clothes and was relieved when he didn't act as if it hurt him. Then she watched TV and fought to stay awake so she could take care of him. For more than two hours, she poured over the books the diabetes association had sent her. Then she examined everything in Jack's glucose meter kit until she found a piece of paper with an insulin scale written on it.

At 8 A.M. the next morning, Jack's sugar was finally under 200mg percent. He woke up when Laurel was sticking his finger again. He was completely bewildered when he realized they were in a hotel room. He searched his mind and found the previous day to be a complete blank.

"What happened?" he asked.

Laurel jumped at the sound of his voice and sat back on her heels as he sat up in bed. "Don't you remember?"

"I don't remember at all." He pressed his hand against his head. "Do you have any ibuprofen? My head feels like someone hit it with a sledge hammer."

"You had a low blood sugar," she told him as she dug into her purse for the pills. "You came to the hospital desk and had them page me. The volunteer said you looked really strange, like you were sick, and then you passed out. The doctor said your blood sugar was one of the lowest he had ever seen. He thought you had been drinking." She closed his hand around the pills and poured water into a glass on the nightstand. She expected to hold the glass for him, but he took it and swallowed the pills.

Slowly the memory of the restaurant returned. With it came a wave of depression so severe that he relived the memory of contemplating suicide after being diagnosed. He pressed his hand to his face trying to control his emotions. Laurel put her arms around him and held him.

"If I had been with you, it wouldn't have happened," she said. "I don't see how you can do this right all alone. I've been reading about it all night. One of the books says stress can make your blood sugar go up or down. You knew it would be bad meeting your father."

"Alyssa came," he said slowly. "He brought her to facilitate our reconciliation. She talked all the way to the restaurant. When we got there, I knew I was low. I went to the bathroom and took some glucose tablets. I remember drawing up my shot." He shook his head. "That's all I remember."

"You need to eat," Laurel said firmly. "I'm going down to the men's shop and get you a change of clothes and some food." She took a piece of paper from her purse. "The emergency room doctor said you need to call your endocrinologist this morning. You said his name was Carpenter, right?"

"Tracy Carpenter," Jack acknowledged. "I'll bet I'll get a rounding chorus of 'I told you so.' He's been warning me about this for the last two years."

Jack became inexplicably angry even though his doctor was simply trying to find out what had happened to him. His anger spread to Laurel because he felt she was taking charge of his life when he was in no shape to make decisions.

"It's over, and we won't let it happen again." She had felt very comfortable in taking care of him until that moment. Something in Jack's face pushed her away more effectively than what he said.

"I'm the only one who can keep it from happening, and I can't do it." He walked to the bathroom and closed the door between them. When he emerged, he sat on the bed again. He looked at Laurel. He was irritated because he felt as if she were intruding too deeply into his life. The whole idea of needing a caretaker made him feel pitiful, and he voiced what he had feared from the second he had accepted his diagnosis.

"I don't want anyone to take care of me because they have to take care of me. It makes me feel like I'm disabled. If I have to live that way, I'd rather be dead."

Laurel pressed her back against the door and said a prayer before answering him. His attack was vicious and completely unexpected. She felt as if she had done something wrong and couldn't fathom what it might have been.

"I'm a caretaker, Jack," she stammered. "You didn't know that when you met me, but I've told you that's how I am. My mom was a caretaker. The reason my dad and I fell out was because he wouldn't let me take care of him anymore. I don't think I could not be involved in taking care of a person I loved. It would hurt too much."

"I don't know if I can let you," he said sharply. "Really, I don't need your help. I've been taking care of it alone for three years, and I've made more mistakes in my self care in the past week than I've made in the last year. For the next week, I think I need some space to do it right. I can't keep screwing it up, or I won't have any chance in Houston."

Laurel cried, but she made no sound. She picked up her bag and left the hotel room without another word. By the time Jack made it to the door, she had disappeared. For that moment, he couldn't make himself care.

Chapter 7

Laurel was alone in a strange city with no idea of how to get back to Gatlinburg. She walked for a long time and found herself at Mercy Hospital late in the afternoon. She went to the waiting room and stood in the doorway like a lost child. Mary Wolfe came to claim her.

"Laurel, you look terrible. What's wrong?"

"I had a fight with my boyfriend. It wasn't even really a fight. He doesn't want me to take care of him. He..." Laurel broke down and crumbled into Mary's arms. Her stepmother let her cry. When Laurel could draw a breath without sobbing, Mary sent her daughter, Suzanne, to fetch wet paper towels and a soda.

"Why does he not want you to take care of him?" Mary asked quietly. "That's a part of loving someone, Laurel. You're supposed to take care of each other."

"He's diabetic. He takes insulin. It started only three years ago, and he hasn't gotten used to all of it. He had a terrible low blood sugar yesterday. That's why they paged me. They didn't let us out of the emergency room until six o'clock. I had to take care of him all night. He was too out of it to test his blood sugar or give himself insulin. This morning he was terribly upset. He said he had made more mistakes taking care of himself in the past week than he had made in the last eighteen months. He meant he was making mistakes because of me."

"Laurel, my first husband was diabetic. He was half white, and he had the insulin dependent kind of diabetes. You know Native American people usually get the non insulin dependent kind of diabetes. Warren couldn't accept being diabetic. I think it is harder for men to have an illness because they think it makes them less a man. He hid his shots from us, and he wouldn't test his blood sugar. Finally, his kidneys failed, and he refused to take dialysis even though I would have done anything to keep him alive.

"At least your friend is trying to take care of his body. You can't help him accept what's wrong with him. You'll just have to pray acceptance will come. Until then, you can't help him. Losing him now would be easier than watching him die over the next twenty years. That's the difference between loving someone and being codependent."

Laurel was exhausted and emotionally drained. She stayed with Mary and slept with her head on her stepmother's shoulder. When evening came, Peter drove her back to her apartment in Sevierville.

Laurel changed her clothes and went to work. She had to keep praying just to get through her evening shift without crying. Her heart told her Jack was home, but she didn't call. She held her chin up until the next morning when she found her belongings sitting at her apartment door. She knew she had been ejected from Jack's life. She was devastated. Only her prayers made it possible for her to get through Sunday and go on with her life.

Jack was well aware he had hurt Laurel. He was so angry at himself and his disease, however, that he didn't care how he deepened Laurel's wounds when he left her belongings outside her apartment door. It was self preservation to remove all traces of her from his home. Seeing her things made him remember to miss her voice and how she had filled the emptiness inside him.

Jack remembered he had been irrational when he left Knoxville. He hadn't called his doctor. He had checked out of the hotel, flown to Sevierville, driven home, packed up Laurel's belongings, and headed to her apartment. When he returned home, he turned off the ringer on his phone and decided he would live the way he had existed for the previous three years, except he didn't pray. He didn't bother to attend church on Sunday either.

Logic told him he didn't have any reason to be angry with Laurel. Still, he closed his heart and his mind very successfully until he went to sleep each night. His dreams betrayed him because they all involved Laurel.

Later, when his reasoning power returned, Jack realized his anger came from being in a situation in which he had no semblance of control. He felt responsible for the low blood sugar and embarrassed by how Laurel had been forced to care for him. He had wanted to take care of her. He felt he was less of a man because he knew he could never be the main caretaker in a relationship. He also felt victimized by his father and Alyssa. He figured his father probably knew he had spent the rest of that day in the emergency room. Jack ignored their messages on his answering machine. He had intended to also ignore Laurel's messages, but that wasn't an issue because she didn't call. He began to feel uneasy.

His endocrinologist had called him every day, and Jack thought long and hard about not returning his calls. Finally on Tuesday he returned the call because he wanted a letter to take to Houston. While dialing, he realized the thought of Houston no longer seemed compelling. Actually, nothing seemed compelling anymore. As he waited on hold, he knew he missed Laurel more than he had ever missed anyone. When he thought of her, the emptiness created by her absence was painful.

Dr. Carpenter answered the phone. "Jack, we need to talk. You were supposed to call me on Saturday."

"I was wasted on Saturday," Jack replied. "And I wasn't sure I could stand the 'I told you so' refrain."

"Jack, that wasn't the usual insulin reaction. That wasn't even the worst case scenario reaction. You were out for six hours even when your sugar came up."

"I was out for eighteen hours," Jack replied. "I was just in the emergency room for six hours."

"You should have been back to normal within a few hours. When you weren't, the emergency room doctor called me. We screened you for alcohol, drugs and other hormonal causes of prolonged hypoglycemia. Your blood contained a very small amount of alcohol, but your drug screen had chloryl hydrate, mescaline, and an animal tranquilizer in it. Did you take anything on Friday?"

"No! I was flying on Friday. I wouldn't do anything to jeopardize my license. I've never done drugs. Are they sure they didn't make some sort of mistake in the lab?"

"We're sure. The combination is a variant on the 'date rape' drugs. It can be bought on the street. Someone must have slipped it to you for some reason. Do you have any idea who could have done it? We need to report it to the police."

"Don't report it yet," Jack said as the realization hit him. "I'm pretty sure it must have been my ex-wife. She's the queen of manipulators. She flew down here with my father and tried to talk reconciliation. She's crazy to think it could ever be an option. I was having lunch with her and my father when I made the last glucose test. I don't remember anything after that."

"She could have killed you, Jack," Dr. Carpenter said grimly. "There's no way you could have taken care of your blood sugar with that kind of medication on board. If we could have found you Friday night, we would have admitted you. I've been trying your house since Saturday. How did you manage?"

"I have a friend," Jack said, feeling sick as he remembered how he had treated his friend. "She sat up all night checking my sugar and giving me insulin."

"That's the kind of friend every man needs," Dr. Carpenter replied. "You might want to hang onto her."

"I hope I still can." A wave of panic washed over Jack because he knew he had treated Laurel like Alyssa had treated him. "Dr. Carpenter, can you fax me a copy of that report? I was completely insane on Saturday, and I may need some way to defend myself from the well-earned title of 'prince of jerks.'"

"I'll have Lila fax it now. If you need other verification, I'll write on the report that the combination causes paranoia, depression, and agitation when the sedation wears off."

"That might help," Jack said. "Try to keep this minimized in my records because Houston wants another letter. I don't think this would reassure them about my ability to manage my diabetes."

"Jack, eventually every insulin dependent diabetic is going to have an assisted reaction," the doctor said patiently. "The tighter you control it, the more risk you accept. You're in very tight control, but you couldn't have prevented this one. You were drugged. Your judgment was nonexistent when you needed it most. My personal opinion is that your friend probably kept you from dying. I'm going to call in some glucagon for you since you're lucky enough to have a friend. Do you still use the same pharmacy?"

"Yes. The Sevierville Drug Mart. I think you have the number on my chart. I'll e-mail you some blood sugars tonight. Thanks for your help."

"Stay away from your ex-wife," the doctor said.

"No problem," Jack said.

He hung up the telephone and anxiously glanced at the clock. Then he dialed Laurel's number, praying she would answer. He heard the phone click and say, "Hi," and he started talking before realizing he was pleading with her new answering machine.

"This is Laurel," said her musical voice. "I can't come to the phone right now, but please leave your name and number. I'll call you back as soon as I can." A metallic tone gave Jack permission to speak.

"Laurel, this is Jack. If you're there, please pick up. I need to apologize, and there's too much I need to say to just leave a message." Another tone cut him off. He could almost sense she was listening and had decided not to pick up.

"Help me, God," Jack prayed. "Help me make her listen."

He tested his sugar and after getting a decent reading, he collected the fax from Dr. Carpenter and closed shop for the evening. He ran to his truck and drove through the rush hour traffic to Gatlinburg. It was well after 6 P.M. when he reached Laurel's apartment building. A quick search of the parking lot told him Laurel wasn't there. Without any clear plan in his mind, he drove to the restaurant. He prayed that her car would be there, and it was. The parking lot was completely full. He had to park two blocks away, but the distance allowed him time to formulate an apology.

A line greeted him at the door, and he stood for thirty minutes before it was his turn to ask for a table. Her pain was very evident when she asked, "One?"

"For now," he said.

"We're completely full right now. You'll have to wait for at least an hour."

"Some things are worth waiting for," he said intently. "Have you got a coke machine?"

"The closest one is across the street," she said with barely suppressed emotions. "Why don't you wait outside? I'll call you when we have a table."

He went to the gas station and bought a diet soda and a package of peanut butter crackers. Time passed slowly in the parking lot. Jack sat on a curb and relived what he had said and done to Laurel. Every replay made him feel worse and convinced him no apology could ever make up for his bad behavior.

"Jack, we both know you don't want a table," Laurel said from behind him. "Why don't you just go home?"

"I can't do that," he said as he stood. "It's not home because you're not there."

"I can't be there, Jack. We don't have compatible needs. You made that really clear on Saturday and Sunday." Her voice caught in her throat. "I can't handle what happened between us. I've never had anything hurt me more. Even what happened with my dad wasn't as bad as your reaction to me was. He never blamed me for his problems."

"Laurel, I remember what I said, and I would give anything to take it back. We both know I can't. I have something I want to show you."

"I don't want to see it," she interrupted. "I can't open my heart to you again. Go home, Jack, or I'll ask the manager to call the police."

"Then I'll get arrested and have an insulin reaction, and it will be your fault." The words provoked a furious response, and she turned back to confront him.

"It's your problem, remember? You don't want my help. You don't need my help. You said you'd rather die than live that way. In fact, you said you'd never had that kind of trouble until you met me."

"None of that was true," he pleaded. "Laurel, my doctor called me today and said I was drugged on Friday. He sent me the report to show you. He said it was probably given to me in something at the restaurant. He said it might have killed me if you hadn't been with me. The drugs are like the 'date rape' stuff they talk about on television. He said those drugs make you crazy, and I was. I didn't even call him. He had to call me six times. Please, just look at the report, and then if you want me to leave, I'll leave. Remember, I called out for you when I couldn't remember anything else to do.

"I love you, Laurel, and I want you to take care of me. I don't want to do it alone. I never really did, but none of the people I thought loved me would help me. I guess I said what scares me the most about being with you. It's hard to be a man who loves a woman and know you won't ever be able to just take care of her. That's what I hate the most about being diabetic."

She was shaking all over when she took the paper from his hands, but she didn't look at it. "I have to get back to work, Jack. Come back at midnight."

"I don't have anywhere else I want to be. I'll be out here for as long as I have to be." He sat down on the sidewalk with his hands clasped. His feeling of desolation was all consuming in the two hours that followed. He thought she was probably going to tell him to get out of her life, and he was certain he deserved it despite the drugs. He had voiced his own problems accepting his condition and his lingering rage at his ex-wife and father. The venting had been directed at the one person who couldn't understand why and didn't deserve it.

"Please let her listen," he prayed incessantly. He thought of Houston and knew he wouldn't go if she weren't with him. It just wasn't as important as having Laurel in his life.

Her hand on his shoulder startled him, and he jumped to his feet. "Did you read it?"

"I read it, and I called your doctor." She sat down on the sidewalk. "He said it probably made you paranoid and agitated. He also said it wouldn't make you lie. It's kind of a truth serum thing. I've been talking to Mary. Her first husband died from insulin dependent diabetes because he couldn't accept what he had to do. I wonder if you can."

"Not by myself," Jack said as he sat beside her. "I can't do it by myself, Laurel. I can control my blood sugar without any variation if I don't have any variation in my life. That's not the kind of life I want. I did mess up a lot in the last week, but it was more because I was trying to act like I'm not diabetic. I was afraid you wouldn't want to be with a diabetic man. I'm not comparing you to Alyssa, but, realistically, you're taking a leap of faith to be with someone with a condition that could disable or kill him. You could have anyone you want. I don't know why you would want it to be me." He looked at her.

"I feel like I should just let you go, but I can't stand the thought of being without you. I can accept that I might die from this or go blind or need a kidney transplant, but I can't accept that one stupid, crazy tirade when I was drugged by somebody else could cost me the only thing that has made me feel happy. I love you. I want to marry you, Laurel. Please forgive me."

"I fell in love with you, Jack. I fell in love with you even though you're diabetic. I think that means God wants me to deal with your diabetes. I'm not afraid to do it if you want me to. Why would anyone have done this?" Her response gave him hope.

"My father brought Alyssa with him so we could talk about getting back together. I had told him I was serious with someone else when I talked to him Thursday night. He didn't want to hear it. He's a control freak, Laurel. He ran my life until I had diabetes, and then he stopped because he didn't think I had a life anymore.

"I think he brought Alyssa with him to try to break up you and me. Her family is really wealthy and political. That's why he wanted me to see her in the first place.

When he told me he didn't have time to meet you, I did
what he hoped I would do. I went alone so he couldn't
treat you badly.

"I'm sure the drugs were Alyssa's idea. Maybe she
thought she'd get me in a hotel room when I didn't
know what I was doing and that would get us back
together. She probably thought the drugs would make
me crazy so I'd drive you away. All I can do is pray it
didn't work." He reached for her hand and felt an
emotional rush when she allowed him to take it.

"I thought I knew what I wanted, Laurel," he said. "I
thought I wanted to be in the space program, but I'm not
going if you're not with me. I'll just stay here and keep
praying God will inspire you to give me another chance."
He was shaking as he stared at his hands. "And now it's
anybody's guess if I'm low, high or just more upset than
I've ever been before."

Laurel reached into his jacket pocket and took out
the test kit. "You won't know if you don't check," she
said slowly. She held his hand while he did the check,
and it read 90mg percent.

"Now you know. All the shaking is for you."

She put her arms around him and kept holding him
as they stood up together. They stood in that embrace
until they had both stopped shaking. He held her face in
his hands and looked into her eyes.

"I love you, Laurel. I'm going to spend the rest of my
life making you believe me."

"I believe you now." She smiled through her tears.

"Let's get married tonight," he said. He had no
doubts that it was the right thing to do, and his certainty
came through in his voice. "We can have a real wedding
later if you want to, but let's go to the wedding chapel
and get married. I don't think I can stand waiting until
tomorrow."

His eyes were in her soul saying all the things she
needed to hear. All she could say was, "Yes."

Chapter 8

Jack drove to the wedding chapel and convinced the preacher to wait for them. Then he went to an all-night department store and purchased a wedding ring. Laurel's waitress friends accompanied her to her apartment and helped make her a beautiful bride in a violet evening dress she had worn as a bridesmaid. The women drove her to the wedding chapel. They were prepared to serve as witnesses. The manager loaned Jack his sports coat. Jack and Laurel were married at midnight on Wednesday, July 24.

Taking the vows seemed dreamlike, but Laurel knew they both meant every word. She emphasized the words "in sickness and in health until death do us part." The only surprise was when Jack had a ring to place on her finger. It had obviously been a hurried purchase, but the sight of the gold and diamond wedding band brought tears to Laurel's eyes. It felt very right to be in his arms as Mrs. Jack Driver.

Laurel had left her car at her apartment. She had brought along a suitcase, so they left the wedding chapel after the ceremony and drove toward their new home in comfortable silence. Jack held her hand all the way and seemed to need that security as much as she did. They were in Sevierville when he said, "I guess we need to find an all-night pharmacy somewhere. I should have thought of that earlier."

It took her several minutes to understand what he meant, and then she blushed in the darkness. "I'm on the pill. I used to have terrible cramps. I had to miss school because of the pain, so my doctor prescribed the pill. It's not because of anything else. Actually this is going to be one of those firsts we talked about." She hesitated. "I do want kids."

"So do I," he said. "I was afraid of passing the diabetes on, but it isn't a big risk. It's only 6 or 7 percent lifetime risk from a parent to a child. If it did happen, it would bother me, but—"

"We know what to do," she said. "It isn't a terminal illness, and our baby would have a role model in you. God will take care of it, Jack. We both know He will."

"You wouldn't be sitting beside me if He wasn't taking care of us," Jack said. "I always thought about having two or three kids. How about you?"

"Three." They were approaching Jack's house, and suddenly Laurel felt apprehensive about their wedding night. Jack sensed her anxiety.

"I know we made a quick decision, Laurel. Don't feel like you have to do anything you aren't ready to do. I just want to be with you. I can wait on everything else. I'm pretty nervous, too." He pulled into the driveway and turned off the ignition. "And to put an end to all this romance, I've got to eat."

"So do I," she said. "I'm famished."

He carried her suitcase to the porch. Then he picked her up gently and carried her over the threshold. She hadn't known a diabetic could be physically strong. Inside, she held onto him for several minutes before he led her through the dark living room to the kitchen.

Kennedy followed them and stayed underfoot until Jack banished him to the den.

They made an omelet and split it between two plates. Jack ate first and then tested. The reading was 86mg percent.

"See. It's perfect when you're around, Laurel Fairlight." He took out the insulin and smiled at her. "I love your name. How did your parents come up with it?"

"The Laurel is for mountain laurel. It's my dad's favorite flower. My mom got the Fairlight from a book called *Christy*. The main character's best friend was Fairlight Spencer. My mom said she always planned to name her daughter Fairlight after she read the name.

"Mom was wonderful. You would have liked her, and she would have liked you. She was fascinated by the stars, too. I guess I got that from her. When I was little, she saved all her nickels and dimes and bought a telescope. The two of us would go out and look at the stars. We did that every night until just before she died. I hadn't star gazed since then until you took me to the observatory. It was like a sign from mom." She bit her lip as tears rose in her eyes. Jack didn't miss the expression on her face and chose to redirect her.

"I guess it's time for you to learn about insulin."

"I read all about it the night you were sick," she said. "The cloudy bottle is like sustained release. It's called N. That stands for neutral protein Hagedorn. It starts working in about four hours and lasts for up to twenty-four hours, but the peak effectiveness is at eight to twelve hours. It's usually given in the morning and at night."

"I'm impressed," Jack said. "You got all of that in one night?"

"I was scared," Laurel admitted. "I learn better under pressure. Why do you take it all day?"

"People with insulin dependent diabetes are really sensitive to insulin, so it's better to take a little bit several

times than it is to take a whole lot once or twice. I take
two or three units of the N when I eat and then eighteen
units at bedtime.

"There's really only one kind of insulin. The cloudy
bottle has a carrier protein attached to the insulin so
your body can't absorb it as fast. The clear insulin is just
insulin so it gets in your system right away. Did you
figure out why I have to take so much sustained release
insulin at night?"

"Something about other hormones your body makes
when you're asleep," Laurel said. "I didn't understand
that part. The book called it 'dawn phenomenon,' so I
guess your sugar starts to go up when the sun comes up
even if you haven't eaten."

"It's because of cortisone and growth hormone,"
Jack explained. "Human bodies make a lot of those at
night, and they make you resistant to insulin. Your body
just makes more insulin so your blood sugar won't go
up while you're sleeping. I have to take more insulin
that will peak in the night to compensate for what the
hormones do. That dose is tricky because I need less if I
stay up late and it can get me if I oversleep.

"That's why I'm so anxious to get an insulin pump.
You can program a pump to give you more insulin
during the night and change it if you're sleeping late.
The only down side for me is not being able to wear it in
space. The company doesn't think it would be safe with
the pressure changes. So if I got a mission, I'd be back to
shots for the duration."

"How do you figure the clear insulin and why do
you draw it first?"

"The clear is called Humalog™, and it works really
quickly. It starts working in fifteen minutes and peaks in
an hour. I count units by how high my blood sugar is
and by how much I eat. Then I subtract units if I'm going
to be more active and add units if I'm less active. I have
to draw it first because if I got N in the clear bottle the

sustained release compound in the N would mix with the Humalog and make it work slower." He showed her a folded sheet in his logbook.

"I take one unit of Humalog for every 25 points over 100 my blood sugar is at the time. That means if my sugar is 125, I take one unit. Since it's under 100, I won't be taking extra to correct for how high I am now. I'll still have to cover the food I eat because my body won't make insulin to keep my sugar down after I eat. I take one unit for every ten grams of carbohydrate I eat. Those are the foods that turn into sugar quickly."

"I read about them. That's bread, potatoes, cereal, pasta, rice, fruits and sugars." She looked at the meal. "You didn't have any."

"Yet," Jack said. He drew up two units of the Humalog and drew eighteen units of the cloudy insulin on top of the clear. Then he gave the shot and removed a bowl of fruit from the refrigerator. "You can have half of that. I get the other half. If you eat my half, I'll have to find two units worth of something else."

"Eat. I'm going to change clothes." She went to the bedroom and carefully removed her evening dress. She slipped on an ecru lace robe and gown her mother had given her for her hope chest. She was feeling tremulous as she walked back toward the kitchen. Jack was sitting in the living room at the piano. His eyes caressed her as if he were touching her. His gaze didn't feel threatening.

"You're really beautiful, Laurel." He could feel her apprehension and said, "Did you bring your flute? Get it, and let's play a game."

"A game?"

"A game," he repeated. "When I was into piano competitions, we used to try to distract each other while we practiced so we'd make a mistake. Get your flute, and I'll show you."

He was playing when she returned, and he continued playing while she assembled her flute.

"You're good, Jack. My chamber music group would be incredibly impressed. How did you become so accomplished?" She laid down her flute and fed him some fruit. He stopped playing.

"My mother started teaching me to play when I was four. I took lessons all my life. Actually I had two scholarship offers. One was to the Air Force Academy and one was to Julliard. For me it was a hard decision. For my father, it was easy. He doesn't understand the attraction to music. It's funny because math and physics draw me the same way. They say math and music are both right brain activities. Have you ever read about the Native American ruins in North and South America?"

"Just when I was in school. We studied a lot about ancient Cherokee history and then about the Mayans and Aztecs in world history," Laurel said.

"All those cultures were like the Egyptians. They were very advanced in math and astronomy. Lucien and I used to think the music and math talents came from our Navajo side." He smiled and put his arm around her. He could feel she had relaxed. "Ready to play?"

"Tell me how," she said.

"Okay, the rules are you play until you make a mistake. The other person can do anything he or she wants to distract you."

"Anything?" Laurel echoed. The suggestion was exciting.

"We're married. Anything goes." He ate two strawberries and then handed her a quarter. "Flip it for who goes first." She flipped it and looked at Jack to call it as she covered it with her hand.

"Heads," he said. He looked over her shoulder. "You're first. Play whatever you want to play."

Laurel closed her eyes and then turned to face the keyboard. "If I look at you, I know you'll make me laugh." She took a deep breath and began playing a

Mozart concerto. She expected Jack would clown around in some way. Instead she felt nothing until anticipation took over. His hands touched her hair like the wind stirring it. He removed the pins one by one until her hair cascaded down her back. He ran his hands through it and then moved the heavy mass over her shoulder. His breath was against her ear, and he kissed her earlobe and then her neck as he removed her earrings. His fingers caressed her throat and the silken skin over her collarbones. She shuddered, missing a note as a wave of desire washed over her.

"It's your turn," she said reluctantly.

Jack took a seat at the piano and started playing a concerto's third movement. The music was softly seductive in her ears. Laurel let her hands slide over Jack's shoulders and forward to unfasten his collar buttons. She moved from one button to the next until his shirt was open. As she brought her hands back to his collar, she caressed his bare skin with her fingertips. She leaned forward and kissed his earlobe and then his neck. When her mouth reached his shoulder, Jack missed a note. Without a word, he patted the bench beside him. Laurel let her robe slide to the floor before taking the seat.

She started playing the theme song from *Titanic*. Jack's hands returned to her hair and then moved to her slender neck, caressing her skin as he removed her necklace. His hands slid over her ribs, and the thin gown let her feel the warmth of his skin. His fingers moved forward and touched her where she had never been touched. It was exquisite torture to attempt to play when all she wanted was his touch. She made a mistake, even though she didn't want him to stop.

"Take off your shirt first," she told him. She had to admire his body; he was underweight but very well muscled. His skin under his shirt was almost as copper as her own, which surprised her. Later she couldn't remember what he was playing because she was so focused on the feel of his skin under her hands. She wanted to make him want her as much as she desired him. She was too young and inexperienced to realize Jack was already struggling to hold back. He wanted the experience to be mutually satisfying, and he knew Laurel hadn't been with anyone else.

He lost his ability to focus on the music when she was kissing his back while her hands raked over his chest. He stopped playing and turned to pull her into his arms, meeting no resistance. When he caressed her gown off her shoulders, they moved to the floor together. Laurel hadn't believed she could want a man so very much, but alien desire continued to intensify as Jack kissed her and caressed her body. Finally, she felt as if there were an aching need inside her that only his body could satisfy. She pulled him as close to her as their flesh would allow. There was no pain in the final consummation. The only sensation was a rapidly growing ecstasy. There was a perfect moment when he made her feel as if she had become a part of him. She held onto him, wishing she could hold that moment in time.

"Jack, I love you so much," she whispered. "I didn't know it could be like this. I feel like you're in my soul."

He couldn't answer except to hold her very tightly in his arms. The gift of Laurel was overwhelming because she had woven a spell of tranquility around him. It had never been that way with Alyssa. After their wedding night, he had been left with the beginning of the end. Alyssa had made it clear that he wasn't the first or the best lover she had been with, but Laurel made him feel like making love was new.

"Nothing else matters now, Laurel," he vowed. "It's just you and me."

She didn't want to move when they were lying entwined, but she was cold from the ceiling fan. When she shivered, Jack carried her to the bed. He returned to get the fruit and put the bowl between them. She fed it to him until he protested. "I may not have taken enough insulin for this much fruit," Jack said.

"You're forgetting to figure physical activity, Jack," she whispered. She took his hands and put them on her body as she touched him. It was after 4 A.M. when they finally slept.

The telephone rang at 9 A.M. Since Laurel was lying closest to it, she answered it.

"Hello."

A woman's voice had called her a series of foul names before Jack snatched the telephone from her hands.

"Who is this?" he demanded. A harsh click was his answer. Jack reached across Laurel and picked up the telephone. He shoved the telephone under the bed and left the receiver off the hook.

"That was probably Alyssa. She's one of those words that Christian people don't say. We'll get an unlisted number." He pulled her close and kissed her. "Don't let her come between us. I love you, Laurel. I feel like everything in my life is right now because of you."

She wrapped her arms around him and could feel he was a little shaky. She pulled on her robe and brought him a glass of juice and the glucose test kit.

"I'm not sorry she called," Laurel told Jack defiantly. "We slept a little late considering how much energy we expended."

"I'm not that low, and it's not dropping that fast. The fast drops are the ones that really get you." He drained half the juice and offered the rest to Laurel. She took a sip and returned it to Jack to finish. She laid down, propped on her elbow, and examined his medical identification tag.

"Why did you get a necklace?" she asked him.

"I was used to dog tags for the last decade, so it seems natural to have something around my neck. I don't wear jewelry all that well."

"I want to buy you a wedding ring. Will you wear that?"

"I'd really like to wear that particular piece of jewelry." He tested his blood sugar and showed her the reading of 68mg percent. "I've had 20 grams of carbohydrate so I can either go running or stay here with you. Those two forms of exercise should have a similar energy expenditure. My bias is being with you."

She allowed her robe to slide to the floor and slipped into his arms. It felt good to hold him and to feel his skin against hers. He made her feel more pleasure every time they made love. She didn't want to let go.

"I'm sorry about last night, Jack. I knew we were meant to be together. I spent the last four days praying you would come back."

"I'm sorry for being a jerk in Knoxville." He held her with his hands in her hair. "I can promise it won't ever happen again. I'm here for the rest of our lives. I just hope your dad won't hold a grudge. I was thinking we could go see him in Cherokee as soon as he gets out of the hospital. If we go then, he won't be in good enough shape to chase me with a gun."

"I don't think he'll mind. I told Mary all about you, and I think she'll probably let him know. She was really nice to me on Saturday. Even my brothers apologized and said to tell you they were sorry about how they acted."

"In the great scheme of things, I probably outranked both of them in acting like a jerk. I definitely won't hold their temporary insanity against them." He sat up. "Let's get a shower. We have a lot to get done in the next few days because we'll have to fly out of here on Saturday at the latest."

They showered together. Laurel was surprised it felt natural to bathe with another person. When they were drying each other, she voiced her insecurity about their physical relationship. Jack's response astonished her.

"Do I make you feel as good as you make me feel?" she asked.

"Yes," he said immediately. "It wasn't like this before." He made her sit down on the bed while he was dressing, and later Laurel knew it was because of what he was going to tell her. He didn't look at her when he spoke to her.

"I was the only one having a first-time experience when Alyssa and I got married. I didn't know until afterwards, but she told me when she gave me suggestions on how I could better my performance. I lost all my illusions about how she felt that night. I left for Saudi Arabia a week later and spent the next three months trying to convince myself divorcing her would be the wrong thing to do. I didn't want to come home, Laurel. I went to the chaplain and got counseling. I tried to make it work because I believe marriage is forever.

"Every time I did come home, I left knowing we didn't have the same values or dreams. After the first night I was with Alyssa, I always felt like I was trying to prove something to her. Sometimes I felt angry after I was with her. It's been different with you from the first time I touched you. Last night felt like the first time I ever made love. I only had sex with Alyssa.

"In my heart, I know you're the one God meant for me to marry, and our marriage is going to be forever." His face revealed how bad his previous experience had been, but she had to struggle for the words to tell Jack how he made her feel.

"I didn't know what it would be like to make love," Laurel said. "I was almost scared, but you made everything wonderful. When we make love, I just want you to keep holding me. I couldn't ever want anything more than how you make me feel."

His expression told her that she had chosen the right words. It was a moment when he let go of the bitterness that was Alyssa's legacy. He lay down beside her and held her without thinking about letting her go.

They finally had breakfast at noon and then went to Laurel's apartment by way of the liquor store to pick up free boxes. She owned very little furniture so it was a matter of packing her clothes, books and other personal items. They loaded her cedar chest and rocking chair on the first load. After two loads, they had lunch and finished packing.

"We'll clean it tomorrow," Laurel said. "I've had all the fun I can stand, and I need to put some of it away at your house."

"Our house," Jack corrected her. "You have class tomorrow. We'll get over here early and see how much we can do." He tested his blood sugar and took her hand. "Let's go home." That night, it felt like coming home for both of them.

Chapter 9

Laurel knew Jack was really pushing himself to be ready for Houston. He had to be tired. She was eleven years younger and completely worn out. They had eaten lunch late so they had fruit and cheese and planned to eat supper later.

While Laurel was unpacking, Jack was in the garage working out for an hour of calisthenics and another hour of weight lifting. He came into the bedroom at eight o'clock and headed for the shower. He didn't say anything to her, and that was Laurel's only clue other than intuition. When she followed him into the bathroom and touched him, she ran for the juice and the test kit. He was bathed in icy perspiration. It was Laurel's first experience with the irritability of a very low blood sugar. Jack argued with the need to do anything.

"I'm not in the juice mood," he snapped as she returned to the bathroom. "I just want to take a shower. Can I do that?"

"I'm just nervous," Laurel said uneasily. "We haven't gotten that other medicine yet. Just check for me, and I promise to lighten up."

"I'll check when I get out of the shower." He stepped away from her and then sat down on the floor. Laurel knelt beside him and lifted the glass to his face, praying he would drink it.

"Please, Jack. Just drink this. You don't have to test. Remember you told me how your muscles keep using sugar when you work out. You'll need it later anyway."

He drank the juice while glaring at her and set the glass down so hard that it shattered on the tile floor. His hand was shaking, and he stared at it as if it weren't his own. Laurel leaned across him as she tried to pick up the glass shards. She was afraid Jack would cut himself. He was barefoot, and she knew if he cut his foot it could cause serious problems. When she leaned across him, Jack pushed her back unexpectedly. She lost her balance, and her palm landed on a shard in the process.

"Just leave me alone," Jack said sharply. "I'm fine."

Laurel was on the verge of tears but managed to gather the glass pieces in a towel as her blood flowed into the same towel. She carried the broken glass to the kitchen, wondering what to do next as she tried to hold pressure on her hand. She called Dr. Carpenter's answering service because it was the only thing she could think to do. She told them it was an emergency. The doctor returned the call immediately.

"This is Laurel Driver. I'm Jack Driver's wife. I'm very sorry to bother you, but I think Jack's sugar is too low. He won't let me test it, and I don't know what to do." Her voice was unsteady, a fact the diabetes specialist didn't miss.

"He's probably under 40mg percent," the doctor surmised. "When the blood sugar goes under 40, the person is intoxicated. Sometimes they're happy. Sometimes they're incredibly irritable. Were you able to give him anything to bring his sugar up?"

"He drank a glass of juice under duress. We've been

very busy today trying to move my things to his house, and Jack's been working out to get ready for going to Houston."

"If you got him to drink eight ounces of juice, he should be fine in a little while," the doctor reassured her. "You can't help him if he won't let you, Mrs. Driver. Do you have glucagon? If he won't let you help him now and he keeps dropping, he'll eventually pass out. Then you could give him glucagon. Don't try to reason with him because he won't be reasonable, and he could hurt you without meaning to."

"We don't have any glucagon yet," Laurel said anxiously. "As soon as he's better, I'll go to the drugstore."

"Then if he does pass out, call 911, Mrs. Driver. Don't try to give him anything by mouth when he's unconscious because he won't be able to swallow. When he sobers up, tell Jack he needs to start a little slower on the exercise so we can adjust the insulin as his requirement drops. One extra unit can drop Jack fifty points. Have him call me tomorrow, and feel free to call back if you need me."

Her hand was still bleeding, and she struggled to tie a kitchen towel around it before hurrying back to the bathroom. Jack was sweating more, but he looked at her apologetically.

"I think I could use a glass of juice."

"I'll be right back," Laurel said.

He was trying to test his blood sugar when she knelt beside him. She steadied his hand as he applied blood to the strip. The reading was 27mg percent, and Jack drained the glass of juice without any discussion. Laurel sat beside him holding his hand and wiping his face until he pulled her into his arms thirty minutes later.

"Well that was great for me. I hope it was good for you."

She had to laugh and sat back to survey his face. "It

was fabulous, but don't feel like we have to do it again."

"I can think of better ways to have fun." He closed his eyes. "Turn on the shower. I feel like I've been out in the rain."

"Just sit there until your sugar is better," she begged. "You weren't real steady a little while ago."

"I don't remember a little while ago. I remember working on the weight machine and then nothing else until I was sitting here."

Laurel wiped his face again, being careful to hide her injured hand from him. "I should have come out to check on you sooner. You aren't used to doing this much exercise at night. I think you should check it every hour when you're doing something new."

"That's probably a good idea." He stood slowly. "I think I'm going to eat and then take a shower." He shuffled his way to the kitchen, and Laurel made him a sandwich knowing he was still not himself. At 9:30, his sugar reached 100mg percent. Then for the first time, he noticed the blood-soaked bandage on Laurel's hand.

"What happened to your hand?" he asked with concern.

"We broke a glass," she told him as he unwound the towel. The cut on her palm was a half inch long and gaping open.

"Laurel, this needs stitches," he said. "We need to go to one of the clinics."

"Let's just wrap it up and go to sleep," she said. "It will be all right."

Jack agreed only because he was afraid to drive. He collected antibiotic ointment, gauze pads, and tape. He wrapped the wound securely and then gave her a rubber glove to cover the bandage in the shower.

"Let's go shower and get some sleep," he said.

Laurel knew he was depressed by the reaction, and she put her arms around his waist.

"I'm not ready to sleep. Let's go shower and then see how we feel."

He made no response to her overture until they were in the shower, but the warm water relaxed both of them. Laurel's touch made Jack forget his other concerns. When they left the bathroom, getting dressed seemed unimportant. Making love distanced both of them from what had happened. Laurel was very glad Jack didn't seem to remember how bad it had been.

"It won't always be this way," he said as he held her. "I'm still learning, but we'll get it together. I would have been in a lot of trouble if you hadn't been here."

It was an admission Laurel hadn't expected, but it went a long way to undo the residual hurt from Knoxville. She snuggled close with her face resting on his chest.

"I know we'll learn what we need to do, Jack. Everybody has problems to conquer when they first get married. This is just one of those problems." She kissed his chest and then went to retrieve the glucose meter and his insulin. He took his insulin, and they slept in each other's arms.

When Laurel awakened, Jack wasn't beside her. She pulled on her robe and went looking for him with more than a little panic. It was a little past eight. Jack was sitting at his computer in the den with Kennedy lying at his feet. The dog came to her to announce her presence.

"Good morning," Jack said. "There's coffee if you want some."

Laurel hesitated as she approached him. She feared he was putting distance between them, but she relaxed when he pulled her close to him.

"I'm okay. Are you? I just talked to Dr. Carpenter. He said I was prince charming while my sugar was low."

"You weren't your usual warm and fuzzy self," she acknowledged. "I know it wasn't really you, Jack, and I

did get the juice down you." Jack pulled her into his lap.
"You did great. We're going to fly to Knoxville in the
morning and pick up the insulin pump. I think that's
going to make a real difference and so does Dr. Carpenter. Then I'll be able to turn off the insulin when I'm
exercising. The long acting insulin is unpredictable, and
I just can't figure out what to do with it. It absorbs faster
when I'm active, and it absorbs faster when I get hot. I
didn't even take any Humalog with the snack we had,
so it had to be the long acting that got me. Dr. Carpenter
told me to stop taking any N in the daytime while I'm
doing so much more exercise. If we pick up the pump
and start working with it, I could start using it before we
go to the next appointment."

"That sounds good," Laurel said with relief. "I also
want to pick up that glucagon today. I could give you a
shot if I had to do it."

"You're doing so well with all this for having had
only two weeks experience." He kissed her. "Let's get
some coffee and then I want to show you what I got in
the e-mail." He signed off his computer and picked up a
stack of papers. While they were sitting at the kitchen
table he gave them to her.

Jack,
    I wanted you to know Julissa and I got married on
Tuesday. I had told dad we were getting serious, and he
flew down supposedly to meet her. He treated her like
a gold digger. We had a really terrible argument, and
when he told me I had to choose between Julissa and
him, I called him a bigot. He threatened to have me court
martialed so I told my commanding officer that I won't
be reenlisting next month.
    I have a really good offer with an aeronautics firm in
Houston, and we'll be there this coming week to look for
houses. If you end up in Houston, that might be really

cool for having our own codependent sons of a control freak support group.

I'm having a hard time understanding dad's attitude, Jack. I went to White Sands two weeks ago, and I stopped at the Navajo reservation while I was out there. I just wanted to know more about our grandfather. I found him on the tribal rolls, and I also found our grandmother there. Our mother was full-blooded Navajo, Jack. We're half Navajo and not a quarter. I think dad never told us because he wanted us to have to list ourselves as Caucasians. I don't know how I'll list myself after this, but I need to know more about my heritage. I thought you would, too. The attachment on this e-mail is the documentation from the Navajo tribal rolls.

Pray for me. I'm a little stressed out right now."

Lucien

"I tried to call him," Jack said. "His letter even sounds stressed out. Usually Lucien doesn't let things get to him. I sent him an e-mail to tell him about us."

"You could be listed as a Native American, Jack," Laurel said excitedly. "Do you want to?"

He took her to the den and pulled out a photograph album. The pages fell open to a section with photographs of Jack and Lucien with their mother. Their mother was Native American in appearance.

"That's my mother. Her name was Rachel. I always felt really close to her. Knowing dad is rejecting who she was makes me want to be listed as a Native American, but that's a lousy reason. I need to know more about that part of my heritage before I claim it. I think being Native American isn't just a name. It's knowing all the traditions and history that make your people unique. You know those things and I don't."

"You will," she assured him as she looked at the

pictures. "Maybe that's why you and your brother are both being directed to Houston."

"Let's go running," Jack said. "Running helps me get rid of the need to deck my father."

They had a good day. Laurel was able to turn in her apartment keys at noon. They forwarded her phone number to her new home and changed the answering machine to a mechanical voice that said, "Leave a message after the tone."

Jack drove Laurel to her class and then went to his office to collect the receipts Buddy had garnered. Laurel remained at Dr. Cotham's desk when the other students had departed. He quickly noted her wedding ring.

"Congratulations, Laurel. You know you need to file a name change form, don't you?"

"I will when we get back. My husband is interviewing to be in the space program, so we have to fly to Houston this weekend. I wonder if you would consider letting me take the final examination early."

"Can you be ready tomorrow?"

"I think so," Laurel replied.

"Meet me here at 9 A.M. then, and we'll get it done. When you return from Houston, let me know about the scholarship."

"I will," Laurel promised. "And thank you for all your help, Dr. Cotham."

She left through the back door of the building and hurried across the street to a strip of small shops. One was a jewelry store. Laurel purchased a broad gold wedding band for Jack. She couldn't wait to give it to him. She ran back across the street to the where his truck was parked. Jack was reading in the driver's seat, and she slid across the passenger's side to embrace him.

"I missed you, Jack. Did you stay out of trouble while I was gone?"

"That's a loaded question," Jack said as he set his

book on the dashboard. "I was reasonably well be-
haved. I'm only terrific when I'm with you." He reached
to start the truck, but she caught his left hand and slid
the wedding band on his finger.

"Does it fit?" she asked as he examined it.

"Everything about you fits," he said. "This is my first
wedding ring. That fits since I never felt this married
before." He kissed her for several long minutes before
starting the truck. Laurel was reluctant to release him.
As they drove toward the main highway, she examined
the book *A Brief History of Time* by Stephen Hawkings.

"What's this?" she asked as she scanned the pro-
logue.

"He's the Einstein of this generation," Jack said. "He's
a professor of astrophysics at Cambridge University.
When I was stationed in Europe, I was able to attend one
of his lectures because I was taking graduate course
work even then. He has Lou Gehrig's disease, and he's
in a wheelchair. He can't use his arms or even breathe on
his own. He has to use a computer to communicate, but
he sits in that wheelchair and figures out the secrets of
antimatter and black holes. When I think about how
many things he's had to overcome, I know I don't have
anything to complain about. Especially not since I met
you."

She felt happy and complete. She held his hand until
they reached Sevierville. He drove to the drug store and
said, "Let's have everything we need from now on."

He took her hand and tried not to see the bandage on
her palm. "Is your hand better?"

"It's sore, but it will be fine. We probably need some
more gauze."

"I was thinking gauze, tape, and antibiotic ointment.
Unbreakable glasses might be good, too." He looked at
her anxiously. "Did I hurt you, Laurel? I really don't
remember what happened. Dr. Carpenter said people

sometimes hurt even the people they love when they're that low."

"No. You weren't very lovable, but I fell on the broken glass when I was leaning over you." She put her arm around his waist. "Let's get our shopping done and go home. I have my final examination in the morning. When I pass it, there won't be anything except my dad standing between us and Houston."

"Let's not cause a panic attack in a public place." Jack picked up a basket and led her to the first aid supplies. He gathered a selection of bandages. "Brace yourself," he said as they approached the pharmacy. He picked up two boxes of one hundred glucose test strips, two boxes of lancets, four rolls of glucose tablets and a box of fifty unit syringes. The pharmacist raised his hand in greeting.

"Hi, Jack. How are you doing?" He flipped through his filled prescriptions and extended a sack. "Three insulins and two glucagons." He smiled as he saw Jack's left hand. "I guess you've made some changes in the last few days."

"Walt, this is my wife, Laurel. Laurel, this is Walt Davis. We're on a first name basis since I pay a large part of his rent."

"He's lying through his teeth, Mrs. Driver." The pharmacist laughed. "He's only here for insulin. That's the first prescription other than insulin I've ever filled for him."

Jack looked at the insulin. "I might need another bottle of Humalog, Walt. I'm about to get an insulin pump, and the syringe for it takes 300 units at a time. Could I get another one?"

The pharmacist pulled it up in the computer and shook his head. "You're out of refills. I can give Dr. Carpenter a call if you want."

"Don't bother. We're going to Knoxville tomorrow,

and I'll get a new prescription then. See you later."

They walked to the household goods section where Jack picked up a six pack of plastic glasses and a pack of juice cans. "Bring me the unbreakable stuff since I'm untrustworthy."

She turned him to face her. "Don't dwell on it. It makes both of us unhappy. Let's just take lemons and make nutrasweet lemonade." His eyes smiled into hers, and they walked to the checkout counter. When the total appeared, she finally understood the reason for his "brace yourself" comment. It was almost three hundred dollars. Jack wrote the check and gave his driver's license to the cashier.

"Diabetes is an expensive disease," he said as they walked to the truck. "I'm luckier than most people who have it. I developed it while I was in the service, so I could get everything at the VA. I don't go to the trouble of driving to Knoxville every time because I have insurance through the university, thanks to working as a teaching assistant for the last six months. Insurance will reimburse eighty percent of this. If I don't stay with a large company, I'm uninsurable because the insurance companies know I could cost them a lot of money.

"In America it's legal to discriminate against anyone unlucky enough to get sick, and nobody wants to do anything about it. The inalienable rights are life, liberty and the pursuit of happiness. Letting me have life is expensive." Laurel started to interrupt, and he silenced her with his expression.

"When I was wondering if I would have a life, the chaplain brought a friend of his to talk to me. His name is Herb Sloan, and he's had insulin dependent diabetes for forty-two years. He's not blind, his kidneys still work, and he has both legs. He developed diabetes when he was twenty-nine, just like me. He had been married for two years, and they had a new baby. His wife said people kept asking her what she would do having a baby and a sick husband. She admitted they were scared but they just took lemons and made a little lemonade.

"On their fortieth wedding anniversary, they were playing golf. A friend started talking to them on the fairway. He told Mrs. Sloan he really admired her for staying with her husband all those years. Herb overheard his comment. Mrs. Sloan told the jerk that she hadn't done as much as his own wife had done just by putting up with him for so many years. If you can hang with me, Laurel, we'll be here in forty-two years, telling everybody that they were wrong."

"I can hang with you, Jack. You're not sick and you aren't going to be unless you make yourself sick worrying about it. You don't know what tomorrow will bring. I could get sick and die like our mothers did."

"Please don't," he said. "I need you. This is the first time I've been able to talk about all this since it happened. I guess that's why I can't stop talking about it. I'm telling you what scares me."

"I'll just have to be brave with you." She pulled him to the truck. "I just realized that I need to change my driver's license."

"And I need to put your name on the bank account. You know there's a lot to this getting married stuff." His arm slid around her shoulders, and he kissed her hair. "And we probably ought to go to the grocery store to buy some lemons and nutrasweet."

"You're nuts, Jack." She laughed. They met on the seat and embraced with the same thought in mind. They were anxious to head home. It was a challenge to drive the twelve blocks and even more challenging to move from the truck to their living room where Laurel pulled Jack into her arms. She held him as he closed the front door. In the solitude of their first home, they made each other forget to be afraid or to worry about what another day might bring.

The phone rang without being answered. Kennedy followed the trail of their discarded clothing until Jack closed the bedroom door in the dog's face. Laurel pulled him down onto the bed and let his body envelope hers. Every time they made love the sensations were more intense and the communion between them became more complete. The world could be completely closed out. Afterwards they lay in the hazy afternoon light, still caressing each other until sleep seemed a part of the bliss.

Jack made himself get up without disturbing his wife when he remembered leaving the pharmacy supplies in the truck. He pulled on his jeans and sandals and ran outside. It was a hot afternoon, but they had left the truck windows down. Thanks to a cool breeze and being sheltered under the seat, the insulin and glucagon had been protected. Both could have been rendered useless by temperatures over eighty degrees. He rolled up the windows and locked the truck.

He was returning to the house when a horn resounded. The mailman brought him a thick package bearing the NASA insignia along with an envelope containing their marriage license. Their simultaneous arrival was not a coincidence to Jack.

Chapter 10

Laurel was sleeping with both arms hugging Jack's pillow when he kissed her ear and said, "Wake up, Laurel. It's time to study photography."

She exhaled slowly and rolled over smiling. "I think I was out for the count."

Jack set a tray on the bed. "I've never provided this kind of service before, but I thought you'd forgive me for whatever I forgot. Meanwhile, you can eat and study. I'm going to do some exercises right in front of you. I tested ten minutes ago and I was 149, which stinks for a premeal. But it's low enough for me to exercise without driving it up even more. I figure I'll do thirty minutes and eat. The unbreakable glasses and orange juice are in the kitchen ready to assist you."

"Jack, you're melodramatic." She smiled and sat up with the tray carefully balanced as he handed her his tee shirt. She pulled it on.

"Don't get too dressed. I'll need to burn off supper in a couple of hours." He laid her photography textbook on the bed and moved to begin his calisthenics. Laurel opened her book and ate her sandwich while trying to keep her eyes off her husband. She had to try to distract herself in order to ignore her memories of the previous night. She kept her eye on the clock. After Jack had tackled an hour of intense push-ups, crunches and assorted weights, Laurel brought him supper and his meter. His reading was 79mg percent.

"That's better."

"Eat before it gets too better," she said. He took his insulin and started eating. When he had finished the sandwich, he pointed to the mail on the nightstand.

"Our license came. Look under it. Our Houston invitation arrived. They even arranged the hotel reservations. I sent Lucien an e-mail. I'd really like for him to meet you, and I'd like to meet his wife."

"What's the rest of it?" Laurel asked as she opened the large envelope.

"The agenda of tests and interviews. I can tell you it wore me out last time, and I wasn't dealing with diabetes then. I was told a big stress can trigger an autoimmune disease. If it can, the interview in Houston three years ago did it. Let's pray they only use the boot camp tactics with the pilots."

Laurel read through the pages. "What's this about zero gravity simulation?"

"Also known as the vomit comet. They take you up in a modified bomber and do some altitude shifts that defy gravity for the passengers. If you have motion sickness, that simulation will bring it out or up."

"Do you have motion sickness, Jack?"

"No. I've been on their roller coaster, and it didn't bother me. Actually I had a blast being weightless, but I've had to roll my plane and fly inverted. I just focused on my target, and I never got motion sickness. I didn't care for the pressure wraps we had to wear to tolerate it. When you go inverted, the g force can drop your blood pressure enough to make you pass out. To keep the blood in your head, the legs on the flight suits are built to automatically inflate and compress your legs when you invert. The pressure is very uncomfortable. They say it's nothing compared with g force taking off into space. That g force is supposed to push you almost through your seat."

Jack was very excited when talking to Laurel. She, on the other hand, had trouble sharing his excitement because she was thinking about Jack being launched into space for the first time. She did her best to conceal what she was feeling, but it came through on her face.

"Do you ever get nervous about going into space, Jack?"

"No," he said with assurance. "That's been my dream all my life so getting this close is an incredible rush." He scanned her face with concern. "Are you all right with it, Laurel? I mean, you've already taken on a whole lot of forever because of me. If this is too much for you, I'll call Houston and cancel."

He was offering to sacrifice his dream for her, and Laurel knew she would never doubt his feelings for her again. She put her arms around him and held him.

"I'll be all right with it, Jack, if it's what you want. Just make sure you always find your way back home. I'll pray until you do."

"There's no way I'd let anything keep me from coming home to you." He sat back and handed her the photography book again as he ate the fruit on his plate. "I'm keeping you from studying."

"I think I know it. You can quiz me if you need proof. Just hold onto me while you do it." He laid down and pulled her back against his body.

"This feels so right," he said. "I've never had anything feel so right."

He encouraged her to study until they were both too interested in touching to keep reading the photography book. Before Laurel set aside her book, she handed Jack his test kit and insulin. It had already become their bedtime ritual.

They were jolted awake by the alarm clock, and Jack sat up reluctantly. "Hit the shower and I'll make coffee. We need to get going if we're going to get you to your exam on time."

"When we return from Houston, how long will we have before we'll have to move?" she asked as she stretched.

"If I make the cut, we'll have to report in thirty days, but it's a big if, Laurel. Let's just pray we'll get shoved in the right direction. God may not want me to be in space."

She wrapped her arms around his waist and pressed her face against his chest. "I really believe that when God closes a door, he opens a window, Jack Driver. This is our window."

"You know what a window is, Laurel?" he asked as he held her face in his hands.

"Tell me because I can think of a lot of definitions."

"A window is the angle that allows a spaceship to escape the atmosphere and leave the earth's gravitational pull. You never know if you'll make your planned window for a launch until you see how conditions develop. We aren't going to know until I get through the screen so let's just be up for the possibility." He smiled into her eyes. "Why are you so sure?"

"I know you," she said simply. "No one in their right mind would turn you down." She took his hand and led him to the shower. They pushed their time to its limit before leaving the house. Before their departure, the answering machine recorded that Laurel's father was being discharged from the hospital in Knoxville.

In the truck they said a prayer together for Laurel to pass her test. Jack stopped at the bank with the marriage license so he could add Laurel to his accounts and pick up the paperwork to merge her funds with his. He left with a stack of forms for Laurel to sign and drove back to wait for her. He used a pay phone to call his insurance company to request Laurel be added to his policy. She appeared at 10:30 just when he was beginning to worry.

"How was it?" he asked.

"I passed. All I need to know now is where I'll be registering in September."

"The countdown is at seventy-two hours and counting." He tested his sugar. "Let's go get your driver's license and get the banking done. Then we should go over to Cherokee and see how your dad is doing."

"Jackson, the lion hearted. Maybe you should let me call Mary so she can break it to him gently."

"The longer we hide it, the more upset he'll be. Let's go. We need to keep mending your fences because I think mine are pretty well razed. When we have kids, we'll want them to have at least one set of grandparents."

"We'll keep praying, Jack, and maybe your dad will come around. You and Lucien are his only children. He isn't going to want to give up both of you."

"I can't know what he'll do, Laurel. He can be a real hard case. Let's fight the battles we can win." He drove to the bank and led her to one of the desks. They merged their financial lives and were given a book of counter checks.

"You won't have the permanent checks and the new debit cards for a week," the teller told them. "If you need any help between now and then, just let me know."

"We'll be out of town on our honeymoon," Jack said. "I think we can make it without checks until then. Thank you for your help." He gave the paperwork into Laurel's keeping, and she placed their marriage license in her purse.

They drove to the highway patrol station, and the line of teenagers awaiting testing was winding around the building. "Your call," Jack said. "I'll be happy standing in line with you. Or we can try over in Gatlinburg."

"Let's get lunch and try in Gatlinburg. I know it's

stupid, but I'll feel better when I can prove we're married." She sighed. "Okay. I'm paranoid."
   "About what? I'm here with you, and I'll be your
witness." He kissed her hair. "I'm ready for some lunch.
Let's go to Gatlinburg."
   "Are you too low?" Laurel asked. "Because I'd like
to stop at your office and get rid of that picture on your
desk."
   "Good idea. I wish I'd thought of it. Let's grab some
fast food and say hello to Buddy on the way to Gatlinburg. Maybe we can get a picture made of the two of us
for my desk."
   Jack let Laurel shred the photograph because he was
afraid she might mistake his emotions for some sort of
unrequited love. It was actually rage, and it grew when
he looked through the office mail and found the expensive stationery Alyssa had always favored. He tossed it
unopened into the trash, but Laurel fished it out.
   "Her?" she asked.
   "Probably. If you want to open it, Laurel, open it. I
don't have anything to hide from you." He sat on the
edge of the desk and opened the other envelopes as if he
had no concerns about the letter's contents. Laurel's
sharp intake of breath rendered that impossible. Her
face was unreadable as the pornographic photograph of
Alyssa fluttered to the floor. Jack snatched it up and tore
it into tiny pieces. He had to read the letter over her
shoulder.

Jack,
   Why don't you stop the pretense? We were good
together. I know you remember what I could do for you.
Keep this picture close to your body for old times sake
or call me, and I'll let you have the real thing. All it
would take is one time, and you'd remember why you
almost missed your flight to Korea. I could always keep
your mind on me. Don't pass up this chance. We have

everything in common. How long can an ignorant Indian girl with a high school diploma keep your attention? I'll be waiting to hear from you. We both know I will.   Alyssa

It wasn't easy for Jack to take the paper out of Laurel's hands gently. The rage Alyssa's letter provoked was unbelievable. He was able to be gentle because he loved Laurel and didn't want to frighten her. He tore the paper into many pieces and threw it into the trash can. Then he pulled his wife into his arms.

"I know I can't make those words go away, Laurel, but just know she's a sick person or she couldn't do something this perverse when she knows I've remarried. The only thing I can say about the rest of it is I would have missed that plane to Korea if I'd been with you. There's no comparison." He felt her relax into his embrace and held her until Buddy came to the door. He saw the newlyweds and grinned broadly.

"I'll just step outside," he grinned. "I don't want to interrupt anything."

"Okay, Buddy. Don't act your age," Jack said with good humor. "This is my wife, Laurel. This smiling, happy pilot is Buddy Rogers. He's in the Air National Guard so he's got quality helicopter time."

"I'm going after Jack's old job," the young pilot said assuredly. "As soon as I get my degree I'm applying to flight school."

"He'll do it, too," Jack said. "He's very good or I wouldn't trust him with Big Red."

"You saw the deposits," Buddy said. "We're doing real good. I was in the air ten hours yesterday. I'll do the maintenance on Sunday if you want me to."

"Please," Jack said. "We're flying to Houston this weekend."

Because of his expression, Laurel knew Buddy was aware Jack had been accepted into the space program.

Jack nodded slightly. "I'm trying for a spot as a mission specialist. I guess it's a wait-and-see deal. But they do know I'm on insulin, and they haven't been scared off yet."

Buddy extended his hand. "Good luck, Jack. Do the deed."

"I'm giving it my best shot. Thanks, Buddy. We'll see you next week."

"It was very nice to meet you," Laurel said. She was still feeling unnerved as they walked to the truck, and Jack sensed her emotions with a fresh surge of anger at his ex-wife.

"Let's go sit in line and get your driver's license," he said as they climbed into the truck. Jack did a glucose check and drove toward Gatlinburg knowing the rise in his glucose was in no way related to what he had eaten. He didn't share the results with Laurel and drew insulin at the highway patrol station. He gave the shot just before they took their place in line. Minutes later he was tapped on the shoulder by a highway patrolman.

"Can I see your license, sir?"

Jack was already irritated, and he took out his wallet without making a response. The highway patrolman looked at the license and scanned Jack's face. Jack's license was color coded to indicate he was diabetic.

"Were you taking insulin, Mr. Driver?"

"Yes, sir. I have a monitoring record if you need to see it." Jack's voice was sharp, and Laurel squeezed his hand, knowing instinctively that he was reaching the end of his fuse. His irritation was being transmitted to the officer who took it as a sign that another substance might be involved.

"I think I should see that and whatever else you have in your truck."

Jack pulled the kit from his jacket pocket and gave it to the officer very deliberately. "You know, officer, I have to take injections. It isn't a choice, and I resent every one I give. It doesn't help when I'm treated like a criminal for trying to stay alive."

The officer examined the kit and then gave it to Jack. "If I don't ask, Mr. Driver, the roads won't be safe for you or your friend."

"Let's go, Jack," Laurel said quietly. "We'll take care of this next week. We really need to get to Knoxville. I'd forgotten about your appointment."

"So had I," Jack admitted. They walked back to the truck, and he climbed in on the passenger's side and tossed the keys to Laurel. "You drive."

Laurel pulled herself into the driver's seat and said nothing until they were on the highway. "Should I go to the airport?"

"Just drive to Knoxville," Jack said. "The plane isn't that much faster, and I'm not in the right mental state to fly or drive. You don't have to be diabetic to be an impaired driver. Road rage fits the bill, too."

She couldn't think of any way to comfort him so she just drove. It was a little after 1 P.M., and they were in Knoxville by 2:15. No words had been spoken during that time.

"Tell me where to go, Jack," Laurel said tentatively.

"Get off at the hospital exit and turn right at the bottom of the ramp." He reached to take her hand. "I'm sorry for losing it. I guess I should have warned you that I have a bad temper no matter what my blood sugar is. I was on the edge because of the letter, and that little violation of my constitutional rights pushed me over the edge. I don't think that will ever get any easier."

"Why don't you do some public education?" Laurel suggested. "If he understood, he might not do it to anyone else. I won't ever ask anyone about that kind of syringe again." She watched him out of the corner of her eye and relaxed when he smiled.

"I'd forgotten about that," he admitted. "At least you did it when we were alone. You're right. If every diabetic in America became less ashamed of owning syringes and became more proactive, that kind of confrontation might not happen. I have to have a letter from my doctor to get through customs and airport security. It gets on my last nerve." He exhaled slowly. "Let's go have some fun when we get through with Dr. Carpenter. We'll get your driver's license when we get back from Houston."

"That sounds good. Then I'm going to give you the Laurel Driver ritual for relaxation when we get home." She stopped at the bottom of the ramp and smiled at him. "Smile, Jack. It's just you and me now. And test your sugar. Your hand is cold."

"Cold hands mean a warm heart." But he did test and was relieved to see he had dropped back into the normal range. "Stress sends me in more than one way."

They were on time for his appointment despite the obstacles, and Jack filled out a new information sheet for his chart listing Laurel as his wife and emergency contact. The nurse called Jack fifteen minutes later. He took Laurel's hand.

"Lila, this is my wife, Laurel. Can she come along?"

"Sure, Jack," Lila smiled. "It's nice to meet you, Laurel. You should come along. I've got some reading material for you on insulin dependent diabetes, giving glucagon, the insulin pump, and mixing insulin. Jack's always been really compliant, but every spouse needs to know enough to help protect the one they love."

Laurel watched with fascination as Jack's glucose meter was downloaded and his blood was taken. The nurse also asked when his eyes had last been checked. She explained it was a yearly necessity to look for any damage from diabetes. They did another finger stick. His weight was recorded on a chart with his height and a blood pressure reading. The nurse also checked his feet and did a test on them to prove his sensation was normal. They checked his urine for glucose and protein.

Both were negative. When the examination was complete, she brought in a box the size of a briefcase. It was marked MiniMed 508.

"This is your pump, Jack," Lila said. "What we like to do is let you take it home and play with it for a week or so. When you feel comfortable with the programming, you can come back and spend a day in Knoxville while you try it out. It's not difficult, but it's a different way of doing things. You already do a good job counting carbohydrates, so this isn't going to be a big challenge for you."

"If I feel comfortable with it sooner, can I go ahead, Lila?" Jack asked. "I'm having tons of fun trying to adjust my insulin when I exercise. I'm taking shots or glucose tablets almost every hour. I've also had a really bad unsensed reaction. I didn't feel it at all until after Laurel got a glass of juice down me. We've got glucagon now, but I really don't want to have one like that again."

"I understand," Lila said calmly. "I've been insulin dependent for twenty-four years, Jack. Reactions are the bane of our existence." She reached under her coat and pulled out a black rectangle. "This is my third pump. Once you get used to it, you'll never go back. It's the closest we can be to non diabetic until they find the cure. When you think you're ready to use it, just call me." She smiled as she replaced her pump. "Laurel, let me teach you about glucagon while Jack and Dr. Carpenter talk."

She led a reluctant Laurel from the room. The nurse sensed the emotion.

"Always give Jack some space to talk to the doctor," Lila explained. "When you have diabetes, sometimes things scare you. Men try to hide those feelings from their wives because diabetes makes them feel emasculated. Our society makes men feel like they have to be invulnerable, and diabetes makes that impossible. A lot of men try to ignore the diabetes because they can't accept feeling that way. Fortunately, your husband seems to be realistic about what he has to do to be healthy."

"He's still angry sometimes," Laurel admitted. "He told me something like what you just said. He even said he didn't know why I would want to love him."

"I've said the same thing to my husband more than once," Lila said. "Diabetes is a burden, Laurel. It costs money and time, and you never get a vacation from it. It takes a special kind of love to live with it one day at a time. It takes a special kind of courage to control it one sugar at a time. Don't worry. Jack's in perfect control even though he's very sensitive to insulin. If he can hold his sugar like this, he'll never have any complications."

"Just tell me how to help him," Laurel said. "I'm not afraid to know."

Chapter 11

Laurel was introduced to Dr. Carpenter at the end of the appointment. He didn't seem much older than Jack, and he was very open and friendly.

"Your husband is doing a good job, Mrs. Driver, and I think we have a plan about the exercise. Jack really needs to gain some weight. He's six two and he weighs 168. Jack, you weighed 190 for several years before you were diagnosed, didn't you?"

"About that," Jack admitted. "I think it will be easier when I can eat because I want to eat and not because I have to eat." He took Laurel's hand. "We're going out tonight and find something totally fattening and bad for us. I can eat it without guilt because you guys told me to gain weight. Thanks. I'll be calling you in a week, Lila."

Laurel knew Jack was feeling better when he let her in the passenger's side and climbed behind the wheel himself. She finally had to ask.

"Did Dr. Carpenter think you were doing well?"

"He thinks I'll do better with the pump. I agree. I'm only supposed to have no more than two unassisted reactions per week and no assisted ones. Assisted means the one where I didn't see it coming and you had to bail me out. I'm having a few more than we want." He glanced at her. "Is that what you meant?"

"I'm just worried about you," she admitted. "You didn't mind me coming with you, did you?"

"No. I want you to be well informed, and you have a right to know since this affects both of us." He stopped at a traffic light and took her hand. "I won't ever hide anything from you, Laurel. It's just easier emotionally to ask Dr. Carpenter certain things when you aren't there. There are aspects to diabetes that freak me out even now. That reaction I didn't feel is on top of the list."

"What else is on the list?" she asked without wondering if she should.

"Avoiding the complications. When you finish reading that book they sent you from the American Diabetes Association, you'll know what I mean. That's why I'm trying to keep the levels as close to normal as I can." He paused. "One of the neurological complications is sexual problems. At least half of the men who have diabetes get those kinds of problems. That's a terrific incentive to stay controlled, especially now."

She laid her hand on his leg and leaned across the seat to kiss him. "If you have that kind of problem, I haven't noticed. If you ever do have it, we'll find a way to get around it." She was glad to see him smile. She knew his expression wasn't forced.

"Next time stay with me if you want to," he said. "I don't think I'll be afraid to tell you anything after this."

They drove to the university to pick up Jack's cap and gown and his graduation invitations. Then they went to a lively Mexican restaurant in the mall. Neither of them had known they shared a penchant for Mexican food. They talked as they ate their meal and enjoyed the time away from their worries. While Jack was paying the bill, Laurel went to a specialty shop. In the large mall bookstore, they purchased a book on the Navajo people.

She read it aloud as she and Jack started back to Sevierville. They were both unaware of the time until Jack turned into the driveway.

"Your relaxation program is working great," Jack said. "You are different from any person I've ever known."

"I think that's how love's supposed to be," Laurel said. "This isn't my relaxation program though. Let me in, and I'll get everything ready while you walk Kennedy."

"This is one of those mysterious woman things, isn't it?" Jack pulled her across the truck seat into his arms. "Don't wear us out too much. We need to get packed and be ready to head out in the morning."

"What about Kennedy?" Laurel asked.

"We'll take him to the kennel. He gets stressed if I'm gone more than one night." He reached around her to pick up their packages including the insulin pump. "Let's go in. I'm really curious about this surprise."

He fed Kennedy and took the dog for a twenty-minute walk. The day had started on a sour note. But finally he felt at ease as he walked out to the mailbox. That feeling ended when he flipped through the mail. There was a letter addressed to Laurel, and Jack recognized the handwriting as Alyssa's. He opened it as they walked back to the house and then had to turn around and walk another half hour to calm down.

Dear Laurel,

I learned your name the day Jack and I had lunch in Knoxville. I feel like you need to know more about him since you have only really known him sexually. I've known him a long time, and we've never gotten over each other. You're just a rebound for him. Everything about you is opposite of me. I have my masters in music, and my family could buy and sell yours. I'm sure you're very pretty in an ethnic way, but you aren't what Jack's

dad wants for him. Jack is his father's son. You might
want to get out now, Laurel. I love Jack, and he still loves
me. I'd hate to see you get hurt. You'll get hurt if you
stay with him.   Alyssa Driver

It was night when Jack sat down on the back porch
with Kennedy at his feet. He was tired from walking,
but his frustrated anger was still fresh. He felt pursued
in a way that made him very uneasy for his own sake
and Laurel's sake. He tested his blood sugar and watched
the starry sky until Laurel touched his shoulder.

"I'm ready. Are you?"

He looked up at her and forced a smile. "That depends on how much exertion is going to be required. If
your plans are incredibly physical, I may need a snack."

"I'm not giving any hints." She pulled him to his feet
and led him into the kitchen. Jack locked the door and
sent Kennedy to his bed.

"Close your eyes," she said. "No peaking."

"Then let me hold your shoulders because I don't
want to break a leg this weekend."

Laurel placed his hands on her shoulders and led
him into the bathroom. The scent startled Jack, and he
opened his eyes. Laurel had filled the bathroom and
bedroom with flickering candlelight. Sandalwood incense was burning in a vase, and the bathtub was full of
hot water.

Jack was speechless for several minutes.

"It's sandalwood," Jack said. "My mother used to
burn sandalwood incense. She'd go find it in whatever
country we were in even if she didn't speak the language. They say men marry their mothers and women
marry their dads if they're going to be happy."

Her smile was luminous. "Come get in the bath with
me. I'll turn on the music." She disappeared while Jack
was undressing and returned with her boom box. As
Jack stepped into the tub, the sweet strains of a violin

concerto filled the bedroom. Laurel came in wearing her lace robe and carrying two cups of hot tea. She set the tea beside the tub and allowed her robe to slide to the floor as she slid into the water behind him.

She used oil to massage him while they were in the water. She started with his neck and shoulders. The pressure of her hands seemed magically able to erase the tension he couldn't hide. Jack relaxed and let her pull him back against her body as her hands moved to massage his chest and abdomen. Her touch caused a different kind of tension then. He held back as long as he could, but he had never wanted to make love as much as he did when her hands were sliding all over his body. She kept massaging his back even when he turned and pulled her into his arms with excited impatience. He kissed her until kissing and touching weren't enough for either of them, and then he led her into the bedroom. When they made it to the bed, waiting was not an option.

It was the most intense, overpowering sexual experience Jack had ever had. Laurel was empathic to his physical responses and used that ability to heighten everything he felt. She had added honey to their tea, so there was no need to stop and test his sugar despite activity that persisted well past midnight. Then all the negative feelings were a dim memory.

"You're like the answer to all the prayers I couldn't pray," he told her. "Laurel, I didn't know I could ever feel this way."

"Happily ever after can be real," she whispered. "It already is."

"I love you," he said intently. "I've never loved anyone like I love you. We're a part of each other already." He pulled her close and held her while they slept in a place where Alyssa couldn't hurt them.

Jack awakened first feeling a little shaky. He walked to the kitchen to get juice and make coffee. When he returned to the bedroom, he found the letter and destroyed it so completely that it couldn't have been reconstructed. He was packing when he heard Laurel stirring. He went to hold her.

"Good morning," he said.

She stretched and wrapped her arms around him in one motion. "Did you have a good sleep?"

"I feel absolutely ready to take on anything today," he said. "I've got coffee brewing. Let's get packed and head over to Cherokee. If we fly out this afternoon, we can make it to Memphis tonight. I have a good friend in Memphis. I thought I'd call him and see if we could stay at his place. He lives near the private airport in Shelby County."

"That sounds good," she agreed. "Will you show me some more about flying?"

"I promise. No matter how Houston turns out, we'll get you a pilot's license by next year." He kissed her several times and had to force himself to release her. "Don't get me started. I'm still thinking about last night. Last night was a first for me."

"Good," Laurel said. "I really wanted it to be."

"You were incredibly successful." He retreated to the kitchen and returned with coffee for Laurel. "What gave you the idea to do all that?"

"I read an article about making a spa in your home. It sounded really—well, I thought you would like it."

"I did. I'd like to plan on numerous repetitions." He couldn't stop smiling because Laurel was so genuine. Everything she did was sending him a message of how much she cared about him. He had never experienced those feelings from another person, and he was most appreciative of her gift.

"Why are you smiling?" She wondered if he thought the gesture was silly or immature.

"You make me happy, Laurel. I've never been this happy, so it's kind of hard to wipe the smile off my face." He kissed her again and then stood. "Call Mary and make sure it's okay if we come. You might want to give her some advance notice of the news. I'd hate to be killed when I feel this good."

Laurel was a little leery about making the call, but she dialed her father's number and prayed her news would be well received. Mary answered on the third ring.

"Hi, Mary. It's Laurel. I was hoping I could come see my dad. I want him to meet Jack, if he's feeling up to it."

"He's doing well, Laurie," Mary reassured her. "I know he'd like to see you. Is everything all right with Jack?"

"It's really all right now," Laurel said. "We got married, Mary, and I've never been so happy. We want to tell dad, but if you think we shouldn't—"

"He'll be very happy," Mary assured her. "I'll pave the way. We'll expect you around lunch."

Laurel heaved a sigh of relief as she went to the bathroom and showered away everything but memories of the previous night. Jack's reactions and words had made her feel secure in the face of Alyssa's letter she had read at the office. She dressed and French braided her hair before going to find Jack. He was sitting at the computer, and he handed her a letter from the printer.

"Lucien and his wife are going to be just down the street from our hotel. I asked him to call us so we can go out Monday night. I haven't seen him since Christmas. We had our traditional, miserable time together at our father's house." He signed off and shut down the computer. "You were fast. Get your clothes together and pack your camera. I was thinking you could look around the Houston suburbs while I'm being tortured."

"Let's house hunt when we know. I'm going to research the Navajo for you."

At 9 A.M. they left the house and took Kennedy to the kennel. Jack drove to the highway patrol station in hopes of getting Laurel's license, but it was closed.

"Do you want to try Gatlinburg again?"

"Absolutely not," Laurel said. "Let's go see my dad and go to Memphis."

"Want to fly to Cherokee?" Jack asked. "The landing is a little tricky, but the scenery is terrific."

"Where would we land?" she asked.

"There's a private airport over by the river near Bryson City. I know the guy who owns it. He rents cars to private pilots."

"Okay. I've got to admit I'm getting addicted."

"To me or my plane?" Jack smiled. "I think I know the answer, especially after last night. Sandalwood is going to be a major turn-on for the rest of our lives."

"Piano music is pretty great for me." She took his hand, noting it was warm and dry. "I bought a whole lot of sandalwood at the mall."

"The question is did you pack any?" Jack asked.

"I wouldn't forget something that important."

Jack did the walk around while Laurel was loading their luggage. It was a bright and clear August day, and Jack resorted to sunglasses as they taxied to the runway. He checked his blood sugar, which was 134mg percent, and took off into the wind. The flight took thirty minutes. Jack set the plane down on the short runway with no difficulty. As they taxied to the hangar, an older man came to greet them.

"Major Driver. It's good to see you. Of course, your lady friend is better on my eyes than you are."

"How are you, Billy? This is my wife, Laurel. Laurel, this is Master Sergeant Billy Rivers. Billy was one of the best jet mechanics in the Air Force when I was stationed in Germany. When the FAA decided insulin dependent people could get a waivered license, I started looking for an instructor. Everybody said Billy Masters was the man. I didn't realize it was the Billy Masters I knew until I drove over here."

"Except Jack didn't need my help or instruction," Billy remarked. "We just tooled around the mountains having a good time until we had jumped through all the FAA hoops. It was fairly entertaining being a flight instructor for a guy who has flown every aircraft the Air Force has. Jack could climb into a commercial airliner and take it to Paris."

"Not anymore," Jack said with a small degree of bitterness. "Hey, Billy, can we rent one of the cars to go over to Cherokee? Laurel needs to see her dad."

"Sure." Billy tossed him a set of keys. "Take the convertible. I'll see you when I see you."

They left their belongings in the plane and took the vintage convertible to Cherokee. Laurel knew most of the people in the small town and, though she had been gone for three years, many folks called out and waved to her. Jack pulled the convertible into her father's driveway twenty minutes later. To her surprise, her father was sitting on the front porch and stood to meet them.

Lawrence Wolfe was still weak, but his physical illness didn't show on his face. He extended his hand to Jack and shook it firmly. Then he embraced Laurel.

"Congratulations, little girl. Mary told me you'd found your soul mate." He looked at Jack. "You'll still have to pass inspection, Mr. Driver. Please come inside."

Lawrence Wolfe took Jack to the den, and Mary ushered Laurel to the kitchen.

"It's all right, Laurel. He was really fine with it when I told him about Jack. I'm sure he's hoping you'll move closer to Cherokee, but he just wants you to be happy."

"We may be moving farther away," Laurel said hesitantly, "but I don't want dad to know yet. Before Jack developed diabetes, he had been accepted into the space program as an astronaut pilot. Now he may be accepted as a mission specialist. If they take him, we'll have to move to Houston."

With some trepidation Jack sat down across from Lawrence Wolfe. He had never been impulsive, and his military background made him dislike being unprepared. He didn't know how he would be received. Lawrence Wolfe gave him several moments to ponder what he would be asked.

"My wife tells me you're a pilot, Mr. Driver."

"Yes, sir," Jack replied. "I was in the Air Force until three years ago. I flew jets, but I was grounded when I developed diabetes. I took a discharge and just finished my doctorate in aerospace engineering."

"You don't have to prove you have value, Mr. Driver," Lawrence said quietly. "My daughter has always been a good judge of character. I just want to know you care about her and will take care of her.

"Laurel is just like her mother. She's tenderhearted and doesn't know how the world can be. At one time I tried to push her to marry a young man here. I did it to make sure someone would be around to take care of her. That was when I first knew I had heart disease, and I was worried about her future. Instead of keeping her safe, I drove her away. I've missed her a little more every day. My wife said you encouraged her to write to us."

"I don't have a good relationship with my father now," Jack admitted. "I didn't want that for Laurel when you mean so much to her. Sir, I want to apologize for not asking your permission to marry her. I know it seems sudden, but I've never been more sure of anything. I've been by myself for a long time, and I've never felt like Laurel makes me feel."

Lawrence nodded slowly. "Someday I hope you and Laurel have children, Mr. Driver. Only then will you understand that my daughter is the greatest gift I could give any man. My only worry is how you will feel in ten years with a Cherokee wife in a white world. Your children will probably look Cherokee instead of white, and Laurel isn't going to want to hide her heritage. Are you sure you can be happy with my daughter then?"

"I'm half Navajo, Mr. Wolfe," Jack said. "My mother was a full-blooded Navajo, and even though I wasn't told about my heritage until recently, I'm proud of it. When I know enough about my mother's people, I intend to list myself as a Native American. Then our children won't have to worry about where they belong. They'll have two tribes to claim."

"I think you know more about being Native American than you think you know, Mr. Driver. I won't worry about my daughter anymore. I do think we should be on a first name basis. My family and friends call me Larry."

"Mine call me Jack." Jack sat back feeling accepted in a way that was comforting. "Knowing I have diabetes, you're probably worried about Laurel's future, but I'm in good shape now and I'm going to keep myself in good shape."

"You can take care of diabetes then?" Lawrence looked relieved. "I'd like to know more about it. While I was in Knoxville, the doctors told me I have it. They call it non insulin dependent diabetes, but they gave me insulin to take. I was still drugged because of the surgery, and I don't understand the information they gave me. I have a machine to test my blood sugar, but Mary and I can't make it work. It tells us 'error' every time we turn it on."

"I can definitely help you with that," Jack said. "Don't worry. When you get used to it, diabetes isn't a big deal. They just won't let you fly fighter jets or the space shuttle when you have it.

"You do need to learn everything you can about it," Jack said. "We don't have the same kind of diabetes. I have the insulin dependent kind. My body doesn't make any insulin anymore. I have to take insulin or I'll die. Your body doesn't use insulin right, but you make a whole lot of insulin.

"Your pancreas is starting to fail in keeping up production so you need insulin to keep your blood sugar normal. You won't die if you don't take insulin, but you won't be healthy. The best way to treat your kind of diabetes is cutting down on how much carbohydrate you eat and also losing weight. The more you exercise, the less insulin you need."

"So I might not always need this shot?" Larry asked.

"I always will, but you might not. Did they give you a pill to take?" Jack asked. "Some of the new pills for non insulin dependent diabetes can help your pancreas make more insulin."

"They gave me several kinds of pills." Larry handed Jack three bottles. "These and an aspirin every day."

Jack examined the bottles. "This one is to make your cholesterol lower because your kind of diabetes causes heart disease in most of the people that have it. This is for your blood pressure, and this one makes you more sensitive to insulin. The magazine the American Diabetes Association sends you when you join says this kind of pill can get you off insulin if you take it long enough. If I had that option, I'd definitely take the pills."

They were inside long enough to become well acquainted and long enough to make Laurel and Mary uneasy. The sound of laughter drew them to the den door just as Lawrence opened it.

"Mary, come here. Jack has finally made this machine work. He says both of us should take insulin before we eat. Bring mine."

Laurel helped Mary serve lunch while Jack taught Lawrence about insulin and glucose monitoring. Lawrence was on an insulin pen that contained an insulin called Humalog mix 75/25™. Jack explained it was a combination insulin that contained both the short acting insulin he used and a new long acting insulin. The dose was dialed up on the pen.

"I used to use the pens," Jack explained. "It's much

more convenient than mixing, but now I need an odd combination so I had to go back to syringes."

"I'm glad not to have to draw up the insulin," Lawrence admitted. "I don't feel like I know enough to do it right."

"Every day you'll learn more. I have a lot of books, and we'll bring you one when we get back from Houston," Jack promised. "I'll bring you a card from one of my *Forecast* magazines so you can join the ADA. Then you'll know about all the new things as soon as they come out. We should be back next weekend."

They stayed until three o'clock. Joseph and his wife stopped by to check on Lawrence, and Joseph apologized to Jack. They left just as Peter and his family arrived. That meeting had to occur in the driveway because Jack and Laurel's deadline had long since passed. They reached Billy's airport at 4 P.M. and took off into misty skies.

"We may have to change our plans," Jack said as he flipped on the radio. "Knoxville Tower, this is 1740 Alpha Tango asking for weather conditions between Knoxville and Nashville."

"1740 Alpha Tango, this is Knoxville Tower. There is a heavy haze surrounding the airport at this time. IFR conditions apply. Other pilots are advised to take an alternate route. Forty miles west of Knoxville conditions are clear to Nashville."

"IFR means you have to use your instruments to fly," Jack told Laurel.

"Knoxville Tower, we are IFR rated. Please advise altitude and heading to fly through Knoxville airspace on course to Nashville."

Laurel couldn't see through the haze. It made her feel more than a little anxious as they flew on the course and heading designated by the Knoxville Tower. Jack fully concentrated on piloting the plane for almost an hour while Laurel prayed. When the horizon began clearing, they both heaved sighs of relief.

"How did you know where we were going?" Laurel asked.

"You don't look out the window," Jack said. "You just have to trust your instruments and the guys in the tower. Check my sugar, Laurel. I can't tell if I'm incredibly tense or getting low." He pulled out the kit and gave her his right hand. Laurel almost didn't want to know, but the reading was 126mg percent.

"You're incredibly tense. Your blood sugar is fine."

Jack shook his head. "It ought to be higher than that from the stress. I think it's dropping, and I'd rather be high than low. Give me a couple of glucose tablets."

Laurel gave him the tablets. As the horizon around them continued to clear, they both relaxed.

"It's still daylight," Laurel said in amazement. "I was sure it was getting dark."

"I've flown through those conditions a thousand times, but not with you next to me. I miss the radar in my F-16." He squeezed her hand. "I've never been afraid something would happen to me, but I couldn't stand letting anything happen to you. And I promised your dad I'd take care of you. I hope he likes me as much as I like him. He's absolutely crazy about you, Laurel. He seemed relieved when I told him I'm half Navajo. While we were working on his glucose meter, he told me that he knew some Navajo soldiers when he was in the service and that they had good heads on their shoulders. You didn't tell me he was in the Air Force.'"

"I was sure he would tell you. He served in Vietnam, and he's really proud of that. I knew you had been in the Air Force before you told me because the uniform you were wearing in the picture on your desk looked a lot like his. It's odd that both of you have diabetes after what you said about girls marrying their daddies if they're going to be happy."

"Are you happy, Laurel Driver?"

"I'm really happy, Jack Driver." She glanced at her watch. "It's only 5:30. Where are we?"

"About an hour from Nashville. We're flying into the wind so it's slowing us down." He spoke into the radio, "Nashville Tower, this is 1740 Alpha Tango on route from Knoxville to Memphis requesting weather conditions in the Nashville area. We are IFR rated."

"1740 Alpha Tango, this is Nashville Tower. The weather in Nashville is clear with a light rain. Winds are southeasterly at 15 miles per hour."

"Nashville Tower, please advise course and altitude through Nashville airspace toward Memphis." Jack made a course adjustment and pointed to the mountains below them. "Those are the Cumberland Mountains. We'll see how the weather looks, but we'll probably be fine going on through to Memphis tonight. If you're tired, get some sleep."

"I'm totally awake. Give me my flying lesson and tell me about how you could see through the haze."

For the next hour, he explained about instrument flight and then let Laurel take the controls as if he were her flight instructor.

"You're a great teacher. Maybe you should give flying lessons."

"They won't let me," Jack replied. "I was a flight instructor for a while before I moved up to fighter jets. I always thought I'd do that full time when I was older. I have a waivered license. I can fly but that type of license won't let me teach. There are a lot of things they won't let me do because of the diabetes. That's really why I left the Air Force. They grounded me, but they didn't kick me out. I resigned. After I pulled myself together from the shock of knowing I was diabetic and Alyssa's letter, I applied to go to any of the space-affiliated bases. They denied my request for transfer. Then I applied to work in the control tower. They denied that request on the basis that I couldn't be trusted with such an important job. I felt—well, I felt like my life was over. They moved me to a desk job. I did ordering and inventory on plane parts and oversaw their maintenance. It was a clear message that they weren't going to trust me with anything requiring independent decisions.

"That was when I stopped taking insulin. The first two times, I just got sick and spent a day in the base hospital. The third time, I just about got my wish. I went into a coma again. They sent in a psychiatrist when I was out of intensive care, and I asked him to tell me what I had to live for. He said it was my duty to keep fighting.

"That wasn't the answer I needed. I had done my duty to God and my country all my life, and I felt like I was being punished. I remember thinking they were going to lock me up. I was thinking about more reliable ways to take care of my problem when Captain Norwood came to see me." His eyes told her he was speaking of suicide. Laurel was appalled because Jack always seemed so in control.

"What stopped you?" she asked.

"Captain Norwood and God," Jack said simply. "Captain Norwood was the base chaplain. I wasn't glad to see him. I asked him the same question I had asked the psychiatrist. I expected another pat answer. He said God gave me my life as a gift, and I owed my life to Him. He said Jesus had been tortured to death at my age to give us all the gift of life, so I didn't have any right to complain about something that was in my power to manage.

"I hadn't cried or vented until then because no one had given me the chance to do it. Macho aside, sometimes men need to cry. I think I hit bottom that night, and Captain Norwood prayed with me all night long. When he left, we both knew I was going to survive in some fashion.

"I resigned the next week because I felt I could handle civilian life better than I could handle feeling demoted. My father never called to ask why or even to ask what I was going to do. I kept going without knowing where I was going. Now I do. I owe my life to you and God."

Laurel was too young to understand complete desolation, and Jack's confession frightened her more than she wanted to admit. She took his hand and held it tightly.

"What if they won't take you at NASA, Jack? You won't feel that bad again, will you?"

"No." His voice was very self-assured. "When I left the Air Force, I had to make my own way when I didn't know if I could. After getting so many doors slammed in my face, I started to wonder if I had made it to major because of who my father was. My confidence was at an all-time low when I finally got a job as an airplane mechanic at the private airport in Knoxville. While I was feeling positive about having a job, I enrolled in the university graduate school on my GI bill. I already had half my credits toward a doctorate in aerospace engineering, but I felt like a freshman in college.

"For the first few months I had the feeling everybody was looking at my medical record and thinking, 'Why bother? No one is ever going to let you around a plane again. You've got the bad kind of diabetes. Face the fact that you're going to die.' Even the commuter airline didn't really trust me at first. They had another mechanic check my work for the first year. I had to pray my way through one day at a time.

"A year passed, and finally people began to look at me as an ordinary human being and not as a diabetic. The airline asked me to check the other mechanics because I was the only one who hadn't made any mistakes. I was promoted to chief mechanic after eighteen months, and they transferred me to their commercial line to work on jets. At the same time, I was doing really well in school, and I received a grant to work with lasers as a new form of instrument flying. I think those successes and a whole lot more praying helped me start viewing the other setbacks as stereotyping and discrimination.

"It's a terrific rush just to have this chance at NASA. I really thought they would turn me down flat. At least I'll know I've given it my best shot. And like I told your dad, I can support you even if they don't take me. I've got nine other job offers that are all aerospace related. All of them have terrific insurance and better than decent salaries." He grinned at her. "I can always go back to being an airplane mechanic. You won't believe how much money I made doing that. It kind of makes me wonder why I wanted a Ph.D."

"My dad would say you're a warrior," Laurel said. "When you know more about being Native American, you'll know being a warrior is your life's work."

Laurel stared out the window at the starry night and caught a glimpse of a falling star. When she closed her eyes to make a wish, she realized all her wishes were coming true without any need for a falling star.

Chapter 12

"Wake up, Laurel," Jack said. "We're about to land."

She stretched and sat up, surprised to see they were circling the bright lights of an airport. "What time is it?"

"It's almost nine o'clock," he said with audible fatigue. "We're in Memphis. I couldn't raise my friend in Shelby County, and there wasn't a visible runway. This is the international airport, and we've been in line for a half hour. Check my sugar, would you?"

"1740 Alpha Tango, this is Memphis Tower. You are number two behind a heavy for runway 11R."

Laurel quickly tested Jack's sugar. "It's ninety-three."

"We'll eat when we get to the terminal hotel," Jack said. He pointed to the commercial plane landing just below them. As soon as they clear the runway, we can land."

"You were dropping before. If you hadn't had those two glucose tablets, you'd be forty now."

"Probably," Jack said. "I'm just glad to know a machine isn't infinitely better able to decide about my body than I am."

"1740 Alpha Tango, this is Memphis Tower. You are cleared for landing on runway 11R."

"Roger that, Memphis Tower." He glanced at Laurel. "Watch the controls now. When I make my turn, I'll be lined up with the runway lights. You have to have flaps on the wings to increase the lift when you're landing because you slow your air speed." He brought the plane down effortlessly, and in minutes they were taxiing to the hangars.

An airport official met Jack on the tarmac as Laurel gathered their belongings. Jack followed him to fill out paperwork and pay for their tie-down for the night. Ten minutes later they were in a cab on their way to a hotel.

"I'm ready for a nap," Jack said. "You've already had yours."

"I don't even remember going to sleep," she said.

"You just tapped out. I was talking to you, and when you didn't answer I saw your eyes were closed. Was your blood sugar too high or too low?"

She laughed and gave him a shove. "I was tired. Sometimes you just have to give in to your body."

"I'll have to agree." He put his arm around her and pulled her close beside him. At the hotel they walked straight to the restaurant and ate supper. Afterwards they went to their room and began settling for the night. Jack fell asleep immediately, but Laurel was wide awake. She took out the insulin pump and began reading the books accompanying it. She was mastering the art of programming it when Jack reached over and turned out the lights with finality at 2 A.M.

"Go to sleep, Mrs. Driver. I like company when I fly. If you're dead tired tomorrow, I won't have company."

She moved to lay her head on his shoulder and her arm across his chest. It felt very safe and secure to sleep close to him, but she wondered if it made him uncomfortable. When she started to move away, his arm tightened on her shoulder.

"I like holding onto you. I don't want to wonder where you are," he whispered.

"I'll always be right here," she promised. "It was a good day."

"With you, they've all been good," Jack said with no reservations.

Jack had the weather report on television when Laurel awakened. She heard the word thunderstorms and bolted upright. Jack raised his hand to silence her question as the weatherman continued showing a storm system on the map. It was headed across Arkansas and their flight plan. It was predicted to last most of the day.

"Get packed," Jack advised her. "We don't have much time. I don't fly in that kind of weather."

Laurel showered, dressed, and then dashed to the hotel's dining room for two takeout breakfasts. Jack met her in the lobby with their bags, and they checked out while awaiting a cab. They ate in the cab after Jack did his routine testing and insulin. There was a line waiting to get into the airport.

Jack loaded their bags and refueled the plane. He performed his walk around and went over the checklist. Then he left Laurel with the plane and spoke with the officials at the hangar. When he returned with the official documents Houston had sent him, Laurel knew he had been pleading their case.

"They're going to let us break line. Let's go."

They were in the sky an hour later. With the city's skyline out of sight, Laurel could see the thunderheads looming in the west. At frequent intervals, patches of murky clouds were illuminated by lightning.

"Wow." She looked at Jack. "What do we do?"

"Fly south as fast as we can." He completely focused on the plane for the hour that followed. Laurel took out the insulin pump and continued playing with it.

"This is really easy, Jack. It makes microwave and VCR programming look like graduate work. You have basal rates, and they run all the time to give you what your N gives you now. If you decide you're more active,

you can make a temporary basal rate of zero or whatever you want. You have three ways you can give
amounts all at once. That's called bolusing. You can give
them all at once, some now with some over time or all of
it over time. That's called a square bolus. If you gave it
all over time, when you got tired of eating, you could
cancel the rest."

"Really?" From his expression, she knew she had
piqued his interest. "I'd really like to have diabetes
locked out of my eating pattern."

"You'll love this part." Laurel held up a remote
control. "You can program your bolus with this and not
even take your pump out. No one will know what
you're doing."

"That would be great," he said. "I could lose my
drug addict image. Of course I'd lose that terrific rush
when I shoot up."

"Very funny, Jack." She kept reading the book until
they were well away from the storm clouds. As they
entered Texas, the sky spread out like a vast blue ocean
dotted with white clouds. She followed Jack's example
and donned her sunglasses.

"We're making good time," he said. "We should be
there by two o'clock. If we don't have to stop to feed my
insulin, we'll go straight through. Go ahead and check
it."

"You're eighty-seven," she said and passed him two
glucose tablets.

"So much for the straight-through flight. We need to
test again in thirty minutes," he said grimly. "I didn't
have any protein to keep it from falling, and I took some
N because I knew I'd be sitting most of the day."

Laurel dug into her purse and produced a package
of peanut butter crackers. She opened them and gave
one to her husband.

"You're a godsend, Laurel Driver," Jack said. "It's
really nice to know I have a backup system now."

She took a bottle of water from her tote bag and opened it. When she had taken a drink, she passed the bottle to Jack. "Have a drink before the crackers choke you."

"Thanks." He handed her the bottle and waited until she capped it. "Time for your flying lesson."

Laurel felt like she actually flew some of the way to Houston. Jack's blood sugar was high enough to stop worrying about it when she tested it an hour later. They landed at Houston just after 3 P.M. As they taxied up to the hangar, Lucien Driver strolled out to meet them.

Lucien was in his air force uniform, but Laurel would have known him as Jack's brother in any attire. They looked very much alike except Lucien's coloring was more Native American. His eyes were dark brown, and he wore his hair in a military crew cut. Close beside him was his new wife, Julissa. She was Hispanic and had long curly dark hair.

Jack embraced his brother and then brought Laurel forward. "This is my wife, Laurel. Laurel, this is Lucien and Julissa." While Lucien was taking Laurel's hand, Jack was meeting Julissa Driver.

"You realize we got married on the same day," Jack told his brother. "When I got your e-mail, it blew me away."

"I think we gave dad a double headache," Lucien said. "He must have figured the mutiny was planned." Lucien walked over to Jack's plane and surveyed it with a pilot's eyes. "You traded up. Nice wings, Jack."

"I've had it since January, and it was definitely a trade up." Jack climbed back into the plane and lifted down their luggage. "Let's go get some supper and get checked into the hotel."

"We're in the same hotel now," Lucien said. "They had a vacancy so Julissa and I checked in. I've got my interviews tomorrow and Tuesday, so I thought the girls could be looking around for houses." Lucien picked up one of the bags and led the way to his rental car. They drove toward downtown Houston, passing the Space Center along the way.

"What's your gut feeling, Jack?" Lucien asked.

"I don't know. There's no precedent for an insulin dependent mission specialist as far as I know. It depends on what sorts of policies and procedures they want to implement. If I get to go, you can bet I'll be hanging out with the pilots."

Laurel had been feeling a rush of fear for her husband that she couldn't suppress, but his voice made her focus on how much he wanted to go up. Lucien spoke to Julissa as she was thinking of the shuttle launches she had seen. She was trying to avoid thinking about Challenger.

"Jack was accepted as a shuttle pilot before he found out he was diabetic," Lucien said.

"You must have been really disappointed," Julissa said.

"I don't think I had gotten over it until I met Laurel," Jack said. "I knew there had to be a reason why I wasn't allowed to go. I just had to wait a while to know what it was." When he smiled at Laurel and squeezed her hand, she pushed aside her fears for him.

They checked into the upscale hotel and walked to the restaurant. They were seated well away from the crowd so they could talk. The waiter took their order, and Jack tested under the table as Lucien explained his job offer.

"I'll be working as a pilot at first testing their prototypes, but they want me to do like you've done and get my degree in aerospace engineering. They have contracts with the space agency and with commercial corporations, too. If you end up here, I'll probably be asking you for study help."

Jack drew up his insulin and put the syringe between Laurel and him. "I'll be happy to help you, but my best advice is start reading now and brush up on your physics and your calculus. Most of the older professors want you to be able to do it all with a slide rule even if they let you use a calculator."

"What did you write your dissertation on?" Lucien asked.

"Using lasers as a form of instrument flight," Jack said. "They have a really good aerospace facility in Tennessee. It's affiliated with the Air Force and the university. I spent a lot of time there. Actually I had a hard time not focusing on astrophysics. I'd like to keep taking course work in that area and astronomy if I'm accepted into the program. Then I might get to work with the telescope projects."

"Jack took me up to a telescope in Gatlinburg and showed me the moons around Jupiter," Laurel said. "That was our first date."

"I didn't know she liked astronomy until then. We've got a lot of things in common." Jack smiled at Julissa, drawing her into the conversation. "What do you do, Julissa?"

"I'm an accountant," she said. "I just graduated in June, and I work for a large CPA firm in Cocoa Beach. I play the violin with the local symphony, and that's how I met Lucien."

"Lucien plays the violin, too," Jack told Laurel. "Our mother was Julliard trained so she started teaching both of us early. She played the violin and the piano. Since we had a little talent, our dad let us keep it up even after she died. If we all end up here in Houston, we'll have our own chamber ensemble."

The waiter served their salads, and Jack took his shot under the table. They kept talking long after the coffee was poured. There was the instant rapport of people not together by chance.

Jack began to feel uneasy when Lucien excused himself from the table twice and drank both his water

and Julissa's. He kept watching Lucien and noticed his
brother had lost weight since Christmas. When Lucien
excused himself a third time, Jack followed him to the
men's room and waited until his brother had washed
his hands.

"Lucien, did you have your flight physical yet this
year?"

"No, and I won't now because I'll be leaving before
it's due." He didn't meet Jack's gaze for several moments and then he said, "I have it, Jack. I haven't done
anything about it yet, but I'm pretty sure. I've had all the
symptoms for a couple of months."

Jack took out his test kit hesitantly. He remembered
that in two weeks Lucien would be thirty. His brother
was the same age Jack had been when he developed
diabetes.

"Your siblings have the greatest risk," Dr. Carpenter
had told Jack when he had gotten up the courage to ask
about children. "They have the same genetic background
and are more apt to have the same exposure to whatever
starts the antibodies."

"Let me test your blood, Lucien. You don't want to
end up in the hospital in a coma. I've done it, and it isn't
something anybody wants to experience. If you have to
live with diabetes, live with it on your own terms and
not at its mercy."

Lucien extended his finger and watched as Jack
used the lancet to take a drop of blood. He jerked
involuntarily at the feel of the stick and then, without a
word, he held pressure on his finger. The machine read
587mg percent. Both men looked at it in silence.

"Let me give you some insulin, Lucien. I can show
you what to do until you get back to Cocoa Beach.
Maybe you can buy insulin without a prescription here
and get it under control even before you get to a doctor."

"They'll ground me, Jack," Lucien said desperately.
"Don't you see my job here depends on having an

unrestricted pilot's license? I can't have that kind of pilot's license and be insulin dependent."

"You're already insulin dependent, Lucien," Jack said gently. "You can deal with it now or get sick and deal with it then. One way or another you have to learn to live with it. I can still fly. I can even still be in the space program or they wouldn't be interviewing me. I can still have a wife and a family."

"And pass this on? I couldn't do that. Julissa can't have kids. She had cancer when she was thirteen. She's cured now, but the radiation made her sterile. I was actually glad when she told me last month. I couldn't live with it if I gave this to a child." He pressed his hand to his face, and Jack embraced him for a long moment. "I should have told Julissa before I asked her to marry me. I was afraid to tell after what happened to you and Alyssa."

"Julissa isn't Alyssa," Jack said. "Laurel has been there for me. I didn't think she would want to be, but she does. God can get you past how you're feeling, Lucien. Let me give you some insulin. Then we'll go to church and pray. I want you to promise me you'll open your mind and listen for the answer." Jack drew up the amount of Humalog™ he knew would bring Lucien down and eighteen units of N. He didn't cover the food his brother had eaten because he knew that drop would make Lucien afraid of a normal sugar. Lucien flinched when the shot was given but accepted the insulin without protest.

"I've always hated needles," he told Jack.

"And you think I like them?" Jack closed the kit. "It gets to be second nature. You don't think about it like you are now. They're going to cure it, Lucien. Being insulin dependent means we'll get the first chance at being cured."

"I can't see that far ahead yet. Don't tell Julissa," Lucien begged. "I should have told her, but I couldn't. I still can't. I want you to swear you won't say anything to dad, the Air Force, or Julissa. I've never asked you for anything, Jack. I'm begging you now."

"I won't tell anyone," Jack said, "but, Lucien, I want you to promise you'll go to the doctor. Lie about who you are and pay them cash if you have to, but promise you'll go. I'm giving you what you need to avoid ketoacidosis and coma, but every day with diabetes I learn something I didn't know about my body. I think you have to do that to stay on top of it. Julissa will help you, and it's good to have help. Since I've been with Laurel, I've felt almost like I did before I had it."

"Almost isn't a reassuring word," Lucien said. "You mean almost normal."

"I feel normal," Jack said intently. "Almost to me means I'm not the same man I was three years ago. I've had to get past being angry and feeling sorry for myself, and I'm not going back there again. I'm also happier than I've ever been, Lucien. I'm happier than when I had an unrestricted license. Maybe I wouldn't have ever been this happy if I hadn't learned how good it is to be alive."

"I promise I'll go to the doctor." Lucien drew a deep breath. "I thought about not meeting you here, Jack, because I was afraid you would guess, but maybe God meant for me to come." He walked out of the bathroom abruptly, and Jack started praying for his brother.

They took a cab to an evening church service. Laurel sensed something was terribly wrong. She could feel the tension in Jack's hands even before she knew he was praying all through the service. Afterwards, he seemed normal. His blood sugar told her she wasn't wrong in thinking he was upset. It was 227mg percent. Jack drew up another two units of Humalog with his night dose of N as they rode back to the hotel.

In their room, Jack sat down at the desk and covered his face in his hands. Laurel was frightened by the gesture and put her arms around him.

"What's wrong, Jack? What is it?"

"Lucien has diabetes," he said. "He's known for a while by the symptoms, but he hasn't done anything about it because he knows the Air Force will ground him. His blood sugar was almost six hundred so I gave him some insulin, but he made me swear not to tell our father, his wife, or anyone in the service. He could die, Laurel. He doesn't understand how much it's affecting him even now. He doesn't understand that he can't hide it." Tears were in his eyes as he looked at Laurel. "Pray for him, Laurel. Don't pray for me. No matter what happens with me tomorrow, I still have you and my degree. We can make a life and be happy even if I never see space. Lucien's life is so much more important to me."

"We'll both pray," Laurel said. Jackson sat beside her on the floor, and they prayed together for a long time. When Jack could release his pain, they lay down to sleep and Laurel continued praying for her husband.

Chapter 13

Jack was awake when Lucien knocked on his door early the next morning. He closed the bedroom door before admitting his brother.

"Please tell me you've decided to ground yourself," Jack said.

"I'm going to the doctor, Jack. I don't know about the rest of it yet. I didn't get up to go to the john last night. It was the first time in six weeks that I didn't get up." Lucien sat down on the couch. "Why couldn't I control it and keep flying? Why does anybody have the right to know? It's not fair to ask someone to make a decision between their life and treating a disease."

"I have a life, Lucien," Jack insisted. "It's a good life, and if someone told me I could go back to my F-16 tomorrow, I wouldn't give up what I have now." He sat down and placed his hand on his brother's arm. "It's a long way from where you are to where I am. Your body can still make insulin now. When your sugar comes down, you'll go into the honeymoon phase and not need much insulin. Over the next two years most of your insulin making cells will die. The doctors believe you can preserve some of those cells if you get your sugar as near normal as you can from the minute you're diagnosed. If that's true, I screwed myself over by not controlling it well for those first six months.

"My endocrinologist says I'm very sensitive to insulin because I don't have any insulin production on my own. He measured a protein called C-peptide that tells him how much insulin I make, and it was undetectable. I have big swings in my blood sugar over little changes in what I eat or what I do. I try to keep my sugar in what they call 'tight control.' That means I'm keeping my blood sugars as close to non diabetic readings as I can. That will keep me from having any complications, but it comes with the risk of low blood sugars.

"When I fly, I have to test my sugar every hour to make sure I'm not impaired. We both know you can't take your eyes off the controls of an F-16 long enough to test your sugar. If you're too high, you get sleepy and your reactions slow down. If you're too low, you're drunk. I can know what my sugar will be for a couple of hours if I'm really careful about eating and my insulin. After that, it can change fast. No one is going to guarantee an air force pilot will only be up two hours. For Julissa and me, let go of this part of your life."

"How much insulin did you give me last night?" Lucien asked.

"Eighteen units of the long acting and ten units of the short acting." Jack took out his meter and tested Lucien's sugar. The reading was 237mg percent. Then he took his own sugar. The reading was 94mg percent.

"Normal is 80 to 120 before you eat," Jack said. "I have an extra bottle of each insulin and an extra meter. I can give you those and enough syringes for the next couple of days. If I do, you'll have to promise me not to fly until you go to the doctor."

"Show me what to do." Lucien looked defeated. Much later Jack realized his brother had never made the promise he had requested. Jack was too concerned about getting his brother's blood sugar down at that moment to think about Lucien being in denial. He wrote out his own sliding scale and the dose of N he took at night. He was very sure those amounts wouldn't be too much when Lucien was so terribly out of control. Lucien didn't know how to mix the two types of insulin so he would be getting less daytime insulin than Jack took.

"You need to test a lot, Lucien. The strips can be bought without a prescription. If you drop under a hundred, you ought to start cutting everything back by two units at a time. When are you going back to Cocoa Beach?"

"Tomorrow morning. We came on a commercial airliner." Lucien placed the kit in his pocket and then embraced Jack for a long minute. "You're stronger than I am, Jack. I never realized how strong until I knew I had it, too."

"The hardest thing to get past is feeling sorry for yourself. We could have had a terminal illness. We could have died on a mission. We don't have a right to complain about just having diabetes. In time, you'll see it isn't so bad. I love you, Lucien. When you feel like giving up, keep going for me."

"Keep praying for me," Lucien said quietly. "I love you, Jack. Having you as a brother has made up for having J.R. as our father." He left the hotel room for his meeting. Jack sat praying for him until Laurel entered the sitting room of their suite.

"Did you make any headway?" she asked him.

"I don't know," Jack said helplessly. "He promised he'd go to the doctor, and he promised he wouldn't fly. I'll have to pray that's enough." He stood and looked at his watch. "I have to be ready in an hour. Can you order some room service while I take a shower?"

"I will." Laurel put her arms around his waist and held him. "I'll pray all day, Jack. Just stay focused on your interviews. If you make it into the space program, the message to Lucien will be that anything is possible."

Jack left the hotel at 8:30 A.M. Laurel read her Bible, then showered and dressed. She sat on a bench in front of the window and prayed for Lucien, Julissa, and Jack. Julissa's knock interrupted her. When Laurel opened the door, Julissa walked into the hotel room and burst into tears.

Jack knew he was under the gun from the minute he walked into the space agency, but he had been a pressure player all his life. The first two hours of interviews were obviously designed to put him at ease or off guard. They did nothing more than review his application and his training in aerospace engineering.

He tested his blood sugar at the second break and found he was holding in the normal range. His physical examination took place just before lunch. He took two glucose tablets before he tackled the treadmill. The medic conducting the stress test seemed surprised when Jack completed the test without any observable problems. His vision was still twenty-fifteen, and his urine tested negative for sugar, protein, and drugs.

Jack accompanied the four other candidates to lunch. It was obvious his medical history was no secret because everyone was watching him when he sat down with his food. Jack took the observation as a challenge and tested his blood sugar without making any attempt to conceal his actions. He drew and gave his insulin with the same in-your-face attitude. The action seemed to discourage any further surveillance. He ate without thinking about the food and said a prayer for Lucien.

The afternoon began with an interview by an air force flight surgeon.

"Dr. Driver, I've reviewed all your medical records, and you seem to do a remarkable job in taking care of your diabetes. I still have reservations about your inclusion in the program. Your type of diabetes requires intensive monitoring, and I don't know how you'd have the time during a shuttle flight."

"With all due respect, sir, I can test my blood sugar in about thirty seconds. If I carry predrawn syringes and glucose tablets, I can treat the results in less than thirty seconds. If we have time to empty our bladders in space, I can monitor myself."

The surgeon coughed to cover his real response to the answer. "I need to see your glucose meter, Dr. Driver." Jack extended it without hesitation.

"There are two readings that aren't mine," Jack said. "I had supper with a friend last night, and he had all the symptoms. I talked him into letting me test him last evening and again this morning. Hopefully he's going to the doctor today. I checked him at the same time I had monitored so that should be evidence that I'm not lying. You can't be under 150 and over 500mg percent at the same time."

The doctor backed up the meter and scribbled the readings into the grids of a glucose log.

"What are these hourly readings?"

"Those were taken when we flew here from North Carolina. I test very frequently when I fly. That's an FAA regulation for pilots with diabetes." Jack extended his fingertips and made certain the doctor could see they had been in frequent contact with lancets.

The flight surgeon gave Jack his meter and sat back with his hands folded.

"I can't find any reason to reject you, Dr. Driver, but keep in mind it isn't my decision. Good luck. I think you go to the simulators next. You may need to test every hour," the doctor said.

Julissa was a bright lady, and she had a family history of non insulin dependent diabetes. After a week of living with Lucien, she had become convinced he was sick. She spilled her concerns to Laurel in a tearful torrent. Laurel felt helpless as she listened, and then she reassured Julissa that Jack was healthy in spite of having the condition. It was lunch time before they left the room. Laurel took her sister-in-law to the hotel dining room where they settled in for a getting-to-know-you lunch. Then they went for a walk and window shopped. As the afternoon passed, the two women were in control of their emotions.

Jack was surprised by the simulators because he was given the same tests he had taken as a pilot. He still had very quick reflexes and was able to handle the testing without any problems. As some of the testing was physically demanding, he took a glucose tablet every hour. At 5 P.M. he was directed to his exit interview. Colonel Asher called his name. He followed the man who would have been a superior officer and waited until the colonel was seated.

"You've done well thus far, Dr. Driver. I'm curious about how the testing has affected you."

"I haven't had any feelings about it one way or another, sir," Jack replied. "It's not very different from what I did three years ago. I passed it then, and I'll pass it now. I just wonder why I'm taking the pilot's test when it's obvious I'll never be flying the shuttle."

"The pilot's test is much more difficult than the one we give mission specialists, Dr. Driver. I'm sure you surmised you would have something to prove here. You've done well today. Let's see how the rest of the testing goes and then we'll talk about the outcome." The colonel stood and extended his hand to Jack, who shook it firmly. He was feeling good as he exited the interview.

Laurel was alone when Jack entered their hotel room. He gathered her into his arms and kissed her.

"So far so good," he told her. "I passed the flight

physical. I think the medic was expecting me to drop dead." He kissed her for several more minutes until he remembered his brother. "Have you heard from Lucien?"

"I spent the day with Julissa," she said. "She's convinced he has diabetes, and she cried all morning because he won't do anything about it. I didn't tell her anything, but I've never felt so sorry for anyone in my life. If Lucien knew how he was torturing her, he couldn't just ignore it anymore."

"He's not rational right now," Jack conceded. "I remember being in the same place. I think I'll call and see if they want to go out again. Would you mind?"

"I think that might be your best hope of being calm enough to sleep tonight," she replied. "Call, and I'll get changed."

There was no answer in Lucien's room. When Jack attempted to leave a message, the hotel operator informed him that Julissa and Lucien had checked out.

Jack walked into the bedroom and leaned against the door. "They checked out. I guess he didn't want another sermon."

Laurel emerged from the bathroom in her slip and struggled for the right words to console him. "Maybe he knew he was distracting you, Jack. He already has his job. He had to see how upset you were about his condition."

"Maybe so. I'm sure he could tell I was frantic for him. He would do something like that."

Laurel walked over to him and took his hands. "Let's just get room service and burn some sandalwood. I think we really should celebrate. You made it through day one."

"I'm ready to celebrate," Jack said. He ran his hands through her hair and pulled her close. She pressed her body against him until he could feel every curve through the filmy fabric. They made love before calling room service. After supper, they lit the incense and went to utilize the whirlpool tub in the bathroom. They were both relaxed when they slept that night.

Jack expected the second day would be more intense. The instructors met his expectations in every way. The only sedentary activity was a two-hour session that involved calculating all the orbital and reentry parameters for the shuttle using a slide rule.

In the afternoon, he was given fifteen minutes to study the op manual for the shuttle arm. With that limited information and no prior experience, he was given another forty-five minutes to take the arm through a simulated task. It was tedious work, and at one point Jack was sure his sugar was dropping. He took a glucose tablet and kept working.

Lunch was late and deliberately hurried. Jack undercut his insulin dose to ensure his sugar wouldn't drop excessively. He was back in the simulator area ahead of the other candidates. He thought about Lucien. Then the instructor took the candidates through a workout that rivaled anything he had done since flight school. One candidate became too ill to continue. Jack and the other two left the workout in sweat-drenched flight suits. They were taken for a ride in the modified bomber known as the vomit comet.

Jack had time to test his sugar during takeoff. The reading was 114. He knew his sugar would continue to drop from the workout, so he took another two glucose tablets. He was the only candidate who didn't experience the comet's usual side effect. When he stepped off the plane, the colonel met him on the tarmac and escorted him back to his locker.

"You've been quite a surprise to us, Dr. Driver. We knew you were acceptable before you developed diabetes. Your performance is actually better now than it was three years ago. You've passed every simulation."

"Two down and one to go." Jack unzipped his flight suit. "I know you'll probably have to politely decline my application, Colonel, but before you do I'd really like to sit in the simulator's pilot seat. It's as close as I'll ever get to flying her, but I can deal with that."

"Put your flight suit back on, Dr. Driver, and I'll take you over there now," the colonel said. It didn't take Jack two seconds to decide.

Laurel was starting to worry about Jack when he called her from the space agency offices. "Laurel, I'm running late, and I didn't want you to worry. I'll be back at seven. Can you wait that long to eat?"

"I'm waiting patiently," she said. "I bought another book on the Navajo tribe, and I picked up a real estate guide because I have a feeling we might need it. Did it go well?"

"From my standpoint it did. I made it through everything. I'll call back if anything else happens." He paused. "Have you heard from Lucien?"

"No, but we will. I love you, Jack. Don't make me wait all night."

Jack left the borrowed telephone and met the colonel by the shuttle simulator. The colonel took the commander's seat and gave the pilot's seat to Jack. "Did you ever go through the pilot's manual?"

"I think I memorized it," Jack said. "I sent it back when it was obvious I'd never get to use it, so I haven't looked at it in three years."

"Take us through the initial launch procedure as best you remember it." The colonel strapped himself in and surreptitiously flipped on the vox switch. Inside the control unit, nine officers and astronauts could hear everything Jack said and see everything he did. With two prompts, he went through the launch window procedure until the simulator had achieved an acceptable orbit. Then he took it through the dead stick landing without any prompts.

"How did it feel?" the colonel asked as he switched off the simulator.

"Probably like it felt for you the first time you did it. I've been waiting a long time to sit here." Jack unbuckled the restraint and climbed out of the simulator. When the colonel climbed out, Jack extended his hand to the officer. "Thank you, sir."

The colonel shook his hand and made it clear he was dismissed by saying, "We'll see you at 0800 hours, Dr. Driver. Have a good evening."

Jack returned to the locker room and dressed hurriedly. He tested just before leaving, catching himself at 77mg percent. He took another glucose tablet and caught a cab for the hotel. He didn't know he was the subject of a heated discussion at the agency at that very moment.

Laurel met him in the foyer of their hotel room and embraced him. They fed each other supper in bed. Laurel had felt terribly lonely during that long day, but Jack made her feel completely essential to his success.

"I got to pilot the shuttle simulator," he told her with undimmed excitement. "I can't tell you what it felt like. I mean it feels like you're really up there when you have the stick. I got through a takeoff and a landing without any mistakes. I could have done it, Laurel. I know I could have." He was silent for a long moment.

"I didn't read Jim Lovell's book that they made into *Apollo 13* until after I left the Air Force. I do know how he must have felt when he looked down at the lunar surface and realized he would never get to set foot on it. Being in the simulator was like that."

"When God closes a door, Jack, He always opens a window. Even launch windows get opened that way." She kissed his chest and snuggled against him. "I'm glad they let you fly the simulator. You earned it."

"We earned it." He gave himself to the comfort of her arms for that night.

Chapter 14

Jack was locked into combat mode, and he handled the tests on Wednesday with increasing confidence. At the end of the day, he was assigned to the pilot's seat and was asked to perform another simulated landing. During the simulation, the ground crew caused multiple system glitches that allowed the shuttle simulator to tumble out of control. Jack had gone through similar problems while flying fighter jets, and he corrected the spin competently without any wasted time. When he completed the landing, the colonel met him beside the simulator.

"You might want to test your sugar, Dr. Driver. You are about to start a two hour exit interview."

"I checked about a minute ago. Let's go."

He walked into the interview room and took his seat across from the panel of space agency hierarchy. The colonel was seated in the center seat, and the interview began with a series of verbal problems being presented. Jack worked his way through one scenario after another until two hours had passed.

"Step outside for five minutes, please, Dr. Driver," a team member requested.

Jack took that opportunity to test his sugar, which was slightly high at 174mg percent but acceptable for the moment. A major summoned him back to the room. As soon as he sat down, the colonel said, "We've decided to accept you, Dr. Driver. You'll need to begin training the first week of September. The agency will help you with your relocation plans. For now, you'll be a mission specialist, but we want you to keep up your time in the flight simulator. You never know when we might have a new policy that would let you step into the pilot's seat again." Documents were placed on the table in front of Jack. It was his contract. He prayed a silent prayer of thanksgiving and tried to suppress the rest of his emotional response.

"I'm certain you'll want to review the documents. You'll have two weeks to mail them back to the agency. Then you'll be sent a stipend to help you with the cost of relocating. The agency uses the moving company and Realtor listed on the back page. We'll also provide transportation back and forth if you need it."

"I flew here in my plane. My only cost was for fuel." Jack stood. "I intend to accept, but I do want time to read the contract. Thank you for the opportunity."

"We'll see you in thirty days." The colonel walked with Jack to the locker room. When they were alone, he continued a private discussion. "Don't assume you won't be flying again, Dr. Driver. You did an advanced simulation today. Only 50 percent of our pilots can correct that spin the first time, and your time to correct it was remarkably good. After the powers watch your performance and see that you can keep your blood sugar from being a major variable, they may give you a chance. After all, the FAA rules don't apply in space. At any rate, congratulations."

Jack was flying high when he left the agency. He had the cab driver take him to a copy service with fax capabilities so he could fax the contracts to his attorney in Sevierville. Then he made two copies of the documents and walked the rest of the way to the hotel. He tried to enter quietly, but Laurel snatched the door open before he could retract his key.

"Tell me," she demanded.

"We're in." He was almost afraid to see her reaction, but it was one of complete joy for him. She wrapped her arms around him and held him tightly. "That's wonderful, Jack. I can't wait to call my dad."

"I need to call Lucien," Jack said. "I'm sure my dad already knows, but I know he didn't have a hand in this because they tried too hard to make me fail." He stepped back and took her hand. "Let's go celebrate and look for houses."

He placed a call to the Realtor listed on the contact list and received an answer before room service could deliver their food. By the time they had eaten, the Realtor arrived and drove them to the suburb where most of the NASA employees lived. They looked at three houses before Laurel fell in love with a ranch style brick home with a large landscaped yard. When she looked at Jack, he grinned.

"This is it, isn't it?"

"Yes," Laurel said as if she were accepting his marriage proposal again. "It has a good aura. Why did the last family move?" she asked the Realtor.

"They retired," the agent told them. "They wanted to live in Florida. They've only been out four days."

"We'll take it," Jack said. "If you can fax a contract to my attorney in Sevierville, I can handle everything else from there. I've had seven offers on my house in the last six months, so that part will be easy."

Laurel and Jack were both feeling very much at ease until they reached the hotel at 10 P.M. Jack flipped on the television to hear the weather, but the lead news story was about a jet crash off the coast of Florida.

There are moments when the emotions of a terrible

tragedy can be carried on words. Both Laurel and Jack turned to hear the story, and later Laurel realized she had known before the story played out.

"A tragic training accident occurred off the coast of Florida just before noon today. Two U.S. Air Force pilots were conducting a routine exercise over the Atlantic Ocean when one F-16 crossed the jet stream of the other, losing power in both engines as a result. Passengers on two ships witnessed the jet crash into the ocean. Neither the passengers on the ships nor the second plane's pilot visualized a pilot ejection or a parachute. At this hour a search is ongoing for the downed pilot, but hopes for his survival have dimmed due to the condition of the wreckage. Captain Lucien Driver is an experienced pilot with more than eight years experience flying high performance jets. He is the son of Major General J.R. Driver, a U.S. Air Force member of the Pentagon staff."

"Oh, no," Jack whispered. He snatched up the telephone and made three tries at dialing the number with shaking hands before handing it to Laurel. "Dial for me. It's 561-743-1663."

Her hands were trembling, but she was able to get the connection. She handed the telephone to Jack. All she could do then was hold onto him when a stranger answered and told him Lucien was dead. Jack kept his composure and promised they would arrive in Florida Thursday afternoon. When he hung up the telephone, he broke down.

Laurel was terrified for Jack that night. He was too upset to think rationally. She monitored his sugars and gave him insulin when the stress made his blood sugar go over three hundred. When he could sleep, she hung onto him and prayed to know how to help him through it. She unplugged the telephone and let him sleep as long as he could the next morning. He was on his knees and praying when she emerged from the shower at 9 A.M. Even then, his face was wet with tears. Laurel ordered two fruit and yogurt drinks for their breakfast, hoping she could get him to eat. She packed fruit and cheese crackers for their journey.

In all those hours, Jack hadn't said anything about what they both knew had played a role in the crash. When they were loading the plane, he said, "I should have turned him in."

"When would you have done it, Jack? You were tied up from sunrise to sunset for the last three days. You told him what the risks were, and you begged him to go to the doctor and turn himself in—for himself, Julissa, and you. He just couldn't absorb it all so fast. This is not your fault."

Jack did the walk around slowly and then closed his eyes before starting the checklist. "I'm praying both pilots made a mistake. If it was just Lucien, it will haunt me for the rest of my life."

"And for the rest of my life, I'll be praying for you to put it behind you," Laurel said.

He pulled her close and held her. "I'm only getting through this because I have you, Laurel. God knows I'm telling you the truth." He released her to do his glucose check, and they took off as if the reason for the trip weren't so terrible.

The wind was behind them, and they made it to Cocoa Beach by 5 P.M. Since Jack had filed a flight plan, they were expected. General J.R. Driver met them at the private airport. He didn't wait for the plane's engines to die. He was beside the plane when Jack climbed from the cockpit, and the general embraced his son with desperation.

"You're all I have now, Jackson. You're all I have left." His voice broke as he released his son. Laurel climbed from the plane and gathered their luggage. They were in a limousine before the general looked at her. She felt intimidated as he surveyed her from head to toe. His eyes rested on her wedding ring before he looked at her face. Jack didn't miss the look, and he put his arm around her shoulders protectively.

"Dad, this is my wife, Laurel."

The general extended his hand and took Laurel's briefly. There was no warmth in the handshake. "J.R. Driver," the general said tersely. He turned his attention back to Jack, dismissing his daughter-in-law. Laurel studied him as if his appearance might give her some clue to who he was.

J.R. Driver was dressed in an immaculate dress blue uniform marked by numerous medals. He was Jack's height but thirty pounds heavier, weight he carried well for his age. He had gray eyes and black hair clipped in a crew cut. Laurel thought he was surprisingly dark complexioned for a white man. His skin seemed to have a different tone than just tanned Caucasian skin. His expression was stony as he spoke to his son.

"The funeral is tomorrow afternoon, Jack. They recovered Lucien's body late yesterday but after nine hours in the water—well they did what autopsy they could. Did you know he was diabetic?"

"I found out Monday," Jack said. "We had dinner, and he had the symptoms. I got him to let me test his blood sugar, and it was really high. He'd been having the symptoms for a couple of months. He promised me he would ground himself and see a doctor as soon as he got back to the base. He made me promise not to tell anyone. What caused the crash, Dad?"

"The other pilot had an engine flame out," the general said impassively. "He veered too close to Lucien, and Lucien was caught in the jet stream. He lost both engines. The witnesses said he went into a flat spin and was trying to correct it. He didn't eject. He should have been able to correct the spin."

"You don't know that," Jack said sharply. "You

didn't fly F-16's, Dad. We're talking seconds to an unre-coverable spin. Anyone can hit a jet stream. It wasn't his fault."

"They're signing it out as pilot errors on both pilots, but the official report will say Lucien had a very high blood sugar at the time. They estimate it was over 500."

Jack took out his glucose meter and tested his sugar in front of his father. The reading was 98mg percent, and he held the meter up so the general could see it. "It doesn't have to be high when you have diabetes. It can be under control. I couldn't make Lucien believe it. I gave him insulin and a glucose meter, but he obviously didn't use them or he wouldn't have been that high."

"We can't bring him back," the general said harshly. "He's gone. When the funeral is over, we need to talk."

"When the funeral is over, we'll be leaving for Sevierville. I graduate on Saturday."

"Before you leave, we need to talk," the general said without acknowledging his son's words. "I arranged for two rooms at the hotel closest to the funeral home."

Jack pulled Laurel even closer and braced himself for what he knew was coming. Laurel prayed the rest of the way to the hotel and was glad for the chance to close the door on her father-in-law.

"I told you he's a control freak," Jack said as he set their suitcases in the bedroom. "I'm not going to let him run us, Laurel, and I'm sorry for how he treated you. We've just got to get through this for Lucien."

"He didn't ask how it went in Houston," Laurel said weakly.

"He already knows," Jack said. He kissed her and held her close. "Pray me through this, Laurel. It's the worst thing I've ever lived through."

The worst thing for Laurel was watching Jack struggle to eat when they rejoined the general. He hadn't eaten enough supper when he pushed his plate away. She instinctively knew he wouldn't want to have blood sugar trouble in his father's presence, so she excused herself from the table and walked across the street to a frozen yogurt shop. She returned with two protein fruit shakes. In her absence, General Driver made his first attack.

"When are you moving to Houston, Jackson?"

"We have thirty days," Jack said. "I've had a buyer for our house that I've been holding off, but I need to sell the helicopter and get us moved. We found a house in Houston Wednesday night."

"Have you thought of reenlisting, Jackson? You could go back in as a major and progress from there. You would still be grounded, but I could make certain your career wasn't affected in any other way if you were back in."

"I don't see any advantage, Dad. I'll make more money as a civilian, and the benefits aren't any better in the service. Since I have my doctorate, I'm going to be Dr. Driver. What's the point?"

"Family tradition," the general said adamantly. "You could be in the Pentagon when you leave the space program. There's no limit to how far you can advance."

"That's not what I want, Dad. Laurel and I want a family, and I'll have more control of my time if I'm a civilian. To be honest, I'm more interested in astrophysics than I am in politics."

"I was there for you and in the Air Force," the general argued. "As for the astrophysics, how far do you think that will take you? There are diploma mills cranking out doctorates all over America. There aren't very many generals. I want you to do this for me, Jackson. I stayed out of your life when Lucien was alive, but you're my only son now."

The beginning of the argument had been insulting but tolerable. The last words were a blow that Jack hid with tremendous difficulty.

"I'll think on it, Dad. That's all I can tell you."

"Don't let her run your life," the general said harshly. "She's your wife, and it's her duty to follow what's best for you. It isn't as if a Cherokee high school graduate has any real opportunities."

"I thought anyone twenty-two years of age had opportunities," Jack said with unsuppressed anger. "Laurel is the most important person in my life now. Don't ask me to make a choice between the two of you. Your choice for me poisoned me the day we had lunch. I spent the night in the emergency room, and my doctor said it could have killed me. It was one of those combinations they call date rape drugs. He wanted me to report it to the police, but I didn't—just to protect you. Why don't you return the favor and get off my back?"

He stood as Laurel returned to the table. Her purchases were carefully concealed in a plain brown bag.

"I thought I'd go up to the room, Jack," she said.

"I'll come with you," Jack said. "I'll see you at the visitation, Dad." He held Laurel's hand until they were in the room and then hung the do not disturb sign on the door. He locked the door behind them, and he removed the phone from the hook. Laurel took out one shake and placed the other one in the kitchenette's refrigerator.

"Drink this, Jack," she said gently. "You didn't have nearly enough food. Just drink it and take some insulin."

"Okay," he said. "If you'll sit with me. I feel like I've been whipped." He sat down on the sofa and pulled her close. Laurel held the shake and watched as Jack drank some of it.

"It wasn't Lucien's fault," she said. "It doesn't matter what his blood sugar was with everything else that happened."

"He killed himself, Laurel," Jack said slowly. "He could have ejected. He must have thought it was his fault, and so he stayed with the plane until it was too late. It was either that or he just couldn't live with losing

his wings." He closed his eyes. "I'll never do this to you.
I swear I'll never do it no matter how hard it gets."

"Drink," she prodded him. "I know you won't.
We'll always be there for each other. We're a family." At
that moment Jack realized how much he wanted the
security of his own family, which had never seemed an
option before Laurel. He found himself wanting a child
that was a part of both of them.

"What would you think of stopping your birth control pills?" he asked her. "I know we haven't been
together that long, but I'm thirty-three." He was speaking out of his pain, and Laurel's eyes told him she would
do anything to make him happy.

"I'll be due to start a new pack next week," she said
with her heart pounding in her throat. "I'd really like to
have your baby, Jack."

"I do so want you to," he said. Laurel moved to his
lap and kissed him with all their deep needs running
like a river between them. She unbuttoned his shirt and
her own and pressed her body against his until their
skin seemed melded together. They moved to the floor
because the bedroom seemed too far away. Laurel gave
herself body and soul to the man she loved. In the
sleepy, relaxed aftermath, she urged him to drink the
rest of the shake. After he took insulin, they slipped into
the shower and stood under the soothing water. It felt
good to release the grief even for a little while. Before
they left the hotel for the funeral home, Laurel threw
away her birth control pills as Jack watched. Theirs was
the ultimate commitment any couple could make.

"Just keep thinking about us tonight," she told him.
"We have us, and we'll have our kids. Don't let him
make you feel isolated. I'm with you."

"Don't let him make you feel alienated," Jack said.
"He'll try just like he did in the car. Don't let him. You
know how I feel. What he thinks isn't important."

Julissa met them at the door of the funeral parlor

and pulled them away from everyone else. "I've cried all the tears I have," she said. "I've been praying for you, Jack. It wasn't your fault, and it wasn't Lucien's fault. He didn't break his word to you. After you talked to him Monday, he came back and told me. We went home early because he called the company and told them he couldn't take the job. He was very upset, but we talked through it. He was going to stay in the Air Force until he got the diabetes under control and then take his GI bill to get an advanced degree. He was still very stressed, but we had a plan. We were going to make it work.

"In the morning, he called in to say he was sick, but his commanding officer ordered him to report. He was so sick. He was dizzy just getting out of bed, and he couldn't get his blood sugar to come down. It was over five hundred when he left.

"I've read the book Laurel gave me, and I think he was in ketoacidosis. He was sick to his stomach all night Tuesday. He couldn't eat or drink anything, but he still kept going to the bathroom. He didn't take insulin that night because he thought he wouldn't need any when he couldn't eat. From what I've read, he needed insulin even more then. His only crime was not telling them why he didn't want to go up. He had scheduled an appointment with the flight surgeon for this morning. I'll always wonder why he had to die, Jack, but I know his only chance was you."

Laurel had struggled through the day she had spent with Julissa. But now she knew that the time they had shared together was the reason her sister-in-law had garnered the courage to help Jack. She could feel Jack release some measure of his personal agony as Julissa's words sank into his mind.

"You do need insulin even more when you're sick," Jack told her. "If Lucien was in ketoacidosis, his reflexes and his vision would have been affected. He probably lost his orientation and couldn't think fast enough to correct the spin. That's why he didn't eject in time. I know he loved you, Julissa. I couldn't let myself believe this was deliberate. If he had gotten through it, he would have lived for you."

"I'll have to believe that. I have his violin. I know he would want you to have it because it was your mother's. I'll send it and some other things over to the hotel in the morning." Julissa kissed each of them and walked away looking very small and alone.

Laurel and Jack sat with Julissa for the visitation even after the general, his wife, and stepdaughters arrived. The general's second family spent their time with the other officers and military personnel. None of them showed any interest in meeting Laurel or Julissa. Laurel first assumed it was due to prejudice until her instincts told her the general's second family was also jealous of Jack.

Jack led Laurel out a side entrance at 9 P.M. without a word to anyone other than Julissa. They were walking to the hotel when the general's familiar voice rang across the parking lot.

"Jackson. Don't you think you should at least speak to your family?"

"Don't react," Laurel whispered as she felt his arm tighten. "Don't listen to him." She could feel Jack wasn't going to be able to heed her request even before he turned to face his father.

"Dad, why don't we stop pretending? It's not easy for you to have a half Navajo diabetic son. I'm a terrific embarrassment in Charlene's wonderfully white social circle, and she is obviously first in your life. Why don't we just say good-bye to Lucien and then to each other? You don't like who I am, and neither of us can change that. The only question I have is why did you marry my mother if she wasn't good enough for you?"

The general looked stunned and then stepped back as if Jack had hit him. Laurel realized the confrontation had been building for years. "I loved your mother, Jackson," his father said.

"You have an odd way of showing it. You hid her heritage from us. I wouldn't have known she was a full-blooded Navajo if Lucien hadn't looked at the Navajo tribal records. Maybe I wasn't cordial enough to Charlene and her spawn, but my wife is the newest member of this family. Charlene could and should have come over to meet Laurel. Our color isn't contagious, you know. I'm only here because I love my brother, Dad. That's it. If you want more, then learn to take me as I am." Shaking with rage, he saluted his father and walked into the hotel.

Laurel didn't know what to do or say, so she sat watching while Jack paced their room like a caged animal. He was furious, and Laurel was aware people in pain can't sit still. He had been walking for a half hour when she knew he was in trouble. He was sweating out of proportion to the humidity in the room. Before she could reach him, he sat down on the carpeted floor. She ran to the kitchenette and brought the other shake. She fed it to him one spoonful at a time until he had eaten enough to bring him up. By then he was drenched in sweat. It had soaked through his clothes and plastered his hair to his head.

"Can you stand up, Jack?"

He nodded and stood up unsteadily. She assisted him to the bathroom and helped him undress. She stepped into the shower with him and gently washed off the sweat. She toweled him off as if he were her child and walked with him to the bedroom. He had stopped shaking enough to test, and the reading was thirty-nine.

"Drink the rest of the milk shake." She held it as he drank it. "I'll give you the night insulin in a little while. Get some sleep, Jack. I'll take care of you."

"Thank you for being here. I need you, Laurel. I'll always need you." He held her until he could sleep, and then she went to the other room and called Mary.

"Laurel, we were worried about you. What happened?"

"Jack's brother was killed in a plane crash Wednesday. We came to Florida for the funeral. It's been terrible for Jack."

"Do you need us, Laurel? You sound terrible, too." Mary's voice offered the genuine concern Laurel had expected Jack's family to have. It was a great relief.

"We're coming home tomorrow. Jack graduates from UT on Saturday." She glanced into the bedroom and spoke as quietly as she could. "It's awful, Mary. His family is terrible. I think his father is prejudiced even against Jack and Lucien for being half Navajo. He's tortured Jack ever since we got here. His stepmother and stepsisters haven't even spoken to us."

"Tell him he has a family here, Laurie," Mary said. "Any man who would reject such a fine son doesn't deserve the honor of having a son." She paused. "Do you want to come here when you get home? We have the spare room."

"No, but we'll come after the graduation. Everyone needs to have a family celebration when they graduate. Then we can all go to church together on Sunday. Tell daddy I love him, and I love you, Mary."

"We love you, Laurie. Both of you are in our prayers. Call when you get home."

Laurel held the phone several minutes and then went to sit beside Jack while she prayed he would make it through the funeral.

Chapter 15

Jack's sugar was surprisingly good the next morning because Laurel had given him two extra doses of insulin before she went to bed at 2 A.M. Jack had slept through most of the testing and didn't mention it when he woke up. They prayed together and then went for breakfast. Laurel watched everything her husband ate.

"Don't give your dad the opportunity to say you can't control your sugar," Laurel urged. "Eat enough to hold you until we get out of here."

He ate only enough to cover the insulin. They arrived at the funeral home just before the services were due to begin. It wasn't late enough to avoid meeting Charlene Driver and her daughters, Charlotte and Caroline. They approached Jack and Laurel as they entered.

"You must be Laurel," Charlene purred. "I'm so sorry we didn't meet yesterday. We felt so awkward after we saw how devastated Jackson was. It's just wonderful to finally meet you."

"Thank you," Laurel said, wanting to believe Jack's explosion could have made a difference. Jack's hand on her arm communicated his opinion. She tried to ignore the negative feelings and said, "It's very nice to meet you."

"These are my daughters, Charlotte and Caroline. Girls, this is Jackson's bride, Laurel." Charlene's voice was just a little too sweet even for Laurel. As Laurel scanned their faces, she was sure they had been pushed into courtesy. She greeted both of Jack's stepsisters and watched as Jack acknowledged them as if they were strangers.

"The service is about to begin," Jack said. "We need to be seated."

It was a terrible day, as any day when a thirty-year-old man is buried must be. Lucien was eulogized by his commanding officer and his chaplain. Julissa collapsed as the casket was taken to the hearse. Jack picked her up gently and carried her to the car. In the military cemetery, Lucien was buried with full honors including a twenty-one gun salute. The flag on his coffin was given to Julissa. When the last prayer was said, Jack led Laurel to Julissa, and they both embraced the young widow.

"We'll be in Sevierville for another month, and then we'll be in Houston if you need us," Jack said.

"I'm going to move back to my mother's house," Julissa explained. "I don't have any claim on Lucien's things. He hadn't changed his will yet, and his will left everything to your father and you."

"You can have my share," Jack said tersely. "Come with us to the hotel, and I'll sign a paper and get it witnessed now. You were Lucien's wife, and I won't let anyone take that away from you." He took her arm, and they rode together to the hotel. The manager was willing to witness the simple document Jack wrote out.

"I, Jackson Daniel Driver, hereby relinquish any claim on the estate of my brother, Lucien Roman Driver, with the understanding that everything bequeathed to me in his will shall hereafter be the property of his wife, Julissa Driver. Given this day by my hand."

Julissa held the paper to her heart and then embraced both of them. They were fighting back their tears when she left. Laurel led the way to their room, but as they reached the hallway, Jack said, "Let's get out of here."

They packed hurriedly and left their room, hoping to escape unnoticed. Jack's family was waiting in the lobby like predators. They descended on Jack and Laurel.

"Jackson, dear," Charlene said. "We haven't gotten to spend any time with you and your little bride. Don't rush off. We all need to get to know each other."

"I don't think it's necessary, Charlene," Jack said politely. "We see each other only when there's a disaster. Since just dad and I are left, if there's another disaster it won't matter if we've gotten to be good friends or not." He looked at his father. "You know where we'll be, Dad. The ball's in your court."

"Jackson," the general protested, "I don't know what you want from me."

"What any son wants, Dad," Jack said sharply. "I want love and acceptance on my terms. I want you to like who I am, including my Navajo blood and the diabetes. I want you to accept my wife and believe she's the best thing that ever happened to me. If you can't, then write me out of your will and forget you ever had me. I don't need to spend my life waiting for what I never had until Laurel came into my life.

"You know, I should have expected how Alyssa treated me when I got sick because you treated me the same way. When I wasn't sure if I wanted to live, Dad, when I was thinking about killing myself, you had other things to do. The only reasons I didn't put myself out of your misery were God and a chaplain who went above and beyond the call of duty. Did you hope I would just die so you wouldn't have the shame of a sick son?

"I know you're disappointed because I'm the one

who lived, but I won't stay around to remind you that you're stuck with me instead of Lucien." He had started off calm, but he was venting years of resentment. His tone remained controlled, but his raw emotions continued to multiply. Even Laurel cringed with his next statement.

"While you're sitting there in your superior WASP world, remember Native Americans don't get insulin dependent diabetes. Lucien and I didn't get the diabetes from our mother. We got this from you, Dad. Lucien died because of something you gave him. Every day of my life is a fight because of your white genes. Live with that."

He walked to the desk and pushed his credit card across it. "Dr. and Mrs. Driver checking out of 414. I believe you have that room charged to General Driver, but it needs to be charged to me. We need a cab to get to the private airport."

Laurel walked over to the general, praying Jack would forgive her. The general jumped as she touched his arm, and then he looked at her with distrust and suspicion.

"He didn't mean it," she said softly. "He's just hurting terribly right now. I'm sorry for your loss, sir."

Jack's expression shamed Laurel as she climbed into the cab beside him. She bowed her head to avoid his angry gaze. Several miles passed before he asked, "What did you tell him?"

"I told him you didn't mean what you said," she whispered. "He's hurting, too, Jack. I don't like him for what he's done to you, but he's still your father. The Bible says you have to honor him no matter what he's done."

The silence between them was deafening for several moments, and then Jack put his arm around her. "You're right. I'm turning into him. Don't let me do that. You are so much like my mother. She was everything he couldn't be. Maybe I need you to do that for me."

"It's all right, Jack," she said quietly. "Let's just go home."

After they left, Alyssa Driver entered the lobby and sat down among the other Drivers. "That obviously didn't go well," she said.

"He loves his wife, Alyssa," General Driver said tersely. "You need to give this up."

"You're losing him, J.R.," Charlene said. "If you don't get him away from that Indian girl, you'll lose him forever. Listen to Alyssa."

"I've talked to my father," Alyssa said calmly. "There's a protocol in Canada that's curing insulin dependent diabetes. My father is willing to pay whatever it takes to get Jack cured if he comes back to me. As Jack said, General, the ball is in your court."

"I want to talk to your father, Alyssa," General Driver said. "If you're telling the truth, I'll help you in any way I can."

"Call him," Alyssa said. "I'm headed back to D.C. I'll see you there." She lifted her brocade bags and walked out of the hotel to a waiting car. "Did you take care of the plane?" she asked the driver.

"It's done," the driver replied. "They'll have to land within two hundred miles of takeoff. There's a plane waiting for us at the private airport. We can track him with the equipment on board. We'll call you when we've taken care of the girl."

Jack did his walk around uneasily and checked everything twice before climbing into the plane. After running the checklist, he got out and walked around again.

"What's wrong?" Laurel asked.

"I don't know. I'm just uneasy. I don't suppose that has anything to do with my brother being killed in a plane crash." He examined the engines and then climbed into the pilot's seat. "The weather is rotten north of Atlanta so we may have to land there for the night. There's a big front coming through with thunderstorms." He pulled out a map and checked the airfields along their route. "I don't even want to contemplate the line to land at Atlanta. We might try Macon or this private strip in Buckhead."

He started the engine and taxied to the end of the runway. They were airborne in the late afternoon with the setting sun off the tip of their left wing. Jack circled over the ocean, looked down at the water, and then turned north.

"I talked to Lucien's copilot. Usually there are two men in an F-16—a pilot and a navigator. We usually flew the F-16C's, and they're dual controlled, but one man can fly them. They were just practicing maneuvers so the two pilots went alone. Lucien's copilot feels almost as bad as I do. If he had been in the plane, he could have made sure Lucien ejected. It pays to have a partner." He took Laurel's hand.

"My dad isn't likely to come around, Laurel. He has to have everything his way or not at all. I can't make myself try to placate him anymore. I'm too much like him. You and I have to be second behind what God wants and not third behind God and J.R. Driver. This has been coming to a head ever since I developed diabetes. He couldn't deal with it, and he abandoned me. I shouldn't have said what I said, but you weren't around for when he told me I had to follow in his footsteps because he didn't have Lucien any more."

"He hurt you, Jack, but you need to pray for him," Laurel said gently. "He really doesn't have anyone but you. Think of what it must be like living with Charlene."

"I've lived with Brunhilda, thank you. I'm surprised she didn't introduce Lucien and me as her houseboys. She sent us somewhere every time she had a party. She was probably afraid we would scare off the right kind of men for the princesses. You notice nobody has been stupid enough to snap at that bait yet. One of her biggest parties was on my sixteenth birthday. I wasn't invited. Dad didn't care. He just wanted to make Charlene happy no matter how Lucien and I felt."

"Jack, don't dwell on it. You're going to have your sugar up to 400. Let's think about the house and getting moved. Tell me about the last day you were tested."

Jack smiled slowly. "Okay, I give. I'm being a jerk again. I'll be all right when there's enough distance between J.R. and me." He told her about the last simulations he had done and what the colonel had advised him about keeping up his flight simulations.

"So you think you might get to pilot the shuttle?" Laurel pulled out the insulin pump. Talking about space flight made her nervous, and keeping her hands busy kept her mind off the uncomfortable parts of the conversation. On impulse she took out the bottle of Humalog and filled one of the pump syringes.

"I don't know. Probably not, but maybe they'll let me command a mission, which would mean being the backup pilot. That would be fantastic." He glanced at her. "What are you doing?"

"I'm playing with your insulin pump. I have it all filled up and ready to go when we get home." She attached an infusion set to the syringe.

"I haven't really looked at it yet," Jack protested. "You'll have to show me what to do with it." He looked at her and then at the bottle of Humalog sitting between the seats. "That's all the Humalog that I have left, Laurel. I gave the other bottle to Lucien. Go easy on it. We'll have to get some more in the morning."

"Why don't we just let you start wearing the pump tonight?" Laurel asked. "These books say the basal rate is the same amount as how much long acting insulin you take. So about a half unit an hour should be right for the daytime. I guess you have to put in a higher rate during the night because of dawn phenomenon. Then you bolus just like you do now. You just press this select button and the first screen comes up. Then you press activate, push the up arrow to dial up your dose, and activate again. It's really easy."

"Dawn phenomenon starts about four hours before you get up, so I guess that would be at 2 or 3 A.M.," Jack said. "If you figure three quarters of my long acting is at night, then I'm getting at least nine or ten units in dawn coverage. Maybe two units an hour from 2 A.M. until 7 A.M. I bet a half unit an hour will be way too much when I'm active, but I guess I could turn it off then." Laurel started programming the rates.

Suddenly, one of the engines missed, and even Laurel felt the disturbance in the smooth rhythm of the plane. Jack leaned forward and looked at both engines. Before he had time to decide what might be wrong, the left engine sputtered and missed again. Seconds later, it cut out. The plane lurched slightly, and Jack made several rapid adjustments, which seemed to steady it.

"We need to set down somewhere and see what happened. We could fly the whole way on one engine, but I don't like not knowing why it failed." He looked at their heading and then pulled out the map. "We're pretty close to Brunswick. Let's go for that."

"Brunswick Tower," he said into the radio. "This is 1740 Alpha Tango. I have an engine failure about thirty miles southwest of your position. Request permission for an emergency landing."

"1740 Alpha Tango, this is Brunswick Tower. Are you declaring a Mayday?"

"Negative on that, Brunswick Tower. I have a left engine failure on a twin engine plane. Request permission for an emergency landing."

"1740 Alpha Tango, you're clear for an emergency landing on any available runway. We have you on radar and will follow."

Laurel held the insulin pump with both hands and prayed as they turned east. She had never felt uneasy while flying with Jack, but at that moment she was terrified and couldn't hide her feelings. They had five minutes of tense silence before the second engine lurched and sputtered. Laurel knew it was going to fail.

"We're landing," Jack told her. "Get braced, Laurel. This is going to be rough." He pushed her head down, and she lost her headset. As the second engine cut out, she could hear him say, "Mayday, Mayday, Brunswick Tower. This is 1740 Alpha Tango. I've had a second engine failure. We are landing at these coordinates."

Laurel was praying out loud without realizing it. Later she remembered their descent wasn't plummeting as she had expected. It was almost as if they still had power. She felt the landing gear hit the rough ground and then a series of bounces. She kept praying that the plane would roll to a stop, but it seemed to take forever. When they stopped, she sat up slowly.

"Are we alive?"

Jack started laughing and embraced her. "Yeah, we may need a couple of changes of underwear, but we're alive." He opened the door and climbed down. "I've got to figure out why we've had the problem. You would think we were out of gas. The odds against two clogged fuel lines are way up there."

Laurel stuffed the insulin pump into her pocket and climbed out to help him. Her legs were so wobbly that she had to hold onto the fuselage for several minutes.

"Great!" she heard Jack exclaim. "We've got popcorn in both fuel tanks."

Laurel stepped away from the plane and looked at their landing site for the first time. They had come to a stop under trees at the end of a field. Their position was making them invisible from the air. A river was flowing just in front of them.

"Where are we, Jack?"

"Five miles west of Brunswick," he said as he de-
tached a fuel line and stripped it. "Not likely to get any
closer by air any time soon."

"What's wrong with the plane?" Laurel asked.

"Somebody put popcorn in the fuel tanks. The popcorn expands and soaks up all the fuel. Some of it got
sucked into the fuel lines and cut off what might have
gotten through." He stripped the second fuel line and
then closed the engine cowls. "I'll have to have some
way to flush the lines and the intakes. Then we'll have to
flush the tanks. We're going to be here until help comes
or until we walk out."

"Who would do something like that?" she asked.
"Your father wouldn't, would he?"

"No," Jack said. "He's a jerk, but he's also a pilot.
This kind of sabotage could have gotten us killed. If we
hadn't had an open field under us, the landing wouldn't
have been as good." The question disturbed him, and he
was still thinking about it as he walked around the
wings. Laurel glanced at her watch.

"It's five o'clock, Jack. Should we walk?"

"I'd be all for it except the Brunswick people are
going to be looking for us, and they won't be amused if
we wander off." He took his tools back to the plane and
wiped the grease off his hands. He tried to use the radio
but could hear only static. When he climbed back out of
the plane, he pulled out a wrapped package Laurel had
never noticed. He gathered the pieces of his test kit and
said, "The Humalog bottle was killed on impact. That's
a problem."

"What can we do?" Laurel asked.

"Get some more Humalog in Brunswick. We can
call Dr. Carpenter and beg for mercy. I'll bet he'll be glad
to see me leave for Houston." He shoved the test kit in
his left pocket and the package in his belt under his
jacket.

"What's in the package, Jack?"

"My gun." He took it out and unwrapped it, revealing a semiautomatic handgun. "I'm the general's son. Paranoia is an inherited tendency."

He walked into the field and scanned the skies. "There's another plane. It's coming from the south." Again an uneasy feeling welled up in him, and Jack moved back under the trees. He reached into the rear of the plane and pulled out a large package and then moved farther into the trees.

"Come on, Laurel. I don't know who these people are, but they aren't from Brunswick, and they're landing." He propelled her into the water, unwrapped the package, and hurriedly inflated the raft contained inside. "If these aren't FAA kind of guys, we're hitting the river." He put the oars together and left Laurel holding the raft while he looked out through the trees. Even from a distance, Jack could see the men who climbed from the plane were well armed.

Jack moved quickly as he and Laurel jumped into the raft. He pushed off from shore and began rowing for the denser underbrush. Laurel laid down and used her arms to pull them into the current. Because it was late summer, the water level was low. The current did little to help them escape the people who were obviously pursuing them. Only the darkness and the willows around the edge offered protection. They made it under a veil of willow branches as the two men reached their plane and began searching it.

"We've got to go," Laurel whispered. "We're a target here. There's a rock face just over there. If we climb it, we'll at least be in a better place to protect ourselves."

Jack nodded, and he quickly tied the raft to a tree. They moved through the willow branches and across a meadow of deep grass. Laurel was just ahead of him. With great agility, she began climbing the rock face. Jack heard the men coming and turned in time to see them raise their guns. In that instant he knew they had targeted Laurel. He ran across the distance between them and tackled Laurel, dragging her to the ground. Somewhere during their fall, two bullets hit Jack in the back. Due to the force of the impact, he rolled away from Laurel. He struggled to breathe for less than a minute and then lost consciousness from the pain. Laurel pulled the gun from his belt and moved into the rocks as she released the safety. The two men couldn't see her when they reached Jack, and one of the men bent over Jack as Laurel watched.

"He's hit bad. We need to get him out of here. We might not get the rest of the money if he dies. Where's the girl?"

"She got away, but she shouldn't be hard to catch." He held his gun readied as he moved toward the outcropping where Laurel was hiding. She tried to remember every lesson her father had ever given her. When she had a perfect target, she remembered her father saying, "If you ever have to shoot, be ready to kill, baby girl. If you don't, they'll kill you."

"Drop your gun," she said clearly. She knew he wasn't going to drop it as he advanced on her. She said a prayer and pulled the trigger. That man fell, and she took his gun before scrambling up into the rocks. She could sense the second man was close behind her. When she found new cover, she barely had time to take aim. Her aim was very sure nonetheless, and the man fell from the rocks to the ground below. She was ready to continue firing as she climbed down. She disarmed the second man and checked both bodies. The first man was dead, and the other was seriously wounded. She held her breath when she reached Jack. At first glance she knew her husband was also critically wounded. His face was pale and reflected his pain.

"Jack, where are you hurt?" she cried frantically.

"My back," he gasped. "Get out of here, Laurel. They'll kill you."

"I shot them," she said fiercely. "We can take their plane, Jack."

"I can't fly it," he said. "We need to get to help. We don't know why they did this, and we don't know if there will be others."

"Can you get to the raft?" she asked. "I can use a pole and push us down the river. The map shows this river goes to Brunswick."

"Yes. It does." Jack rolled to his side and made an effort to rise. He couldn't breathe when he tried to sit up. The attempt to move increased his pain and made him cry out. He fell back knowing he didn't have the strength to try again. "I can't, Laurel. Go on and get help."

"No," she said adamantly. "I won't leave you." She searched her mind for a way to get him out and realized she could drag him on the raft across the meadow. "Wait. I'll bring the raft and get you on it. I can pull you down to the water."

She ran to the raft and untied it with unsteady hands. It was eight feet long and bulky but light. She pulled it across the meadow grass. When she reached Jack, she knelt on the ground beside him and lifted his chest onto the raft. Laurel wasn't a big woman. She was five feet five inches in height but small boned, and she weighed only 115 pounds. It took all her strength to lift Jack's chest, but adrenaline and prayer gave her the needed muscle to do it. Her hands were covered with blood when she pulled them from beneath him. She shuddered as she moved to lift his legs.

He was shaking as she moved him into the center of the raft. "Is your sugar low?" she asked frantically.

"It's not that. I'm bleeding a lot," he said through clenched teeth. "You can't do anything about it."

"If I wrap it really tight, it might stop," she said.

"We don't have time. We're only four or five miles from the ocean. The Coast Guard will be patrolling along the port. You can get us there. Just go!"

Laurel grabbed the ropes, which were woven through the edges of the raft. She dragged the raft with Jack on it over the hundred feet that separated them from the water. She was so desperate, she was able to cross it in five minutes.

Laurel was panting when she pushed the raft into the water. She climbed on with a long stick in her hand and straddled Jack's body to steady them. Then she pushed with all her strength. They began moving down the river to the sounds of the white water ahead and Laurel's prayers.

Chapter 16

They had covered close to two miles when Jack whispered the words, "I love you," and then lost consciousness. He was still bleeding. Laurel's blue jean knees were soaked in blood. At first Jack was in too much pain to think or help his wife, but as he lost progressively more blood, the pain eased and was replaced by intense cold and a feeling of disorientation. Then he prayed for Laurel to be safe and to be all right if he didn't make it.

She didn't understand he was dying. If she had understood, she might have lost determination and given up her effort to propel them downstream. She told Jack she loved him and went on to say, "Don't worry. We're making good time now. Just hang on."

She expected a response. When he didn't speak, she realized he was unconscious. Laurel was terrified he might be having a low blood sugar with no possibility of an antidote, but when she tested his blood, it was almost three hundred. He needed insulin and she knew the N wouldn't help him for hours. On the river in the murky light of evening, she put the insulin pump site into

Jack's abdomen and programmed the pump to deliver a half unit every hour. Then she gave him four units as a bolus because he was so high. The pump clicked efficiently, and Laurel went back to her primitive propulsion system. They came out of the tributary and into open water a half hour later. She could see lights on a highway above them. She started screaming for help and continued until she was hoarse. She was feeling for Jack's pulse when a bright light came out of the darkness. After several minutes of being blinded by the floodlight, she heard a loudspeaker.

"Unidentified boat, this is the United States Coast Guard."

"Help us!" Laurel screamed. "We're on a raft. My husband has been shot."

"Stay right there," the voice ordered her. "We're coming."

Then the time seemed to blur. Men in uniform in a motorized launch came alongside them and lifted Jack into their boat. They helped Laurel out of the raft and let her sit beside Jack as they sped back to the main boat. As soon as they were loaded, Jack was taken to a stretcher and seen by a medic.

"What happened?" the medic asked as he examined Jack hurriedly.

"Someone tampered with our plane. We lost both engines and had to make an emergency landing."

"Call Brunswick Airport and tell them we have their plane crash victims." He cut Jack's jacket away and uttered an oath. "I have two large caliber gunshot wounds in his left chest. There aren't any exit wounds. Get on the horn and get an ambulance or a rescue helicopter on the dock." He took Jack's vital signs and prepared his arm for an intravenous line. "How did he get shot?"

"Another plane landed behind us, and the men had guns," Laurel explained. "They chased us to the water and shot at us. I think Jack jumped in front of me. I knew he was hurt so I grabbed his gun and climbed up in the rocks. I shouted to the men to drop their guns, but they shot at me. I shot them, and I think they're dead. I had to do it so they wouldn't kill us."

"It's all right," the medic assured her. "They probably mistook you for a drug run. Small planes come out of South America into this part of the country all the time. What's your husband's name?"

"Jackson Driver," Laurel stammered.

"Can you give me a date of birth, Mrs. Driver?"

"September 18, 1966. He's an insulin dependent diabetic," Laurel said. "He's wearing an insulin pump. We hadn't really been taught to use it yet, but his only bottle of short acting insulin got broken when we landed. His sugar was 289 so I put the pump on him."

"Good thinking," the medic said.

Laurel picked up Jack's cold hand and tried to take a reading, but she couldn't get enough blood. The medic applied a drop from his intravenous start site.

"He's in shock, Mrs. Driver," the medic said. "His blood pressure is too low for you to take a reading from his finger."

Laurel didn't understand the idea of shock so she dealt with the diabetes because it gave her a sense of control. She held the meter tightly until the reading appeared.

"His sugar is 195. I need to give him another two units," she said.

The medic nodded his consent and with admiration he watched Laurel handle the pump. He attached a bag of saline to the intravenous line and opened the volume up. Seconds later they were at the dock, and a rescue helicopter stood waiting. Laurel wasn't allowed to fly with her husband, but she told the paramedics about Jack's diabetes and how the pump worked before they took off.

A police officer drove her to the local hospital, but when she arrived at the hospital, she was informed Jack had been transported to the regional trauma center in Macon. Before they would allow her to follow her husband, the police took Laurel to the station for questioning and drove her to the crash site. She gave them the guns she had taken from their attackers and showed them the two bodies. She also showed them the popcorn Jack had stripped from the fuel line. They allowed her to take the luggage from Jack's plane and transported her to the bus station so she could make the ninety minute trip to Macon.

The bus delivered her at 9 A.M., and she used the last money she had to take a cab to the hospital. When she inquired at the information desk regarding Jack's room number, a security guard approached her.

"Don't make any trouble, lady," he said brusquely. "We were warned you'd be coming. You did a good thing in helping that guy, but his wife is with him. They don't want you here."

"I'm his wife," Laurel said in bewilderment. "I'm Laurel Wolfe Driver. I'm Jack's wife."

"Let me see your ID," the security guard suggested. "I have to have proof. The woman who claims to be his wife has ID."

"That's Alyssa!" Laurel drew a deep breath. "They're divorced. We've been married only two weeks, and I don't have any new ID yet. Please. Ask Jack. He'll tell you who I am."

"I can't," the guard admitted. "He came out of surgery at 6 A.M., and an air ambulance took him away. I can't tell you where they took him. If you were his wife, I'd think you'd know that."

Laurel sat down in the hallway and stared at her hands. Jack's blood was still on her fingers, caked around her wedding band and under her fingernails. For that moment, she thought it might be the only part of Jack she would ever have again. She sat in the hallway and cried until the security guard went to the phone. She heard him calling someone and realized she was in danger.

Laurel grabbed the two suitcases and ran out of the hospital. She kept running until she saw a church. The building promised sanctuary and, once inside, she begged the minister to call her father. That night she was on a bus for home without knowing where home would be. She never stopped praying for Jack, but she never allowed herself to realize how serious his injuries had been either.

Jack had been critically injured, but Laurel's efforts to get him help and the surgery in Macon saved his life. Two thoracic surgeons worked for five hours to close the torn arteries in his chest and repair the damage to his pericardium, the covering of his heart. It took eight units of blood to get him out of shock.

The following morning, transport wasn't in Jack's best interests, but General Driver could not be dissuaded from his intention to take his son to Washington, D.C. He hired a medical plane and paid $7,000 to take Jack out of the Macon Hospital while he was still on life support. Alyssa flew with them.

Jack required a ventilator to breathe for him the first three days after his arrival at the Air Force Hospital in Washington. For a week, he had no consistent awareness, and then he was dazed and confused by the medications he had been given. Alyssa and his father encouraged the liberal use of pain medication in an effort to keep him confused. Every time Jack asked for Laurel in their presence, he was given more medication. Alyssa and J.R. took turns staying with him.

General Driver was sitting beside him when he remembered being awake. "Dad?" he said. "What happened?"

"You were in a plane crash," the general explained calmly. "You had engine failure, and your plane went down in Georgia. You were injured." His eyes were piercing. "Don't you remember, Jackson?"

"I don't remember," Jack said slowly. He looked around the room. "Where am I? Where's Laurel?"

"She left you, Jackson," the general said slowly. "She walked off and left you injured. It's a miracle you didn't die." The words were much more painful than the pain in his chest, and for a minute Jack couldn't breathe because of them. When he caught his breath, he wasn't sure he wanted to continue breathing.

"She wouldn't leave me," Jack protested desperately. "I know her. She wouldn't have left me. Even if she did, I still need to see her. She's my wife."

"She had the marriage annulled, Jackson," the general said impassively. "She sent this letter, but I don't think you should read it now."

Jack tried to reach for the letter and was rewarded with a stab of pain that cut off his breath. His father called for the nurse, and he was given something through his intravenous line. Time blurred, and Alyssa was sitting with him when he awakened the next time.

"I can't believe you're awake," she said softly. "You've been here for over a week, Jack."

Jack scanned the room frantically. "Where am I?"

"You're at the Air Force Hospital in Washington, D.C. Your father had you flown here after your surgery. You were close to death, Jack. You might have died if he hadn't brought you here." She caressed his forehead, and Jack pushed her hand away.

"Don't touch me, Alyssa. We aren't married now, and we aren't ever going to be married again." He closed his eyes fighting to remember anything about the plane crash. There were only fragments. All the fragments revolved around Laurel's face.

"She left you, Jack," Alyssa said. "She left you bleeding to death in a field. If the rescue helicopter hadn't seen you, I know you would have died. You hated me for leaving you when you found out about the diabetes. That was nothing compared to what she did."

Jack closed his eyes and thought of Laurel. Alyssa's voice kept droning in his ears, but he could only think of Laurel. After a while Alyssa finally stopped talking, and he heard his father come in and sit beside the bed.

"I'm going to read this letter to you, Jackson, even though it isn't in your best interests to hear it when you're still sick. Alyssa said you still don't believe Miss Wolfe left you. I hope hearing this will let you put the relationship behind you."

Dear Jack,

I haven't been fair to you. I let you believe I could handle your diabetes, but it's just too much for me. It's always there like a shadow hanging over our lives. Now with your new job in Houston, I'll be all alone. I can't handle all your problems with no help. When the plane crashed I knew it was a sign to end our marriage. I've filed for an annulment. Please don't fight me. It will be for the best.

Laurel

The general folded the letter, stuffed it in his pocket, and waited for some response from his son. Jack kept his eyes closed and spoke only to demand that his father leave.

"Bring her here, and let her tell me to my face. I'm a grown man. I've been told to shove off before. You can't do it, can you, Dad? I don't remember what happened, but I know Laurel didn't leave me. Not by choice. When I can get out of this bed and away from whatever you're giving me, I'm going to Cherokee."

"You don't need to go back," the general said haltingly. "All you'll do is cause yourself more pain. I've taken care of everything for you, Jackson. I've sold the helicopter and your house. Your belongings are being packed right now. I had Miss Wolfe's belongings shipped back to her. That's what she asked me to do. When you're well enough, we'll get you to Houston."

"No," Jack said. "I'm not going if Laurel doesn't go. I told her that the night I asked her to marry me. I guess you can't understand that kind of commitment since you've never loved anyone like I love her."

"Jackson," the general began.

"Don't," Jack said sharply. His eyes pushed his father away as strongly as his words. "Just leave me alone. If you want to help me, you'll leave me alone."

He closed his eyes and kept them closed until he heard his father walk out of the room. Then he pressed the button to call the nurse. She came with a glucose meter.

"You had good timing, Major Driver. I was just coming to check your sugar. You have a tray ordered for lunch if you want it. As soon as you start eating, we'll get that IV out of your neck." She stuck his finger and pressed it to the machine. The reading was 104mg percent. "Your insulin pump sure does a good job controlling you," she commented as she took the pump from a pocket in the hospital gown. She recorded the total daily amount and then tucked the pump into his gown. "We'll need to give you a carbohydrate bolus when you finish eating."

"When did you put the pump on me?" Jack asked in confusion.

"You came in wearing it," the nurse said. "Don't you remember?"

"No." Jack shook his head and thought of the pump. Laurel had been playing with the device on their flight to Houston and then during their flight from Florida.

"That's all the Humalog I've got," he said as if to himself.

"What?" the nurse asked. "What did you say?"

"I was thinking about the flight. Was my sugar all right when I got here?"

"It's been good most of the time." She flipped through his chart. "Here it is. You were 110 on arrival. It was so good that they just changed your pump site and kept it running even when you were in intensive care."

Jack slid to his feet and held onto the bed as his legs threatened to buckle. The nurse steadied him.

"Don't go so fast, Major Driver. If you fall and break something, you'll be here a lot longer."

"I've already been here too long," Jack said. "If you bring that tray, I'll eat." He got into the chair and picked up the telephone with difficulty. Even his arms were weak, but he held onto the telephone as if it were a lifeline. He quickly learned that his calling card had been canceled, making long distance calls impossible unless they were collect. He dialed directory assistance asking for Lawrence Wolfe's phone number and was trying to call it when Alyssa came into the room. He hung up the telephone and set it back on the nightstand.

"Who were you calling, Jack?" she asked.

"Not you, Alyssa," Jack said. "And I won't be calling you. You've kept me here like a prisoner, and I'm sure you've kept Laurel away. When I can leave here, you won't be able to keep us apart. Even if the lies were true, I wouldn't come back to you."

"Not even for a cure, Jack," she suggested. "There's a cure for insulin dependent diabetes. It has already worked in almost twenty people, but it isn't being done in this country. My father has your ticket for a cure. You could still pilot the shuttle. You could be normal again. The only price is you'll have to be my husband to get it." She smiled at his expression and bent to kiss his hair. He was too stunned to shun her touch. "Just think about it, Jack. I'll be back for your answer tomorrow."

Jack waited until she had left the room, and then he

summoned the nurse. "I need my wallet," he said.
"We don't have it, Major. Your father probably has
it. He was with you when you were transported."
"Then I need to see the hospital chaplain, please."
Jack ate what was on the tray because he knew he would
have to eat before they would discharge him. When he
had forced down the last bite, he took out the insulin
pump. He could almost hear Laurel telling him how it
worked. He pressed the "select" button, calling up the
bolus screen, and then pressed "activate" to program a
bolus for his food. When he had pressed "activate"
again, the pump began delivering insulin. He could feel
traces of Laurel on the pump and closed his eyes remembering the terrible insulin reactions and Laurel's
face hovering over him.

"God, please let me remember." His simple prayer
was answered almost before the plea had left his lips.
Suddenly he could remember lying in an open field and
telling Laurel to leave him.

"No," Laurel said. "I won't leave you."

"I'm not leaving you either," he said to himself.
When he looked up, the bemused chaplain was standing in the doorway.

Laurel was in hiding because of the obscene phone
calls. She had gone to her father's house after returning
to Cherokee. She had regretted her homecoming because her father was still recovering from his bypass
surgery. Lawrence had tried to help her locate Jack and
was given the same story Laurel had been given. Laurel
and Jack hadn't told Lawrence about Jack's divorce.
When he learned his son-in-law had been married before, Lawrence's estimation of Jack's character plum-
meted. He wondered if Jack had deliberately deceived
his daughter to sleep with her. Every phone call he
made convinced him further that Jack was deliberately
hiding from Laurel. Finally he told Laurel it was time to

see what her husband would do. They didn't have another option.

The telephone calls began that night, three days after she returned home. The phone would ring, and a verbal assault of Laurel's character began for whoever had answered. Laurel had never seen her father get so angry. Every phone call seemed to put him at risk of further heart problems. He changed the telephone number, made it unlisted, and added caller ID and call block. Nothing stopped the calls. After a week, a letter arrived stating Laurel and Jack's marriage had been annulled. Several boxes containing Laurel's belongings followed.

Lawrence was convinced the telephone calls were because of Jack, and he could see they were destroying his daughter. Laurel was losing weight every day. She was a hollowed-out version of the happy, loving daughter Lawrence had known. He feared she would be emotionally destroyed by what was happening to her. He sent her to Joseph's home and then Peter's home in an effort to protect her, but the calls followed her to each place. Finally Lawrence drove Laurel to his sister's rural home, which bordered Maggie Valley.

Laurel's Aunt Nan was a widow who lived alone on a mountainside farm. Her two sons lived and worked in Cherokee, and she enjoyed being close to her extended family. She was glad to have Laurel's company and made it her mission to take care of her wounded niece. Out of her father's sight, Laurel cried for a week. Then she started feeling sick in the mornings and threw up more than once. Nan suspected another person might need protection and took Laurel to the women's clinic in Maggie Valley. A pregnancy test was positive, and an examination confirmed the test.

"How?" Laurel whispered in disbelief. "I was taking birth control pills."

"They were progesterone only pills," the nurse said gently. "They aren't as effective as some of the others. I gather your husband won't be happy about this."

"I don't know where he is," Laurel whispered. "I haven't heard from him in two weeks."

The nurse's face was somber. It wasn't the first time she had seen a young woman abandoned in such a way. "Do you want to keep the baby?"

"We don't believe in abortion," Nan answered for her. "Just tell us what we'll need to do, and we'll take care of Laurel even if her husband doesn't."

"She needs to start these prenatal vitamins," the nurse said. "I'd also like for her to have an ultrasound at the hospital in Cherokee. You're full blooded so your care will be free if you go there. You may have a cyst on your right ovary. That's not uncommon in early pregnancy, but it's something we need to know about and watch."

Laurel was silent all the way back up the mountain. As Nan stopped the car she said, "I need to go away. I'll just be an embarrassment to dad and the others. I know we have cousins in Oklahoma. If I go there and change my name, the calls would stop. Later we could come back. When Jack returns, you could tell him how to find us."

"No," Nan said quietly. "You can stay with me. The caller won't find you here, and I'm alone now. I'm glad for your company. Pray, Laurel. You don't know what God has planned. All life is a gift, and this baby is no different."

"I just wish I could know if Jack is alive." She started crying again because she missed him and needed to believe their separation was out of his control. She cried all the way back to her aunt's home. She thought the pain in her side was from her pelvic examination. That night, the pain made it impossible for her to sleep.

Laurel lay in Nan's guest room thinking about being pregnant and having a baby all alone. She remembered Jack asking her to have his baby and knew he couldn't have been lying. She told herself he would come back when it was in his power to do so. She prayed for a sign to get her through the separation. When she finally slept, she dreamed of feeling Jack's arms around her. She didn't want to stop dreaming.

The next morning Laurel had to drag herself out of bed because she felt so weak. While she was in the shower, the pain hit with increased intensity. For a minute it was so intense that she couldn't breathe. She doubled over, unable to stand up straight. She began to feel light headed while she was under the hot water and then she felt nauseated.

She got out of the shower and laid down on the bathroom floor because she wasn't able to walk to the bedroom. Her vision began fading in and out of focus. She could only hear a buzzing in her ears when Nan bent over her. Then darkness closed around her.

General Driver arrived at the hospital expecting a problem. Jack's doctor had called the general and told him his son was requesting discharge. He didn't expect to find a crowd of people in Jack's room. They were people he didn't know with the exception of Lucien's widow, Julissa.

Jack was pale but resolute as he walked to the door and closed it.

"We need to talk, Dad, and I wanted witnesses I could trust. I'm remembering a little more every day about how I got here—and you aren't. Somebody sabotaged my plane. The fuel tanks and lines were full of popcorn, and I lost both engines before we could get to Brunswick Airport.

"Right after we landed, another plane came in from the south and landed. The men on that plane were armed. They came after us, and we had to run across a field to get away from them. I saw them aim at Laurel, and I jumped in front of her. I couldn't get up after that, but I remember Laurel shooting them and dragging me down to the river. I told her to leave me, but she wouldn't do it. I know that's how it happened because I hadn't started using my insulin pump when we were in Florida. Laurel kept working on it while we were down there. In the plane she had filled the syringe. My insulin bottle broke when we landed, and I know the stress of being hurt would have run up my blood sugar. Since it wasn't up and I had the pump on, I know she stayed with me and put the pump on me.

"I called the Brunswick police and my attorney got the police report. I was picked up on the dock in Brunswick. It seems that the Coast Guard fished me and my wife out of the river. The police report says my wife shot two men who had shot me. I was taken by rescue helicopter to the regional trauma center in Macon. After questioning my wife, the police put her on a bus to Macon.

"The security department at the Macon hospital said a woman claiming to be my wife showed up the next morning and fell apart when they refused to give her any information about me. She told them her name was Laurel Wolfe Driver. They also said her father called every day for the first three days after my surgery. I've tried calling Cherokee, but her father's number and her brothers' numbers are unlisted now. I want to know what you did," Jack said.

"Who are these people?" the general asked tersely.

"This is Jeff Bennett. He's my lawyer. This is my doctor, Tracy Carpenter. This is my sister-in-law, Julissa. I'm claiming her as family, even if you don't. These two people are from the FBI, and they helped get everyone else here so we could find out who sabotaged my plane and tried to kill me and my wife.

"They're like me. They don't understand why the other events didn't upset my father. Like the time I was drugged after I went to lunch with you and Alyssa. Dr.

Carpenter brought those records to add to the investigation. I want my wallet, all my belongings, my money, and an explanation. Then, you're never going to see me again."

The general sat down weakly. "I didn't think about why, Jackson. I just took care of you. I had just lost Lucien. I didn't think about anything after Alyssa called me."

"Alyssa," Jack said to the agent beside him. "I know she did this, and I know she'll hurt Laurel. She would have had her killed if I hadn't jumped in front of her." He extended his hand. "I want my wallet, Dad."

The general reached into his coat pocket and drew out the wallet and Jack's keys. "Your belongings are in storage in Houston. The receipt is in your wallet. Jack, I didn't think about anything except your health. Alyssa's father has made arrangements for you to be cured."

"So she told me. You know what, Dad? I'll wait my turn," Jack said sharply. "I can live with being diabetic. I can't live without Laurel. I think what hurts the worst is knowing I've lost my father.

"My father was an honest man. He taught me that freedom was worth dying for. He taught me that a man's word was his honor. I never wanted anything more than to please my father, but I never could do it. I'll always miss him, but I know I'll never see him again." Jack sat down slowly as if his words had drained the last of his strength. "Please tell me where Laurel is."

"I don't know, Jackson," the general said dully. "I never saw her. I didn't know she stayed with you."

"Give the letter to these agents, and then they're going with me to Sevierville and Cherokee until they have enough information to send Alyssa to prison."

General Driver took the letter from his pocket and gave it to the FBI agents. "It came in the mail post-marked Cherokee, North Carolina." He looked at Jack. "Your plane is here in D.C.; I had it repaired."

"If anyone here can fly it, I'll take it back with me," Jack said.

"I can fly it," the general offered.

"I don't trust you," Jack said.

"Then let them go with us," the general said. "I want to fly you home."

Chapter 17

They landed in Cherokee at 3 P.M. Billy loaned them the convertible to drive to the city proper. Jack wished his father were still in Washington, but he could only really think of Laurel. He was praying when he walked down the sidewalk to Lawrence Wolfe's house, but no one answered his knock there or at Peter Wolfe's house just down the street. He had no idea where to find Joseph Wolfe. As dusk fell, Jack's spirits fell with the night.

"Where now?" General Driver asked as they sat in Lawrence Wolfe's driveway.

"I don't know," Jack said hopelessly. "Just leave me here. They'll have to come home sooner or later."

"You can't sit out in the night air when you just had major chest surgery, Jackson." The general exhaled slowly. "I'm sorry. I didn't know you felt so strongly about her. We'll find her."

"You can't know that, Dad," Jack retorted. "I've been abandoned, and you don't have positive feelings about the people who do it to you. She may not ever let me find her." He scanned the neighborhood desperately and on impulse he knocked on the neighbor's door.

"I'm looking for Lawrence Wolfe," he said to the man who answered. "It's very important that I find him."

"He's in Knoxville," the neighbor said. "I can't say when he'll be back. His daughter had to have emergency surgery. It was pretty bad. They said she almost bled to death. I haven't heard anything since they left two days ago."

"Thank you," Jack managed to say as he hurried back to the car. He could hardly breathe when he reached it, but he climbed into the passenger's side and said, "We've got to get to Knoxville. Laurel's in the hospital."

They flew to Knoxville and the general rented a car. Jack guessed Laurel would be at Mercy Hospital. He breathed a sigh of relief when the woman at the information desk told him Laurel was in intensive care but in stable condition. The helpful attendant then called security just as she had been instructed. The Wolfe family had warned hospital security not to let anyone near Laurel, and Jack met heavy resistance at the door to surgical intensive care. The resistance intensified when Lawrence and Mary Wolfe appeared. Jack was flushed from the effort of walking through the hospital and looked to be in much better shape than he was.

"You need to leave," Lawrence said curtly. "You've hurt Laurel more than enough, and I won't let you hurt her again."

"I didn't leave her by choice," Jack pleaded. "I was out for a week, and then I wasn't told the truth about what happened. As soon as I could get up, I came here. I didn't even know she was sick."

"She was pregnant in her tube," Lawrence said. His expression bespoke his hatred without need for words. "It ruptured on Friday, and she almost bled to death. She's still very sick. I don't think she cares if she lives or not, and if she dies, Mr. Driver, you killed her."

"Please," Jack said desperately. "I have to see her. I don't know what I can say to make you believe me. None of this would have happened if I'd had any choice. At least let Laurel decide. Just tell her that I'm here. Please."

Lawrence hesitated because Jack's emotional plea was compelling. He looked at Mary. "Do you think we should tell her?"

"I think she would want to know," Mary said as she scanned Jack's face. "Don't go in just to settle your conscience, Mr. Driver. She got a letter telling her you annulled the marriage. She knows you shipped her belongings back to Cherokee. She said it was like what you did before you married her."

Jack leaned against the wall to keep from falling down. "I didn't do those things. I swear to you I didn't do them. I love Laurel. I couldn't ever do anything to hurt her."

As the general stared at his son, he remembered losing the only woman he had ever loved. Jack looked very like his mother the day her husband had destroyed her will to live.

"He didn't do it," General Driver said reluctantly. "I did it. I did all of it, and I've lost my son because of what I did. Jackson was unconscious for most of the first week, and then he couldn't remember much about how he got hurt. I didn't approve of his marriage to Laurel, and I didn't believe Jackson really loved her. He didn't know what I had done until it was done."

"I suppose you did the phone calls, too," Lawrence accused. "Day and night calling her a whore and a slut and worse. Changing the telephone numbers didn't stop it. I had to send her away, and then this." He looked at Mary. "See what Laurie wants, and then, Jack, I want your word you'll abide by her wishes."

"I promise," Jack said. "I promise I'll leave if that's

what she wants." He gripped Mary's arm, and she could feel he was trembling. "Tell her that I love her." He held up his left hand. "Tell her I never took this ring off. Tell her she's the only thing I care about. Tell her I can't ever see another sunrise unless I see it in her eyes."

Mary looked at Jack and knew he was telling the truth. She looked at Lawrence. "He should tell her those things, Larry. He couldn't speak from his heart if it weren't the truth."

"Go see her," Lawrence said reluctantly, "but if she sends you away, I won't let you in again."

Jack walked slowly, but he still had to stop and catch his breath before following Mary into the intensive care unit at the end of the hallway. Laurel was in the closest glass cubicle. She was gray from loss of blood and the suffering she had endured for two weeks. Her face revealed she had lost at least ten pounds. Her hands were pale on the bedclothes, and her wedding ring was gone. Mary touched her hand gently.

"Laurie, you have a visitor." Her eyelids fluttered for a moment, and then she looked at Mary with the hopeless eyes of death.

"Laurie, Jack's here. He wants to see you."

"There's no point to it," Laurel said slowly. "We're too different. We can't make it work."

Mary looked at Jack and shook her head.

"Please," Jack said soundlessly. "Please."

Mary closed her eyes in prayer and then nodded. Jack came to the bedside and put his hand on Laurel's hand. "Laurel, I love you."

She had been through too much to see he was telling the truth. Her face contorted, and tears streamed down her cheeks. "Don't say it, Jack. Don't say it when it can't be true. You let them send me away. You sent my things back in a box. Even then I kept hoping until I lost the baby. I prayed for God to give me a sign, Jack, and I lost the baby."

"No," Jack said desperately. "The sign was when I remembered everything that happened. I was in a hospital in Washington. I didn't even know where I was, and when I woke up they told me you left me after I was shot. They brought a letter they said you wrote saying you wanted an annulment. I knew it wasn't true. I knew it was all a lie, but I couldn't remember. I prayed to know what to do. Then I remembered telling you to go for help and hearing you tell me that you wouldn't leave me. I called everyone I could. I tried to call your brothers and your father, but the numbers had been changed. I made the doctors discharge me so I could come here." He put his hand on her face.

"I remember why I got shot. I remember seeing they were aiming at you, and I remember jumping in front of you because I'd rather die than lose you. I know I only lived because you were there. Don't make me live without you. I don't want to do it. I can't do it." His voice broke. "Laurel, you know me. You know I wouldn't have left you, just like I knew you wouldn't leave me."

In her heart, she did know and would have known just from the agony of his expression. She drew a shuddering sobbing breath as she reached out to him. "I love you, Jack. I couldn't ever leave you." It took all Jack's strength to hold her, but he reached across the bed and held her in his arms. The emotional relief overrode the pain of her arms against his chest and allowed him to keep holding her.

Mary pushed a chair behind Jack and let down the bed rails so he could sit close beside Laurel. Then she returned to the waiting room and sat down with her husband. "She wanted him to stay, Larry. It's what she wants."

Lawrence nodded slowly and then looked at J.R. Driver. "Will you always be coming between them? I won't let you hurt my daughter anymore. I don't care who you are and what power you think you have.

Laurel is an innocent young girl. She doesn't deserve how she's been treated, and I will fight you to my last breath if you try to hurt her again."

"I didn't intend to hurt her," the general said slowly. Even he knew he was lying because he hadn't cared about Laurel's feelings. At that moment, he had to remember Laurel had cared about his pain. "I don't know anything about any telephone calls. When I was Jack's age, I would have given my life for someone very like your daughter. I lost her, and I've never let anyone else become that important to me again. My sons should have been, but they weren't. I didn't let them." He looked at Lawrence Wolfe.

"Jack almost died. One of the bullets was lodged against his heart. When they called me from Macon, they had taken him to surgery. They said they didn't know if he would make it. I had only two sons. My daughter died when she was born. I lost Lucien just days before Jack was shot. I took Jack to Washington to give him the best possible care.

"I know your daughter has been sick, but until you've buried one son and seen the other one dying, you can't know how desperate I was to keep Jack with me." The general stood. "He's still very weak. The doctors in D.C. said he wasn't strong enough to do this, but he said nothing mattered but coming here. Please take care of him. Tell him I'll come if he needs me."

"Who did this to them?" Lawrence demanded. "Who could have done it?"

"I don't know," the general said. "When I get back to Washington, I'm going to find out." He walked out of the waiting room slowly and in the posture of a defeated man.

"Your son is a grown man," Lawrence said just as the general reached the door. "The decision to marry should be his own. Why can't you accept that?"

"You wouldn't understand," J.R. Driver replied.

He left them. Larry and Mary Wolfe could only feel pity for him. Because of what the general had told them, they were worried about their son-in-law. When they joined him during the next visiting hour, they knew they had reason to worry. Jack was clearly with Laurel only by force of will. It was easy to see he didn't have the strength to do it. He stood with an effort as Lawrence and Mary entered the room. He had been somewhat slender at their first meeting, but he had lost enough weight to be thin. He was visibly tremulous.

"Sit down, Jack," Mary said with concern. "Have you eaten anything today?"

"This morning. I didn't have time after that. I just had to get here. Nothing else mattered." He sat down still clutching Laurel's hand. "I called my lawyer when I was in Washington, and he came to help me get out of the hospital. He came back to Sevierville this morning, and he's gone to see if there was an annulment. I didn't agree to an annulment, and I didn't sign anything. If there is one, it can't be valid. I don't want Laurel to ever think I had any part in it."

"She won't," Larry said. "When she can come home, you can have another wedding."

"If our marriage is made invalid, people will always talk about her and this baby. I don't want anyone to ever think that about her. We weren't together until we were married." Jack stood again and placed his hand on her forehead. "Is she going to be okay? I haven't talked to anybody." His hand was trembling on her head, and Laurel opened her eyes.

"Jack, your hand is cold." She reached up to touch his hand. "Are you all right?"

"I'm all right." He sat down again and fumbled with the insulin pump to put it in suspend. He found the roll of glucose tablets in his pocket and took two before checking his sugar. The reading was fifty-three.

"You need to eat," Mary said firmly. "Laurie, I'm

taking him to eat. We'll be back in a few minutes."

Laurel looked at Jack with concern. For the first time, her face looked alive. She could see he was still very sick, and she protected him.

"Go eat, Jack." She smiled faintly. "I'll wait for you."

"I can't leave you," he said. "You lost your wedding ring, and the other guys won't know you're mine." Laurel knew the words weren't a joke. They were more in response to the low sugar and Jack's desperate need to erase what his father and Alyssa had done.

"It's in my purse." Laurel looked at Mary. "Please get it for me."

Mary dug into her tote bag and pulled out Laurel's small brown purse. The ring was in the zippered inner lining, and she gave it to Jack. He slid it onto Laurel's finger and held her hand in both of his.

"Do me a favor and don't take it off again."

"I promise," Laurel said with tears in her eyes. "Go eat, Jack. I can't bail you out if you crash tonight."

He kissed her forehead and walked very slowly with Mary to the cafeteria. He forced his food down with difficulty. The meal took much longer than it should have because eating still made him feel sick. When he finished, he bolused with the insulin pump. His lawyer came into the cafeteria with a grim face as they were preparing to leave.

"I'm sorry, Jack. It's more than an annulment. Someone destroyed all the records of your marriage. There's no license. There's nothing at the wedding chapel. The minister remembers marrying you, but there's no legal evidence. All you can do is marry her again."

Jack buried his face in his hands. "Make a new will leaving everything to Laurel, and let me sign it tomorrow." He looked up with frustrated anger on his face. "We had a copy of the marriage license and the certificate from the wedding chapel, but they were in my house. I'm sure they found it when they packed my belongings. Why can't they just issue us a new one? We know everyone who was there. Why?"

"I'm sorry," the attorney said quietly. "I wish I could do it for you. I'll bring the will by tomorrow. I have the contracts for Houston. What do you want to do?"

"I need to ask Laurel what she wants," Jack said. "I'll let you know tomorrow." He was too exhausted to stand as the lawyer departed. It was a battle for Jack to walk back to the intensive care unit. He had to stop twice to rest and catch his breath. Mary put her arm around him before they reached the bedside, and she was frightened when Jack made no protest. It was a relief to have him sit down.

Laurel's doctor came into the room before anyone said anything. Mary saw Jack's expression when the doctor called Laurel Miss Wolfe. She felt like she should comfort him because his pain was so obvious.

"Your blood count is stable now, Miss Wolfe. I think we can move you to the regular floor and let you get on your feet. You could go home as early as Wednesday."

"This is my husband, Jack Driver," Laurel said. "I know it sounds strange when I'm listed as Miss Wolfe, but we're married. He just got here today. He was seriously injured when our plane crashed. Can you explain to him what happened to me?"

"We need to get your admission papers corrected," the doctor said. "We went by your driver's license. They'll need something to prove you're married."

Laurel pulled her purse across the bed and took out a folded paper. "This is our marriage license. Is that good enough?"

"You had it?" Jack asked. "Thank God." He leaned back in the chair, finally able to relax.

"I'll have a copy made and get your record corrected. I assume you have different insurance information."

"I added her to my policy the same day we got the

license," Jack said. "I can give you a card. Is she going to be all right?"

"She lost about five units of blood, her right tube, and her right ovary. I didn't transfuse her, but she's at the limit for missing the transfusion. For now this won't affect her fertility, but blood is inflammatory. It may cause scarring, and if it does the other tube may be affected. If you want children, you may want to think about trying later this year."

"We'll worry about that another time," Jack said. "Just tell me what we need to do to take care of Laurel."

"She just needs rest and time," the doctor said. "She'll need to be on iron and prenatal vitamins for the next few months, and you should use some form of contraception until she's stronger."

"I'll take care of that," Jack said.

"We also need to know your blood type," the doctor continued. "Mrs. Driver is B-. If your blood is Rh+, she needs to be given a shot to prevent antibodies against Rh+ blood from developing."

"I'm O-," Jack said.

"Well, there's no compatibility problem between you." The doctor smiled. "You're very lucky. The outcome could have been much worse. I'll bring this license right back."

Jack took out his wallet and passed an insurance card to the doctor. "This is our insurance. They said the number would be the same as my social security number but with 02 behind it. It doesn't require pre-certification for emergencies."

"That's good," the doctor said. "I'll see you in the morning." He exited to the nurse's station and consulted the charge nurse.

"Miss Wolfe is actually Mrs. Driver," he told the nurse. "Do you know what's up with that?"

"Some sort of traumatic separation, I think," the nurse said in a hushed voice. "If you ask me, the husband is in no shape to be here. He must be in an HMO die-at-home plan. They said he was in a plane crash two weeks ago. I'll bet she has more blood than he does, and he's a diabetic. I've been letting him sit with her because I was honestly afraid to have him walking back and forth between here and the waiting room."

"Keep an eye on both of them," the doctor said as he copied the two documents. "I've written transfer orders, but let them go to step down. Let him stay with her."

They were transferred to step down at 9 P.M., and Laurel sent her parents to the hotel. Her motives were clouded by a need to know what had happened to Jack in the previous two weeks. She didn't ask until they were alone.

"What happened to you, Jack? I never saw you again after the helicopter took you off the dock."

"What happened before that?" he asked. "I don't remember anything except seeing your face, and I obviously can't trust my father to tell me the truth."

"I hid in the rocks and shot the two men. You tried to get up, but you couldn't so I got the raft and put you on it. I dragged it to the water and used a pole to push us down the river. When you passed out, I thought your sugar was low so I tested you. It was high so I put the pump on and gave you insulin. I couldn't think of what else to do. I started screaming when we made it to the ocean, and the Coast Guard picked us up." She held his hand tightly. "Did you jump in front of me?"

"They were aiming at you. I wasn't going to let them hurt you if there was any way to stop it." He closed his eyes for a long moment. "I don't remember what happened. I woke up in D.C., and my father said you had left me. At first I thought maybe you had. Don't get mad at me for thinking that. I'm just paranoid, and dad and Alyssa know it. He read me a letter that said you didn't want to stay married. When the drugs started wearing off, I knew he was lying because I had the pump on, and you were the only one who could have put it on me. I think they were deliberately keeping me drugged. Every time I asked for you they gave me more medicine. Alyssa kept trying to get me to agree to marry her again. She actually said she could get the diabetes cured if I would agree to be with her.

"I finally called the chaplain for help. Dad had my wallet, and either he or Alyssa had canceled my calling card so I was at their mercy. The chaplain told the hospital administrator, and he called my lawyer and Dr. Carpenter. I was afraid if I didn't have some backup, they would send me to a psychiatric hospital when I started talking conspiracy. Dr. Carpenter and my lawyer convinced them that I was sane.

"Then they called the FBI. My father hadn't even reported any of it. Not the sabotage. Not why I was shot. He just took me out of Georgia and held me like a prisoner. He sold our house and the helicopter and had my things shipped to Houston. I've got a receipt, a new glucose meter, and what I'm wearing. I don't even have any extra insulin or pump supplies."

"I have our suitcases at my aunt's house. We'll just have to get someone to bring them here tomorrow. How badly were you hurt?" Laurel forgot her own pain as her anger grew for what Jack had endured. "The Coast Guard medic said you had been shot twice and that you were in shock."

"I know what the records say. I don't remember any of it. They said I was shot twice in my left chest. One of the bullets was lodged against my heart. It tore the covering around my heart and collapsed my lung. They gave me eight units of blood before I was transported to D.C. I was on a ventilator for the first three or four days. I'm still having a hard time keeping the days straight."

"Are you supposed to be out of the hospital?" Laurel asked anxiously.

"No," he admitted, "but I didn't—and still don't care. I had to get here. When we got to Cherokee, I thought I'd lost you. I can't ever make it up to you, Laurel. I know you've been through two weeks of hell on earth, but I couldn't keep it from happening. I told my father that I don't ever want to see or hear from him again. I think Alyssa still presents a real threat, and I'm filing for a restraining order.

"This whole thing is so bizarre. I've spent the past three years alone struggling to rebuild my life. Just when I've finally found my place in the world, my father and my ex-wife appear and act like I abandoned them." His eyes riveted on her. "I don't know if the cure they told me about is real or not, Laurel. I told them how I feel. I'd rather be diabetic for the rest of my life and have you. It was an easy choice. I'm not leaving you unless God takes me."

"I know," Laurel said softly. "Really I knew all along. I didn't take off my ring, Jack. They took it when I went to surgery. Mary put it in my purse."

"I need to tell Houston what we're going to do," he said. "I want it to be your decision."

"We have to go," she gave him a wan smile. "We already bought a house."

"When my father read the letter he said you wrote, it said you couldn't deal with the diabetes anymore or the idea of being all alone in Houston. I didn't believe you wrote it, but I still needed to hear what you wanted. That's how it's supposed to be when people love each other."

"That's why I want to go," Laurel said simply. "I want to go because I love you. I never stopped loving you, and I never stopped praying for us. I never will."

Chapter 18

The doctors discharged Laurel on Wednesday. Her parents drove Jack and her to see Dr. Carpenter. Dr. Carpenter summoned a surgeon to his office. They both examined Jack. Laurel had her first look at the incision that was wrapped around Jack's left chest. She had to sit down when she saw it because it became apparent just how close she had come to losing him. The surgeon vocalized his concerns bluntly. He read the results of a new chest X-ray and sonogram of Jack's heart before he was satisfied.

"If that bullet had gone into your heart muscle, you'd be dead now," he said. "In the long run, you shouldn't have any impairment, but you won't be ready to train in a month. I'd say October at the earliest, and November is more reasonable. I'll have my secretary type a letter to that effect if you want."

"That would help," Jack admitted. "This is already hard to explain."

"What are the federal investigators doing with this mess?" Dr. Carpenter asked.

"I'm not sure," Jack said. "I've filed a restraining

order against my ex-wife, for all the good it will do. We're going up into the mountains until I can fly us to Houston."

"I need to check you again in four weeks," the surgeon warned. "If you have any trouble breathing or any chest pain other than the incision site, you need to come in immediately."

"He will. I can promise he will," Laurel said.

"He needs to gain fifteen pounds bare minimum," Dr. Carpenter asserted. "I was suggesting a weight gain last time, Jack. It's an order this time. You've passed below ideal body weight and moved on to malnourished. You won't heal if you don't eat."

Laurel was glad when Jack pulled on his shirt and covered the stark souvenir. When he was dressed, she clung to his arm and let herself realize he had almost died to protect her. Lila came to review the pump with them and confirmed what Laurel and Jack had guessed. His daytime basal rate of insulin was much too high. Lila explained the way to test a basal rate was to skip a meal. If the rate was correct, Jack's blood sugar should not change even if he didn't eat unless he was more active. Lila decreased his daytime rate to 0.2 units per hour. She and Dr. Carpenter were otherwise pleased with his control and made no other suggestions.

Laurel's parents drove them to a car rental lot. They wanted to drive Jack and Laurel home, but Laurel thanked them and explained they needed to reclaim Kennedy. She promised they would come straight to Cherokee afterwards. In the car, she sat close to Jack with her hand on his leg because she needed the comfort of touching him. They retrieved Kennedy. Before they were allowed to pay the bill, they had to explain that the dog had not been abandoned. Then they drove to the highway patrol station.

"We're getting a license or spending the night in line," Jack said. Fortunately the line was short. When they left the station, Laurel's driver's license read Laurel W. Driver. Their next stop was Jack's attorney's office, where Jack signed the revised will and the contracts with NASA. They took certified copies with them, leaving the registered mailings to Mr. Bennett.

"Did you get the marriage license straightened out?" Jack asked.

"It's legally recorded, and I've asked for the records to be sealed. That way they can't be tampered with again." The attorney gave Jack an official envelope. "This is the restraining order. If she calls, writes, or contacts you in any way, have her picked up. Don't show her any more mercy than she showed you."

"God's going to have to forgive me for how I feel," Jack said. "Mercy isn't a part of it. My only problem will be not shooting her if she shows up." His expression was almost frightening to Laurel.

"Do you have a gun permit, Jack?" she asked when they were outside.

"Yeah, I do, and although I'm a better shot with missiles, I'm not too bad with semiautomatic handguns." He looked at her. "And you're a decent shot yourself if I remember who saved my life." He placed his arm around her and walked her back to the car.

Two hours later they were in Qualla Boundary, having stopped only one more time to buy Jack some clothes. Lawrence Wolfe insisted Jack and Laurel stay at their home at least for a few days. He helped them settle into his upstairs rooms so they would have a bedroom, bathroom, and living room of their own. Kennedy came with them and stayed under Jack's feet until he finally tripped his master. Jack sprawled on the floor and grimaced as the dog licked his face. Laurel fell to her knees.

"Are you hurt?" Her voice trembled.

"I'm sore. Really sore." He sat up slowly and rubbed the dog's head. "I made you feel abandoned, didn't I,

Kennedy? Try to remember if you kill me with kindness you'll be in the kennel forever." He climbed to his feet slowly and sank down on the sofa with Laurel beside him. Kennedy rested his head on Jack's knee.

"How much do you weigh?" Laurel asked. He felt even thinner than he looked.

"Not enough," Jack said cryptically.

"I want a number, Jack," she demanded.

"One fifty-three," Jack admitted reluctantly. "I've been on a two-week fast."

"You can't train if you don't gain weight, Jack. If you don't eat—"

"I will," he interrupted. "I was too upset to eat, but I'm getting over it." He pulled her head down on his shoulder. "Your dad is a good man, Laurel. Don't ever forget how much he loves you. I wish Lucien and I could have received that kind of love from our father. I used to tell myself we didn't need our father because Lucien and I had each other. You're all I've got, Laurel. If I didn't have you, I don't know how I could have gotten through all this." He closed his eyes, and she curled close against his right side for comfort. Mary had to awaken them when she had supper on the table.

There were no further telephone calls, and no one tried to contact them. After the first few days, they started walking through the town and then hiking in the nearby national park. They began with the easy climbs. Laurel knew most of the hiking trails in the national park and carefully selected their earliest walks. By the third week, she was taking Jack to hike the level three climbs. Her endurance returned much more quickly than Jack's, but he never let fatigue get the best of him. The activity made him hungry, and Laurel could see he was regaining some of the weight he had lost.

It was during that month that Jack and Lawrence became good friends. Jack still felt guilty for what his family had done to Laurel and her family. In an effort to show his appreciation, he did all the handiwork around the Wolfe house that had been awaiting Lawrence's recovery. He labored even when he didn't have the endurance to work more than an hour at a time. His tenacity impressed his father-in-law, but the way Jack treated Laurel allowed Lawrence to overlook Jack's divorce and the general's behavior.

Every night Lawrence talked to Jack about being Native American and being Cherokee. His acceptance helped Jack get past the loss of his whole family. They didn't hear from General Driver, Alyssa, or the federal investigators during those four weeks.

Jack and Laurel drove back to Knoxville for his checkup four weeks later. Both the surgeon and Dr. Carpenter gave him the go ahead to step up his exercise. He had gained ten of the mandated fifteen pounds. His blood sugars were almost all in range. As they left the office, Jack looked at Laurel.

"You want to fly back?"

"Can you keep us in the air?" she asked not entirely teasing.

"Hey, I got us down in one piece," he said. "The landing wasn't our problem."

"Let's fly home then." She was relieved that he felt well enough to fly again. He hadn't discussed the future, NASA or flying very often for four weeks. "Can we return the rental car here?"

"Yes, we can. We'll use Billy's convertible while we're in Cherokee." They drove to the airport, and Jack paid for the extended tie-down before doing a meticulous walk around that took over an hour. He tested both engines on the ground and then checked the fuel tanks and lines a second time.

He ran the checklist twice and then looked at Laurel. "Ready to go?"

"I'm saying my prayers now." She passed him his test kit. "You only forgot one thing."

"That's your checklist," he said. He checked his blood sugar and recorded the number. They took off into the wind and a sapphire blue sky. The plane showed no signs of its previous misadventure, and Jack showed no signs of flight anxiety even though they had crash landed only six weeks earlier. Even for Laurel the flight was too short. She wished they could have kept on flying over the mountain tops on that bright September day.

They touched down on Billy's airfield and taxied up to the hangar. The grizzled master sergeant greeted them effusively and agreed to keep the plane under lock and key. They rented the convertible for a week and drove back to Cherokee with the wind in their faces.

Jack stopped at a drug store and collected strips, syringes, and insulin using a new prescription. He also added contraception to their basket, and Laurel attempted to remove it.

"You don't need that," she said. "Let's just see what happens."

"You get clearance from your doctor, and I'll be happy to do just that. In the meantime, we're going to follow directions." He took her hand and led her to the checkout counter.

They drove to her parents' house and went for a walk. They ended up near a church where an afternoon wedding was taking place in the open air. The bride and groom were wrapped in white shawls, and the preacher stepped forward to tie the two ends together.

"That's the old way," Laurel smiled. "That's where the term 'getting hitched' came from."

Jack wrapped his arms around her, and they watched until the ceremony ended with a prayer. Then he kissed Laurel's hair and closed his hands over hers. "Do you want to have a church wedding before we leave here?"

"Sometimes I think it would be nice, but I know it would be a lot of trouble when we're already married."

"Tell me what you want, Laurel." He turned her to look into his eyes. "I want what makes you happy." "You make me happy." Her dark eyes caressed him until he could almost forget they weren't alone. "Let's go home," he suggested. "Let's go make chamber music. There's a grand piano at the church. We can stop and get my flute." "Let's make music like we did on our wedding night," he whispered in her ear. She shivered under his touch. "Are you ready to make that kind of music?" she whispered. When he smiled his answer, she led him back to the house.

She was glad that her parents were at work. They locked the house doors to keep out the outside world and the upstairs door to keep them safe in their two rooms. Laurel leaned against the door and unbuttoned her blouse slowly. Her skirt slid to the floor in a graceful puddle of silk. Her slip straps were sliding over her shoulders when Jack caught her to his body. His arms felt strong when he held her, and he kissed her with all the deep undercurrent of feeling she knew she couldn't ever forget. Desire rose in her and made her hands shake when she was removing his clothes.

They made love without any intrusions other than the birth control and brief uncertainty about what to do with Jack's pump. Ultimately he disconnected it and set it on the nightstand. Afterwards, they couldn't stop touching each other, and they spent the afternoon in bed. Laurel brought him the pump and his meter when they went to shower.

"That's the first time I've felt weird about being connected to it," Jack admitted. "Otherwise it's been the best part of being diabetic."

"Can you tell a difference?" Laurel asked.

"I don't feel like I'm on a roller coaster any more," Jack said. "I can't tell what the actual reading is, but I can feel my sugar when it changes fast either up or down. I'm not constantly having that feeling since I went on the pump. I can tell when it's dropping a lot sooner. I thank God for you and MiniMed every day. It just felt strange trying to figure out where to put it."

"Unless it doubles as a camera, I don't think that matters," Laurel said as she laughed. "Use those other things to wrap it up so it can't watch us." She was rewarded by a swat on her behind and hurried into the shower to escape further retribution.

When they had showered and dressed, they walked to the church. Laurel carried her flute, and Jack carried a case of sheet music. The preacher was leaving for the evening, but he seemed happy to allow them the use of the piano.

It was the first time Laurel and Jack had played together, but they both had chamber music experience. Laurel was again impressed by Jack's skill. He was very talented and well taught. They played several Bach selections and moved to Mozart. Laurel paused to choose something else just as Jack started playing a nocturne. The music seemed to envelope her. Though it had not been written for her, she could feel it was being played for her. When he stopped, she clapped.

"You're so good, Jack."

"Only because I'm playing for you. Play for me, and I promise not to distract you here." She lifted her flute, and he pulled it back down. "No *Titanic* music please. The guy's name was Jack, and he dies. I'm not thrilled with the concept."

She laughed and pulled out a sheet of music. It was her favorite classical piece also by Bach. She played it as an expression of her feelings for Jack Driver. When she finished, Jack held her in his arms.

"We're in harmony, Laurel. I don't think that happens very often." They played together for another hour and then locked the church building. They walked home in the cool of early evening and met Lawrence in the driveway. Laurel's face was radiant, and her father smiled when he saw her happy face.

"How was your day?" he asked.

"It was good," Laurel answered. "They gave Jack a good report, and we flew back in the plane. How was your day?"

"Any day I'm alive is good," her father smiled.

They entered the house together as Lawrence sifted through the mail.

"You've got a letter, Jack." He extended an official NASA envelope to his son-in-law.

Jack opened the envelope and read the letter on the front steps. Laurel hung over his shoulder. "It's okay. They've approved my training to begin November 1." He handed the letter to Laurel. "I'll have to pass another flight physical. I'd better go run before supper."

"Test first and suspend your pump," Laurel said.

Jack tested and gave her the reading. He suspended the operation of the insulin pump and ran down the driveway. Laurel felt anxious.

"I don't think he should run alone yet," she explained to her parents. She whistled for Kennedy and climbed into the convertible to follow Jack.

Jack liked to run, and he was grateful to be able to run again. His endurance still reflected his injury. He could handle only ten minutes before needing to rest. That limit didn't bother him because he could feel his strength returning every day. He jogged until he could catch his breath and then ran again until he was winded enough for pleurisy to make him stop.

He sat down on a picnic bench by the river to catch his breath while watching the sunset. A hand slid over his shoulder provocatively, and he turned expecting to see Laurel. He was at a tremendous disadvantage when he looked up into Alyssa's face. When he jumped back, he hit against the edge of the concrete table, striking the ribs the bullets had broken. The pain made escape impossible as Alyssa leaned over him.

"You shouldn't have left D.C., Jack. You know you didn't want to leave. She made you leave. She's trying to keep us apart, and it won't work. We're supposed to be together." Her hands were on his chest and shoulders.

Jack shoved her away and moved around her before she could regain her balance. "Get away from me, Alyssa. I don't want to see you for any reason. I have a restraining order against you. If you don't want to go to jail, you'd better get away from here." Her face turned to ice as she pulled a gun from her pocket.

"Don't move, Jack," she ordered her stunned ex-husband. "You don't have a choice. You can be with me or die." It was the first time Jack had allowed himself to believe his ex-wife was dangerously unbalanced and capable of killing. Her face told him she would kill him with little or no remorse. He didn't have any way to defend himself, but he knew going with her would be a fatal mistake. He stalled for time while battling his panic at the thought of being shot again. Alyssa's finger was curled around the trigger, and the gun was aimed at his chest.

"Where are we going, Alyssa? How do you think you'll take me out of here without anyone seeing you?"

Before she could answer, he saw Kennedy racing across the grass behind Alyssa. The dog hadn't been trained as an attack dog, but instinct told the German shepherd that his owner was in trouble. Alyssa whirled just as the dog reached her, but she had no time to avoid attack. Kennedy hit Alyssa and sank his teeth into her arm savagely. Alyssa fell to the ground screaming. The gun bounced toward the river and went off as Laurel drove onto the grass. Jack vaulted into the convertible and called Kennedy. The dog jumped into the back seat as Laurel backed up and turned. The tires squealed and threw gravel as they entered the highway. Laurel began honking the horn to draw attention. Neither of them could garner the courage to look back. A police car approached them with lights flashing and pulled them over.

"My ex-wife is here," Jack explained. "I have a restraining order against her. She caught me down by the river and pulled a gun on me. You need to pick her up. She's crazy."

The officer looked skeptical until he called in using both of their driver's licenses as a reference. Then he returned to their car looking apologetic. "I've called it in, Mr. Driver. Another car is investigating the park. I need both of you to come with me to the station and file a report." Laurel stayed behind the wheel because her husband was in no condition to drive.

"I wanted to believe she would quit," Jack said. "When I looked at her face, I knew she's crazy. She would have shot me."

"I don't understand why the federal agents can't arrest her," Laurel said. "When we get through, we need to make our plans and get out of here, Jack. A part of me wants to stay, but I don't want to put my dad and Mary at risk. The Houston house is in a gated community."

"You're right. Do you want to check into a hotel tonight?" His voice revealed his stress.

"Test your sugar, Jack. You're shaking." She said a prayer to know what to do and then said, "Dad would want us to come home, and Alyssa will be running away tonight. Let's make a flight plan and leave tomorrow."

He tested his sugar and it was 67. He knew the shaking was more related to what had happened with Alyssa, but he took two glucose tablets while suspending his pump.

"I'm going to call my father. Alyssa's father and my father are friends. If they know she did this, maybe her father will do something with her," Jack said.

They filled out a report, filed charges against Alyssa for assault with a deadly weapon, and then remained at the police station while the federal agents were summoned. The agents' comments convinced Jack and Laurel they would have to leave Cherokee.

"We haven't made much progress in the investigation, Dr. Driver. I know you're convinced your ex-wife is involved, but there's no definite connection between her and what happened to you in Georgia. The men were contract criminals, but since they're dead, we have no way to find out who hired them. I would suggest that you put as much distance between yourself and her as you can."

"We understand," Jack said tersely. "Obviously we aren't safe. We'll leave in the morning and fly without filing a flight plan. Can you get us to our plane?"

"I'm sure the Cherokee police will be happy to help you," the agent replied. "We'll contact you in Houston if we learn anything helpful."

Jack stood and put his arm around Laurel's shoulders. "Thank you for your help."

They drove to the Wolfe house under police guard, but they knew they were really on their own. Jack left Laurel to explain to her parents what had just happened. He went to the upstairs phone and said a long prayer before dialing his father's phone number. His prayer was answered when his father picked up the phone.

"Dad, it's Jack. I need your help." The silence almost made Jack hang up. Then when his father spoke, the general's voice broke with emotion. Jack was as surprised by the emotion as he was by the words that followed.

"I've been praying you would call me, Jack. I'm sorry for everything I did. I hope someday you'll be able to forgive me. Tell me what I can do to help you."

"Alyssa followed us to Cherokee," Jack said. "I was

running tonight, and she came after me with a gun. The police are looking for her now. She's crazy, Dad. It's like she's stalking me. She said I'd be living with her or I wouldn't be living. You can send for the police report if you want proof."

"I believe you, Jack. I think she was making the telephone calls your father-in-law was talking about. I'll talk to her father. I spoke with him once before, but I don't think he believed me. I'll try to convince him. Are you going to Houston?"

"In a while," Jack said cryptically. "We haven't had a honeymoon yet so I thought we would go somewhere first. I won't be filing a flight plan, but I'll let you know I'm all right."

"Can you forgive me, Jack?" the general asked. His voice trembled. "Can we talk eventually?"

"I still love you, Dad," Jack admitted with a twist of pain. "I just can't be who you want me to be, and I can't keep living with the feeling I've failed you. I know it's because you care about Charlene and how she feels, but I haven't been a part of your life since you married her. We'll talk, and maybe we'll be friends and go from there."

"Please call me," the general begged. "I do love you, Jack. I just haven't been very good about showing you."

A part of Jack knew he should respond to his father's plea, but he was still too angry and bitter because of Lucien and his mother.

"I won't close you out of my life, Dad, but that's all I can promise you now. Thanks for your help." Jack hung up the telephone and sat down on the bed. Laurel came in while he was lost in his memories of Lucien and his mother and in his regrets for losing his father. Laurel sat beside him knowing she shouldn't ask. She held him until they could both sleep.

Chapter 19

Laurel hadn't allowed herself to think about leaving her folks until the next morning when she knew they would be going. When their bags were packed, she placed her personal belongings in the boxes in which they had been shipped to her. Jack gave Lawrence a check to arrange for the shipping and then he and Lawrence embraced spontaneously.

"Take care of my girl, Jack," Lawrence said hoarsely.

"I will," Jack promised. "We'll get home as often as we can." He stepped back and watched Laurel fight back her tears.

"I love you, Daddy. Even when I'm not here, I'll be thinking about you every day."

"You'll always be in my heart, Laurie. Please call us so I won't have to wonder how you are." They embraced with the pain of parting on their faces, and Jack felt a surge of guilt for taking his wife from her home. It eased when Laurel moved to his side and wrapped her arm around his waist.

"Don't worry about me, Daddy. Jack will take care of me." She turned to Mary and then embraced her stepmother. "We'll come home to visit. I love both of you."

They left just after 8 A.M. and drove to the airstrip. Billy met them at the plane and watched as Jack did his walk around. When Jack tried to pay him, he shook his head. "This will be my wedding present to you, Major. You come back and visit me when you can. Bring me some of that Mexican hot sauce. You can't get the real thing here."

Jack patted Billy on the back and then climbed into the plane beside Laurel. Kennedy was lying behind them with his nose on his paws. He looked unconcerned as they taxied to the field. Laurel's eyes were on the mountains, and their takeoff into the wind allowed her to keep watching the mountains until they turned west.

"Don't worry, Laurel," Jack said. "We'll visit as often as we can. I want you to be happy and not look back because we're going on our honeymoon. We're going to Window Rock, Arizona."

"The Navajo reservation." Laurel smiled in recognition of the site. "Are we looking for your roots, Jack?"

"Yeah," he said. "I think it's time for me to know who I am."

They had good weather, and they made it into Oklahoma that first day. They camped at the airport inside the plane and ate breakfast at a diner at the airstrip. There was no place to shower, but Jack used a map to locate an airstrip in Arizona adjacent to the reservation and a hotel. They bought sandwiches to eat for lunch and then flew across country and landed in Arizona at 8 P.M.

They took Kennedy to a kennel. They had a bath and room service at the hotel and then slept. They felt safe from Alyssa for the first time. When Laurel awakened the next morning, she found Jack reading the Navajo book they had purchased in Knoxville. He was sitting in front of the window facing the desert sunrise.

"Good morning. It's early to be daydreaming."

"Good morning," Jack said as he closed the book. "You know, I don't remember ever having been here, but I feel like I have been. I never really liked the desert, but I feel like I'm drawn to it now."

"I feel that way in the mountains," Laurel said. "I think it's because my people have always been in the mountains." She moved to sit behind him with her hands massaging his shoulders. "What are we doing today?"

"Doing the self-discovery journey, I think." He put his hand over hers. "They said the tribal office opens at 8 A.M. Let's be there."

The hotel manager provided a map, and Jack was good with directions. They found the offices of the Navajo tribe with no difficulty and were the first people to approach the clerk.

"May I help you?" she asked.

"I hope so," Jack said. "My name is Jackson Driver, and I was hoping to get some information on my family. My mother was full blooded. Her maiden name was Rachel Batisse."

The clerk typed information into the computer screen. "Here you are. Jackson Daniel Driver, date of birth September 18, 1966."

"I'm in there?" Jack asked, leaning to look at the screen. The clerk turned it so he could better view the information.

"You were placed on the tribal roll in 1967. Your father is Jack Roman Driver. He's half Navajo." Jack did a double take. "His father, Samuel Lucien Driver was full blooded." She smiled. "He was a code talker during World War II, but I'm sure you know that."

"I didn't know," Jack said. "For as long as I can remember, I was told I was only a quarter Navajo."

"You're a lot more than that," the girl commented. "Your father's mother was only a quarter, but everyone else is full blooded. That makes you at least three quarters." She scanned the screen. "Your mother was Rachel Rose Batisse. Her father, Daniel, was also a code talker. She was an only child, but your father's brother, Samson, still lives on the reservation. Would you like to contact him?"

"I would," Jack replied. "May I have a copy of all that?"

"Sure. We encourage all the tribal members to keep track of their genealogy. It was difficult to compile some of it because so many records were lost at the turn of the century. You're lucky. Yours is complete back into the 1700s." She printed three pages of pertinent information and gave them to Jack.

Laurel touched Jack's arm as he stared at the paper. "Why don't we walk around for a while?" He nodded and managed to thank the clerk. Outside, they sat on a bench and read through the papers.

"I don't understand this," Jack said under his breath. "I just don't understand why he would hide it."

"Jack, you don't know what it is to live as a Native American," Laurel said gently. "There are so many stereotypes and so much prejudice still out there. Maybe he was afraid for you to face that when you were living off the reservation."

"He still could have told us." Jack traced the name Samson John Driver with his finger. "He told us his family was dead. Whenever Lucien and I asked him about them, he said they had died when he was young."

"His parents did," Laurel said as she pointed to J. R. Driver's record. He would have been twenty-three. They must have been in an accident because they died at the same time."

"Let's find a pay phone. I want to meet my uncle." Jack stood like a sleepwalker and crossed the street with Laurel watching out for both of them.

The telephone was answered by a woman, and Jack

struggled to ask his questions. "I'm sorry to bother you. My name is Jackson Driver, and the tribal office told me this is my uncle's residence."

"Yes, yes," the woman said. "Please hold on. I know Samson would want to speak to you."

Minutes passed, and Laurel noticed Jack's hands were sweating. She checked his sugar, and the reading was 112mg percent. She could feel his pulse quicken when a deep voice spoke into the receiver.

"Is this really Jackson?" The voice was very much like his father's voice.

"Yes. I'm J.R. Driver's son. The tribal office said you're my uncle. Please forgive how I sound. I didn't know I had an uncle until ten minutes ago."

"I understand," Samson Driver said. "Could you come over? I would like to meet you."

"Give me directions, and we'll be right there." Jack gestured to Laurel who gave him a pen and paper. He scribbled down the instructions and ended the call. "Let's go. Am I safe to drive?"

"From a blood sugar standpoint, yes. Emotionally, I can't say." She put her hands on his face. "This is good, Jack. He'll be able to answer all your questions."

Laurel drove at Jack's request, and the trip took only twenty minutes. The address brought them to a single story brick house equipped with ramps. The reason for the ramps became obvious when Samson Driver rolled his wheelchair out on the porch to meet them. He was strongly built from his chest up, but his thin legs told them he had been confined to a wheelchair for many years. He had shoulder-length black hair that was almost devoid of gray. It was tied back with a plain leather band. Laurel smiled on seeing his hair. It was the mark of a Native American who was committed to preserving the old ways. As they walked up the sidewalk, Laurel could see Samson shared Jack's unusual eye color.

"You look like my father," Samson said in greeting.

"I'm Samson Driver. This is my wife, Olivia."

"Jackson Driver." Jack grasped his uncle's hand. "This is my wife, Laurel."

Samson smiled as he took Laurel's hand. "You're not from a western tribe, are you?"

"I'm Cherokee," Laurel said.

"The ones who study us say we all came from one man. Welcome to Navajo country. It's good to meet both of you. Please come inside, and we can talk out of this heat." Samson turned his wheelchair with practiced ease and led them into a room decorated much the same as Jack's office had been. When they were seated, Olivia brought them iced tea.

"I can see you didn't know about me," Samson said. "I haven't heard from your father for more than twenty years. After your mother died, he never came home again. You know he brought her here to be buried."

"I didn't know," Jack said slowly. "I thought she was in Arlington. We were living in Washington when she died. He wouldn't talk about her at all after she died. It was like she hadn't ever existed."

"How is your brother?" Samson asked.

"He was killed." Jack hesitated. "He died in a plane crash a couple of months ago. It was just the two of us."

"I'm so sorry," Samson said. "I'm the oldest. I'll be sixty-one in a few weeks. I was also in the U.S. Air Force. I served in Vietnam. My helicopter was shot down, and this was the outcome. I came home, and your father took my place. We didn't expect him to stay in the service, but then our father had often wished he had stayed longer in the Marines. He returned here to work in the airplane factory. I was an architect until last year. I thought it was time to retire. Are you in the service?"

"I was," Jack said. "I served until I was twenty-nine. Then I developed diabetes. I was a pilot. Now I'm taking a job with the space program as a mission specialist."

"I'm impressed," Samson said. "That's a family

dream." His face showed an unspoken longing when he asked, "Where is your father now?"

"He's a general. He works in Washington, D. C." Jack's hand tightened on Laurel's. He was caught up in his own pain and didn't see Samson's. "He remarried when I was fourteen, but they didn't have any children of their own." He paused. "Do you know why he hid being Navajo from me?"

"I can only guess," Samson admitted. "He was angry about the prejudice. He didn't think there was a future for Native Americans. Of course, every man deals with discrimination in his own way. It made me more determined to be Navajo, but then I was living here. He was in the world. How did you find out?"

"Lucien came to the reservation before he died. He must not have given his name. He must have just asked about our mother. He found out she was full blooded, and he called me. When I gave my name, they told me I was on the tribal roll," Jack said.

"You would be a little more than three quarters. J.R. and I are a little more than half. Your wife will tell you that quantum of blood means nothing. What you are in your heart decides if you are Navajo. I am Navajo, and I will live and die as my forefathers did." Samson took a glass of tea from his wife and waited until Jack and Laurel were served before taking a sip. The first taste told Jack it was sweetened. He used the pump's remote control to give himself insulin.

They couldn't stop talking, and Laurel could have listened forever. When Olivia went to make lunch, Samson directed Laurel to bring him photograph albums from the bookcase. He had pictures dating back to the early 1930s.

"You've been able to pass because my mother was very fair," Samson said. "She was three quarters Norwegian. She had light brown hair and very pale gray eyes. Our eyes are from her." Samson passed a picture over to Jack. "These are your cousins, my daughters, Eve Marie and Sarah Anne."

Jack looked at the unfamiliar faces feeling as if he had a family again. He had felt angry, lost, and confused since Lucien's revelation, and every interaction with his father had intensified those feelings.

"I want to list myself as Native American," Jack said, "but I want to know what it is to be Navajo when I do it. If I don't, it will just be a word and not who I am. I told Laurel's father how I felt, and he thought it was the right thing to do."

"You're on the right path, Jack," Samson said. "In this place we call ourselves diné. It means the people. We believe we were always in this place. Our traditions were always passed like our language from father to son. My father was Sam Driver, and I'm Samson. For the same reason, you're Jackson.

"My father taught your father and me the ways of the Navajo, but a man should learn all his life. J.R. and I lost that gift when our parents were killed in a car crash. Your father was twenty-three. I don't think J.R. ever recovered from their loss. It was the first stage of his separation from being Navajo. Our father could have kept him focused, but when he died there wasn't anyone to do it. I tried—"

Jack took the statement as rejection of his veiled request to be taught, and he nodded his acceptance of the tradition.

"There's a tremendous distance between my father and me just now. I'm not sure I'll ever be able to close it or that I want to close it. He rejected me," Jack said.

"I don't have a son to teach, Jack," Samson said. "You don't have a father to teach you. Maybe we can help each other. After my father died, Olivia's father and some of the other tribal elders became my teachers. It was a gift I've wanted to return."

Jack and Laurel moved in with Samson and Olivia

the next day. For a month, which included Jack's thirty-fourth birthday, they both learned about the Navajo tribe. Laurel learned to weave in the traditions of the Spider Woman, and she learned the legends of the Navajo people. By choice she spent a great deal of time with Olivia and her daughters because she was wise enough to know Jack needed his uncle very much.

Jack learned the traditions and became very familiar with the language. It was a difficult language for a man who had been raised as white, but he became fluent rather quickly. He remembered having heard the words from his mother.

Jack flew Samson and Olivia around the reservation to see the sacred places not easily accessible to a man in a wheelchair. Laurel made a photo diary of everything they saw and did. They attended a large powwow that took place in Window Rock and flew to Mesa Verde to see the ruins of the Anasazi world. Because they lived for a month in the Navajo world, Laurel's vision of the world outside her reservation broadened. She also saw her husband find his place in the world where he had felt orphaned and rejected. At the end of their respite, she felt he had begun the healing process of dealing with the death of his beloved Lucien.

They were packing to leave for Houston. Laurel sensed Jack had some reservations about what was to come. She wasn't privy to the exit interview Jack had with Samson, but she knew it took place the same day they drove to the tribal office where Jack could obtain a card identifying him as a tribal member. On the way, Samson stopped at Window Rock to watch the sunlight spreading over the desert.

"All of life is a gift, Jack," Samson said. "I was very angry when I came back from Vietnam. I was angry because I could not walk. I felt I was no longer a man and could never be a warrior. I almost lost Olivia while I was fighting my greatest battle. I remember thinking death would have been better. It was how I learned the greatest lesson.

"Being a warrior and a man doesn't come from the strength of your limbs or how much insulin your body makes. It comes from your heart. It comes when you have the courage to face every challenge God gives to you with the belief you will answer it as a man. The outcome is not important. It is how you fight that matters. You've had one of those challenges in being diabetic. Your father is another challenge. He was the challenge I failed because I faced it in anger."

"Why do you think my father has hidden who he is?" Jack asked.

"I think it was to advance his career and his sons' careers. You don't remember the days before the Civil Rights movement. Then we were only a few steps away from The Long Walk and The Trail of Tears. A Native American man could not have become a general. His sons might not have been admitted to the Air Force Academy. The code talkers lived the Navajo prophecy and saved the free world, but none of them were allowed to advance. I was passed by for promotions during the four years I served.

"Your father saw all of that. He never learned that there is no medal for knowing you have done your duty. He needed the gilt of his uniform to fill the empty places in his heart. Ache for him, Jack. He has lost everything he valued. He lost your mother because of his decision. He lost the child she was carrying. He lost Lucien, and now he knows he might lose you. I was still too angry myself when I tried to talk to him. We argued, and he never came home again."

"Are you saying I should continue passing as white?" Jack asked.

"You should follow your heart, Jack. Being Navajo off the reservation is something like being a Christian outside of church. It might be easier if you continue to pass as white. You might lose your father if you choose to be Navajo."

"To hide who I am dishonors everyone who lived before me," Jack said. "Some day, I'll make my father understand that. I'm not afraid of what NASA will say, Samson. I'm already marked by being diabetic. I want to take this step and believe God will show me the right path."

"If you go for the glory of God and the honor of your people, you will be triumphant." Samson pointed to the rock. "Keep this place in your heart, Jack, and don't be a stranger to us."

"I couldn't be. This was the first home I've had since my mother died. You never really leave your home." He absorbed his surroundings as they drove to the tribal office. He walked beside Samson to obtain the card that would change his racial status forever.

Chapter 20

Jack and Laurel had both recovered from their infir-
mities when they flew into Houston. Jack could honestly say he was in the best physical condition he had
been in since being diagnosed. He weighed 182 pounds,
and none of the gain was visible fat. He could run ten
miles without resting and do a hundred push-ups, chin-
ups and crunches. Because the stress level had been so
much lower for both of them, Jack had kept near perfect
glucose control. After a month in the Arizona sun, he
was also much darker skinned than he had been. He
was dark enough that Laurel was sure Jack could be
accepted as a Native American with less difficulty than
he could continue passing as white. Only his eye color
marked him as genetically different from the full-blooded
Navajo people they had met.

They flew into a private airport the agency had
recommended and arranged for long-term tie-down of
their plane in a secured hangar.

They rented a car and, with Kennedy sitting between them, they drove to the gated community that
would be their home. The house had been filled with the

boxes and crates holding their stored belongings, and the task of unpacking seemed daunting. Leaving the mess for the following day, they went to the grocery store and to a car dealership to purchase a car. The highway patrol station was on the road to the dealership, so they stopped to get new driver's licenses. Laurel's license was duplicated on a Texas format. Jack had to produce his tribal membership card to have the square for race changed to Native American.

They bought a four-wheel drive dual cab truck using the money Jack's truck and Laurel's car had brought. It was bright red in memory of the helicopter. When they pulled into the driveway, a crowd of people began gathering in their yard bearing a banner that read, "Welcome to the NASA family."

Two men met Jack with their hands extended. "You must be Jack Driver. I'm Stuart Bradford, and this is Russell Chou. We're on the same crew. The other guys will be here in fifteen minutes. They're bringing the beer and pizza. The crews help each other with getting settled. We figured you guys could use some help."

Jack shook hands with both men and introduced Laurel. Russell Chou and his wife were Chinese Americans. The rest of the crew included an African American, Odell Hughes, and four other Caucasians, Jim Graham, Roger Lawson, Ted Meers and Blake Arnold. Russell and Stuart were navy pilots. Odell Hughes and Blake Arnold were air force pilots, and the other team members were civilians. Jack fit in with both groups for obvious reasons.

For the rest of the evening, Jack and Laurel's house was crowded with adults and a host of small children. Two of the wives acted as baby-sitters, but the rest joined in cleaning and unpacking. The stereo was set up hurriedly, and they played rock and roll CD's while they worked. Laurel forgot to feel nervous in being hostess. She remembered to watch the time for Jack. He had set his pump rate at zero units per hour because of the increased activity. Laurel gave him a glucose tablet every hour until he stopped to eat pizza. They both shunned the beer.

The party broke up at midnight after everybody sang another chorus of "California Dreaming." Sleeping children were collected, and the seven couples departed one by one, promising invitations for the weekend. When Jack returned from locking the doors and turning on the security system, he found his wife still fully clothed stretched out on the bed.

"Well, well. It seems my little kid is worn out just like the others," Jack remarked from the door.

"Don't pretend. You're tired, too," she said without moving.

"I'm totally pumped up. I could keep going all night." He snapped his fingers sending Kennedy to his dog bed. "I've got all sorts of ideas about how to unwind."

"You'll have to come here to tell me about them. I can't move." She did embrace him as he stretched out beside her.

"I'm going tomorrow to get the flight physical. Why don't you come with me? Then we can stop at a furniture store and get the rest of what we need. We can also find a gynecologist for you and see when you can be cleared for baby making. I was thinking we should wait another few months just to make sure all the blood they gave me didn't cause a problem."

"Can it cause a problem?" Laurel asked anxiously.

"Probably not, but you can get infections that way, and I'm not taking any chances with you." He leaned over her and kissed her. Their eyes were communicating when he said, "If I can do this, Laurel, I'll be doing it because you're with me. I feel like I can do it when I wasn't ever sure until you came into my life."

Because of Jack's words, Laurel forgot to feel tired.

They had never felt any closer than that first night in their Houston house. Everything seemed so perfect that Laurel could forget the purpose of being there and how afraid she was of having Jack go into space. She left that part of their life in God's hands because it was the only way she could manage the worries.

They were both greeted by name when they arrived at the space agency. A guide assigned to them ushered them to the proper office to secure identification badges. That first stop was where Jack initiated his change in racial status. The intake official was startled by Jack's request and brought his superior officer. Jack gave them his card from the Navajo tribe and the genealogy he had obtained.

"I wasn't aware of this when I was in the Air Force. I knew my mother was part Navajo, but I didn't know about the rest. I don't have enough Caucasian blood to continue claiming that race. I need to be listed as a Native American. I don't know what my father will think, if that's what worries you, but this isn't his decision. He's only half Navajo so he can claim either race. This is my decision."

"You realize this is an unprecedented change, Dr. Driver?" the official asked.

"I'll accept whatever consequences I have to take," Jack said. "My personal information would have been correct from the beginning if I'd known the truth. I can't take lying about something that makes me proud. Surely there are other Native Americans in the program."

"It's your decision." He made the change in Jack's file and sent them on to the flight surgeon. As they were led across the compound to the infirmary, Laurel moved close to whisper to her husband. "When will your father know?"

"Right about now. Did you feel the sonic boom? I'm almost sorry the telephone's connected. I guess I'll call him before he uses the CIA to get our number."

Laurel was allowed to watch some of Jack's flight physical. She wanted to be there to hear their opinion of his injury. The flight surgeon whistled as he reviewed the report.

"You're lucky, Dr. Driver. You were about a quarter inch from seeing eternity. I'm glad you brought the echocardiogram reports or I'd be afraid to run you." He examined the scar and listened to Jack's chest for a long time. "I can't hear anything I'm not supposed to hear. Let's see how the system works under stress."

Jack tested his blood sugar and disconnected his pump. He was on the treadmill for fifteen minutes, and he showed no signs of excess stress during or after the test. His maximal heart rate after a ten percent grade at five miles per hour was only 160. Laurel could see it was a matter of pride when he finished the stress test. The message was being sent that he was no less a man because he was diabetic.

"You've got my stamp of approval," the surgeon said. "We'll draw a glycosylated hemoglobin and the routine blood work."

"Can you draw the tests for hepatitis and the AIDS virus?" Jack asked. "I had eight units of blood, and they said I needed to follow that for a year."

"No problem," the doctor said as he passed Jack a lab slip. "Go down the hall to the lab. I'll have my nurse get you an appointment with Dr. Kurt Jarman. He's the local insulin pump guru."

They were finished at the agency by 1 P.M., and Jack was given two boxes of ops manuals and uniforms. They had lunch at a Mexican restaurant and went to the office of a gynecologist Danielle Chou had recommended. Laurel made a new patient appointment for December and was given a registration packet. Almost as an afterthought, Jack went back to security at the agency and gave them Alyssa's picture.

"This is my ex-wife. She's been stalking us, and I

have a restraining order against her. I'll bring a copy on Monday. If she shows up, detain her and call the police."

"No problem, Dr. Driver," the officer assured him. "You won't be the only astronaut who has been stalked. You guys have been known to get celebrity status."

"I doubt that," Jack said, "but I don't want any more contact with Alyssa."

They spent the afternoon at several furniture stores and then a department store where they ordered drapes and other decorative items. Jack's sugar was 110 when they were on their way home, and they both forgot to think of the effect of the exercise testing. It was supper time when they reached their house. Jack unloaded a number of purchases in the late afternoon heat while Laurel started cooking. When he came in the last time, he went straight to the refrigerator and poured juice.

"How low are you?" Laurel asked as she tried to remember where the glucagon was. "Suspend your pump." With a blank expression on his face, Jack sat down holding the juice.

"It's getting there fast wherever it is."

Laurel extracted the test kit from his pocket, but he shook his head. "Not yet. I don't want them to see this kind of reading. I should have turned my rate down after the stress test. I forgot."

"So did I," Laurel said. Jack still hadn't turned off his pump so she took it off his belt and suspended its action.

Jack sat at the table until he started sweating profusely and had to pull off his jacket and shirt. "Why don't you get the other meter? I'm thinking forty right now."

She tested his sugar because his hands were so unsteady. While the meter counted off the time, the telephone rang, and Jack answered it. Five seconds later Laurel wished she had answered it because she could hear the general shouting through the telephone. Jack's sugar was thirty-eight, and his ability to tolerate his father's attack was at a low point.

"Do you have any idea what you've done, Jackson? What you did affects me as well as you. You had no right to tell them my background."

"It's my background, too, Dad," Jack shouted. "You took it away from me all my life. I never had the right to pass as white. I lived a lie for thirty-four years because of you. I just spent a month with Samson Driver. He's the kind of man I want to be when I figure out who I am. He's the brother you haven't seen or spoken to in the last twenty years. You know if I could have Lucien back for fifteen minutes, I'd spend the whole time telling him how much I love him.

"Sometime why don't you tell me why Charlene is worth so much more than the rest of us. You've pushed everyone who should matter out of your life for her. This will just make the break between us even cleaner. I'm Navajo. You're white. You can't be my father." He slammed the phone down and had to restrain himself from throwing the juice glass at the wall. Then he took the phone off the hook. "Who needs glucagon? Talk to a jerk and get your adrenaline flowing."

Laurel put her arms around his waist and held him until the rage began to subside. Several minutes passed before he turned and held onto her.

"The fall out begins."

"Are you sorry, Jack?"

"No," he said adamantly. "I wish I had known to do it sooner. I'm just leaving it in God's hands. Samson said to go for the glory of God and the honor of the Navajo nation, and that's how I'm going."

Neither of them would realize the other side of Jack's leap of faith until months later. The fallout of being a minority in a government agency was no longer a dampened career. Even that day, Jack was being pushed closer to the head of a long line.

They had two weeks together and then Jack entered the training program with the rest of his team. Laurel had the house to occupy her mind and help keep her from worrying about the man who had become her best friend. The other wives spent time with her to forestall the isolation all of them felt.

Laurel never considered herself a talented interior decorator, but she was determined that their home would pay tribute to their roots. Accomplishing the task required a complete paint job, which she did on her own throughout the week. The other wives taught her how to wallpaper and undertake other decorating tricks. When the house was finished, Laurel was proud of her accomplishment. She also felt a part of the NASA sisterhood. The crew wives went out to lunch at least twice a week and attended craft classes together throughout the spring and early summer.

Laurel had her own life, but she lived for the moment when Jack walked through the door each night. He was tremendously happy in living his dream. He told her all about every day with the undimmed excitement of a first grader. Even when he had to study his manuals at night, he would lie down with Laurel and hold her while he read.

They had the weekends, which often involved outings with the other crew members. Fall became Laurel's favorite time of the year because of the recreation instigated by the highly competitive air force, marine, and navy pilots. They had created football teams that played each other every Saturday before the college games came on television. Odell and Jack both played for the Air Force. Odell was a quarterback, and Jack was his favorite receiver. Laurel and Odell's wife, Angela, were cheerleaders. When the Air Force won the astronaut Super Bowl that fall, Laurel took one of her favorite pictures of Jack. He and Odell were giving each other the high five while the other team members held up the trophy. She mailed a copy of the picture to Jack's father without knowing why it seemed important to do so. The gesture made her feel good. It was the beginning of a one-sided correspondence with Jack's father.

After football season ended, Jack took Laurel to the beach. He snapped photographs of her as she viewed the ocean for the first time. Every weekend, he let her choose a location and then flew her there to practice her photography. He escorted her around the base to take pictures in the non classified areas. Her natural talent showed in the quality of her work. They purchased the digital camera and computer equipment to allow her to be a professional. In December, she sold two of her photographs to a local magazine.

They had time off to fly home to Cherokee for Christmas. They remembered to take Billy a case of Mexican hot sauce and were offered free tie-downs indefinitely. They flew to Window Rock for New Years. Laurel enrolled in the local college beginning in the winter semester and finished enough credits to become a senior by the end of their first year in Houston.

Jack had worried about the blood transfusions he had received. He had delayed discussions of a baby because he feared he might have contracted a virus from the eight units of blood he had received. In August of 2000, he had a negative one-year blood check for the hepatitis and AIDS viruses. He came home early on a Friday afternoon with the lab report and airline tickets to the Virgin Islands. They flew out that night and spent six blissful days at a secluded resort on St. John.

They had both thought they would be quick to conceive because of the speed of the first pregnancy. When Laurel started her senior year in September, she wasn't pregnant. She was the only crew wife who didn't have children. It became the focus of her prayers because she knew Jack's team had been training long enough to be slated for a mission. She couldn't bear the thought of having him at such risk when they didn't have a child.

The teams were trained to handle the shuttle and all its equipment for a year before they knew they would be considered. The first year was like flight school, and Jack approached it with all the aggressiveness of a fighter pilot. He had become more experienced at managing his blood sugar and had never had a low anyone else had detected. He used his very limited free time in the flight simulator until he had logged more hours than the pilots. The simulator made computer recordings of pilot competence and pilot error. Jack's errors were few and far between, but he didn't expect what happened in December of 2000. When he was signing out on Friday night, Colonel Asher caught up with him and ushered him out to the airfield. Night had fallen, and none of the astronauts were at the field. A readied T-38 stood on the tarmac, and the colonel handed Jack a helmet and a suit.

"Take me up, Dr. Driver."

Jack thought the offer was a joke until he scanned the colonel's face.

"Sir, I haven't flown at this level for over four years."

"You do the simulator almost every day, Jack. I know how many hours you had before you left the Air Force, and I'm fully qualified as an instructor. Take me up. I want to see your non-simulated skills."

Jack paused almost a minute as he thought of Lucien and Laurel. Then he tested his blood sugar, suspended his insulin pump and suited up. Their wheels were up fifteen minutes later. Jack forgot everything except the feeling of the jet. His reflexes were automatic and confident as he took the jet through every maneuver the colonel gave him.

He didn't know his performance was being monitored on the ground, as well as from the second seat. He just felt a sense of reconciliation for having been grounded and took that time in the air as a gift. He could have flown on through the night, but the colonel asked him to land two hours later.

"Not bad, Jack," the colonel acknowledged. "I wouldn't have guessed it had been four years. Keep up your time in the simulators."

"Thank you, sir. I will." He felt elated by Colonel Asher's comments because every pilot knew flight instructors were stingy with positive comments of any kind.

He didn't realize how late it was until he was in the locker room. He had neglected to call home. It was almost 9 P.M., and he was usually home by 7 P.M. He had never been later than seven without calling Laurel. The line was busy when he called, so he drove home without trying again. His test before driving let Jack know that his sugar had climbed to almost two hundred, but he bolused with insulin when he started his pump.

He couldn't wait to tell Laurel about the flight. He almost expected her to meet him in the driveway. She was on the phone with the agency operator when he entered the house. When he heard her voice, Jack knew his wife was terribly frightened.

"He just walked in. Thank you for all your help." Laurel hung up the phone and wiped her tears with her hands as she moved to the stove. "I was really worried, Jack. I was afraid you had gotten low somewhere. I was afraid you'd had a wreck."

"Colonel Asher asked me to stay over," he explained as he put his arms around her shoulders. "I'm sorry, Laurel. I didn't have time to call, but I should have made time." She was stiff in his embrace and didn't return it.

"I guess I worry too much. The others say I do, but they haven't seen their husbands almost die. They haven't buried a brother-in-law."

"I'm sorry, babe," he said sincerely. He was overwhelmed with guilt when he turned her to face him. Her face was tear streaked and her eyes were swollen from two hours of crying. "I just didn't think of how late it was when Colonel Asher called me. You know I don't ever do this to you. Please forgive me."

He cradled her face in his hands and kissed her until she began to respond almost against her will. His mouth was warm and persistent on hers, and his hands slipped into her clothes and pulled her tightly against his body. Wanting him merged with Laurel's relief at knowing he was all right. He carried her to the sofa, and they made love there. Then they went to their bedroom to lie in each other's arms.

It was close to midnight when Laurel had relaxed enough to think about their cold supper. Jack being so close seemed much better able to fill her heart and soul than any meal could.

"You need to eat," she murmured.

"I forgot to think about it. Being overwhelmed with guilt kills your appetite. I really am sorry for scaring you."

"I know," she said. "You love all this so much. It's hard for me to compete with it." Jack's response was immediate.

"You don't have to compete," he said as he looked down into her eyes. "You and God are first before my job. If I'm not showing you how I feel, Laurel, I've really been screwing up."

"You do show me," she admitted. Jack was much more attentive to her than some of the other astronauts were to their wives. "I'm just really scared for you. I know they'll assign you to a mission soon. Everyone says they will, and I'm scared something will happen. I guess it would be easier if we had a baby. If I were pregnant, I'd have a part of you with me all the time."

"You don't know if I'll get a mission, Laurel, and I don't either. They haven't said anything about scheduling our team yet. There are fully trained astronauts here who haven't been up after three years. I do know I'll quit before I'll leave you feeling like this every day."

"I don't feel like this every day. I just live for you to walk in that door at night. Then I feel like you're mine for at least a few hours." She sat up slowly. "You'd better test and put your pump back on. You've had it off for over two hours. I'll go warm up supper." He pulled her back down forcefully.

"My sugar is fine. I'd much rather hold onto you." He held her so she had to meet his gaze. "Do you want me to resign? This has to make both of us happy or it won't work."

"It doesn't make me unhappy," she said. "I love you so much, Jack. Every day I love you even more. It's like I'm not alive until you come home. When you didn't come and you didn't call, I kept thinking of Lucien and Julissa."

"I won't leave you," he vowed. "Laurel, I love you, and I think of you all day every day. Sometimes I have a hard time keeping my mind on my business because I'm thinking of you. I promise I'll never do this to you again."

"I believe you," she conceded. "It just scares me. I feel like we live on the edge of the envelope you're pushing."

"If I didn't believe I'd make it home to you, Laurel, I wouldn't go. They've never lost an astronaut in space. I know you're thinking of Challenger, but that was a one-time catastrophic failure. There have been over seventy flights since then." He lifted her chin and looked into her eyes. "Tell me what you want me to do."

"Just love me," she whispered. "That's all I want."

"That's easy," he said. "That's what keeps me focused." She held onto him. She knew Jack loved her. He was offering to give up his dream to make her happy. She fell asleep in his arms and, unfortunately, Jack fell asleep without retesting and without reconnecting his pump. He had always disconnected it when they made love, but it was the first time he had fallen asleep without reconnecting his pump. Neither Laurel nor Jack realized what a huge problem that error would bring.

Laurel felt Jack get out of bed just after sunrise. She wasn't concerned because he usually got up before she did. She assumed he would come back to bed, and she went back to sleep. It was some time later when she woke up again and realized his side of the bed was still vacant. It was after 9 A.M., and she checked the kitchen and the den before returning to the bedroom as she called for him. She found him in the bathroom on the floor, and one look at his face terrified her. She thought he was low, but the reading told her he was too high for the machine to read, which meant more than six hundred. He was violently sick twice before he could tell her to get his pump.

"I'm in trouble, Laurel," he managed. "I went too long without insulin. This is like when they found it. I've been trying to make it into the den for three hours. Get a syringe and give me twenty units."

"Jack, you're crazy. Twenty units will make you too low." She ran into the den and returned with his pump. Her hands shook as she reconnected it. "I'll give you ten units and call Dr. Jarman."

"No," he argued. "They'll think I don't know how to take care of it. This was total stupidity on my part."

"You'll have to get off the floor and stop me," she retorted. She ran to the kitchen and drew up ten units. Jack gave himself twenty units through his pump before she got back. When she had given him the shot, she had to hold onto him while he was sick again. Laurel called the doctor and sat with Jack's head in her lap on the bathroom floor. She started to panic. Jack's breathing was fast and deep, and Laurel remembered reading about diabetic ketoacidosis. She also remembered it could kill.

An hour passed before the doctor returned her call.

By then the meter told her Jack's sugar was down to 490.
"He's in ketoacidosis," the doctor affirmed. "His
glucose meter will read ketones, too. Read those."
"They're high," Laurel reported.
"When did he vomit last?" the doctor asked.
"About thirty minutes ago, but I think he was sick
for at least a couple of hours before I found him," Laurel
reported. "What should I do? He's really sleepy now,
and he's breathing really hard."
"You need to get him to the emergency room," the
doctor said. "Some people can get in a tremendous
amount of trouble really fast. If he can't walk to the car,
call 911. I'll be there making rounds, and I'll tell them to
page me."
The threat of an ambulance got Jack off the floor and
to Laurel's car, but he was dizzy and almost fell twice.
He begged her not to ask anyone else for help.
Laurel rued her compliance with his request when
they reached the hospital. Jack couldn't step out of the
car, and he was less responsive to her frantic touches
than he had been on the bathroom floor. In a panic,
Laurel ran into the emergency room and returned with
a seasoned nurse. The triage nurse took one look at Jack
and summoned two other nurses to get him on a
stretcher. He was admitted an hour later, and Laurel
had to release his hand at the door to the intensive care
unit. It was a realization that Jack didn't have to leave
the earth to risk dying.
The doctor came to see her in the waiting room.
"Jack got into a lot of trouble fast. He's very acidotic.
That means his blood pH is abnormal enough to put his
life in danger. A normal blood pH is about 7.4, and that
number is important because all the enzyme systems in
the body only work well at that pH. That pH is neutral,
which means all the acids and bases in the body are in
balance. When the pH is low, nothing works like it's
supposed to work. Jack's pH is 6.9, which is very low.

He'll be in the ICU overnight, but he might be able to go home as soon as tomorrow. What happened? He's really too out of it to tell me."

"It's my fault," Laurel cried. "We had an argument, and he fell asleep without putting his pump back on. It was off for at least ten hours."

"That's definitely long enough," the doctor said. "He has no insulin of his own, Mrs. Driver, and when he takes off his pump, the site insulin is gone in about two hours. Don't let him go any longer than two hours off the pump without testing. He's strong and healthy, but he's also insulin dependent. People can die from keto-acidosis."

She couldn't bring herself to call anyone. It was Saturday, and they hadn't had any plans because football season was over. She sat in the waiting room and prayed for him to be all right. Relief was being able to visit him at two o'clock. He was still breathing hard. His face was haggard, but he could talk to her. Laurel took his hand and held it.

"I love you, Jack."

"I know," he said slowly. "If you didn't, how could you put up with this?"

"I'm still remembering the guy who had it for forty years. You haven't been that much trouble, and you've been worth every minute of it." She kissed his forehead. "It's a reality check for me."

"How's that?" he asked.

"Space isn't any more of a risk than diabetes is." She kissed his forehead again and didn't see she had said the wrong thing. "I'm sorry about last night. I just lost it."

"We both did." He held her hand then and closed his eyes as she stroked his hair.

The nurse looked in and smiled. "I'll close the door. If you're quiet, you can stay with him."

Laurel stayed as close as the hospital bed would allow and held Jack's hand as the day slowly passed. He couldn't tolerate anything other than a few ice chips. His sugar didn't normalize until late that evening, and even then he looked and felt terrible. Early the next morning he was finally able to sip liquids and complain of a terrible sore throat. Dr. Jarman arrived at noon.

"I think you'll live. I'll let you out, but you need to really push the fluids and rest today."

"I don't feel like arguing," Jack said. "I do feel well enough to get out of here. Try not to make me look like too much of an idiot in the record."

The doctor patted his shoulder. "You aren't the only diabetic who takes off their pump at certain times. Just don't forget to reconnect it. That's one of the limitations of the system. If you're disconnecting at night, set your alarm for two hours. Take this as a part of the learning curve. You've only been on the pump for a year, Jack, and this is your first trip to the hospital. That's a good track record. You may have had a virus or food poisoning to help push you over the edge. Your blood count looks like a viral illness, and that's not the usual pattern we see with ketoacidosis. If you had a virus, that would explain why things got so out of hand so fast. You need insulin even more when you're sick."

Laurel drove Jack home knowing their absence and reappearance would be noticed in the tightly knit astronaut community. She helped him into bed before the first knock. She explained to their neighbors that Jack had picked up a stomach virus or maybe food poisoning. The rest of the day was devoted to making Jack drink juice and sport drinks. That evening he made it from the bed to the shower. Laurel was waiting with a towel when he turned off the water. She wrapped it around him and held him.

"I'm sorry, Jack. I should have been taking care of you instead of feeling sorry for myself."

"It's my disease," he said slowly. "It's ironic. When I got home on Friday, I didn't feel like a diabetic for the first time in four years. They let me fly Friday night. Colonel Asher let me go up in an T-38. I guess the powers that be are right. When you let diabetics fly, they crash."

"No," Laurel said adamantly. "You have a condition. We let it be a disease, Jack. We won't let it happen again." He scared her by not echoing her words. Before the night was over, she knew it was because he felt so much at the mercy of diabetes.

The next day, he called in sick for the first time, and Laurel had the uneasy feeling he was ready to quit the program. She called Samson when Jack was in the shower, and then she called their pastor. Both called Jack later that afternoon. Samson's call was the turning point because self pity was not an option when speaking with Samson Driver. When Jack hung up the phone, he seemed to make an effort to overcome the lingering depression. Colonel Asher appeared at 7 P.M. Laurel admitted him with trepidation.

"I heard you were sick," the colonel said as he met Jack in the living room. "I wondered what had happened until Stuart and Russell both had to leave early today because of a stomach virus. Apparently Jim Graham's whole family had it on Sunday. Are you all right?"

"Diabetes and throwing up don't mesh well," Jack admitted. He relaxed visibly in knowing a virus might have sent three men who weren't diabetic to their beds. "I have to tell you, I ended up in the hospital on Saturday because of it. I know you'll have to address it."

"Why?" the colonel asked simply. "Jack, we used to look for perfect physical specimens, and we left a lot of men with the right stuff grounded. The chances of you getting the stomach flu in space aren't that great. If you're willing to take the risk, I'm willing to let you take it. How long will it take you to get over this?"

"I'll be in tomorrow," Jack said with relief.

"Good," the colonel said. "Report to Jeff Scales' team. Phil Slaydon had emergency surgery for an obstructed bowel yesterday. He has cancer. I need a mission specialist to take his place. You have the best competency testing on the shuttle arm. The launch date is January 4."

Laurel felt her heart turn over in her chest, but she forced herself to smile because she loved her husband. In her mind, the countdown began that minute.

Chapter 21

Going home wasn't an option that holiday season. Jack was training in a way he had never trained. He was training more than fourteen hours a day in the simulators for a launch that was four weeks away. Their crew threw Jack a going-up party on the third weekend of the month, complete with a shuttle-shaped cake and sparkling grape juice. They presented him with a series of good luck charms and gave Laurel a tee shirt, which read "My husband is the world's sweetest astronaut."

"You guys are ruining my reputation," Jack commented good naturedly. "There are a whole bunch of definitions of sweet. One and only one applies."

"I don't know," Laurel said as she kissed him. "I think you are pretty sweet." She pulled him under Danielle Chou's mistletoe and kissed him in front of everyone.

"Okay," Jack conceded. "I'll allow two definitions."

They finished the night playing Handel's *Messiah*. They had a chamber ensemble as many of the crew members and their spouses were musically inclined. Jim Graham ran across the street and returned with a guitar while Danielle and Laurel were pouring coffee.

"Okay, we've had enough heavy music," Jim told them. "Let's see if you guys really know how to play." They started out with the Eagles and finished with Elton John's "Rocket Man." Laurel had never heard Jack play that kind of piano, and she applauded along with the others. Eight astronauts with varying degrees of talent sang the last chorus while their wives took pictures.

At 2 A.M. Jack and Laurel walked home wrapped in each other's arms. Once inside their front door Laurel was swept off her feet and carried to bed. When she could catch her breath, she sat up and looked down at Jack's face with barely hidden regrets for his eminent departure.

"What are you thinking?" he asked her.

"My husband is the world's sweetest astronaut," she smiled.

"Let's just keep that between the two of us, shall we?" He held her face in his hands. "The rumor mill has it that I was pushed to the head of the line because I'm a Native American. I don't know how I feel about that if it's true."

"Be honored," Laurel said defiantly. "You didn't try to break line by being Navajo. We thought it might even hold you back. I think that would be another example of God closing a door and opening a launch window, Jackson. Just keep reminding yourself you would have already been up if you hadn't gotten diabetes. Have a little bit of Native American pride and figure this doesn't begin to make up for how many times our people haven't been allowed to stand in the line at all. Just smile and take your window of opportunity."

"The only window I care about is the one that brings me home to you," he said quietly. "Are you going to be okay? It's starting to seem real to me, so it has be feel that way to you."

"It always has felt real to me, Jack." She caressed his

hair. "When I've been scared, I've prayed for God to only let it happen if you'd be safe. I think this is His answer, so I'll be all right." She reached into the nightstand drawer and took out a package. "This is your early Christmas, keep-you-safe present," she said. He opened the box and found a silver cross without a chain. While Jack was still wondering how to wear it, Laurel attached it to his medical identification necklace. Then she kissed him and was pulled into a very intense embrace.

"I thought I wanted to fly on the shuttle more than anything else until I met you, Laurel Fairlight. It can't compete with you." Knowing he was telling her the truth made it easier to forget how soon he would be leaving.

Their house began filling with relatives the week before Christmas. Samson and Olivia arrived from Arizona, and Laurel's father and Mary arrived from North Carolina. It was that week when Laurel missed her period for the second time in her life. She was hopeful as she held her breath and prepared Christmas food. In the evening, they all talked about how exciting the launch would be. Laurel was glad for the company because Jack rarely made it home before midnight. When Laurel went to the grocery store on Christmas Eve day, she bought a pregnancy test and then struggled to hide her elation when it was positive.

Jack was home for Christmas Eve night and most of Christmas Day. He devoted that time to Laurel except for when he had to pack for the journey to Kennedy Space Center in Florida. He was scheduled to leave Christmas night, and the time passed all too quickly. Late Christmas Eve, Laurel sat on the bed and watched him pack. She prayed for the courage to let him go. When midnight ushered in Christmas Day, Jack handed her a package.

"Merry Christmas, Laurel," he said. "I know this

has been a rotten time for me to get the nod, but I wanted
you to know I've still been thinking of you more than
Discovery. Open it."

She unwrapped the package and found a beautiful
diamond engagement ring. "Isn't this a little late?" she
smiled. "We got married almost eighteen months ago.
It's my best memory."

"Mine, too," he said as he slipped the ring onto her
finger. "This is to remind you that I asked you to spend
the rest of your life with me. I'll be back to make sure
you keep your word."

"I'm making your main present," she said shyly. "It
isn't ready yet"

"That's okay," he said. "We can have part two of
Christmas when I land. Do I at least get a hint?"

"Actually we're making it together." She smiled.
"I'm pregnant, Jack. We're going to have a baby."

It was a moment when his response carried her
through the sorrow of their parting. He held her in his
arms and couldn't speak for several minutes. She could
feel he was too moved to voice his feelings, and then he
said, "I'll never be able to thank God enough for sending
you into my life." He held her face in his hands. "Come
to Florida for the launch. I need you to be there. There's
a charter plane for the families. I know you're scared,
but you could get Mary and Larry to come with you.
Can you come?"

She had to swallow hard, but she couldn't have said
no. They had lived their life on wings and prayers, and
she knew it was time to let her faith carry her. "I couldn't
let you go without me."

He kissed her, and they ended up in bed making
love with fevered emotions. The tension was broken
when they both reached for Jack's insulin pump at the
same time. After it was reconnected, they laughed and
held each other, pretending the next night wouldn't be
separating them.

Christmas Day was a desperate day when she just had to keep her hands on her husband. They were together all that day until the car came to pick him up just after supper. Later, when she could ask, she learned he was flying with the mission commander, Jeff Scales, in a T-38. Everyone followed Jack to the door, giving Laurel and Jack no privacy until the last moment.

"Call me when you get there," she begged.

"I will. Laurel, take care of yourself. I think I'm more worried about you than you're worried about me."

"Not possible." She pressed her face against his chest and then kissed him. "I love you, Jack Driver, and I'll be there. Look for me."

"Always," he promised. He kissed her again and walked away because it was what they had to do. The telephone was ringing when Laurel returned to the kitchen, and she answered it. It was General Driver, and even his voice was a shock. They had not heard from Jack's father since the terrible long distance argument he and Jack had fifteen months earlier. In an effort to keep the lines of communication open, Laurel had sent monthly pictures and letters to the general. They had never been answered.

"Laurel, this is J.R. Driver. I was hoping to catch Jack. I didn't know he was going on Discovery until tonight."

"I'm sorry, sir," Laurel said slowly. "He just left for Florida, but I know he would want to talk to you. He still misses you." Larry Wolfe recognized the significance of the conversation and took his daughter's hand reassuringly.

"I miss him," the general admitted slowly. "Every day I feel it more. If I came to the launch, would I be welcome, Laurel? I'd be coming alone."

"I know he would be very happy if you came, sir. We're going on January 3. We'll be at the hotel on the base, if you want to meet us there."

"I will," he vowed. "When you speak to Jack, tell him I'm really proud of him. Tell him I'll be praying for him."

"I will, sir. Good night." She knew that vote of confidence would make the dream even better for Jack, but Laurel still couldn't draw a deep breath as she hung up the telephone.

She sat in the living room and told her parents and Jack's aunt and uncle about the baby. They prayed together for Jack and the baby before going to bed. In the emptiness of their bedroom, Laurel could sleep only when she put one of Jack's shirts over his pillow and pressed her face against it. The telephone rang just as she was starting to doze, and she snatched it up.

"Jack?"

"Oh, no," said a vaguely familiar voice. "This isn't Jack, but he'll soon be right here in bed with me. I'll make him forget all about you, Laurel. I'll make him remember what it was like to make love with a woman and not a little slut." Laurel slammed down the phone, but it rang again almost immediately. She was afraid not to answer because she knew Jack would call. So, apparently, did the caller.

"I know what turns him on. I know what he can't resist, and I'll make him forget you. I've been waiting for this chance, and now he'll be mine."

Laurel was shaking so hard that she could barely hang up the telephone. When it rang again, she prayed it would be Jack.

"He's here now, you know. I've got him in my bed, and I'm sure he's not thinking of anything except my hands. He's mine now, Laurel, and he'll be mine forever."

"Stop it!" Laurel cried out. "Don't call here again or I'll have the call traced."

Laurel slammed down the receiver and held her breath, dreading its next ring. Her heart was beginning to slow when the telephone rang again.

"I told you not to call again," she raged as she answered the phone.

"Laurel?" Jack's voice said. "What's wrong?"

"I had an obscene phone call," she stammered. "I guess it just got to me."

"After we hang up, take it off the hook," Jack said. "Leave the cell phone on in case I can't stand not talking to you. We made it to the space center without a hitch. I'm going to get some sleep because they want us in the shuttle at 5 A.M."

"Test your sugar," Laurel said as she thought of his face.

"I did. It's 119." He sat back on the hard single bed and realized he didn't want to hang up. "You know this is kind of anticlimactic after what you told me. I couldn't stop thinking about it all the way here. What do you think we should name the baby?"

"If it's a boy, I was thinking of Lucien, and if it's a girl, I don't know."

"I was going to ask you what you'd think of Lucien Lawrence Driver," he said. "Call your doctor tomorrow and get an appointment as soon as you can. You don't hurt anywhere, do you?"

"I'm a little sick to my stomach. Everything else feels good." She thought her heart was breaking, but she knew she wouldn't ever let him know. "I'll take an appointment any time after January 11. I'm not going without my husband."

"For my sake, call tomorrow and remind them what happened the first time. If anything happens to you while I am in space—"

"Nothing will happen," Laurel reassured him. The concern in his voice warmed her. "I'll call and tell them. If they think I need to come in, I'll go, but there isn't any pain."

"I love you, Laurel," he vowed. A knock at the door

signaled an end to his free time. "They're telling us to turn in. Sleep well."

"I love you, Jack. Good night." She hung up the telephone and promised herself she'd buy an answering machine the next day. It was a long time before she could sleep. During the night she remembered she hadn't told Jack about his father's call.

Samson and his wife left for Arizona the next day. They were hosting a launch party for other interested Navajos on the reservation. Larry and Mary helped Laurel clean her house and pack for her trip. She drove to a nearby store to buy an answering machine, which also contained a caller ID feature. Her father installed it for her.

The days seemed interminable as she waited to get on the plane for Florida. The nights were unbearable because the phone rang over and over again with the caller ID announcing call blocked. All the machine recorded was a receiver being slammed down.

She was a basket case when Jack called, but she managed to hide her feelings. She was afraid if she told anyone, word of it might somehow reach Jack and put him at risk. She was able to keep her secret, but it showed in her haggard face. When two of the wives of teammates appeared on New Year's Eve to wish her luck, they were concerned.

"Hey, you'll be the calming voice when they all go up," Angela Hughes reassured her. "Just remember he'll be back home in twelve days. Did you see the paper? He got mentioned more than the others."

"I can't stand to think about it," Laurel managed. "I can't read the paper or listen to the news."

"Laurel, don't make yourself sick," Geneva Bradford urged her. "The shuttle is a lot safer than being a fighter pilot." She was genuinely concerned by Laurel's expression. She put her arm around Laurel. "Honey, what else is wrong? You look like death on a cracker."

"I'm pregnant," Laurel said stoically. "I'm just feeling a little sick. I'll be all right."

She was on her seventh night of limited sleep when
the group drove to the airport and climbed on the
charter flight. She drew immediate attention from all
sides because of the dark circles under her eyes and her
weight loss. She brushed off the well meaning questions. She looked forward to sleeping away from a
telephone. The flight took four hours, but it landed on a
runway looking out over the ocean where Lucien's life
had ended. Laurel had to pray for the strength to walk
calmly into the hotel. General Driver was waiting for
her in the lobby. On seeing him, Lawrence Wolfe put his
arm around Laurel protectively.

The general hesitated and then said, "I saw Jack on
the monitor. He looks great. He looks like he used to
look before he got diabetes. You've been good for him."

Lawrence's posture relaxed slightly, and Laurel
managed a tremulous smile. "He's worked really hard.
No one can know how many hours he's put in."

The general gave her the local newspaper. "He did
the right thing, and I guess this will be his confirmation
of that." He indicated the story on the front page.

Discovery Carries First Navajo Astronaut

Tomorrow's launch of the shuttle Discovery will mark
yet another milestone for NASA. Mission specialist, Dr.
Jackson Driver, is an aerospace engineer and a graduate
of the U.S. Air Force Academy. Two distinctions set Dr.
Driver aside from his colleagues on Discovery. He is a
card-carrying member of the Navajo Nation and the
first Navajo to fly aboard the shuttle. He also jumped
through more than the usual training hoops since he has
had insulin dependent diabetes for the past four years.
He will be the first insulin dependent diabetic to travel
in space. Physicians at NASA plan to record his blood

glucose readings to assess the effects of zero gravity on insulin usage.

Dr. Driver was a fighter pilot in the Air Force for eight years. His service in Operation Desert Storm earned him several decorations. He earned his doctorate in aerospace engineering after leaving military service.

Dr. Driver was interviewed early yesterday after a complete simulation of his satellite deployment task was completed. He stated that his presence on the mission was the answer to his personal prayers. He hopes his service on the shuttle will honor his God and the Navajo people. He also hopes to be seen as an inspiration to diabetics all over the world.

"May I have this?" she asked. "I've been keeping scrapbooks for him."

"I want you to have it. Could we talk? Just you and me?" The general seemed vulnerable and looked more like Jack than Laurel would have thought possible.

"Okay," she said. "I'll be right back, Dad."

General Driver led her to the far side of the lobby and then sat on the edge of a sofa facing his daughter-in-law. He had aged in the past eighteen months; he looked older than fifty-nine. His black hair was heavily peppered with gray, and his face was lined.

"I have a letter for Jack. I know you don't trust me, Laurel. I haven't given you any reason to trust me. You can read it before you give it to Jack. I would have tried to call, but we always end up shouting at each other. I wanted to mail this, but I was afraid he wouldn't read it. I didn't know if I'd be strong enough to see it returned unopened. I love him, and I thought if he knew why I've lived the way I have, it might be easier for him to forgive me.

"I always had a much fairer complexion than my brother. Off the reservation, people were never certain if I was Navajo. When I went into the Air Force, I thought

I would have a better chance of advancing if I passed as white. I'm half Navajo so I could have called myself either race, but my wife was full blooded. Rachel was very upset when she realized what I'd done.

"She registered Jack as a tribal member when he was born, and she made me promise I would change my own status. Because she trusted me to keep my word, she asked me to register Lucien when he was born, and I told her I had but never did. She had been admitted to have our third child when she saw the hospital record and knew I had lied to her about changing my status.

"She was already sick from the pregnancy. They used to call it toxemia. We argued, and her blood pressure went very high. She had a stroke and died that night. Jack and Lucien looked so much like her. Especially Jack. Every time I looked at them, I had to remember why their mother and sister were dead.

"I think I wanted to forget I wasn't white. My brother begged me to come home to find myself after my parents died and again when Rachel died. When Rachel died, we argued. I lost my feeling of belonging to Window Rock after that.

"When I married Charlene, I felt I was a white man. She was ashamed of my sons' color, and I allowed her to shut them out of my life. I didn't know the decision would cost me everything I valued until I lost Lucien and saw Jack walk away. Everything Jack said to me the day of Lucien's funeral was the truth except that I never intended to abandon him.

"The doctors told me he had insulin dependent diabetes, and I went to read about it. The books said it's rare in Native Americans. Jack is more than three quarters Navajo. I knew the disease had come from the white part of me. I thought I had brought the curse of it on him by living the lie of being white. I thought he would die from diabetes and if he had died, it would have been my fault.

"I left because I was afraid of showing my feelings. I never thought he might have needed to know how much I wish it had been me and not him. When Alyssa said she could have him cured, I couldn't think of anything but having the curse removed from his life. I'm sorry for what I did to you, Laurel. Jack still has diabetes, but your medicine has healed him from the curse of it. Rachel always said that love is the great healer.

"Tell Jack that I'm retiring. I'm going to live at Window Rock and see if I can remember how my father wanted me to live. Charlene left me when Jack told everyone about his background. The divorce is already final. It wasn't Jack's fault. She couldn't have left me if she had loved me. She did it because she's a bigot. She used me and abused my sons. Jack and Lucien always saw through her facade. I was a fool.

"Tell Jack I will do anything to earn his forgiveness. I need to be a part of your lives, Laurel. For months, I've been praying you could forgive me. I know you've sent the letters and pictures. I'm grateful. They kept me sane when Charlene left." He bowed his head. "Just try to make Jack understand. Thank you for listening."

"He still loves you, you know," Laurel said. She reached out and put a consoling hand on the general's arm. "More than anything, he wanted you to be proud of him. He isn't going to die from diabetes. We work together to make sure his blood sugar is normal, and his doctor says he doesn't have any signs of damage. We're going to have a baby. If it's a boy, we want to name him Lucien."

"I'm happy for you. Jack thinks I loved Lucien more," the general said. "That isn't true. I loved both of them equally. I love Jack more than my life. He's all I have left, but that hasn't changed how I feel about him. Everything he does makes me proud to call him my son. He doesn't know he's doing what I always dreamed of doing. I know he'll never believe it now, but God knows it's the truth.

"You're very like my Rachel was, Laurel. She did everything in her life with her heart and soul. Keep your family together, Laurel. Nothing is more important than your family. Some of us never know that truth until it's too late." He stood and nodded. "I'll see you at the launch." As he walked away, Laurel felt like running after him, but she knew only Jack could mend the remainder of the fences between him and his father. She went to hotel room, and the call awakened her as soon as she put her head on the pillow.

"You thought you'd leave me in Houston, didn't you, Laurel. Don't you see, I'll be wherever Jack is. I'd forgotten how good he is in bed. You taught him a few things, but he still hasn't forgotten what turns me on. If he misses the shuttle flight, you'll know why."

Laurel slammed down the telephone and left it off the hook as she pressed her face into the pillows. Pounding on the door awakened her from sleep, and she staggered to open it. Lawrence Wolfe caught her and said, "You have to get ready, Laurie. They're taking us over to see the astronauts. You'll get to see Jack."

She changed and did her hair to make certain he would think she was beautiful. She knew a glass wall would be separating them, but just to see him seemed essential. There was a mandatory seven day isolation period for astronauts before a flight. It was a precaution to make certain they weren't exposed to an infection since germs grow faster and are more virulent in space.

Laurel was the first off the bus, and she walked as fast as the guide. When she saw Jack, it was the first sense of relief she had felt in eight days. The same expression was in his eyes. The guide showed her how to talk on the monitor and then left her to what privacy was possible.

"I've missed you so much," they said simultaneously.

"Two great minds with a single thought," Jack smiled. "I couldn't wait for six o'clock. I've been in an adrenaline storm waiting for you. Are you okay? You look tired. Have you lost weight?"

"I'm fine." Of course, they both knew it was a lie. "I've had some morning sickness, and our bed is too big without you in it. Have you been okay?"

"I've had a couple of reactions trying to get used to shots again, but I caught them. I miss my pump. Lila was right. I'd never go back to shots if I didn't have to for the mission. They'll bring the pump to you to keep for me because there didn't seem any point in wearing it today."

"I'll bring it to the landing," she promised. "Dad and Mary are going to stay with me until you land. Your dad's here, Jack."

She almost regretted telling him because of his expression, but he only said, "Don't let him upset you. You have to think about the baby now."

"He didn't upset me," she said. "He told me a lot of things to tell you, mostly that he's sorry for how many times he's hurt you. He said to tell you that he loves you and that you're the only thing he's ever done that made him proud. He said you're doing what he always dreamed of doing. I know he was telling the truth. He's all alone now, Jack. Charlene left him. He wanted you to know he's going to retire and move to Window Rock."

"I wish he had called me or come here," Jack said slowly. "They won't let us take calls tonight." He pressed his hand against the glass, and she pushed her hand against it on the other side. "Tell him the diné have no greater responsibility than finding harmony. Ask him to stay, and when I get back maybe we can find it." He paused.

"Laurel, I'm not saying this because of any bad feelings about tomorrow. I just want you to know how grateful I am that you've let me do this. I know it scares you more than anything, and I know it's been a big sacrifice for you. I needed to fly this mission so much. No one ever needs to believe all their dreams are gone. You gave mine back to me. You and this baby are more than I ever dared to dream about. I want to make sure you know how much I love you. For seven days, I'm going be looking down to find you instead of looking up at the stars. Make sure you're on the tarmac when I get back."

"I'll be right here waiting for you," she vowed. "I love you, Jack. Keep remembering you're doing this for both of us. This has been our dream. Take pictures for me."

"I will." From behind him, a uniformed officer summoned the eight astronauts, and Jack looked back at Laurel. Then he told her he loved her in Navajo and in Cherokee.

"I love you," she said fervently. "You're taking my heart with you."

She didn't want to watch him go out the door, but she couldn't look away. The room on the other side of the glass seemed very empty as the wives left their side of the room. Laurel was sure she wasn't the only one who couldn't sleep that night. She prayed all night and managed to not think of Challenger until she drifted off before dawn and heard the fateful words, "Go for throttle up. Throttling up." The explosion appeared in her mind with perfect clarity, and she sat up gasping. She spent the next hour on her knees praying. Then she showered and dressed. She was in the stands before any of the other wives. The general came to sit beside her, and Laurel took his hand.

"I told Jack what you told me last night. He said to tell you that the diné have no greater responsibility than making harmony in the world. He said he hopes you'll be here when he lands so the two of you can make harmony between yourselves. Please stay."

The general nodded slowly with relief evident on his face. "I'll be here when he lands. Nothing is more important to me than being here."

The countdown proceeded without any delays. Several times, Laurel was tempted to pray that it would be delayed or even canceled.

Her father's arm held her even more tightly when the engines fired. The rockets shuddered as the pressure necessary to overcome gravity was achieved. The shuttle and its three fuel supplies rose slowly into the sky and began picking up speed. Laurel saw it roll and heard the pilot receive permission to throttle up. It accelerated, and her eyes followed it until it was a tiny speck in the blue sky.

She remembered Jack talking about the g force making the astronauts feel like they were being pushed through their seats. She knew that force couldn't be any greater than the pressure in her chest as she watched the shuttle disappear from view.

She had to sit down before she could face the walk out among reporters who still considered NASA newsworthy. She was their favorite target because Jack had given them a new angle for their stories. She smiled and told everyone she was praying for a successful mission and a safe return.

In her room, she threw up and spent an hour praying before she could gather her emotions.

Chapter 22

Lawrence and Mary moved into Laurel's suite to take care of her. By that afternoon Lawrence had tolerated all the telephone calls he could stand. He left Mary standing guard over the telephone while Laurel slept. He went to seek out General Driver. The general answered his knock and invited Lawrence into his room.

"I'd hoped I would have the chance to apologize to you," the general told Lawrence. "I mistreated your daughter, and even knowing what I did, she forgave me. She's been a blessing for me and my son."

Lawrence sat down at the table and said, "Laurel is a good wife to Jack. She lives for him." He paused. "I believe Jack's ex-wife is causing a problem again. Someone has been calling Laurel day and night for the last eight days. They say terrible things to her. It's a terrific stress, and I'm worried about her since she's pregnant. Jack told us you helped make Alyssa stop calling when they first married. I've come to ask your help for Laurel."

"I don't know if I can this time," the general said. "Alyssa's father was controlling her, but he died three

months ago. I haven't seen her for the past year and a
half. Doesn't Jack have a restraining order against her?"

"Laurel told me it may have expired. They hadn't
heard from her, and Laurel doesn't even know where
the paperwork is. We can't take out a new one when
Jack isn't here unless we have proof she is the culprit."

"We'll call the space agency," General Driver said.
"They'll help us protect Laurel. The last thing they want
is a wife getting sick when her husband is in space." He
picked up his coat. "Let's take Laurel to administration
and see what can be done."

Laurel was still sleeping when Lawrence and the
general returned to her room, but the telephone rang as
they came into the suite. Mary nodded to Lawrence, and
they answered simultaneously. The general listened to
Lawrence's line as Mary said, "Hello."

"Laurel, I saw you at the launch. That was a nice
dress, but you know Jack spends more money on my
clothes. He probably spends more time taking off my
clothes."

"Alyssa, stop calling," the general said. "We know
it's you, and I'm going to the police and NASA. Jack has
made it clear he doesn't want to see you."

The response was a series of vile epitaphs that even
embarrassed the two men. The general gestured to
Mary, and they both hung up their receivers.

"We need to record the next call," the general said
grimly. "I know it's Alyssa because I know her voice,
but we need proof." He dialed the space agency and
asked for security. Laurel was awake when the security
police arrived. She described all the phone calls, wring-
ing her hands as she did. Mary and Lawrence kept their
arms around her until the questioning ended.

"It might be better if we just move you to another
hotel, Mrs. Driver," the guard suggested. "We'll plant a
guard with caller ID in here and trace the next call."

There was a knock, and the general answered it. A

florist with a dozen roses was at the door. "I have a delivery for Mrs. Laurel Driver."

The flowers were from Jack who had obviously placed the order prior to the launch. The card read, "Day one. Only six more until I see you again. I love you. Jack." His words helped her make a decision.

"I want to stay here," Laurel said. "I just won't answer the phone."

"I'll arrange for the hotel to change the number," the general said. "These calls are very disturbing," he said to the guard. "You will take them seriously?"

"Yes, sir," the guard replied. "We're on it. It will be better if you don't leave Mrs. Driver alone at any time. We'll keep someone here around the clock."

Laurel and her parents decided to take a walk on the beach that afternoon. They were trailed by security. They remained on the beach until the stars came out over the ocean.

"He seems so far away," Laurel said under her breath. "I keep thinking it isn't real. I wish I could hear his voice."

"I never thought of how hard this part must be," Mary said. "Like Jack's card said, it's only six more days now. We need to get some sleep, Laurie. Let's go to bed."

The attendant at the front desk called out to them as they reentered the hotel. "Mrs. Driver, we have a package for you. It's from your husband."

Laurel was afraid of what the package might be until she recognized Jack's handwriting. She opened it when they were in their room and found his pump, a cassette player and a tape. She placed the tape in the tape deck and sat down with the headphones over her ears.

"Hi, babe. I was thinking you might want to hear my voice by now. I sure wish I could hear yours. I made a tape for every day except the day we land. Then you get

the real thing. I can't tell you everything about the
mission, but tonight we'll be getting into our final orbit
and preparing to deploy the satellite we brought. That's
when I get to go to work. I'm going to have to work
really hard to focus on my job and not to think of you
and my Christmas present. If it's a girl, what would you
think of Miriam Rachel after our mothers? I keep wondering if there has ever been another joint Navajo-
Cherokee production. I love you, Laurel. Don't be surprised when you get something to make you remember
me every day. Sleep well, and please dream about me
and the littlest Driver." She could sleep when she was
listening to his voice, and she played the tape until she
could almost forget he wasn't with her.

The space program had become less open to the
media because of the classified nature of some missions.
Wives were no longer given radios for listening to daily
life in space as the Apollo wives had. They were invited
to come to Florida's mission control every evening and
watch what was happening inside Discovery.

Laurel had received a pair of gold earrings shaped
like half moons along with a second tape. Seeing Jack on
the screen was the best gift of all. He and the other
astronauts were floating unrestrained through the
shuttle's cabin and tossing weightless food to each other.
Three of the other families were in attendance, and
Laurel thought the other four men looked sad to know
they didn't have visitors. Each of the astronauts who
had family listening had a turn speaking into the camera. Jack spoke to Laurel in Cherokee, provoking some
good-natured harassment. Laurel blushed and smiled
because his words meant, "you're the brightest star in
my sky."

"Before she asks you," he said to the microphone,
"my blood sugars are great. Activity doesn't do much
when you're weightless. I can't wait to send a logbook to
Dr. Carpenter and Dr. Jarman."

Too quickly his turn at the microphone was over, and Laurel had to be content to watch his animated face. "He speaks Cherokee well now," Lawrence said. "I hope they will record something for his tribe to see."

"We've made a tape," one of the men told them. "He said greetings to the Navajo in their language and held up the tribal seal. We sent it to Window Rock this morning. He's a pretty good linguist, isn't he?"

The controllers turned off the video screen at 10 P.M. and told the astronauts to turn in for the night. As the visitors walked back to the hotel, Laurel couldn't bring herself to look at the stars. Five more days seemed an eternity. The general joined them in the lobby and rode with them up the elevator.

"I spoke to Samson," he said. "He received the tape, and they've played it all over the reservation. I asked him to send a copy so you could take it home to the Cherokee."

"That would be good," Lawrence said. "The children need to know they have the power to do anything."

The elevator door opened on the fifth floor, and Laurel saw a man in the hallway turning slowly toward them. Before she could see more, General Driver threw himself over her and took all of them to the ground. Laurel heard a loud pop as she fell, but she couldn't see anything except the dark blue of General Driver's uniform. She didn't know they had been fired on. She didn't know her father-in-law was mortally wounded until the elevator reopened on the ground floor and they were surrounded by guards. Laurel crawled from under General Driver, thinking he was still trying to protect her. When she turned him over, his eyes told her he was dying. She had never realized his eyes could be as mesmerizing as Jack's.

"Tell Jack," he pleaded. "Tell him that I love him."

"No," she said as she grasped his hands. "You can't

leave him. He still needs you. Don't leave him."

The general held onto her hands, and his hands felt like Jack's hands. He lost consciousness before help arrived, but Laurel still held his hands and prayed for him. Paramedics came in a blare of sirens, and the general was taken to the base hospital. The guards surrounded Laurel and her parents, shielding them from the curious and the reporters.

Laurel was bruised from the fall but otherwise unharmed. Learning she was pregnant, the doctors checked her carefully at the hospital before they would release her. No one else suffered injuries from the attack.

When she could pull herself together, Laurel called Samson Driver. She made no effort to locate Charlene and wasn't surprised when she was told the general's military records listed Jack as his next of kin. In Jack's absence, Laurel signed permission for emergency surgery. General Driver was in surgery most of the night and on a ventilator when he came out. Colonel Asher flew in by T-38 and met with Laurel and her parents.

"I have to ask you to make a hard decision, Laurel," the colonel said quietly. "I don't think Jack should know until he lands. He has to stay focused more than the others. If he doesn't and anything happens with his diabetes, there isn't a doctor up there. You know and I know that stress is a big player for him. He took a very limited amount of predrawn insulin, and he could need too much of it and run out. If his diabetes causes him problems while he's in space, he won't be allowed to remain in the program on the active astronaut roster."

"Can they hear the news reports there?" Lawrence asked.

"I've radioed the commander, Jeff Scales, and asked him to make sure no newscasts of any kind are played. He wasn't told why, and he knows it won't do any good to ask. They'll all suspect something has happened to a family member, but none of them will know whose family member, so they'll try to keep each other from worrying. I've been on the wire with the Associated Press, and they're cutting us some slack for the time being. They won't if General Driver dies. I'm praying he won't, but God doesn't always see things the way we do."

Laurel closed her eyes in prayer. She knew the colonel was absolutely correct in his thinking, and she made her decision to protect Jack. "Don't tell him. They've had terrible arguments, but they love each other. This will be as hard as Lucien's death."

Laurel was supported by her parents as she sat with the general and read the Bible to him. They were all surprised when he seemed to want her there. The nurses told her it was the only time he seemed comfortable. Before the end of the second day, Laurel knew why J.R. Driver had risked his life to save hers, as if the general had told her himself. When they were alone, she spoke to him and promised she would make sure Jack understood how he had felt.

"You took care of me to tell him how much you love him," she said. "I'll make sure he knows." He squeezed her hand while his eyes expressed his gratitude.

When Samson arrived, he was immediately brought to the intensive care unit. Laurel was sitting with the general and he held her hand with all his strength as Samson approached. Samson took his other hand and said, "I've come to beg your forgiveness. I should have come much sooner. I wasn't strong enough, J.R. Forgive me. I need to have my brother back."

Tears ran down J.R. Driver's face, and he shook with the effort of crying. Samson held his hand in the only embrace possible to him. Tears were on his face as he and Laurel formed a prayer circle around the bed.

The doctors came that evening to explain to Samson the extent of the general's injuries. The family knew the report was grim because they were taken outside of the intensive care unit for the conference. The doctors were thorough in their explanations. A 9mm bullet had lacerated the general's liver and caused irreparable damage to his right kidney. His left kidney had failed due to prolonged low blood pressure and the numerous transfusions he had required. He was holding fluid because of renal failure and that had kept his lungs from functioning normally.

The doctors felt he still had a fair chance of surviving his injuries, but they were guarded in their prognosis for his kidney function. It seemed likely that Jack's father might suffer from permanent renal failure and require permanent dialysis or a transplant. The transplant option was limited by the general's age and the availability of Native American organs. Samson immediately offered one of his kidneys for transplant. Later that evening, he explained to the general everything they had been told.

"I have told them you can have one of my kidneys, Jay," Samson told the general. It was the first time Laurel had heard the general's childhood nickname.

The general shook his head at the offer.

"If you are Navajo, then I am the head of the family," Samson said. "It is my right to give this to you. The doctors are making the tests to see if we are compatible. I've told them that we must be compatible by blood because we were never compatible by nature." He was rewarded by the general's attempt at a smile.

"If I give this to you, Jack will not be tempted to offer his. It would be dangerous for him because of the diabetes. This is the best choice and, if it's God's will, we will be compatible."

Laurel breathed a sigh of relief when the general nodded slowly. He asked for paper. With a trembling hand, he wrote, "It's your decision." They all let themselves believe everything would be alright in time. It was the only way to bear the waiting for his recovery and for Jack's return.

The hotel employees brought Laurel a gift and a new tape from Jack every day, and she walked under guard to watch him every evening. On the tenth of January, the hired assassin was captured as he tried to cross into Mexico. He implicated a blond woman who had called herself Allison and picked Alyssa Driver's picture out of a series of unmarked photographs. An all-points bulletin was issued for Alyssa. She seemed to have vanished.

The general stabilized on the ventilator, and some progress was made in weaning him off. His left kidney continued to be nonfunctional, but the tissue typing proved he and Samson were a perfect match. They began testing Samson to clear him as a donor.

On January 10 when the doctors were again discussing the timing of transplant, J.R. Driver had a massive heart attack. Clot-breaking drugs couldn't be used because of his recent surgery, and the cardiologist was unable to reopen the occluded coronary. The general went into congestive heart failure and required maximal drug and balloon pump support to stay alive. Another family conference was called.

"He's in God's hands now," the trauma surgeon said. "There's almost no chance he'll survive with so much against him, and I don't think he would want to survive. His heart is irreparably damaged. He doesn't have enough pumping surface in his heart to come off life support."

"How long can you keep him alive?" Samson asked.

"Maybe twenty-four hours with luck and blessings," the surgeon replied.

"He needs to see his son," Samson said. "Jack needs to see him. Please do what you can to make that happen."

Samson was with his brother almost every moment for the twenty-four hours that followed. J.R. seemed aware only when Jack's name was mentioned, and Laurel knew he was waiting to see his son.

The weather cooperated despite heavy winter storms to the north. Discovery made its primary window and landed on schedule in the afternoon on January 11.

If they had let her, Laurel would have run across the tarmac to hold onto Jack. She stayed with the other families and kept praying for his father to remain alive. Colonel Asher met the astronauts as they climbed out of the shuttle, and they froze at his approach. His presence meant a serious problem and something personal. They had all known a crisis was a possibility when their news connection had been terminated.

When Colonel Asher reached Jack, Laurel saw terror on her husband's face. She ran toward the shuttle crew until Jack saw her. He reached out to her with fear and grief marked on his face. Laurel threw her arms around him and held onto him as they were ushered to a limousine and driven to the hospital. In the car, he held Laurel while she tried to tell him what happened.

"It was evident to us that something had happened. They wouldn't allow us to listen to the news, so we knew there was something they didn't want us to hear. When I saw Colonel Asher coming toward me, I panicked. I was terrified something had happened to you." His face spoke his agony. "God forgive me. I was relieved it was my father. What do the doctors say?"

"He's dying, Jack," Laurel said slowly. "They say he isn't going to live." She could feel the tension in his hand, but his face seemed frozen. Later, she knew he was just stunned and unbelieving.

"Do you have insulin?" he asked her. "I ran out this morning, and I'm going high. I can feel it."

Laurel had brought his pump. She had loaded with Humalog and had attached a new infusion set that morning. She unzipped his flight suit to his waist to put the site in place. His chest was covered with telemetry leads because his physical response to space had been intensively monitored. He jerked them loose to give Laurel room to work. He stuck his finger as Laurel connected the line and then gave him two units. The glucose reading was 425.

"I'd better give another ten," he told her. After making the statement, he sat immobile. Laurel bolused him through the pump again and zipped his suit. Then she held him until the car stopped at the emergency entrance.

Laurel had prayed for the general to live until Jack could be with him. The nurse looked relieved when they entered the intensive care unit, and she ushered them into the room. Samson was holding one of J.R.'s hands when Jack reached his father's side. The general opened his eyes as if he knew his son were there. Jack gripped his father's other hand. Their gaze transcended words.

"I love you, Dad," Jack said. "Stay with me. We can put everything else behind us. It was just words. I've always been your son. I've always loved you, Dad."

Laurel saw the general's hand tighten on Jack's, and two tears ran down J.R.'s cheeks. His lips moved around the ventilator tube almost imperceptibly, but Jack, Samson, and Laurel knew he was saying, "I love you," to his son. As if his last task was complete, his monitored heartbeat began slowing. Frantically Jack looked at the monitor and grabbed his father's hand with both his hands.

"Laurel told me how you feel. I forgive you, Dad. I love you. I need you to be here for me. You've got to hang on." J.R. looked at Samson and then at Jack. The restraints had been removed from his wrists, and he tried to put Samson and Jack's hands together but lacked the strength even for that movement.

"I'll take care of him," Samson vowed. "He'll take care of me."

Slowly the general's hand relaxed between Jack's

hands. His eyes were on Jack as the monitor recorded his death.

Samson leaned across the bed from the confines of his wheelchair and closed his brother's eyes. He was crying as he prayed the twenty-third Psalm in Navajo. After several moments of emotional shock, Jack's tears fell on his father's hand. It took a long time before they had regrouped enough to leave the intensive care unit. Colonel Asher was in the foyer with the guards.

"You'll want him buried at Arlington, won't you?" the colonel asked.

"No," Jack said slowly. "He needs to go home. My mother is buried in Arizona in the military cemetery, and that's where he needs to be."

NASA closed its protective arms around Jack and kept the media away from him that night. He was too upset to eat, sleep, or deal with his blood sugar. Laurel kept watch over him while thanking God for the chance to do it. She insisted he take a shower and then ordered a yogurt drink from room service to make sure he had something to eat. She felt triumphant when she managed to massage his back until he fell asleep. He wasn't able to talk about what had happened or even ask questions. He was just doing what had to be done. Laurel did her part and made sure his blood sugar was down to 120 before she could rest.

The story broke with the morning news and papers with the headlines "Astronaut's Father Assassinated." Jack kept his composure and signed everything Laurel had consented to. The debriefing team did a very limited exit interview. Jack had kept excellent records during the flight, allowing them to skip what wasn't absolutely necessary. Samson and Olivia stayed with Jack, and Laurel's parents stood with her as they struggled through discussions of coffins and the funeral service.

In deference to General Driver's years of service, his body and his family were flown to Arizona on a military jet. They were accompanied by a military guard. That evening Jack and Laurel were in a funeral home in Window Rock surrounded by well wishers. After several hours, the last people who were paying their respects departed. Then, Jack had to keep standing beside the coffin. Laurel stood beside him with her hand on Jack's arm.

"I wish I had been stronger," he said slowly. "I wish I had put the past behind me and just loved him because he was my father."

"If you feel up to hearing what your father said, I'd like to share it with you."

"Tell me, Laurel," Jack said.

"He said he hid the truth about his Native American bloodline because he was afraid you and Lucien wouldn't ever advance. He told me he had promised your mother he would correct the part of his military record that indicated he was white.

"When she was admitted to the hospital the last time, she found out he hadn't kept his word. When they argued, your mother's blood pressure elevated to a dangerous level and she had a stroke.

"Your father blamed himself. He said you and Lucien looked like her, and every time he looked at you, he remembered he had caused her death. He was so sorry, Jack. All he wanted was for you to forgive him, and he said he would give his life to have you forgive him. That's what he did. The police said I would have been killed. He died to save me and our baby, Jack."

Jack wiped his eyes, which was a futile gesture, and then he bent and kissed his father's forehead. "I forgive you, Dad. I love you."

Laurel urged him to leave so he could get some sleep. She used her pregnancy as an excuse. Before the funeral, he had lost six pounds on top of the four he had lost in space.

The funeral was attended by senators, ambassadors,

and numerous other dignitaries. Charlene and her
daughters came. They were shunned by everyone. Jack
wore his air force uniform and stood at attention, salut-
ing his father as the coffin was lowered into the ground.
He was presented with the flag. Everywhere he went
reporters wanted to interview him, and the camera
crews focused on him. The media attention drew his
stepmother and stepsisters' attention.

Laurel had prayed for Jack to hold up under the
stress. She understood the agony of burying a parent.
She knew what Jack could voice was only the surface of
deep waters. She was incredibly proud of him when
Charlene oozed her way through the crowd and touched
his arm with a gloved hand. She dabbed at her powdered cheeks with a lace handkerchief.

"He was the great love of my life, Jackson. I think we
might have reconciled our differences in time. I know
you can't understand, but I do hope you'll remember
how many years I was your mother," Charlene said.

"I do understand, Charlene," Jack said quietly. "I've
always understood your feelings. I won't ever forget
what you did for me, Lucien, and our father. Eventually
God will give me the strength to pray for you and your
shallow, narcissistic clones. I just don't have that desire
today. Don't make the mistake of saying we're related
because I'll be quick to set the record straight. Look for
another funeral plot because I won't allow your kind to
be buried here." He took Laurel's hand and walked
away from all the years when he had been a prisoner of
emotions he hadn't understood.

Jack and Laurel stayed at Samson's house because
Jack felt safe there. It was home. He and Samson talked
long into the night, looking through photograph albums from years before the outside world had intruded
on the serenity of Window Rock. He spent a great deal
of time pouring over photographs from the years when
his father had lived as a Navajo. Jay and Samson Driver

looked very happy in those pictures.

"He always dreamed of being an astronaut," Samson told Jack. "We both did. We'd sit out on the desert and look for the Gemini capsules. Jay was going to apply to the Apollo program. They had loosened the restriction on an astronaut's height then. He told me he withdrew his application when your mother died. He said he knew he couldn't take the risk of making you two boys orphans. He loved you, Jack. He just lost himself when our parents and Rachel died."

"Did he talk to you, Samson?" Jack asked. "Before this happened, did he talk to you?"

"He had been calling me every week for almost six months," Samson replied. "The first time he called, he spoke as if we had never been separated. By the third call, he said you had told him how you wished you could have your brother back for fifteen minutes. He said he knew then it was a sign that he and I needed to be brothers again. He was going to retire and come back here to live. He just wanted to make his peace with you first. He believed your diabetes and then Lucien's was a curse on him for hiding who he was. I prayed with him before he went to see the launch. I hope he had forgiven himself at the end."

"It's not a curse," Jack said slowly. "In some ways it's a blessing, like you said it could be. It's forced me to live every day for what God gives me. I know I'll be able to keep fighting to make life good. You have to learn from your mistakes."

"Learn from your father's mistakes," Samson said quietly. "Don't waste your heart on anything other than God, your family, and your people. Martin Luther King said 'if a man hasn't found something worth dying for by the time he's grown, then his life isn't worth living.' God, your people and your family are the only things worth your life." He smiled wryly. "If I could stand, I would hold you in my arms, but you'll have to know I hold you in my heart. For the rest of our lives, I'll be honored if I can be your father."

"For the rest of my life, I'll be honored to be your son." Jack knelt down beside the wheelchair and embraced his uncle.

Chapter 23

Jack and Laurel lived in a strange cocoon the rest of the winter. NASA kept military guards at their home and gave Jack an escort back and forth to the base to complete a full debriefing from his flight. After a month of feeling helpless at Alyssa's mercy, Jack began to fight back and took out a Texas gun permit. Every Saturday, he and Laurel spent two hours at the firing range. He insisted Laurel take a self-defense course. Jack enrolled in an advanced taekwondo course to recall the skills he had learned early in his air force career. Driven by the need to not feel vulnerable, he became competent in karate.

Jack had leave for ten more days after the funeral. During that respite they went to the obstetrician for their first appointment. Laurel's due date was August 28, and the ultrasound showed them a tiny form with a beating heart. It was a much needed celebration of life that carried Jack through the months of going through his father's possessions. Among the items were a box of unmailed letters written to him, a scrapbook of accomplishments of Jack and Lucien that their father had been collecting for years, and two boxes of Rachel Driver's belongings.

His father's divorce had been final for a month before his death, so Jack was the sole heir. He inherited a sizable number of assets when the will was probated, but Laurel knew he valued the letter J.R. Driver had given her more than anything else he received. That letter and the others in the box served to heal the deep rift that had been between Jack and his father for twenty years.

Jack,

I wish I could undo all my mistakes, but there have been too many over too many years. Your mother was my life, Jack. I would have died for her, and if not for you and Lucien I could not have gone on after her death. She died because of me, Jack.

My father left the marines because he wasn't allowed to advance. The code talkers followed the Navajo legend that said the diné would someday save the world, but they weren't rewarded for their service because they were Indians. I wanted to advance for my father so I called myself white. After you were born, your mother found out that I had chosen to ignore my Navajo blood, and it hurt her deeply. I gave her my word to change my status, but that would have interfered with my goal.

Your mother didn't know I had continued the lie until she was already toxemic from being pregnant with your sister. I should have begged her forgiveness and done as she asked. It was the only thing she ever asked me to do. In pride I argued, and I lost both your mother and your sister. Then I was too much of a coward to admit why they had died. The last day of Rachel's life was the last day I ever knew what it was to be happy. I spent all the years after that hiding from what I had done.

I alienated you and Lucien for a woman who never loved me. Charlene only wanted to be with me for a title a white world gave me. In truth, I never loved her like I loved your mother. Rachel was my heart.

I love you, Jack. You've lived the way I should have lived.

You've been a warrior all your life. Your word has been your honor, and you were never afraid of living or dying for the truth.

I hope and pray your courage will let you forgive me. More than anything else I want to be a part of your life and the lives of Laurel and your children. I don't have the right to ask you so I'm begging you to forgive me for wasting so many years. I'll be praying for God to let you give me this gift until I see your face again.

Your father,
Jack Roman Driver

Jack kept the letter in his Bible and read it often that first month.

In May, Jack and Laurel returned to Florida so Laurel could testify in the trial of the assassin who had killed the general. The hired gunman was found guilty and sentenced to death, but there was little satisfaction in the verdict because the person ultimately responsible was still free. Alyssa continued to elude capture despite an nationwide campaign to seek her out.

The federal agents met with Jack and Laurel while they were in Florida. Jack had requested that the meeting take place at NASA with some of his superiors present. The information they were given did nothing to provide closure.

"Alyssa Driver was in a private mental hospital until last August," the federal agent said. "Her father had her committed, and we've been able to obtain her records because of your father's murder. She was diagnosed with psychotic depression and mixed substance abuse. She was released because she was stable on medication and her father's death ended the payment of her bills.

"She was obsessed with you, Dr. Driver, throughout her treatment. Her family denies knowing anything about her whereabouts, but they aren't friendly to your cause. Apparently she convinced them that you were abusive to her and that you left her. Of course, your divorce papers are very clear in that regard."

"You're saying she won't stop," Jack said slowly. "Is that what you're saying?"

"We have a psychiatrist working this case who has evaluated the file. He doesn't think she'll stop until we catch her or until one of you is dead." The agent's voice was matter of fact.

"You've got to think of a way to get her," Jack said with perceptible anxiety. "I've got a wife and baby to think about. You can use me as bait. Whatever it takes, I'm willing to do it."

"Jack, that isn't necessary," Colonel Asher said. "You're a valuable asset to NASA. We don't want you put at risk. These gentlemen can take care of the situation." He looked at the agents. "We'll protect Dr. Driver and his family. Your job is to incarcerate Alyssa Driver. Be aware NASA will use its considerable influence to make certain this is a priority case for you."

This was an unexpected and terrifying blow. Laurel and Jack returned home and entered a counseling program for crime victims. Meeting with their pastor was their greatest solace. Every day and night they prayed together for Alyssa's capture. Aside from that, they made every effort to forget she was still a threat.

In June, all the media attention had died down. Colonel Asher caught Jack on the first Friday night of the month and began a series of Friday night flights with him in agency T-38's. Jack was religious about two preflight procedures. He always called Laurel, and he always suspended his pump and tested his blood sugar. He didn't know why Colonel Asher wanted him to have actual flight time, but he didn't question what was for him good fortune. The flight time was progressively increased until they flew every night during the week.

One night in early July, Jack was allowed to send for Laurel. She had the opportunity to see him fly the trainer jet. As luck would have it, that was the only night they had trouble. The problem was mechanical in nature. It couldn't have been blamed on the pilot, but it assuredly required excellent piloting skills to compensate. Examination of their left engine, after the fact, gave evidence that a bird or bat had been pulled through it. The engine flamed out with no warning, as jet engines do. Jack shut it down, stabilized the plane, and requested an emergency landing. He did it all automatically without any signs of panic, and his landing was flawless.

Laurel was almost eight months pregnant and was panic-stricken for him. Even hearing the controllers remark on how competent Jack was didn't help. Seeing him climb out of the cockpit let her breathe again. He didn't consider it a big deal and walked around the plane before returning to the hangar.

Jack was feeling the rush all pilots feel when they avoid a major problem, but one look at Laurel brought him back to reality. She was pale despite her dark skin. He wrapped his arm around her immediately with unconcealed anxiety.

"Are you all right, Laurel?"

"I don't think I want to watch anymore," she said.

"Let me get my briefcase, and we'll get out of here." He was so worried about Laurel that he went home wearing the flight suit. His blood sugar in the car was 195, and he bolused one and a half units as he restarted his pump.

"They're going to send you up again soon, aren't they?" Laurel asked.

"Our team isn't slated yet, so it would be at least twelve months. Way after the baby." He glanced at her. "I'm sorry I scared you. I should have been thinking about pride going before a fall. I just wanted you to see me fly. It wasn't really a big emergency."

"The last plane I was in that lost one engine lost the

other one, too. Jets can't be landed without engines, can they?"

"Not easily," Jack said. "But I've landed one after both engines flamed out during Desert Storm, and I had to ditch a Huey helicopter when I first started flying in the Air Force. I've been flying all my life, Laurel. I've been in a lot of emergency situations, and God has brought me through all of them." He could see the talk was not reassuring her, so he changed tactics. "Think about it this way. The shuttle is like a jet with no engines. All it has is maneuvering thrusters. That's why we call it a dead stick landing."

"What would happen if you couldn't land the jet? Like Lucien."

"Then I'd ditch the plane, pop the canopy, and parachute." He took her hand. "I'm not staying with the plane, Laurel, unless staying with it is the only way to keep people on the ground from dying. I couldn't save myself and kill other people, and you wouldn't want me to."

"No." She pressed her free hand against their baby as it twisted and turned inside her. Jack laid his hand on her belly, smiling as he felt the movements.

"Do you want me to transfer off the astronaut service, Laurel? You know I will if you ask me to."

"I know." She placed her hand over his hand. "You might want to quit offering because if I didn't know what it means to you, I'd have accepted your offer a long time ago. I love you, Jack, but I don't want to watch you fly anymore."

"Okay," he conceded. "No more showing off. It always gets you showed up instead of shown off." As they pulled into their driveway, he waved at Russell, who lived next door. Russell strolled across the lawn to meet them.

"Do you guys ever come home on time?" Russell asked. "I need your help moving our piano. We're trying to paint, and I can't get it to budge." He looked at Jack's flight suit. "Where have you been?"

"It's a long story," Jack said. "Give me five minutes to change." He climbed out and then helped Laurel out of the car.

"Come with him, Laurel," Russell suggested. "We've got burgers on the grill. You can help Danielle keep the kids out from under the piano. Bring your flute. We'll do some chamber music afterwards."

"Sounds good." Laurel's back was hurting, but she liked their neighbors and considered a refused invitation to be an insult. She followed Jack into the house and stripped off her dress, changing into a pair of shorts and smock. Jack left the flight suit on the bed and came out of the bathroom wearing jean shorts, a Navajo Nation tee shirt, and sports sandals. Before they could leave, he pulled Laurel close and kissed her.

"I love you, Laurel, and I'll tell you a secret. This baby is more of a rush than a shuttle flight."

"That's the nicest thing you ever said to me, Jack." She smiled and took his hands. "I'm okay now. It was just more adrenaline than the two of us could handle."

He kissed her more than once and then said, "Let's not stay too late."

"Early would be good." She kept her arm around his waist as they left the house. Jack stopped long enough to toss their mail onto the living room sofa. On top was his credit sheet from the university graduate school for another course in astrophysics.

"How many hours is that?" Laurel asked.

"Twenty-nine, I think," he said. "Are you graduating in August? You didn't tell me what they said about your transferred credits."

"I'm graduating. I'll probably have to get an extra super-sized gown, but I am graduating *magna cum laude*." Jack stopped walking and kissed her. His expression made her feel ready to celebrate.

"Congratulations. I'm so proud of you. August is going to be a red letter month for the Driver family." He knocked on the Chou's screen door. "Hey, Russ. Let us in."

Danielle came to the door and invited them in. She was wearing an apron over her own pregnant belly and pointed toward the den. "Russ is in the den fighting with the furniture."

"Can I help you with the food?" Laurel asked.

"Go on in. I've got it covered," Danielle said.

Laurel remembered thinking there was a lot of food on the counter for four adults and two kids. When they walked into the Chou's den, the rest of their crew and their families shouted, "Surprise!"

It became obvious they were being given a baby shower. Pastel decorations were hanging all around the room, and a large pile of gifts was stacked on the coffee table. Besides their crew, many members of the ground crew were sitting around the room. Jack started laughing and slapped Russell on the shoulder.

"You're a great liar. Have you thought about going into politics?"

"Hey, Jack, I was under duress. Danielle threatened serious Chinese water torture if I gave you even one hint." He handed a glass of iced tea to Jack. "It's unsweetened."

The party lasted until almost midnight and ended with all the musicians on the team giving an impromptu concert. Jack was the pianist. Laurel was the flutist. Danielle and Russell were violinists. Odell and Geneva Bradford played the viola, and Tricia Arnold played the cello. They had been practicing a Brandenburg concerto, and it came off well.

The sky was a brilliant canopy, and they could see the stars even in suburbia as they walked into the night. The men helped carry their gifts, and after prolonged good-byes, they were finally alone. Jack locked the doors for the night and took their mail to the sofa in the den. "It's like having a whole other family," Laurel said. "I'll be glad you'll be going up with them next time because I'll know the wives. If my parents hadn't been with me last time, I'd have been alone."

"I did my best to make that better," Jack commented as he began opening the letters.

"You did make it better," Laurel said as she kissed his temple. She punched in their security code to turn on the alarm. Kennedy followed her back to the den and sat on her feet when she sat beside Jack.

"Twenty-nine credits." He passed her his transcript. "Just think. If I were really masochistic, soon I could do another dissertation and have a second Ph.D. I don't think so."

He tossed the envelope into a sack of paper recycling and followed it with three pieces of junk mail. Beneath it was a letter from NASA. He opened it with some trepidation. Official letters meant some sort of status change. He was speechless as he read the letter.

Jack,

I'm sure you've wondered about the extra flight time. As always, you've gone with the flow and not asked questions. We have your team slated for a mission next June. You're going to be named commander which, as you know, also means being the backup pilot.

You're one of the youngest men in the program, but you have the credentials necessary to take the job since you have more graduate credit, extensive hours in fighter jets and one previous shuttle flight. We hope to downplay your back-up pilot position in the media because of the questions that will be asked about your diabetes, but should those questions be asked we are still committed to having you command the mission. Congratulations. You've earned this with hard work and not by who your father was or by your race. Al Asher

"Wow," Laurel said. "That's a rush for everyone in the house. I wonder if the others know yet."

"I don't think so. Russ would have said something. You'll have to throw water on me until they release it to the media because I can't wait to tell Samson."

"Which shuttle will it be?" Laurel asked.

Jack counted the missions in his head and laughed. "Discovery. I guess that's fitting." He turned and pulled her close. "How does it feel to be the wind under a shuttle's wings?"

Laurel didn't know how much more flight time Jack would be logging, and he didn't tell her. Three days later, his team was given their assignment, and he and Russ were assigned the T-38 for daily sorties. Russ was always in the first seat, but part of their instructions was for Russ to give the control to Jack abruptly at times. The ground control clocked how quickly Jack could pick up. If the truth had been told, the diabetic copilot had faster reflexes than the non diabetic pilot.

They went from the T-38 to simulator for extra time on all the maneuvers as well as takeoffs and landings. They had to work fourteen or more hours a day at least four days a week for a mission that was almost a year away. Laurel was out of school and would have been lonely if not for Danielle Chou who came every day to help her work on the nursery. They finished just in time for Laurel's graduation from college on August 11. Jack had a two week leave beginning whenever the baby decided to come, but he and Russell still had flight time for every day until then.

They were feeling rushed when they reached the tarmac on Friday, August 10, because their session in the simulator had been delayed by a crew getting ready for launch. Jack checked his sugar and found it was 93. He took a glucose tablet and suspended his pump. When he zipped his flight suit, the zipper caught his pump line and yanked the infusion set out of his skin. It wasn't a pleasant sensation, but it presented a bigger problem because he didn't have an extra infusion set in his locker.

"Great!" he remarked. "Give me a minute, Russ. I need to call Laurel. I have a technical problem." He picked up the telephone and dialed Laurel. "Hey, babe, I've just yanked my pump site, and I don't have one with me. I used the last one a week ago, and I hadn't remembered to get another one. We're just getting ready to take off, and your parents' flight lands at 8:30. We should land at 7 o'clock. Please put a pump infusion set in your purse with a bottle of insulin."

"I'll get it together now. Will you be okay until then?"

"Yeah. I'm actually a little low to fly, but I just took a glucose tablet. How are you and our little baby doing?"

"We feel like a bomb waiting to go off." Laurel laughed. "I've had a lot of contractions today. I was just wondering if I'm going to make my graduation."

"Don't start a Driver tradition," Jack responded. Russell was beckoning him, and he said, "I love you. I'll see you in about ninety minutes." He hung up and put his pump in his locker before following Russell to the readied T-38.

"What's up?" Russell asked.

"I yanked my pump site, and so I asked Laurel to get another one for me. You know, this astronaut is brought to you by Lilly Pharmaceuticals and MiniMed."

Russ laughed and slapped Jack's shoulder. "They're darn good sponsors, if I'm any judge of copilots. Let's go check out the stars."

Laurel was cleaning with a passion inappropriate for the duration of her pregnancy. She wanted to impress her parents, and she was also nesting. The sky was cloud laden. It was tornado season so she had the TV on as she dusted. All she intended to hear was the weather report. The newscaster came on first and said, "In a late breaking story, a T-38 jet on routine maneuvers over the Gulf of Mexico reported losing an engine and then disappeared from radar. At this hour, Navy and Coast Guard ships are searching the sea just off Galveston for the two pilots. Their names have been held pending notification of their next of kin."

Laurel sat down with her heart racing. It was just after 7 P.M. Rational thought told her Jack would be on the ground and on his way home. She dialed his cell phone number and got the message about the cellular customer being unavailable. Then she called Danielle Chou and got a busy signal. Kennedy started barking, and she ran to the front door expecting Jack.

Laurel hadn't been a pilot's wife, and that lack of experience spared her knowing why the NASA car was in their driveway until she saw Danielle and her two children leaving their house. All of them were crying. Another grim-faced officer was walking up Laurel's steps, and Laurel had to hold onto the door when the floor swayed under her feet. She was praying when the officer reached her and confirmed her worst fears.

"Mrs. Driver, we need you to come with us. There's a problem with your husband."

The takeoff had been flawless, and Russell had flown the plane out over the bay on their filed flight plan. They were fifteen minutes in the air and going through a climb to 50,000 feet when their right engine suddenly exploded into a fireball. Jack had been watching the instruments since Russ was piloting the plane, and there were no abnormal readings prior to the explosion. A series of explosions continued up to the engine manifold and sprayed the canopy with shrapnel.

Everything that followed moved too fast for anything other than pilot's instinct. The plane rolled twice and dropped 5,000 feet rapidly. It was in a flat spin before Jack recovered enough to grasp the stick. The pressure-stabilizing devices in his suit tightened painfully as he called out to Russell. When there was no response from Russell over the microphone or via the controls, Jack knew his comrade was either badly injured or dead.

Jack took over the controls and struggled with the stick as he managed to correct the spin. It was a battle to keep the plane upright during the remainder of their 20,000 foot descent. He realized they were headed back toward land so, with great difficulty, he turned the jet back toward the water. As his fight with the controls became even more arduous, he knew they were losing hydraulic pressure and therefore the ability to maneuver the crippled jet. It was taking all his strength to compensate for the drag from the right engine debris and to keep the jet flying straight. He was sure a crash was inevitable. He began slowing their airspeed in preparation to ditch the plane.

"Mayday. Mayday, Houston control. This is Bravo Echo 4269. We've had an engine explosion. The pilot is injured. We're at 22,000 and losing power rapidly."

"Say again," the radio commanded him over static.

"This is Bravo Echo 4269," Jack shouted. "We're a T-38 training flight. We've had an engine explosion. The pilot is injured. We've lost the right engine and hydraulics are failing. We are at 22,000 feet and will crash at these coordinates. Clear this air space. We have limited maneuverability." He couldn't say more.

He left the vox switch on and shouted what he was doing so the tower could hear and the black box would record everything he did. He had no direct vision and made the final decision to ditch as they dropped to just under 20,000 feet. He knew they were over the water and headed out to sea when he began shaking Russell's shoulder and shouting, "Eject, Russell. Eject."

The controls would only allow Jack to eject himself. Each seat was controlled independently. He saw the altimeter go to 16,000 feet before he felt Russell move. Until that moment he wasn't even sure if his friend was alive.

"Eject, Russ. Pull it. Please, God, let him eject."

The altimeter dropped to 14,000 feet, and Jack knew he would have to eject soon whether Russell did or not. He tried to pull up on their descent, but the jet no longer responded to his attempts to control it.

"Eject, Russell. Eject!"

He felt Russ bend slightly and heard the whisper, "Ejecting," just in time to retract his hand. He hadn't been sure the canopy would release even before he realized the forward right side had been severely damaged. As Russell's seat threw him out of the plane, Jack released his seat. The force of the ejection was stunning, but his oxygen continued working and kept him aware as his parachute deployed. He saw their plane crash into the sea and explode. As he descended, he searched the skies for Russell and then focused on his friend until he hit the water.

A heavy gust of wind swept Jack's parachute a hundred feet before he hit the water, rendering it ineffectual. He hit the water sideways, feeling his right ribs pop at impact. He knew he was still in much better shape than Russell. He released his chute so he could swim to his partner. He took his one-man life raft with him, praying the emergency transponder was already calling for help.

Two hundred yards separated them, and Jack battled the tide to reach his comrade. Russell was slumped over his life vest with his face bobbing in and out of the water. Jack was grateful to find a pulse in Russell's neck and held his friend with his head well out of the water as he prayed for the navy to be quick. He had tremendous difficulty pulling Russell onto his raft. Then he could see

Russell's flight suit had been penetrated over his chest and abdomen. The flight suit was heavily stained with blood.

Jack lost his own raft in the struggle to keep Russell afloat. He stayed in the water beside his wounded friend and swam against the current. The approaching storm told him prayer might be his best option for keeping them in the bay. In between prayers, he thought of Laurel and their baby. Those thoughts and his prayers gave him the strength to keep swimming as the storm hit the bay and intensified the current.

They had been down for almost five hours in a driving rain without any close passes from the rescue teams. Jack knew he was already in trouble from no insulin for six hours. Russell had responded to him only once with a groan. The pulse in the pilot's neck was thready. The tide was pulling them out of the bay, and Jack had fought the current as long as his muscles would allow.

The constant physical exertion with no insulin was driving his sugar higher and his blood pH lower even more rapidly. Jack knew insulin dependent diabetics are not supposed to exert themselves if their sugar is over 200 because without insulin the body can't let any blood sugar into the muscles. His muscles were making lactate as a fuel, and it was being turned into more sugar by his liver. Jack was starting to feel sick when he heard a helicopter passing just over them.

"We're here. Help us," Jack shouted, trying to be heard over the howling wind and crashing waves.

The helicopter hit them with a spotlight telling Jack they had been seen. Two minutes later two navy divers were beside him and took Russell from his arms. After the basket carried Russell up, Jack was lifted. He was grateful that he didn't have to climb the ladder. Jack lay down on the chopper floor, keeping his need for insulin from the rescue team as they focused on Russell. He knew he was already in ketoacidosis, but he felt he could handle that much better than Russ could handle his injuries. Bits and pieces of what the medics were saying made him pray his good friend would live.

"We'd just about given up hope for you," one of the Seals said. "We found your raft and transponder out at sea without you. The transponder with you was barely making a signal."

"I couldn't hold onto both of them," Jack managed. He gave his report to the rescuers and stayed on the floor as his own symptoms became overwhelming. No one noticed how he was breathing because Russell was in deep shock and occupied both medics. They were airlifted to the base hospital and arrived just after midnight. Jack was sick several times before they landed, but he was still not considered a priority because Russell had been so badly injured. Before he was seen in the emergency room, he had been to the bathroom three times and vomited another five times.

He was seen by a physician's assistant at 1 A.M., and she focused on the huge bruise on his chest. She was harassed and assumed a pilot wouldn't have any other medical problems. She didn't give Jack time to tell her his medical history. She left the examination room as soon as she checked his ribs and produced considerable pain for her patient. When he was sick again in her presence, she ordered a chest X-ray and gave him meperidine and promethazine, thinking his vomiting was from the pain of broken ribs. His lungs looked normal on the X-ray, so she didn't look any further for a cause of Jack's breathlessness. She moved on to her next patient. Sedated by the shot, Jack couldn't tell anyone his problem. Finally the trauma doctors got to him.

"Did anybody get a history?" the doctor asked with irritation. "He's out from the meperidine."

"He's the civilian copilot from the NASA crash. He said his chute was a streamer from the wind, and he hit the water hard. He's got a big hematoma on his right chest and four fractured ribs. He's been breathing fast since he got here, but his lungs look and sound good." The nurse flipped through the chart. "It doesn't look like there's any other history."

"That's not just fast breathing," the doctor observed. "That's Kussmaul breathing. He must have some sort of metabolic acidosis. Get a blood gas stat. Call NASA and get us a medical history."

The nurse picked up a blood gas kit and moved to Jack's arm. She noticed the chain around his neck and pulled it from under his hospital gown to examine it.

"I think I have your answer," she said. The doctor swore as he read the medical identification tag.

"Insulin dependent diabetes. He's probably in ketoacidosis. Get a test strip in here. What was this guy doing in a training jet?"

Laurel and Danielle were in a room at the agency alone at first, but gradually the other crew members came to form a prayer circle around them. Colonel Asher joined them before the first hour had passed and sent a car to pick up Laurel's parents at the airport.

They prayed without ceasing until an officer burst into the room at midnight. "A Seal team just picked them up. They're both alive!"

Tears of despair turned quickly to celebration. "They're at the base hospital," the officer said. "We have a car to take the wives over."

"Jack hasn't had any insulin for hours," Laurel said. "He accidentally pulled his pump site before they took off. His doctor said he'll be in bad trouble after four hours."

"I'll call them on a secured line," the officer replied. "Let's go."

Colonel Asher went with them with the rest of the crew following. Laurel's parents rode with Jim Graham and his wife. The colonel made the call on an agency cell phone and was given enough information to frighten them again.

"Jack's sugar was really high and he's in ketoacidosis, but other than a couple of broken ribs he's all right. Russell is in critical condition. Jack told them the engine exploded and shrapnel penetrated the canopy over the first seat."

Laurel drew two breaths and wrapped her arms around Danielle. It was a twenty-minute drive to the hospital.

Laurel and Danielle were holding each other as they reached the intensive care unit. A member of the rescue team was standing with the trauma physicians and gave his report first.

"They were just inside the bay with the current pulling them out to sea. Major Chou was unconscious and bleeding from multiple wounds. He was being supported in the water by Dr. Driver. Dr. Driver said the right engine exploded without any warning and put the plane into an angulated dive that produced a flat spin. He said Major Chou made no effort to correct the plane's attitude, and he took the controls. He said they were losing hydraulics, and he had minimal control when they reached 20,000 feet. Radar tracking documents those facts exactly. He was still able to correct the flat spin and turn the plane away from the land, which is a tribute to his piloting skills.

"Dr. Driver was able to get Major Chou to eject himself, and then he ejected. When he reached the major in the water, he was unconscious. Dr. Driver lost his own raft while pulling Major Chou onto a raft. Unfortunately, Dr. Driver's transponder was swept out to sea. We tracked that one first because the second signal was almost too weak to pick up. We worked on Major Chou all the way in. We didn't know Dr. Driver was diabetic. He didn't tell us."

"Dr. Driver is in diabetic ketoacidosis," the doctor

acknowledged, "but he's doing well. He's sedated by the medicine we gave him for pain and nausea. He has four broken ribs but no other trauma we could find." His face was grim.

"Major Chou is in critical condition. He has a closed head injury and a small bleed in his head on CT scan. He suffered a penetrating injury through his right chest that collapsed his lung and tore several vessels. He had a second penetrating wound that lacerated his liver. He inhaled some water before Dr. Driver got to him, but he's ventilated and we can handle that problem. If Dr. Driver hadn't gotten to him, he would have drowned."

They walked in with the doctor, and Laurel felt terrifically relieved on seeing her husband. Jack looked flushed and was breathing very fast and deep, but he was clearly in no worse shape than when he had experienced ketoacidosis nine months earlier. Laurel sat with him and took his hand, thanking God for sparing her husband's life. Her parents and the rest of the crew arrived at 1:30 A.M. They filled the waiting room with their heartfelt prayers. At 6 A.M., Jack was awake and reached out for Laurel when she entered his room.

"I kept my promise," he said hoarsely. "I promised not to die like Lucien did."

Laurel leaned over and kissed him as best she could with the big swell of the baby between them. "They said you saved Russell's life."

"Is he hanging on?" Jack asked anxiously. "I was afraid they wouldn't tell me the truth."

"He's hanging on," Laurel vowed. "The doctor said it will be a few days before we know he'll be okay." She was crying and couldn't even feel her tears. "I love you, Jack. I don't think I knew how much my heart is wrapped around yours until I didn't know if you were alive for five hours."

"I know. I thought about you and the baby the whole time we were in the water. I just kept praying to get home." He smiled. "God definitely heard us."

"I want to stay with you," Laurel said. "They've made me stay in the waiting room."

"You need to go graduate, Laurel," Jack insisted. "I want you to do it for me and the baby. We'll want to see the pictures someday. By the time you get back, I'll be ready for my pump. You can stop at the base and get it out of my locker."

"I don't want to go without you, Jack," Laurel protested. "I've had this mental picture of seeing you in the audience."

"Just pretend," he urged her. "In my heart I'll be there."

Laurel never agreed. It was too fulfilling to just hold Jack's hand and know he was alive. He was exhausted, and the nurse told Laurel his blood pH was still low. The doctor confirmed he would be ready to get out of ICU by that night.

"He's in a lot of pain from his broken ribs, and that's going to get worse when he gets up and moving. Outside of that, he could go home by tomorrow."

"I'm graduating from college today," Laurel confided. "Jack told me to go, but I don't want to leave him."

"I would go," the doctor said. "You can't sit with him in ICU, and you can when I move him out. I'll move him at 6 P.M."

"I'll be back at five," Laurel vowed.

She stopped to hug Danielle and explain where she would be. Lawrence Wolfe drove her to the house to change and get her cap and gown. She received her bachelor of arts in graphic arts at 11 A.M. with her parents shooting roll after roll of photographs. They took her to lunch and then to the house to pick up clothes and pump supplies for Jack. They were at the agency by 4 P.M. Though the controllers admitted Laurel to the locker room on the basis of her driver's license, security appeared before she had removed the pump from Jack's locker. Fortunately one of the guards recognized Laurel and turned on the controller who had summoned them.

"Listen, this is Dr. Driver's wife. What's your problem anyway?"

"This lady doesn't have her badge with her, and his wife was here yesterday afternoon with a valid badge. She's tall and blond."

Laurel sat down discouraged. Her face was pale. "That's Jack's ex-wife. She's wanted by the FBI. She hired the man that killed his father."

"Call personnel and tell them to run every Driver with a badge. What's her name, Mrs. Driver?" the security guard asked.

"Alyssa," Laurel stammered. "Alyssa Winston Driver."

"Ask them to get into the main frame computer and see whose name is listed under spouse in Dr. Driver's file," the guard continued. "If she was here, the plane could have been sabotaged."

They kept Laurel until she proved she had the combination to Jack's locker and a valid photo ID. She took Jack's pump and street clothes before heading for the base hospital. A security officer remained with them and, after receiving a call on his radio, the officer accompanied them to the hospital. Jack had just been transferred out of intensive care on hourly glucose measurements because he didn't have his pump yet. He sat up when he saw the security guard and then grimaced as he was reminded of his broken ribs.

"What's going on?" he asked when he could speak.

"Is this your wife, Dr. Driver?" the guard asked.

"Yes, this is my wife. What's going on?" Jack reached for Laurel's hand possessively, and the guard extended a photograph.

"Do you know this woman?"

Jack's face answered his question. "Call the police and the FBI. That's my ex-wife, and she makes the woman in *Fatal Attraction* look like the Easter bunny. Where was she?"

"At the hangar yesterday," the guard answered. "She and a man claiming to be her brother went to look at your plane."

If he hadn't still been sick, Jack would have exploded with rage when the base police arrived an hour later. Laurel had never seen him so angry, and his anger intensified when they asked him why he hadn't reported his ex-wife's whereabouts to them earlier.

"What do you mean—report to you?" he shouted. "I've been telling you that she's a psychotic death angel since my father was killed. There's been a report with the FBI since our private plane was sabotaged two years ago. She's been on the 'most wanted' list. Are you telling me you made her an ID badge?"

"She had a Texas driver's license listing your address, Dr. Driver," security explained. "We've already notified the highway patrol and the FBI."

"You can tell them if she shows up in or around my house or my family, they'll find her dead on my property." He sat up unsteadily and gritted his teeth against the resultant discomfort. "Help me get dressed, Laurel, and let's get out of here."

The doctor released him reluctantly, and Jack insisted on seeing Russell before he left. Russell was still being ventilated, but Danielle told them he was steadily improving and expected to be off the life-support equipment within twenty-four hours.

Jack demanded and received police escort to their house. Once inside, he got out his gun and sat on the sofa talking to Laurel and his in-laws with the posture of a sentry. Late the next day the investigators confirmed that the explosion had occurred due to plastic explosives. The charge had been detonated from the ground.

Chapter 24

———————————○———————————

Jack had intended to take care of Laurel, but he was in too much pain for the first three days. He had to take ibuprofen alternating with prescription pain pills to tolerate the discomfort. Lawrence and Mary cared for both their son-in-law and their daughter. They turned away reporters more than once.

Security kept watch around their house day and night. A police investigation confirmed that Alyssa had acquired a Texas photo driver's license with Jack's address on it. She had obtained the NASA spouse's ID by using her license and a forged marriage license. A very professional hacking job had changed Jack's personal database in the main frame computer at NASA. Those changes had lead security to issue Alyssa a spouse's ID. She and an unknown man in a policeman's uniform had been allowed to see the T-38 trainer jet. As a result of the sabotage, the astronauts' database was secured to prevent any further tampering. Though it was obvious everyone had done their duty, the mental and physical scars of the victims of Alyssa's crime could not be so easily erased.

Colonel Asher came on the fourth day to communicate the results of the investigation. He met with Jack behind closed doors. Laurel expected shouting, but Jack emerged from the interview looking pale as he walked with his superior to meet with reporters waiting at the security gates. He never told any of them what the reporters asked. Lawrence turned off the television as the evening news began and was rewarded by his son-in-law's grateful nod. He told them what Colonel Asher had told him a week later.

Laurel went into labor ten days early. She had her first real pain at midnight and awakened Jack at 3 A.M. Her husband was very relieved her parents were with them because he was a nervous wreck. Lawrence drove them to the hospital, and he and Mary helped Jack care for Laurel during the long ten hours that followed. Impressing his in-laws greatly, Jack ignored his own discomfort and devoted all his attention to Laurel. He rubbed her back and fed her ice chips. When the time came to push, he was her coach doing all the Lamaze techniques they had practiced.

Lucien Lawrence Driver came into the world at 1:30 P.M., incredibly blessed to have two parents. He weighed in at seven pounds ten ounces and yelled as loudly as his father had a few days earlier. The nurse laid the baby in Jack's arms first, and Jack brought him to Laurel.

"He looks more Cherokee than Navajo," Lawrence teased them as he photographed his daughter's family.

"Give him time. It took me thirty-four years to really look Navajo," Jack said as he held his son. "He's so small. You just don't think about anybody being this small." He kissed the baby's head gently. "You don't think of how lucky you are until you get this kind of gift." He laid the baby in Laurel's arms and kissed her hair while she said a prayer of thanksgiving at having him there.

Lawrence and Mary left the new family alone in the

hospital and retreated to the house to sleep. Laurel was exhausted and slept dreamlessly between feedings. When she awakened the next morning, she found Jack asleep in the recliner with the baby sleeping on his chest and covered with two baby blankets.

"Hey, Jackson, what are you doing with the kid?" she asked as she sat up in bed.

Jack moved carefully, trying not to awaken his son. "We had flight school at 3 A.M. He's a nightshift kind of guy."

"You could have sent him to the nursery," Laurel said.

"No way! He's not getting out of our sight. You looked exhausted, so I gave him a bottle of sugar water and walked him until he settled down. Just think, he's not a day old and he's already hooked on glucose solution."

"Don't try giving him any glucose tablets," Laurel warned. "I don't want him learning how to spit."

"I'm running too low to share. If you feel like it, I'd really like to take my family home today. I've heard too many stories about babies being kidnapped out of hospital nurseries," Jack said.

"I'm ready to go home. I feel wonderful. It's like a great weight has been lifted off my pelvis. He feels a lot lighter on the outside," Laurel said.

"I'm sure." Jack brought her the baby and stretched his cramped muscles while trying to protect his right ribs. "Let's go as soon as the doctor makes rounds." He paused when the room seemed unsteady, and then he suspended his pump. "I think I'm a shade too low." He checked his pockets. "No glucose tablets. I guess you can tell where my head was when we left the house. Ask the nurse to bring you some juice, Laurel."

She pressed the nurse call button hurriedly and watched Jack as he stuck his finger. "What is it?"

"You don't want to know," he said as he sat down in

the recliner. "You might want to call them again."

The nurse came at the second call and brought two juices without asking questions. Jack stayed down until he could feel the effects. By then he had experienced the usual drenching sweat of a bad reaction.

"How low was it?" Laurel asked.

"Thirty-six. I love this meter. It says 'do you need a snack?' on the assumption you can read when your sugar is thirty-six. You know what the first three letters of assume are." He wiped his face. "Let's split your breakfast."

"Go get something to eat, Jack."

"Not until your dad gets here. I guess becoming a father is a good reason to forget to test. Meters don't lie. I haven't checked since last night at six."

The doctor made rounds before breakfast arrived. He discharged Laurel and Lucien after checking both and circumcising the baby. Jack stood guard even then and came back with Lucien in his arms. He didn't see the blond-haired nurse watching him from the stairwell.

They left as soon as Lawrence and Mary arrived. Jack's sugar had rebounded to 200, and he drove them home. He showered, ate, and spent the rest of the day calling everyone they knew. He also held the baby as much as sharing would allow. Laurel took care of the baby whenever the others gave her the opportunity. She was glad to be breast feeding because that gave her at least twenty minutes to hold her son every three hours.

At midnight, they were up with the baby, and she reminded Jack to lower his basal rate. The reaction the next morning was less intense for that reason, but his blood sugar was still too low for Jack's comfort. He called his endocrinologist as soon as the office opened. The resultant conversation involved him giving several weeks of readings to the nurse and then dropping his night rate by 0.2 units per hour.

"If you're up at night with the baby, you might want to take a glucose tablet, especially if you have to do much walking," the nurse warned.

Colonel Asher brought Russell and Danielle home later that day. Then he came to visit Jack and Laurel. "Not a bad looking boy," he told Jack. "It's a good thing he looks like Laurel."

"Thanks a lot, Al," Jack commented dryly. "How's Russ?"

"About like you'd expect. It may be hard to get him to go up again. He's shook up, but he has good reason to be. Walk over and see him between feedings." He took a report from his pocket and gave it to Jack. "The committee report on the crash. The verdict is sabotage, and you get some well-deserved accolades for keeping two astronauts from dying. There's probably going to be a medal involved at some point. You did a good job, Jack. You did a commander's job. You saved your pilot and kept the plane crash from killing anyone else. I don't think anyone will ever question your flying skills after this. You and I will start going up as soon as you come back from your leave. You don't need to lose any flight time." He scanned Jack's face. "You are going back up, right?"

"Yeah. I'm going back up," Jack said slowly. "It just makes you think when you don't know if you're going to come back or not. I don't want to push my luck with God."

"I don't think you ever have, Jack." He patted Jack on the back and left them. Jack told Laurel where he was going and walked across their side yard to the Chou home. A haggard Danielle answered his knock and then hugged him.

"I never had the chance to thank you," she said. "You saved his life."

"God saved both of us," Jack said. "I was hoping to see Russ. Do you think he feels up to it?"

"I think he'd be upset if I didn't take you back right away." She took his hand. "How's Laurel?"

"The baby's here. I called everybody else, but I didn't want to bother you at the hospital. It's a boy."

"Lucien then," Danielle said. "Congratulations."

She led Jack to the bedroom door and said, "Russell, it's Jack. You need to congratulate him. Lucien's here."

Russell Chou looked like he still needed to be in the hospital. His face was sallow from loss of blood. Still, he managed a smile on seeing Jack.

"Hey, Jack. I've been wanting to thank you. Colonel Asher said you held onto me for five hours so I wouldn't drown."

"You would have done the same thing for me." Jack sat down beside the bed just glad to see Russell was alive. Of all the team members, he had felt closest to Russ. "You know it was sabotage?"

"I know. It doesn't really matter why. Catastrophic engine failure is catastrophic by any other name. It's strange. Except for hearing the explosion, I don't remember anything until I woke up on all the equipment." He looked away and then shook his head. "I'm going to resign my commission, Jack. Danielle and I have talked a lot in the last two days. We have three kids to consider, and they need a dad. I'm going to move into the aeronautics division of NASA. I just wanted to tell you before I told Colonel Asher and the navy. I owe it to you since I'm bailing on you. Do you understand?"

"I do," Jack said quietly. "I even thought of resigning from NASA. We were a long time in the water, and I didn't have anything to do but think especially about what would happen to Laurel and the baby. Since Lucien was born, I've had some midnight hours to think even more. Last night I did a lot of praying, and I still feel like this is what God wants me to do. Maybe I'm wrong, but everybody has to follow their heart and soul."

"I think it's what you were meant to do, too," Russell

said slowly. "Maybe I'll let you tell me what it's like when you get there."

"I can tell you that now. It's like the end of that poem the pilot wrote. When I'm up there, I feel like I really am almost close enough to touch God." Jack clasped Russell's hand between both of his. "I'm going to miss having you in the first seat. When you start feeling better, let's get together and keep working on the Brandenburg."

"We will," Russ promised. "I'm too sore now, but give me a week."

Jack walked out feeling a sense of grief he couldn't explain. He put his arm around Danielle. "I'm right next door if you need anything. My ribs are sore, but I can still pick up anything you need lifted. Don't do anything to hurt yourself when your baby is so close."

"I won't," she promised. "Thanks for coming, Jack. He really needed the encouragement."

Jack walked to his back porch and sat down. He felt responsible for Russell's loss. He was sure the sabotage had occurred at Alyssa's direction. He just couldn't think of any way to draw her out. He felt helpless at the mercy of someone who could obviously pick and choose her time to attack him. He was on the steps when Lawrence Wolfe came out and sat beside him.

"Hot day, isn't it?"

Jack smiled. He liked his father-in-law very much. In many ways, Lawrence had a brilliance that isn't appreciated in a computer-driven society. He had a high school education and graduate work in the art of reading people.

"Irony is when people keep congratulating you for salvaging a disaster that was your fault."

"How do you figure that?" Larry asked.

"My ex-wife did it. She almost killed me and almost destroyed my marriage to Laurel. She killed my father, and now she's destroyed my best friend's dreams. I don't know what to do."

"Read Job," Larry said simply. "Sometimes you just have courage under fire until you can fight back. You didn't cause this, Jack. Evil caused it, and God will put the world back in balance. This is not the first time good and evil have battled. Good still survives." He put his arm around Jack's shoulders. "You're a good man, and a good husband to my daughter. I know your heart is with God, and I know you're a warrior. Wait for the right time to fight, and leave the guilt as a temptation from Satan. Evil can't defeat you without help."

He walked with Jack to the house. To their surprise Laurel was at the stove with her stepmother making supper. She made an extra dish and sent it to Russell and Danielle. They sat down to supper with the baby in his carrier on one of the extra chairs. Kennedy sat near the table watching the baby.

After supper, Laurel picked up her flute and cajoled Jack into playing the piano with her. They played "Sicilienne" by Gabriel Faure and then moved on to Ravel. When they made music together, Laurel knew it always relaxed Jack. That night, their baby seemed to be listening to their music. Lucien was asleep in his carrier when they stopped. Laurel carried him to their room because she didn't like having him as far away as the nursery.

The baby never stirred as they locked up for the night and moved through the house turning off lights. With a grunt, Kennedy curled up in their doorway. Jack laid down gingerly because of his sore chest. He began opening their mail. The top brown envelope was from the ground crew at mission control. It held a card congratulating them on having Lucien. Under it was a book entitled *A New Father's Sex Life*. The pages were blank. Laurel giggled

"I work with a bunch of deviants," Jack said. "Freud would have a field day in there."

"Open the rest tomorrow," Laurel suggested. "You're

getting sleep deprived. I've had two naps today, and you haven't had any."

"And I'm tired," he admitted. He threw the mail on the table and tested his blood sugar, which was 86. He pulled glucose tablets from the nightstand and ate one. Then he kissed Laurel. "See you at 3 A.M."

He slept through the 1 A.M. feeding when Laurel got up with Lucien. She changed their baby's diaper with only the moonlight coming through their window to guide her. Then she brought Lucien back to bed and laid down with him between Jack and her. She turned over to offer Lucien the second breast and then moved back until she was snuggled against Jack. He flung his arm across her automatically and continued sleeping.

Before Laurel could go back to sleep, she said another prayer thanking God for sparing her husband. She felt very safe with her family all around her.

Larry and Mary had to return home to Cherokee the next day, but then Samson and Olivia came to see the new baby. When they left, Jack and Laurel had only three more days of his leave to share with each other. They spent those days playing music and reading together on the den floor between feedings. Laurel took roll after roll of photographs, mainly of Jack holding their son. Despite the jokes, Laurel thought the baby already looked very much like her husband.

The Bradfords and their two children, Wayne and Maggie, came over their last night bearing supper. Their kids were old enough to pretend to be waiters as it was served. After supper, Geneva helped Laurel clean up, and Stuart and Jack sat on the patio watching Wayne and Maggie play with Kennedy.

"I received a letter yesterday informing us Russ had resigned," Stuart said. "They want me to take the pilot's seat. I guess I wanted your opinion."

"I'm glad," Jack said truthfully. "Both of you guys are top-notch pilots. I feel really safe when you have the controls, which is a tremendous vote of confidence from an air force pilot to a navy pilot." Stuart laughed.

"Keep in mind a Navy SEALs team found you and fished your sorry air force butt out of the bay."

"I have absolutely kept that in mind," Jack said. "I've thanked God and the SEALs. Did the colonel say who'd be taking Russ' place? We're supposed to be an eight-man team."

"Seven man, one woman now," Stuart remarked. "Her name is Karen Lampley. Lieutenant Colonel and or Dr. Karen Lampley to be exact. She's a nuclear physicist. They hired her to work on power utilization in space. They say she's a genius."

"Does she play an instrument?" Jack asked. "Since she's going to talk so far above us lower life forms, we'll have to find some basis for communication."

"Her bio says she plays the piano, so you can communicate with her." Stuart looked at Jack. "We need to start getting some flight time together. I thought I'd sign us up tomorrow for Tuesday."

"I'm ready," Jack said slowly. "But we're going to insist that our plane stays under lock and key until we're ready to take off. Is Geneva okay with you being the pilot?"

"We've been married for twenty years, Jack. The poor woman hasn't ever known anything but being a pilot's wife. I've been fished out of the Atlantic, the Pacific, and the Sea of Japan. The last time she told me I'd pushed the edge of the envelope so often that she was ready to put it in the paper recycling.'"

"Then leave your luck at home. The rescue team was just a little too slow for me to want to go swimming in their pool again." The baby had been crying and, when no one immediately responded, he began screaming at the top of his lungs. Jack got up and returned holding his son.

"With these lungs, Lucien won't have to resort to

Morse Code, radios, or smoke signals. They'll be able to hear him from 50,000 feet," Jack said.

On Monday morning, Jack was up early and showered before awakening Laurel. For more than a few minutes, he wished he didn't have to go to work. He wished he could stay with his wife and his son. He sat down beside Laurel and kissed her ear.

"Wake up, sleeping beauty. I can't leave without being with you."

She wound her arms around his neck. "I don't want you to leave. Stay with us for just one more day."

"I can't. I'm addicted to you, and I've got to go cold turkey or I'll never make it out of here." He kissed her twice lightly, and Laurel held onto him with both hands as she kissed him with passion.

"Stay addicted to me. I'll make you throw that book away." She ran her hands through his hair and kissed him again.

He extricated himself very reluctantly. "I'm tearing myself away. Don't think it doesn't hurt."

Laurel sighed. "That's not the kind of consolation I'm wanting." She stood and pulled on her robe. "Stop at a pharmacy and bring home supplies."

"You won't have to ask me twice," Jack laughed. The baby squeaked and started his precrying ritual. Jack picked him up and walked him as Laurel made fresh fruit and yogurt for their breakfast. She sprinkled it with granola and placed a serving at his place and her own. She nursed the baby while Jack ate.

"Were you low this morning?"

"No. Dr. Jarman called it right again. I was 100 even." He bolused through his pump and then said, "Don't go out. I'm not worried about me. I'm worried about you and Lucien. Kennedy would kill anybody that tried to hurt you, and he already doesn't like Alyssa."

"I need to go to the grocery," Laurel protested.

"I'll take you tonight. Do it for me, babe. I won't be

able to keep my mind on business if I know you're outside the gates."

"We'll wait for you," Laurel conceded. "Are you flying today?"

"No. Stuart signed us up for time tomorrow." He kissed her and the baby. "I'll see you at six."

Chapter 25

Their lives restarted that morning, and the days fell into a pattern. Laurel wasn't as lonely anymore because she had Lucien, but she still missed Jack terribly. After all, he was her best friend. She worried about him more than ever, thanks to his two brushes with death. Even that feeling eased as time passed without any new signs of Alyssa.

At Christmas, they flew to Cherokee and spent a week introducing their friends to Lucien. In January, they flew to Window Rock and spent a week with Samson's family. In February, Lucien was almost six months old when his father began training intensively for the June launch. At the same time, Russell and Danielle moved to Colorado where Russ had accepted a job with an aeronautics firm. Karen Lampley bought their house.

Some of the wives had been uneasy about having their husbands working with a female astronaut, especially since Karen was very attractive at age thirty-nine. The gossip was she was unmarried and by all accounts she was heterosexual. She moved in with her thirteen-year-old daughter and her seventy-five-year -old mother. Karen's daughter, Carmen, gravitated toward Laurel and Lucien almost immediately. After school she was usually at Laurel's front door. Ultimately she became their baby-sitter, allowing Jack and Laurel to go out occasionally without worrying about their son.

After a couple of months, they learned Karen had been married to an air force pilot fourteen years earlier. He had been a test pilot and had died in a prototype aircraft crash two weeks after their wedding. Rather than becoming afraid to fly, Karen had completed the training herself while raising their baby alone. Pictures of Carmen's father were all over the house. Carmen fully intended to follow in her parents' footsteps.

"I'm going to Mars," Carmen told Laurel. "They'll be ready to do it by the time I finish the Air Force Academy."

"You were born to fly," Laurel said simply. She was glad for Carmen's company because she missed Danielle Chou very much.

Jack was gone a little longer every day. His mission was the installation of parts on the international space station. It had been completed the previous summer, and astronauts were living on it. A new module was being installed to accommodate another experiment. The installation was slated to take nine days. The agency wanted Jack and his crew in Florida two weeks early to handle the actual payload.

Jack urged Laurel to take Lucien and fly to Cherokee after the launch and return to Florida for the landing. Laurel decided she wanted to be in Florida for at least one day so she could see him in the shuttle at night. Carmen was going to stay with her and accompany her to Cherokee. Grandmother Lampley was remaining in Houston due to poor health.

Laurel and Jack hadn't heard anything from Alyssa for almost a year. The FBI had no new leads, though they suspected her mother and brother were helping her hide. They were certain she had a variety of false ID's. Jack made very sure his family was going to have security coverage at all times while he was in space.

The week before they needed to leave for Florida, Jack arrived home at noon on Thursday with a flight plan to San Juan and reservations at a resort on the east coast of the island. Stuart's family had agreed to care for Lucien.

The only delay in their early morning departure was Laurel's surprise meeting with a certified flight instructor at the private airport. Before they left, she took her written test and passed. Her solo flight was scheduled to follow. She hadn't felt ready, but the uncertainty left her when Jack kissed her and fastened her seat belt.

"I don't know if I'm ready," she said.

"You're ready!" Jack held her face in his hands and her heart in his eyes. "I wouldn't shove you out of the nest if you weren't ready. Soar like an eagle, babe."

He stood beside the instructor, feeling nervous for her. Her takeoff, flight, and landing were flawless. He pulled her into his arms when she emerged from the plane. Before they left for San Juan, she had her temporary license to pilot their plane. Jack offered the primary seat to Laurel, but she declined.

"I'm flying even without a plane right now. I can't wait to call my dad."

"Then you'd better call him now," Jack said. "I'd like to have all your attention in San Juan."

"I can promise you'll have it." She couldn't stop smiling as they took off into the bright morning sky. The flight took nine hours because they were flying into a crosswind, and they had landed in Florida to take a break in the afternoon. Their plane touched down in San Juan at 7 P.M. local time. They hailed a cab to take them to the resort. Their supper was already set for them on the private balcony when they checked in.

When they crossed the threshold to their room, Laurel could hardly wait for Jack to tip the bellman. When the door was secured, she was in his arms with the world closed out. It was twelve hours before they left the room. Room service took care of their need for food. Later they hiked to the rain forest. They ended their perfect day in San Juan sitting on the balcony watching the stars emerge in the crystal clear night sky.

Sunday morning, they attended a local church service before they headed to the beach. They played in the water with Jack's pump secured in a waterproof waist pack. He had disconnected it to keep the pack sealed and then reconnected it every two hours to bolus. Due to their heritage, they didn't have to worry about sunburn as did the other tourists. They basked in the sun all day, even eating lunch by the water. Laurel sat between Jack's legs; his arms were wrapped around her while the waves lapped over their ankles.

"You're very quiet," he said. "You're thinking of being separated again."

"I can't help it," she admitted. "Every time the stars come out, I think of you being in space. When you're gone, I feel like I'm missing part of myself."

"I know." His arms tightened around her. "They're about to start the Mars project with a vengeance, and they want all of us to commit to it. Of course, they know I'm not really a candidate for prolonged space flight because of the diabetes. They do want me to commit to time in the space station. That's not days. That would be weeks." He felt her tremble.

"I told them no, babe. I've had a really good offer from the space institute in Tennessee. The people there already know me because I trained there. It's a teaching and research position using the laser technology I designed when I was working on my doctorate. I thought I might take it. What do I think?"

Laurel turned in his arms and pushed him down on

the sand so she could look into his eyes. "Don't say it if you don't mean it," she said. "I've been praying you wouldn't keep going up." His hands were on her face, and his eyes held her. "I told them yes on Friday morning because I knew you would want me to. We can move this summer. I love you, Laurel, and you let me have my dream even though it's been really hard for you. It's your turn. And I want to be Lucien's dad. Every time I take a risk now, I risk losing the most important things in my life. The rush doesn't make up for how that feels."

Three years of fear left her heart, and she knew she could handle one last trip into space because it would be the end. It was hard to leave his arms and walk back to the hotel. When he closed the door to their room, Laurel held onto Jack with the undying love of a woman committed for life. Making love was a reaffirmation of that feeling that made the emotions engendered even more poignant.

"I can just hear the questions now," Jack laughed as the afternoon light faded. "So what did you guys do in San Juan?"

"Tell them to look at our suntans and draw their own conclusions," Laurel said as she caressed Jack's chest to punctuate the statement.

"You know the biggest radio telescope in the United States is here. I was going to take you to see it, but now I think we'll have to do it some other time."

"We'll have forever to go," Laurel said. They missed their scheduled flight time and left at 7 P.M. for the five-hour flight. The weather was perfect, and the stars seemed to make a pathway to guide them home.

"Your blood sugar is really staying down," she said as she tested him again. "Were you out of range this weekend?"

"No. I'm totally unstressed when I'm with you." He smiled at her. "And remember, we were three hours late for our flight home. If we had been flying commercial, we'd have had a problem."

"I don't care about any of that any more," Laurel said. "I just wish they would catch Alyssa and put her away."

"You and me both." Jack radioed the airfield and received clearance to land. They were in their car headed home at 11 P.M. Houston time. They stopped at Stuart's house to pick up Lucien, who crawled to them and pulled himself up on their legs.

"He's just about ready to walk," Geneva told them. "He spent the weekend cruising around the furniture."

"I'm glad he didn't walk without us being here to watch. We've kept the video camera ready for the big event." Jack tossed the baby up in the air and Lucien squealed with delight. "See, Laurel, he's into flying already."

She gave her husband a good-natured shove and thanked Stuart and Geneva for baby-sitting. It was 11:30 P.M. when they headed for home. They had no premonition of trouble until they pulled into the driveway. Laurel thought she saw a light being extinguished in the back of the house.

"Did you see that?" she asked Jack.

"What?"

"I thought there was a light on in our bedroom, and then it went out." She shook her head. "Maybe I'm paranoid."

Jack glanced around the neighborhood and observed only dark windows at the houses of their friends. He tried to dial on the cell phone. The battery was dead. He reached under the seat and took out his gun.

"I guess I'll be paranoid with you. Drive back to the gates and get someone from security to come down here. I'll go in and make sure everything is all right." He got out of the car and pulled her across the seat into his place. He tucked the gun into his belt while he was still behind the car door and then locked Laurel in the car. He watched as she backed out of the driveway. He approached the house, collecting the mail from the box as if he weren't suddenly uneasy. It crossed his mind that Alyssa had tended to attack whenever he had been mentioned in the news, and the upcoming launch had brought him national recognition.

When Jack unlocked the door, the security system didn't beep, and the light switch didn't bring any illumination to the dark house. He assumed there had been a power outage in the neighborhood, so he relaxed his guard to some degree. Kennedy usually met him at the door, but he was at the kennel.

Jack laid the mail on the sofa and left the front door open so the moonlight would light his path across the living room. He was almost at the kitchen door when the front door slammed shut. He moved immediately into the kitchen, taking cover behind the refrigerator.

"I have you, Jack," Alyssa's voice said softly. "I've been waiting to have you for a long time. I've dreamed about it since you threw away a chance to be with me in D.C. I can't forgive you for choosing that little slut when you could have had me. I'm your wife, Jack. I'll always be your wife until death do us part. For you, that's tonight."

Jack was moving toward the back door and escape when he heard someone behind him. Fire ran through his body paralyzing him. He fell to the floor and lost awareness for several seconds. Then he could hear and see but couldn't move as Alyssa and a man leaned over him. The man was holding a weapon Jack recognized as a stun gun. They took the handgun from Jack's belt and rolled him on his back.

Even breathing was a struggle for the first few minutes, and Jack closed his eyes and prayed to know what to do. He heard the telephone ringing as if it were in the distance, and someone ripped the cord from the wall.

The security guard had felt calling in more people
was unnecessary. To prove his point, he loaned Laurel
the telephone to call the house. When there was no
answer, Laurel panicked.

"Something is wrong," she said. "My husband was
going in when I left. He should be answering. Please call
the police. If his ex-wife is there, she'll kill him."

The security guard sighed and reluctantly agreed to
heed her plea while thinking she was being paranoid.
His attitude changed when he and another guard found
the power grid to the Driver's neighborhood had been
shut off.

Jack's hands were bound with tape before he could
move at all. As Alyssa's accomplice completed that task,
suddenly the lights came on almost blinding them and
provoking curses from Alyssa.

"There are security cars outside," the man said.
"They'll know what's going on. Just kill him and let's
go."

"No," Alyssa said sweetly. "That isn't the plan. You
know I have a plan, Gary. I always have a plan." She was
smiling as she approached her partner, and she reached
out to touch him in a lewd manner. She continued
touching him as she looked up into his eyes. Gary
pushed Alyssa against the wall and began having sex
with her. When pounding on the front and back doors
interrupted them, Gary turned toward the front of the
house with his gun held ready. Before he could move
away from Alyssa, she pointed her gun to his chest and
pulled the trigger. He collapsed on the floor and gasped
convulsively. Alyssa moved to his side and, with no
visible emotion, fired a second shot through his head.

"Get away from the doors," she shouted. "I have Dr.
Driver, and I'll kill him if you try to come in." The
knocking stopped, and Alyssa prowled through the
house making certain all the draperies were closed.

While she was gone, Jack tried to move but couldn't generate the power to do so.

"Now it's just us, Jackson," Alyssa said as she returned. "Just you and me for all eternity. We're like star-crossed lovers. A celestial Romeo and Juliet. I told you in Cherokee you'll be mine forever, Jack."

She hovered over him like a black widow spider as she unbuttoned his shirt. She alternated between touching him gently and inflicting pain in any way she could. Jack kept his eyes closed and prayed for escape and for his family if he wasn't able to escape. Praying gave him the strength not to react when she lit a cigarette and burned him with it repeatedly. As she tried to force him to respond, she pinched his skin with a pair of pliers and then cut him with a carpet knife. His silence infuriated her and made her stop after the third cut. She pressed the gun against his temple.

"You should have brought your little slut in, Jack. If she were here, she'd be getting the pain and you'd be getting the pleasure. I tried to kill her, but you got in the way and then your father got in the way. He was cruel to me when he answered Laurel's phone for her. He told me he was going to call the police. He made my father lock me up. It was an accident when your father was killed, but I was glad. I wanted him to die. He deserved to die." She traced the side of Jack's face with her fingertips and then clawed him deep enough to draw blood. She dipped her fingers in his blood and tasted it.

"It's too sweet. I like my blood with a little bite to it." Alyssa stood as sirens wailed in the distance. She disappeared for a minute and then returned with a bottle of clear insulin and a ten milliliter syringe with a very long needle. As Jack watched, she drew the entire contents of the vial—1,000 units.

"You blamed me, Jack. It wasn't me that ended our marriage. The diabetes came between us, Jack, so that's how you'll die. Insulin and the diabetes will kill you."

Outside he could hear the police on loudspeakers and more sirens in the distance. It was a hostage situation, and he knew the S.W.A.T. team would be called. He also knew 1,000 units of rapid onset insulin would kill him long before anyone could come to help him. He tried to move his feet and found his muscles were returning to his control.

As Alyssa raised the syringe, Jack kicked at her with all his strength. The blow threw her backwards and off balance giving him time to scramble away from her. He staggered through the kitchen toward the front door. Alyssa picked up the gun and fired it wildly and, by some miracle, she missed him on the first two shots. The third shot hit Jack in his left shoulder, and the impact sent him to the floor.

Instantly Alyssa was on top of his body pinning him down. She raised the syringe like a weapon and plunged it into his side with all her strength. The two-inch needle went through Jack's clothes and his abdominal wall, allowing Alyssa to shoot the cold insulin into his abdominal cavity. The pain of the injection controlled Jack very effectively for several moments. Alyssa sat back on her heels triumphantly.

"You'll die now. She can't have you now. When you're dead, I'll get her and your son. You owe me their lives."

The threat to his family spurred Jack into immediate response. He managed to turn enough to hit Alyssa in the head with his bound hands. All his rage and anger went into the blow. If he had been at his normal level of strength, he could have ended the confrontation then. He had less than half of his muscle tone, however, due to the electrical charge they had used to paralyze him. The blow stunned her and gave him time to again scramble to his feet. He kicked her in the chest when she dove toward his legs. He was still clumsy from the effects of the stun gun. The kick and move to escape her made him fall against the cabinets. Before he could run, she had the gun in her hands leveled at his chest. They faced each other struggling for breath for a couple minutes.

"You'll be mine, Jack," Alyssa hissed as she curled her fingers around the trigger. "Sit down."

"You'll just have to shoot me, Alyssa," Jack said slowly. "You'll have to shoot me and remember I never did anything to hurt you. I loved you until you told me you wanted me out of your life. You're going to have to look at my face and look into my eyes and know you killed someone who loved you."

"You said you hated me." Her face contorted with indecision. "You said you hated me and would never be with me. You said that when you were in the hospital in D.C. I offered you everything, Jack. I offered you a cure from the diabetes. I offered you my body and my soul."

She was crying then, and the gun moved away from a direct aim. Jack could feel the insulin beginning to hit him. The struggle had increased the rate of absorption and the insulin was injected into a place where the usual dynamics were greatly altered. He started to back away, but Alyssa saw the movement and raised the gun again. "You refused me, Jack. You're a liar. You hurt me."

The back door exploded off its hinges. As Alyssa turned, Jack dove into the living room and rolled away from the door. He heard Alyssa screaming and heard the officer order her to drop her weapon. There were more shots fired and then silence.

Jack remained on the floor hoping help was coming. He felt as if the paralysis were returning to his muscles. He could feel his mouth getting numb and then his hands. His heart was pounding, but he didn't feel any pain even from the bullet wound. He prayed to be able to tell someone about the insulin before he lost consciousness. He couldn't generate the strength to get off the floor.

A police officer bent over him and asked, "Are you all right?"

"She gave me—" Jack couldn't think of the word. "Help me. She gave me something."

"Get the paramedics in here," the policeman shouted. "He's been shot and he says she gave him something."

Jack couldn't hear the people running into the house or feel them cutting his hands free. He kept his vision another two minutes and saw Laurel running into the house. She was on her knees beside him when his vision began to fade.

"Jack, are you all right?" He could barely hear her voice. "Somebody help him. He's bleeding." She pressed her hands against his wound.

"Insulin," Jack said in almost inaudible slurred speech. "She gave..." He gripped Laurel's hand and pressed it against his side just before he lost consciousness. Laurel saw the blood and the puncture wound, and she screamed for help.

Laurel was supported by the other team members in the surgery waiting room. At 5 A.M. the surgeons came to them to report on Jack's condition.

"The bullet wound wasn't all that bad. It damaged a large vein, but there was no arterial damage and the nerve appeared intact. His blood sugar has been a major problem. He must have been given a huge overdose of insulin injected directly into his abdominal cavity because his blood sugar read 3mg percent when you got him here after two amps of 50 percent dextrose in the ambulance and the glucagon you gave him. The police found an empty bottle of Humalog on the bedroom floor. If it was a new bottle, she gave him 1,000 units. If it was all short acting, we should have that problem controlled in the next couple of hours.

"He was very low, Mrs. Driver. He may have neurological damage from hypoglycemia, but we won't know that until he wakes up. You'll need to call the MiniMed helpline to see about getting him a new pump. His pump isn't working at all, and the police found a stun gun in your house. That's a device used to paralyze an attacker. He has a third degree burn on his right shoulder where they hit him with it, and the electrical charge no doubt fried the circuits in his pump."

"It had to be a new bottle," Laurel whispered. "He used the last of the old bottle when he did a site change before we left for San Juan. The idea of such a dose in Jack, who was so sensitive to insulin, was terrifying. He used only 28 units total most days. "Can I stay with him?"

"I can't permit it. I wish I could. He's in critical condition right now. He stopped breathing twice from the low sugar. He's breathing on his own now, but he's entubated just in case he stops breathing again. We have him on a continuous glucose sensor we borrowed from the diabetes team. He was dropping so fast we needed rapid readings. We inserted a central vein catheter, and he's getting a 20 percent sugar solution to hold him out of the danger zone. You can see him now and then again in three hours."

It was the hardest thing Laurel had ever done when she had to go into the ICU and see Jack on so much life support equipment. He was completely unresponsive to her touch, and his face was marked by the lived scratch Alyssa had inflicted. He had multiple cuts, bruises, and cigarette burns on his chest and abdomen and a huge bruise on his side where Alyssa had stabbed him with the syringe. His left shoulder was bandaged from the bullet wound, and his right shoulder was bandaged from the deep burn. Laurel and their pastor and the crew stood around the bed and prayed for Jack until Laurel could feel God was carrying her. When the others had left, she stayed alone to tell Jack how much she loved and needed him. Every three hours she repeated those vows.

Chapter 26

Jack and Laurel were at the "cape" having supper with families of the other crew members. It was their last night together before the flight. A week of isolation and being separated by glass would follow before the ten-day separation of the flight. Their hotel had given them use of the private dining room so families could have that time with the crew. A television set was turned on so they could catch extra coverage the media had given them. Carmen, with her sharp technological eyes of a teenager, caught the beginning of a news story. "Listen, will you," Carmen said.

"We're here at the Kennedy Space Center with Dr. Jackson Driver and his crew who will embark on STS-100 in less than a week. This particular flight has lived up to its number in being unforgettable even before it leaves the earth. Dr. Driver and his family have been victims of a stalking for the past three years. The stalker caused the death of Dr. Driver's father during his first mission in space, and Dr. Driver himself was held hostage and wounded four weeks ago. No one has told us very much about the stalker situation, Dr. Driver. Of

course, we do know the stalker was killed by a S.W.A.T.
team member while you were being held."

Laurel cringed. It was especially difficult to be on
public display as an astronaut or a member of an
astronaut's family just before a launch. The situation
with Alyssa had made the press even more aggressive.
Some of the newspapers had been cruel in their specula-
tions about Alyssa Driver's motives in attacking Jack.
Even when her autopsy had revealed large quantities of
cocaine in her system and evidence of long-term cocaine
and alcohol abuse, some reports had hinted that Jack
had caused his ex-wife's obsessive behavior. NASA had
helped suppress the stories to the degree they were able,
but it was obvious the television reporter was seeking a
sensational interview. Laurel was proud of how Jack
handled the question.

"I'd rather put that behind me," Jack said into the
camera. "I was already injured, so I don't remember
when the stalker was killed. I'm just glad it's over and
that no one else in my family was hurt."

"We've also heard that people in Hollywood are
interested in making your story into a movie," the reporter commented.

"We hope this mission isn't going to be exciting
enough to draw Hollywood's attention," Jack said.
"We're looking forward to the opportunity to go and to
interact with the crew of the space station. For myself,
I'd like to remind everyone with diabetes that the stars
aren't out of your reach. There was a time when I wasn't
sure of that, but now I know it's the truth. Being here
with these people and being able to fly with them is all
the evidence you need. To my people, the Navajo Nation, I'd like to say it's an honor to be representing all
Americans in space."

"Dr. Driver is the first Native American shuttle
commander, and the first astronaut to have insulin
dependent diabetes. While he's being very modest, I'm

sure his journey here to the launch pad was both challenging and interesting. We wish him and the crew of
STS-100 great success."

"Not bad, Jack," Karen said. "Actually that was
pretty classy for a man."

"Everybody has a story, Karen," Jack laughed. "Let's
just leave it at that."

When they had finished supper, Jack sat on the floor
of their hotel room and played with Lucien for an hour.
He held their son until the tired toddler fell asleep on his
shoulder. Laurel arranged for a hotel-contracted baby-
sitter to watch Lucien so she and her husband could
spend the next three hours walking hand in hand.

The moon was full over the ocean, and it illuminated
the shuttle on the launch pad in the distance. Laurel
took several pictures of the shuttle and of Jack with the
shuttle in the background.

"Do the others know you're leaving after this?"
Laurel asked as Jack looked at Discovery.

"No. That's between us and NASA."

"You won't have any regrets?" she prodded him. "I
don't want you to be unhappy."

"I won't be," he assured her. "I guess my only regret
is that I won't have the chance to pilot her. That's the
reason I applied in the first place. On the first mission, I
was sitting behind the pilot. This time I'll be too close to
not be a little envious. Stuart's been harassing me and
saying he might let me take her once around the block
while we're up there—if I pack my learner's permit." He
took her face in his hands. "All things considered, that's
not much of a regret." He kissed her and then held her
close.

Laurel caressed his left shoulder and felt the healing
scar through his shirt. She knew Jack was still recovering from the gunshot wound and the skin graft to cover
his third-degree burn, but he had successfully convinced the flight surgeons to clear him for the mission.

As she held him, she kept reminding herself that it was
the last time he would be going into space.

"I'm not going to Cherokee, Jack," she murmured.
"Lucien and I will be watching you on the big screen
every night. So remember to smile for us."

"It's even harder to leave this time. I just don't want
the shuttle as much as I want and need the two of you."
He took her hand and led her back to their room where
they could be even closer. During the time he was with
her, she was a NASA wife. That courage had allowed
her to prepare a package for Jack and to hide it inside his
bag. He held onto Laurel until the last possible moment.
She knew he was leaving reluctantly. Despite her inten-
tions not to cry, she wept after he left their room.

All of the wives and Carmen held hands a week later
as they saw the boosters ignite and carry Discovery into
the clouds. Stuart's voice was very clear and confident
when he said he was going for throttle up. The extra
push carried them out of sight and into their window of
opportunity.

Carmen was clinging to Laurel's arm as they made
their way through the sea of waving microphones and
inquiring minds. Laurel held Lucien tightly, grateful to
have a tangible part of her husband with her. The
downside was hearing Lucien say "dada" every time a
door opened. The nine days ahead of her still loomed as
an almost insurmountable hurdle to their future.

When the wives returned from supper the first night,
the hotel's front desk produced a dozen roses for Laurel
and a package containing Jack's pump, a tape player,
and his first tape. To Laurel's surprise, the other astronauts had followed Jack's example and sent their wives
a gift every day of the mission. Karen sent a package to
Carmen each day.

They sat around the pool and on the beach watching
the sky while their children swam. Every day they went
to the chapel to pray for their families to be complete

again. Their best time was spent in the screening room where they could see and hear the astronauts.

The mission was on schedule without a hitch when a tropical storm reared its ugly head in the Caribbean. The families were alarmed. After tracking the storm for two days, it was upgraded to hurricane status. NASA communicated the problem to Jack and his crew members, who had already heard some of the details on news broadcasts. That night, the families knew they had good reason to worry because the tension on Discovery came through the video cameras.

When the screen was shut off, Colonel Asher told the families Discovery would have to be brought down a day early or land at White Sands, New Mexico. The crew had been instructed to push to complete their mission in eight days instead of nine. Haste is the mother of all accidents.

Jack and his team worked inside the shuttle until very late that night, cutting their sleep schedule to a mere four hours. They restructured everyone's work to try to complete the installation in sixteen hours instead of the twenty-four hours originally slated. The new schedule put everyone outside the shuttle except for the astronaut designated to work the shuttle's arm. That duty was rotated among Jack, Odell, and Jim Graham, who were the most skilled with the arm. It was tedious work. None of them could tolerate more than three or four hours working the arm without a break.

They were suited up and in space when the shuttle reached the sunlit side of earth. The shuttle arm locked when they had been working only four hours, and it took three hours to repair it. Behind schedule, the astronauts were becoming irritable and frustrated as they were beginning to see their goal as unachievable. As the day dragged on, Karen had been pulled to work on a power upgrade inside the space station, and Jack remained in the shuttle working with the arm.

Fourteen hours into the installation, Stuart and Jim Graham were installing an oxygen tank. Jack was holding the tank with the shuttle's arm while the two astronauts secured it in the module frame and attached the inflow and outflow lines. As Stuart tried to tighten the outflow fitting, it stuck. He struggled with it for several minutes and found it impossible to tighten or loosen the fitting. He had been doing EVA (extravehicular activity) for more than four hours, and he was uncharacteristically tired and frustrated.

"I'll get a different wrench," Jim said. "Jack, put one of those vise wrenches in the air lock."

"You've got it," Jack said. He retrieved the equipment and placed it in the air lock, reversing the pressure so Jim could get it. Then he returned to the window and the arm controls. As he looked out at Stuart, he observed his friend as he hit the fitting with his wrench. Jack saw a sudden tiny jet of oxygen seep out around the fitting and turn into ice.

"Stu, you've got a leak," Jack warned. "You must have a crack in the fitting. Wait for Jim."

"If I wait for every glitch to work out, we'll be here until our kids get out of college," Stuart said.

"Chill out, Stu," Jack said soothingly. "White Sands is a beautiful place. Geneva and the kids might like seeing the desert, and the weather there is definitely better than Florida." Stuart was directly in front of the outflow, and he ignored Jack's implied order to wait for Jim. When he attempted to remove the fitting by hitting it again, it shattered into several shards with a sudden explosive release of gas. Propelled like a bullet by the escaping gas, a titanium shard struck Stuart in the chest.

The space suits were built to resist such impacts because of the risk of penetrating injuries from space debris, but the sharp edge ripped through every layer of Stuart's suit. It pierced his chest cavity and came to rest inside his heart. The puncture caused a complete suit decompression, but the wound would have been fatal on its own. Stuart was dead before they could retrieve him. The force of the explosion blew him a thousand feet from the shuttle and space station leaving a frozen trail of his blood.

Jack saw his friend die, but no one heard him shout, "no!" As the other members of his crew brought Stuart's body into the cargo bay, it was Jack's duty to inform NASA. It was also his duty to rally his crew to complete their billion dollar mission. Both tasks were gut wrenching.

Before there was a press release or any official statement, the wives and families were summoned to Florida mission control. All of them arrived knowing something was wrong. Laurel felt as if she were suffocating as she took her seat. Lucien seemed to sense her fear and fretted incessantly. They had been in the meeting room for five minutes when Angela Hughes noticed Geneva Bradford and her children were absent. Her dark eyes were stricken as she looked at Laurel. "Stuart," she whispered. "It must be Stuart."

"There's been an accident," Colonel Asher said quietly. "We lost Stuart. He was EVA, and something ruptured his suit. It was over in seconds. He couldn't have suffered. I told Geneva and their children a half hour ago. They're doing as well as could be expected.

"The crew is still working, which is a tribute to all of them. Everyone is EVA except Jack because he's the back-up pilot, and we can't afford to risk him now. None of the others have enough simulator time to take over the pilot's seat. They can't make the window for tomorrow. We'll be bringing them down at White Sands on Friday. We'll have a charter plane to take all of you to New Mexico tomorrow night."

Laurel's heart turned over in her throat, and she raised her hand tremulously. "Does Jack have enough insulin?"

"He told me he was taking enough for two weeks this time," the colonel replied. "Everyone else is doing as well as can be expected for now. We'll let you see them as soon as they're back on board Discovery. We don't expect any problems in getting them home. Jack has more cumulative T-38 and STA flight time than Stuart had, and he has logged more simulator time than any other astronaut in the last three years. He can land Discovery. Stay close, and we'll call you when they're back on board."

They waited seven long hours to see their families. They spent the time praying and reading their Bibles together. During those hours when Laurel was living her worst nightmare of fear for Jack, she felt the peace of her faith come over her. She was the calmest of the family members when the NASA officials came to admit them to the viewing room.

Geneva and her children were with them when the viewing screen showed them the inside of Discovery. The atmosphere aboard the shuttle was somber that night, but the other seven families were grateful to God to see their loved ones were alive. Stuart, the comedian and counterbalance for Jack's intensity, was painfully absent. Jack was the last to come to the camera because he was the commander. His face showed his deep regret for wishing he could pilot Discovery.

"We're all pushing to get home now," Jack said. "The rest of this mission is dedicated to Stuart, and we're going to get it done. Laurel, I love you. Give Lucien a hug for me." The screen went black, shutting out Jack's grief-stricken eyes. All the families rose to their feet unsteadily and filed out pretending they would be able to sleep.

Colonel Asher caught Laurel at the door. "They'll be focusing on you and Jack. You know what they're going to say. Just don't listen. If you break down, they'll find a way to make Jack look bad."

"I won't break down," Laurel said adamantly. "I'm grieving for Stuart. I know Jack can do this. You know he can do it or you wouldn't have made him the commander."

"I'm very sure he can do it. He's one of the best pilots I've ever seen. Feel free to tell the reporters that."

Laurel prayed most of the night. She called Samson, who said he would meet them at White Sands. Then she called her parents and asked for their prayers. When their wake-up call came, she and Carmen took showers and packed. They took turns caring for Lucien. The televisions and radios remained turned off.

"I don't want mom to go back up again, Laurel," Carmen said tearfully. "You shouldn't go when you have people who need you here on earth."

"You have to go where you feel God wants you to go, Carmen," Laurel said quietly. "You can die on earth as easily as you can in space. We have to place our lives in God's hands every day." She and the young girl spent their last few hours making plans for a welcome home celebration and trusting for it to happen.

When they left the hotel, they were surrounded by reporters who focused on Laurel. The NASA guards couldn't keep them away, but Laurel was not intimidated.

"Mrs. Driver, is it true your husband will have to fly Discovery now?" several reporters asked at once. "How do you think his blood sugar will affect his ability to bring the shuttle down?"

"My husband's record as a pilot speaks for itself," Laurel replied. "He treats his diabetes the way he treats his duties as an astronaut. Because of the way he manages his sugars, having diabetes doesn't affect his ability to do any job he chooses to do. This landing won't be any different to Jack than the time he's logged training to fly the shuttle. When he lands Discovery, maybe everyone will be able to understand that diabetes is a

condition. Ignorance and neglect are the only things
that make it a disease." There were no further questions.

Discovery's crew was restless during their last night
in space. They were all sleep deprived, but it was cus-
tomary for them to sleep in shifts. No one really wanted
their turn. Jack felt like all eyes were on him when he left
his sleep restraint to test his blood sugar.

"You okay, Jack?" Odell asked tentatively. He didn't
want to voice his uncertainty and that of the other
astronauts about how Jack's blood sugar might affect
his ability to fly. In spite of knowing each other so well
for so long, Jack's condition suddenly seemed a huge
obstacle to their safe return.

"I'm fine," Jack said as he gave himself a shot of
insulin. "I've got one syringe left. I guess it's time to go
home."

"I thought you brought two weeks worth," Odell
said as he floated over to join Jack.

"I did, but I burned all the extra the past two days."
He shoved his test kit into one of his flight suit pockets.
"Weightlessness keeps exercise from bringing it down,
and stress definitely drives it up. It's not high enough to
make me sleepy and I think I've cornered the market on
adrenaline. Don't let me keep you up."

"I think we have the same kind of insomnia," Odell
admitted. "You're ready to do this, Jack. You've always
wanted to fly her."

"Not like this," Jack said slowly. "Not at this price."

"It was Stuart's time," Odell said simply. "It isn't
our time, so you've got to take us home. When you do
this deed, you'll have six new contributors to the American Diabetes Association." He settled into the commander's seat. "Did you fly during 'storm'?"

"Yeah," Jack said slowly. "I flew more sorties than I
care to remember. How about you?"

"That was where I got most of my combat time.

What was your hairiest mission?"

"That's easy," Jack said. "We were on a bombing run, and we engaged six Iraqi fighters. There were only four of us that night, and we ended up in a major fire fight. We got two of them, and they got one of our planes and sent it back to the base. Then they hit my wingman's engine. He crossed in front of me and flamed out both of my engines. We went into a flat spin with an Iraqi right behind us. I let the spin go because I knew he'd target us the minute we pulled out. My navigator thought I was nuts, but he held on until the Iraqi pulled up.

"Later I accused him of holding out only because he would've been parachuting into hostile territory. I think we were below ten thousand feet when the Iraqi finally pulled out. I got both engines to restart and pulled out about four thousand feet off the ground. We went straight up and engaged them again. They didn't see us until we had them in the sights. We got both of them and had one missile left to deliver to the primary target.

"Afterwards Rusty said the reason he didn't eject is I was praying out loud. I don't remember a thing about it being out loud, but I do know I did some serious praying." He looked at Odell. "I can do this, Odell. I know you guys have to wonder about a diabetic sitting in this seat, but I can get us home. If I pray out loud, don't let it worry you. I've always thought any extra help is a good thing."

"We have total confidence that you can do it, Jack, and we'll be praying with you." Odell patted Jack on the back and floated back to his sleep restraint, leaving Jack to focus for his battle.

Alone in the cockpit, Jack opened the package Laurel had marked for his last day in space. It was a pocket-sized Bible. A picture of Laurel holding Lucien was glued inside the front cover. She had marked a passage, and that night it seemed more appropriate than any other verse would have been. It was Isaiah 40:31. "But they that wait upon the Lord shall renew their strength; they shall mount up with wings as eagles; they shall run, and not be weary; and they shall walk, and not faint." Reading the verse seemed to alleviate his fatigue. He ran his checklist three times before sleeping an hour in the pilot's seat.

White Sands was a military installation with a long runway for testing prototypic planes. Ever since the missions began, White Sands and Edwards Air Force Base had been alternate landing sites for the shuttles. White Sands wasn't equipped for families but, due to the circumstances, it was made ready. When Laurel, Carmen, and Lucien reached the viewing area, they were joined by Samson and Olivia. Larry and Mary arrived moments later.

As they were being seated, Russell Chou came to sit among the other crew families. He took Laurel's hand and said, "Don't worry. Jack has tremendous courage under fire. I'm here only because he does."

At the time the families were arriving, the shuttle's crew was going through their checklist. Odell was in the commander's seat. Jack was in the pilot's seat. Using his last test strip, Jack tested his sugar. The reading was 134.

"Will that hold you for landing?" Odell asked.

"Oh, yeah," Jack said. "The shuttle may be going down, but this stress will have me going up in another hour. We'll be enjoying the desert sunshine before I need to do anything about it. That's a good thing since I'm out of insulin." He ran down the checklist again and passed it to Odell.

"Mission Control, this is Shuttle Discovery on final approach to White Sands. We are one minute from reentry and ionization blackout," Jack reported.

"Shuttle Discovery, this is Mission Control. We have your coordinates. We will talk to you in about six minutes. Good luck."